DAY OF NOW

DAY OF NOW

MIRANDA REASON

BLOOMSBURY
LONDON OXFORD NEW YORK NEW DELHI SYDNEY

BLOOMSBURY YA
Bloomsbury Publishing Plc
50 Bedford Square, London WC1B 3DP, UK
Bloomsbury Publishing Ireland Limited
29 Earlsfort Terrace, Dublin 2, D02 AY28, Ireland

BLOOMSBURY, BLOOMSBURY YA and the Diana logo
are trademarks of Bloomsbury Publishing Plc

First published in Great Britain in 2026 by Bloomsbury Publishing Plc

Text copyright © Miranda Reason, 2026

Miranda Reason has asserted her right under the Copyright, Designs
and Patents Act, 1988, to be identified as Author of this work

All rights reserved. No part of this publication may be: i) reproduced or
transmitted in any form, electronic or mechanical, including photocopying,
recording or by means of any information storage or retrieval system
without prior permission in writing from the publishers; or ii) used or
reproduced in any way for the training, development or operation of
artificial intelligence (AI) technologies, including generative AI technologies.
The rights holders expressly reserve this publication from the text and
data mining exception as per Article 4(3) of the Digital Single
Market Directive (EU) 2019/790

A catalogue record for this book is available from the British Library

ISBN: HB: 978-1-5266-8433-2; Export: 978-1-5266-8432-5,
eBook: 978-1-5266-8430-1

2 4 6 8 10 9 7 5 3 1

Typeset by Six Red Marbles India
Printed and bound in Great Britain by Clays Ltd, Elcograf S.p.A.

To find out more about our authors and books visit www.bloomsbury.com
and sign up for our newsletters
For product safety related questions contact productsafety@bloomsbury.com

For Benni

PART 1
THE BLUE HOUSE

1

The first sign of life in the outside world – of other people who are still, at this very moment, living – comes from the radio.

The radio is Dayna's. She found it on one of the family supply runs and took a liking to it. It's a rectangular box, only a little larger than the palm of her hand. It is a shiny silver colour, with some knobs you can swivel this way and that, and other knobs you can push up and down. It has very small holes on one side, where the noise comes out. The noise used to be sound in the past, Dayna knows. People talking about the weather and events happening and, most exciting of all, music. But now it's just noise because all the people who used to do these things are dead. White noise, Father calls it. White noise is both thrilling and a little scary. It is scary because it sounds like an angry monster just before it attacks. It is thrilling because it is connected to the past.

Father didn't want Dayna to take the radio because it is against the supply run rules: only take what is necessary – tinned food, batteries, medical supplies, sometimes clothes or toothpaste or razors or books. Occasionally, Father bends the rules and they go into what used to be department stores, where the dusty shelves are filled with useless, lovely, interesting things, like dead electrical gadgets or puzzle games or small plastic figures, and there Dayna and her brother, Pax, are allowed to choose one thing, as long as it's not too big for their rucksacks. And as long as it doesn't need batteries.

The radio needs batteries and so Father said no. 'There's no use in it anyway,' he said. 'There aren't any radio stations left.'

But Dayna disobeyed him and slipped it into her rucksack when he wasn't looking. She usually never disobeys him, not on the outside at least, where they have to move as a unit and rely on each other and be quick to react. She can't fully explain why she wanted the radio so badly. She doesn't truly believe it will ever be anything but white noise, the ghosts of the dead radio stations and the dead announcers and the dead music. But this in itself is a wonder.

Father soon found out about the radio, but it didn't much matter. He let her keep it, though she has to work for the batteries: skin rabbits or gut fish, which are jobs that she hates. Pax helps her, and once the radio is alive, the two of them will spend the hottest part of the day listening to the white ghost noises, and sometimes they will flinch at a particular hiss, and then they will nudge each other and grin.

And then, one day, the white noise turns into sound. Pax, who is playing with the radio at the time, squeals in shock and drops it. Even so, the woman's voice, a radio voice that sounds nothing like a real voice, continues from the ground.

—*there, come and be welcome,* she says. *Follow the hummingbird. 51 degrees, 35 minutes, 53.88 seconds north, 0 degrees, 7 minutes, 10.92 seconds west. Repeat: If anyone is out there, come and be welcome. Follow the hummingbird.*

Dayna and Pax stare at each other with wide, wide eyes. This radio woman is the first person they have ever heard, aside from each other and Father and, a long time ago, Uncle William and Mother. It's not as if they believed they were the only humans left in the entire world. Father has said there must be others somewhere, getting by much in the same fashion as they are getting by here. He has also said that they have to hide straight away as soon as they see a stranger. But before this moment, this was always just something you were told but would never experience for yourself.

'Father!' they cry, almost simultaneously. 'Father! Father!'

Father comes rushing into the room, his eyes squinting and sleep-sanded.

'What? What—' But he stops then because the woman in the radio is still repeat-repeat-repeating her message, and he hears it.

'Oh,' he says. He listens until the message has repeated itself for the fifth time, then he says: 'Don't get too excited.' He reaches down and turns the woman off. 'It's probably an old message, in an endless loop. From long ago.'

'But what if it's not?' asks Dayna. 'What if there's a village out there, and they want to bring people together so that the village gets bigger and stronger?'

She knows that villages are people living together in small groups of houses. There are abandoned villages and towns everywhere, but they don't count because they are only buildings and no people.

'What do the numbers and minutes mean, Father?' asks Pax eagerly. 'Is it code?'

Father shakes his head. 'Just let it rest.'

They argue about it, Dayna and Father. Dayna wants to

follow the hummingbird (whatever that is) and find the other people, but Father is angry and says: 'No, No, NO.' He is scared of other people because things like the police and judges and prisons only exist in stories now, they aren't real any more. Which means people can be bad and no one can stop them. 'Look at what happened to your mother,' he says.

Dayna and Pax know their mother died when Dayna was little and Pax was littler still, but Father has never told them how.

'You mean bad people killed her?' asks Pax in a very quiet voice.

They know and love Mother through Father's stories, but they don't remember her.

'Yes,' says Father, and doesn't say any more. And this is how he wins the argument.

Dayna and Pax still listen to the radio, but Pax only wants to listen to the noise, like before. Dayna memorises the exact frequency, and when she's alone, she will tune into the woman and her message, and wonder about the hummingbird people.

Dayna was born into the dead world, and Pax was born just before it ended. Exactly how long ago that was can only be guessed. At the beginning, Father tried to keep track with home-made calendars, but forgot more often than not and has long since given up. You can no longer tell just by the weather. Father says there used to be four seasons always in motion: cold, warmer, hot, colder. And then repeat. Repeat. Repeat. Now most of the year is made up of hot days, with a lot of rain and thunderstorms, especially at night. Trees still renew their leaves, but at different times and not all at once, so that you hardly notice. And if winter does come (often it won't), all the difference it brings is slightly cooler air.

Father and Dayna and Pax live in a house they call the Blue House because it has a door the colour of a cloudless midday sky, the only blue like that on the street. The house's other colour is like most things, green, although you can still see traces of the red bricks between the many leaves and vines creeping over the facade. Father chose the street because there's a stream close by, but still far enough away in case of floods, and a wide field with intertwining trees that was a nature area (park, Father calls it) even back when most things weren't. You can catch fish in the stream and small animals in the undergrowth, and you can boil the stream water and drink it. The town supermarkets and kiosks and pharmacies are all gaping empty (contrary to the shops with useless items), but many dead houses still have a good supply of essentials, or used to. There are surrounding towns too, which they have to visit more and more often now to keep up their supplies; a day trip there and back on foot. Father chose the Blue House out of all the other houses on the street because blue was Mother's favourite colour. Mother was already dead when they arrived at the Blue House. Uncle William was still with them. Dayna was so young she can't remember, and Pax was just a baby. That was about a month after the end of the old world. But Father won't talk about that.

He will talk about other things, though. Father is the most fantastic storyteller. The stories are all from the time before, and they fascinate Dayna and Pax, just as the radio fascinates them. The lost world is a marvellous place, if only for all the things that have happened there.

One of Pax's favourite stories is that of King Kong, a

gorilla as tall as a house, who fell in love with a human woman and was killed because of it. Pax doesn't care about the love bit, but he's very interested in the flying machines called aeroplanes that were able to take the gorilla down. He has built miniature aeroplanes out of bits of wood and glue and plays with them a lot. Dayna likes listening to the adventures of her namesake best. She's a heroine of olden times, who didn't want to believe in monsters but fought them anyway.

Dayna is not like her namesake: she does believe; it would be foolish not to, now.

In addition to storytelling before bedtime and supply runs once in a while, the family has other routines. In fact, every day is a routine with only a few changes: indoor lessons and outdoor lessons, hunting and food planting, Father's heat headaches, the radio, games, meals, sleep. Even dangerous things like mist days or the crazed have become part of the routine. Dayna dreams up adventures in her head for her and Pax's entertainment, and will secretly wish that something exciting and new and wonderful might happen in real life; something connected to the hummingbird people. But of course, it never does.

And so, the days go by, and nothing changes. And all that really shows the passing of time are the rising indents on the inside of the wooden doorframe that mark Dayna growing, and Pax trying to catch up.

The endless routine ends with a scream.

2

Dayna and Pax are just returning from a swim in the stream when they hear it, and stop dead in their tracks.

And then run.

Father is curled up on the tiled kitchen floor of the Blue House. He's not dead, he's breathing.

'Father! Father!'

Then Dayna sees something next to him, a small furry heap on the ground. A dead rat. Next to it is Father's cricket bat, with the red mark clearly visible where it made contact.

How did it get in? Did someone leave the door open? Did it burrow into the cellar?

Father stirs and grunts and his eyelids flutter, then blink, then stay open. He pushes himself up and looks at them. 'It's all right,' he pants, although they can see it's not. He's cradling his left arm in his right, and it's swelling already. The bite marks are startlingly red.

'Did it have the craze?' asks Dayna, but of course it did. Why else would a rat attack a human man?

Father nods. 'Must have. Check the eyes.'

Dayna doesn't want to, but she forces herself to bend over the crushed rat. Its glassy eyes are pink. Some rats have naturally pink eyes, so that, as Dayna's namesake would say, is not conclusive evidence at all. But Father's swelling bite mark, and the fact that he's beginning to tremble and sweat simultaneously, all point towards something she doesn't want to be true.

'My eyes, Day,' gasps Father.

This time Pax is quicker, and he peers into Father's eyes with their noses almost touching. Then he pulls back and whimpers. Dayna looks too and sees the whites are bloodshot with red veins.

'You're not going to die, are you?' asks Pax. 'I didn't die when I was little and the crazed cat bit me. Remember, you said? You told me.'

Dayna remembers, vaguely. But that was when they still had a vaccine. In all the time they've lived in the Blue House and gone on supply runs, they haven't found any more vaccine. Father says it's because ordinary pharmacies didn't stock it, as there was hardly any time to work out a good system before things started to escalate very, very quickly. Mother was a doctor in the old world and managed to get hold of a handful of vials. That's why Pax didn't die that day he was bitten. Mother saved him, even though by then, she was already dead herself. But that was a long time ago, and the rest of the vials are no longer liquid at all; they have become hard and crumbly. No one can inject the once-upon-a-time vaccine into a syringe any more, and no one can get better from it.

Father's bloodshot eyes meet Dayna's, and now he's speaking only to her: 'You and Pax have to pack clothes and food and leave. Find some safe place, not too far away, but not too close either. And wait.'

Pax whimpers again but doesn't protest. Neither does Dayna. There are one of three ways things could go now, and all of them know it. Either the sickness will pass after a few days, leaving Father trembly and weak but alive. Or it won't pass, and he'll be dead by that time. Or, and this is what Father is afraid of, he will get the craze himself.

Zombies, he sometimes jokingly calls the crazed. They already existed in the old world, but only as legends and scary stories. Visions of the future, Dayna supposes, because the people of the dead world were magic and could do such things.

They pack their rucksacks quickly, mostly with gear and essentials, although Pax also squeezes an aeroplane in, and Dayna a book and her radio.

'Leave ... now,' Father tells them when they bring him plastic bottles of clean water and a pot of yesterday's boiled potatoes. He's wheezing heavily.

Silent tears are streaming down Pax's cheeks. Dayna mustn't cry because Father has to know that she is strong. Father won't let them hug or touch him, but he says: 'I love you ... very much.'

Says: 'It will be ... all right. Whatever ... happens.'

Says: 'Go.'

They choose one of the tall houses at the other end of the dead town and climb its stairs to the topmost flat. Closed doors are seldom a problem because Dayna inherited a lock pick from Uncle William, and spent many patient hours teaching herself how to use it. The people who lived in this flat were a family. There's a room with faded star wallpaper and old toys still strewn over the floor: small cars, coloured bricks, little square figures with yellow faces. Another room has a leaking beanbag and black-and-white comic books you read back to front, and so many photos. The girl on most of these photos looks so different from Dayna; like all dead-world girls, with their long hair and new clothes and colourful eyelids. Dayna's hair is short enough to stick up at the sides if she runs her fingers through it, and her worn T-shirt and jeans are at least as old as the Echidna fungus, whose arrival changed everything. The photo girl is laughing; she is happy. She doesn't know what is coming in her Now. She doesn't care what is happening in Dayna's.

From the window of this room, you can see rusted cars and gnarled trees and plants creeping up and into buildings. You can see a clump of Echidna spreading over a brick wall, its purple-pink colour and thin, long stems unmistakeable even from this distance; its pulsing caps a ticking time bomb. You can't see the Blue House.

'How long until we can go back?' asks Pax.

'Two days,' says Dayna. 'Father's rule.'

Sometimes the infected become crazed quickly, and sometimes they will take their time about it. Humans hold out longer than animals, Father says, but once humans turn, that's it for them, they won't survive. If Father hasn't turned in two days, then it should be all right. 'It *will* be all right,' says Dayna (because it has to be), and Pax looks at her and accepts what she says (because it HAS to be), and agrees: 'Yes.'

He wanders off, probably to the room with the toys. Pax doesn't suit his name at all, because it means peace in a dead language, and he always has to be moving and doing things. Dust explodes from the girl's bed when Dayna sits down, and it makes her sneeze and sneeze until she opens a window, then calls to Pax to open the others. She takes Mother's palm-sized picture out of her rucksack and studies it. Mother's picture is from before, like every picture is. It's both sleek from what it is and gritty from being touched so often. Along the folding lines, the image has rubbed off completely so it looks like Mother is divided into four pieces which meet just below her neck. Still, she's smiling and happy and so very, very pretty, and her long dark brown hair is the exact same colour as Dayna and Pax's. And when Dayna squints, she can magic the lines away. And when she pretends, she can hear Mother – whose voice is gentle and kind and light because women's voices don't deepen like men's – tell her that it's true: everything will be all right.

3

She is jolted awake by rain spraying into the room through the open window. Outside, thunder rumbles far away.

'Pax,' she moans, jumping to her feet. 'Close the windows!'

He's not in the room, so she does it herself. The dark outside world is briefly illuminated by white. Lightning, but not anywhere she can see.

'Pax!' she shouts again, stalking into the other rooms to close the windows there too. She should never have fallen asleep and left him in charge. Rain doesn't matter, but what if the wind had carried pink mist to them? What then? The mist brings death and craze more surely than a simple bite from an infected animal.

'Pax, you idiot! Where are you?!'

She spots a line of light under a closed door, which must be from his wind-up torch (although another of Father's rules is No Lights After Dark, in case the crazed see). The torch is on the ground, and her brother is standing on a chair, holding something high over his head near an open window. He whips around when she enters, almost toppling off the chair, a mixture of guilt and excitement on his face. The something, she can see now, is Uncle William's black walkie-talkie radio. Uncle William was once a soldier, someone trained to fight and survive, and he left behind all manner of interesting things. They have never seen any great use in this, though. Not without a second walkie-talkie to communicate with. The walkie's ordinarily blank screen is alight, glowing green in the gloom, and there are letters in it, sharp and straight instead of round. With a flash of anger, Dayna sees her beloved radio a few paces away, its back open and exposed, the casing where the batteries are, empty.

'Hey—'

'Don't be mad, Day,' Pax says quickly, hopping down from the chair. 'This is an experiment. If it works, maybe I can help Father.'

'If what works?' she demands. 'That won't, Father said. There's no one else nearby. You're just wasting the batteries, put them back.'

She makes a grab for the walkie and Pax jumps back, still clutching it to his chest. 'That's why I said experiment,' he says. 'No, *listen*, Day. You don't know, and Father doesn't either. But I do because of the book.'

The book, in Pax speak, means a thick textbook chock-full of information and pictures of gadgets from the dead world. Dayna likes reading stories. Pax, on rainy days, reads this.

'Walkie-talkies transmit and receive frequency waves if they're in range,' he explains, obviously reciting. 'And we always said nothing was in range. But we never tried properly. It makes a really big difference if we're higher above ground, so there's less interference with the waves, see? We're high over trees and most buildings now.'

So that's why he insisted on the topmost flat of the building earlier. 'How long have you known this?' she asks. 'You must've known before we came because you took the walkie-talkie with you.'

Pax doesn't meet her eye. 'For a bit,' he mumbles. 'I read it a while ago. I didn't say anything because I knew you'd want to try it out straight away. To try and contact the hummingbird people—'

'What, and you didn't?'

He shrugs. 'I dunno. Father wouldn't've liked it. And I don't really think I would, either. Even if they're not bad. I like it how it is. Just us. But now …'

'Yeah,' says Dayna. She's too excited to be angry at him for keeping this a secret. 'Yeah. If the hummingbird people have a village, they might have doctors. Or even some of the old vaccine.'

Pax is nodding. 'And if they have a radio signal, it makes sense for them to have walkie-talkies too.'

'If the range can be widened … How far's the range on this thing?'

'It says forty miles,' says Pax, pointing out the faded letters. 'But that means best conditions, with no interference. On the ground, there's no way we could pick that up because of so much other stuff getting in the way. It must be better now, but this rain is probably bad for the signal too. I just wanted to try it out already.'

Pax holds the walkie-talkie to his mouth. 'Hello? Hello?'

Nothing, just the faintest crackle of white noise. He shrugs as if to say: See?

'Try the other numbers,' says Dayna. 'They must be frequencies.'

He does, one after the other. Nothing happens.

'Hello?' shouts Dayna into the walkie-talkie, not really believing anything will happen; and at the same time believing that it must. It would in a story.

'Hello?' shouts Pax. 'Hellohellohellohellohello!' He begins pressing all the buttons in turn. 'Hello? Hello-oooh?'

And the walkie-talkie comes to life:

'*Ch-chssschhhhs-chhh-chhhhh* Hell … *chhhhh chhh-shhhh-hhh* … there?'

It's like finding the voice in the radio all over again, right down to Pax screaming and dropping the device. And it's not like that at all, because whoever is talking now is talking to *them*. They haven't in a million lifetimes expected this. Not even Pax, whose idea it was in the first place. Not even Dayna, who half believed something might happen and half believed nothing ever could. The walkie continues to spit and crackle, but there are no more words. Then suddenly, there is nothing at all.

Pax looks at Dayna. Dayna looks at Pax.

They scramble to the walkie. Dayna snatches it up first. 'Hello? Hello? Hello?'

Nothing. Nothing but silence. Have they missed their chance? Has there really been a chance to miss?

'It was them,' croaks Pax. 'This is crazy. It was *them*.'

And Dayna says: 'The hummingbird people.'

They try to contact the hummingbird people again, shouting their hellos through all the different channels, but whoever heard them the first time must have turned off their own radio, or, more likely, is completely out of range now. In the end, there's nothing to do but do nothing.

Pax practises his handstands against a wall. Up, down, up again in an endless, untiring loop. Dayna tries to read the book she has brought by torchlight, which is about a girl who belongs to a farm called Green Gables the same way Dayna belongs to the Blue House. But she can't concentrate on it, not with Father infected, not with the hummingbird people real. White noise murmurs in the background. They have left the walkie-talkie standing on the floor between them, switched on, even though this is a waste of the precious batteries. Just in case.

'Hello?'

From the ground. A man's voice. Crackling, but a hundred times clearer than it was before. Clearer even than the woman's repeat repeat repeat voice on the radio.

Pax comes crashing down from his handstand.

'Anyone there?' the man is still asking. 'Hello? Over.'

Dayna recovers first. She swoops down and picks up the walkie, hands trembling. 'Yes, we're here!' she gasps into the speaker holes, breathless, dizzy. 'Are you the people who said to follow the hummingbird?'

But the man still can't hear her. 'Do you copy?' he keeps on asking. 'Is anyone there? Hello? Over.'

Pax is by her side now. 'Press that,' he says, indicating a big button to the side. He's whispering, in awe.

Dayna presses the button. 'Hello?' she says again. 'Can you hear me?'

She can't hear anything, so she lets go of the button again and laughter crackles through the machine. 'Yes!' shouts the man. He sounds excited. 'Yes! I hear you! How many of you are there? *Where* are you? Over.'

'We're two people,' Dayna hears herself say, and still she can't quite believe that she's actually talking to someone else. Someone from outside. Have people always been this close, and they never knew? Just a walkie-talkie call away? If Pax had only said something sooner …

'Me and my brother. And then there's our father, but he's ill. Have you got medicine?'

'Say over,' says Pax. 'That's to show that you're done talking.'

'Over,' says Dayna.

'Yes! Yes!' The man sounds happy, not just excited. 'We're in a lorry, we must be close to have a signal like this. We heard you before, but weren't really in range. Where exactly are you? Over.'

Pax is tugging at her left arm. She lets go of the button so the man can't hear them, and Pax whispers: 'It is OK, isn't it? To tell him? Father will be angry when he finds out we told someone.'

Yes, because Father is afraid of bad people. But this man doesn't sound bad at all. He sounds cheerful and young, younger than Father. He sounds like he knows a lot of stories and could make you laugh easily. Pax is right, Father will be angry. But as long as he is alive, he can be as angry as he likes.

'Hello?' the man is saying. 'Hello? Still there? Over.'

'Yes,' says Dayna, pressing the button again. 'My father was bitten by a crazed rat. Have you got the vaccine? Or doctors to help him? Are you the hummingbird people? Over.'

'Yes to all that,' says the man. Dayna's heart leaps. She smiles at Pax, who smiles back in return.

'My name's Ryan,' says the man. 'I'm part of the reconnaissance, which means we tour the country and try to find survivors. Amongst other things. You're the first in a very long time. It's not easy, mostly just pure chance whether we run across anyone or not. But we have a safe place. We're building infrastructure as best we can. We have doctors who can help your dad. We have scientists trying to work out a proper vaccine. We need as many people – good people – as we can get. To help with the work. Everyone does their bit at the Hummingbirds. You sound like good people. Are you? Over.'

'Yes,' says Dayna at once. 'Yes, we are.' (And he is too, or he wouldn't have asked, would he?) 'Over.'

'Tell me where you are, and we'll come and meet you,' says Ryan. 'We have some of the vaccine right here in the lorry. When was your father bitten? Over.'

'Today. This afternoon. Um … over.'

'Then there's a good chance he'll pull through. If we give it to him soon. Over.'

This decides it for Dayna. And for Pax too.

She looks at him; he nods.

'Heathfield,' she says to Ryan. 'That's where we are. You can only get in from the east. If you take the big road, you have to turn left by the tipped bus, then right when you reach the bit that's all overgrown. We live in the Blue House. I mean, the door is blue. You have to be careful coming in, though. We've planted thorn bushes so you can't come from all sides, and there are tripwires and noise alarms closer to the house. Cans on strings and buckets and such. To keep away the crazed, or warn us when they come. It might be difficult with a car.'

'It's not a car, love,' says Ryan. 'We'll be there soon. Sit tight. Out.'

4

The Hummingbirds, Dayna keeps thinking. The Hummingbirds are going to help us. Thunder and lightning clash over them, and Dayna and Pax run, heads down, gas masks bumping against thighs, rucksacks seemingly lighter than on their way up.

They reach the Blue House drenched and trembling. No new vehicles are parked there, only the handful of familiar ones people left behind in the old world, the ones that are rusted and dead. The Blue House looks dead too, and although they're eager to get out of the storm and into the dry, both Dayna and Pax hesitate before they enter.

Father is exactly where they left him, curled up and trembling and asleep. He does not wake, even when Pax shouts his name.

'He'll get the vaccine soon,' says Dayna. 'All we have to do is wait.'

It's a long wait, upstairs in their bedroom, or it feels like it is, although there's no way to tell without the sun. Dayna is beginning to nod off when there is a resounding knock on the front door, and she jerks up at once, more awake than she has ever been.

'Is that him?' whispers Pax, his voice higher than usual. 'Is that him?'

But of course it is. What else would knock like that? Knock like people do in Father's dead-world stories, asking to be let in.

They rush down to the door, their torch beams bouncing wildly, and Dayna reaches it first and swings it open and steps back, into Pax, who steps back as well. And here is a man who is not Father and not even long-lost Uncle William. A stranger, looking right at them. Pax's hand suddenly clamps around Dayna's arm. She turns briefly, to give him an it's-OK nod, even when her own heart is pounding. The two of them watch, awed, as the man enters, brushing off raindrops from his waterproof poncho. He's not quite as tall as Father, but almost. He has light hair, so light that at first, he seems not to have eyebrows at all. Another person, here.

'Hello, kids,' says Ryan, grinning wide. 'Took a bit longer than we thought, sorry.'

Through the sheets of rain behind him, Dayna sees a huge vehicle; a lorry.

'Have you got the vaccine with you?' she asks, and tries to push away the strangeness of this new man, and her speaking to him. 'Father's in there.'

'Let's see what we can do, then,' says Ryan. He strides through the hallway and into the kitchen, where Father is, leaving puddles of muddy water in his wake. Father always has strict rules about taking off one's boots by the door, but Father has the fever now, and Ryan doesn't know the rules, so it shouldn't matter, should it? Dayna jogs after Ryan with Pax at her heels.

Ryan is already kneeling in front of Father. He takes out a square object from one of his many trouser pockets and holds it up to Father's face. Numbers light up in the box: *40.1*. Ryan stows the box back into his pocket, pushes one of Father's eyelids up and peers into his eyes.

'Spreading,' he mutters to himself, then looks at them and smiles. 'But he ought to pull through. Won't give him the vaccine yet. If he recovers on his own, it'd do more harm than good.'

Dayna feels dizzy as relief washes over her, and Pax whoops and jumps in jubilation, knocking into her and making her laugh as well. Meanwhile, Ryan has taken hold of Father's limp body and hoisted him up, over his shoulder like a large sack of potatoes.

'What are you doing?' asks Dayna.

Ryan looks surprised at the question. 'Taking him with us, of course. All of you. To our people. That's what you wanted, isn't it?'

Dayna and Pax gape at each other. Yes, this is what they wanted, isn't it? Dayna has just not thought this far. Or dreamed this big. This is unreal and amazing and scary all at once.

No time to take more than their rucksacks, no time to think. Ryan has already opened the blue door. Through the wind he calls to them: 'Go on, run to the lorry. Mart will let you in. Quick!'

The lorry is only a blurry shape through the rain until it is suddenly right in front of them, and another man with thick arms is pushing them towards the back. There are two doors here, and the man pulls both of them open. Dayna hoists herself into the back space and gives Pax her hand so that he can clamber in too. A second later, Ryan hauls Father in and climbs in himself before pulling the doors shut and leaving them all in complete and utter darkness.

'Ryan?' whispers Dayna. She realises that she has grabbed hold of Pax's hand and that he isn't trying to shake it off as he would usually do, but hanging on tight.

'It's OK,' says Ryan's voice. 'We'll get some light as soon as Mart starts the engine. Best sit down, you two, it'll be bumpy.'

Just then the floor beneath them begins to quiver and buck and— 'We're moving, Day,' gasps Pax. 'We're in a car and it's *moving*.'

There's a hissing noise and a thin pipe-like light between wall and ceiling flickers into life. On-off-on-off, before finally deciding to stay on. Another wonder, as for Dayna, electricity beyond their torches has always belonged to the dead world, not to Now.

They're in a long space lined with boxlike, tarp-covered shapes stacked from floor to ceiling, although there are smaller, uncovered boxes too, full of masks and rope and other gear. At the far end is a small mesh window; behind it, the bristly head of the lorry's driver, Mart.

'Don't peek behind the tarp,' says Ryan, as he drags Father's limp body towards the window. 'We've got animals in cages there, and the fluorescent light would set them off.'

'What are they for?' asks Pax. 'Food?'

'They'll help the scientists,' says Ryan. 'You'll see how when we get there. Sorry that I can't offer you any blankets. But hey, this time tomorrow, you'll be sleeping in nice, cosy beds at the Station.'

They watch as Ryan adjusts Father's position to something more comfortable. Watch him tie Father's wrists and ankles together with a thin strip of plastic, a cable tie, and fasten a muzzle-mask of leather bands over Father's nose and mouth. 'Sorry,' he mutters, glancing at them. 'I'll give him the vaccine before anything can happen, but … well. Just taking precautions.'

Pax inches slightly closer to Dayna. 'It's OK,' she whispers. 'It's horrible, but that's the way you have to do it. To be safe.'

Sleep is impossible at first, after all the scares and wonders, with rain hammering against the cargo roof, in a lorry that is actually alive. Impossible, then suddenly here.

And when something jerks Dayna out of her half-dreams, it takes her a few seconds to get her bearings: She is curled up in the shadows next to Pax. The light stick at the far end is still humming and spitting. Beneath it are Father and Ryan, both asleep, Father wheezing on his side, Ryan's head lolling against the wall, bobbing to the lorry's rhythm. Above them, through the small mesh window and past Mart's outline, is a patch of black outside world. The storm has quietened down, and now Dayna can hear little whimpers and mewls close by: the animals in the hidden cages. She should wake Ryan. He should be alert and watching Father and ready to inject the vaccine if—

Tap, tap – tap, tap.

Dayna turns to the cages, frowning.

There, again. *Tap, tap – tap, tap.*

It's difficult to hear through the animals' whining, especially because the taps are so very light, but now that she's separated this sound from the others, it's unmistakeable.

Two taps, pause, then another two. Repeated, and again, and again.

Without thinking, without knowing, Dayna reaches out. Beside her, Pax mumbles something in his sleep and rolls over. Slowly, carefully, so that the plastic material won't crackle, Dayna lifts the tarp.

Cages, just as Ryan has said. A scrawny tabby cat hisses loudly and retreats from the mesh bars. On its cage is another, still mostly hidden behind the tarp, where an unseen animal's movements quicken. Dayna drops the tarp again, quick as quick. She glances over at Ryan and the driver, but Ryan's eyes are still closed, and all that is visible of Mart is part of his back and left shoulder. Not even Pax, right beside her, has woken up, but then again, Dayna has always been the light sleeper of the two. Good survival instinct, Father calls it. Father is a light sleeper as well, usually, when he isn't ill with fever. But Pax is the opposite. You really have to shake and shake him if you want to wake him up before he is ready to—

Tap-tap-tap-tap.

The tapping again, louder, quicker. More urgent. Whatever is making the sound knows how close she is. Slightly to the right of the cat's cage. Another glance at the sleeping Ryan, and then Dayna leans forward again and lifts the tarp, at the right-hand corner now, for a second time.

A big cage, six times the size of the cat's. And inside: a boy.

Dayna freezes, stares. He's older than her by a couple of years, maybe more, and his skin is darker. Darker still because of the bruises, all over. His left eye is almost black, puffy and swollen shut so that not even the tiniest slit of his pupil is visible. He's been gagged with a bandana tied between his teeth and is sitting in this cage with his knees drawn up to his chin and his arms wrapped around them and the frizzy ropes of his hair squashed against the top.

She opens her mouth – to what? Gasp? Scream? Ask him questions?

The boy lifts a finger to his mouth, signalling her to be quiet. She sees that his hands have been bound like Father's. But he can still use them to gesture.

He points to her (you), then he brushes first the index and then the middle finger of his right hand against the flat palm of his left in quick succession (run): You. Run.

Blood pounding in Dayna's ears. *Ba-boom. Ba-boom. Ba-boom.*

She lets the tarp fall again, and the captured boy is gone as if he has never been there. Ryan is still asleep; Mart is still driving. Father is still here, and so is Pax. Nothing has changed. And everything has changed.

Slowly, Dayna lowers herself on to the hard floor again and closes her eyes. Her tiredness has been frightened out of her, and she does not sleep and does not want to sleep. Instead, she thinks, and thinks, and thinks.

Ideas and doubts and fears whirl around her at dizzying speed, and she tries to catch them, to twist, form, force them into shape, into something that will work, that will get them out, that will help them *run*. And when, much later, the low voices of two men break in on her thoughts and shift them back to the lorry (stationary now, only she never noticed it stopping), she knows what she is going to do.

5

Ryan and the driver are whispering to one another through the mesh window, words Dayna can't make out. At Ryan's feet, Father's breathing behind the muzzle is quick and shallow, and she can see sweat on his forehead glistening in the pale fluorescent light of the lorry. Still alive.

'Are we there?' she gasps, her throat tight with fear. If they've reached their destination, then there's nothing to be done.

Both men whip around as if they have forgotten all about her being here. Beside her, Pax stirs and mutters: 'We there?'

Ryan smiles at them. His smile looks so kind and sincere, it makes Dayna doubt herself, and doubt the boy in the cage.

'No, just about halfway,' says Ryan. 'Even if all the roads were still in decent shape, which they're not by a long shot, we still have all the other shit to deal with. Fallen trees, landslides. This is just a quick pit stop, and then I'll drive. You could do with a rest, couldn't you, Mart?'

Mart grunts in acquiescence without looking at Dayna. It strikes her how big he looks, but maybe that's because the only view she has of him is through the tiny mesh window.

'I have to wee,' says Pax, sitting up with a yawn.

'Me too,' says Dayna quickly.

Ryan shrugs. 'Nature calls, I reckon. Wouldn't mind

going myself. But don't be too long and don't wander off too far.'

Dayna relaxes somewhat. She hasn't been sure whether Ryan would actually let them walk off by themselves. She's been wondering if she and Pax were going to be put in cages as well.

'What about Father?' asks Pax.

'He's already done his business, can't you smell it?' says Ryan, and he glances at Mart and they both smirk. Dayna feels a rush of shame, followed by fury. And the doubt from earlier is gone. 'Don't laugh at him,' says Pax hotly. 'It's not his fault!'

'Sorry, kid. Course it isn't,' says Ryan, but his eyes are laughing even so.

Pax senses this too, and he glares suspiciously at Ryan. Dayna nudges his shoulder: 'Leave it. Let's go.'

She picks up her discarded rucksack, looks Ryan straight in the eye and says: 'I need to take some things in here with me. Sanitary towels.'

She waits for Ryan to spot the lie, call her out, but he just shrugs as if to say: What do I care?

Ryan has to unlock the back doors with a ring of jangling keys. Dayna watches as he takes them out of his vest pocket, and puts them back in afterwards. His right-hand lower pocket. All three of them climb out into the dawn sunlight of a new day, blinking in the sudden sky-brightness. The lorry is pulled up next to a brick house in what looks like a small village, surrounded by all manner of weeds and trees. The air is pleasantly fresh and cool after the rainstorm, and there are still a couple of clouds in the sky, but already you can tell that it's building up to be another scorching day. Ryan watches, amused, as Dayna and Pax busy themselves with fastening their gas masks to their trouser loops, another one of Father's rules about going outside.

'Nice masks,' he comments. 'Good quality. Where'd you get them?'

'We always had them,' says Pax.

'Lucky. Most people left only have the thin, flimsy kind. We're different, being soldiers.'

'Is that a hummingbird?' asks Pax, pointing. Dayna looks and sees that someone has spray-painted a black bird with outspread wings and tail feathers on the side of the lorry.

'Yeah, our symbol.' Ryan nods. 'I'd have preferred something cooler, like a tiger maybe, but it wasn't my decision.'

The driver's door opens and Mart slouches out to join them, an unlit cigarette in his mouth. Without taking any notice of the kids, he offers the pack to Ryan, who takes one too, then fishes a lighter from his pocket. He is big, thinks Dayna. Taller and broader than Ryan, and older too. Maybe Father's age. Still, both Hummingbird men look like brothers, with their identical buzz cuts and similar clothes. Not quite matching, but still similar. Like uniforms. Combat trousers, undershirts (Ryan's is dark blue, Mart's a grimy white) and heavy, sleeveless vests with a lot of pockets. Both of them are wearing belts with handguns, and while earlier Dayna might have been glad for the extra protection these offered, now they make her very uneasy ...

Pax is watching the men smoke in fascination. Father doesn't smoke, but they know a lot of people did. There are pictures in weathered magazines and packets in stores, packets with horrible photographs.

'Come on, Pax,' she hisses, grabbing her brother by the hand and tugging him in the direction of the nearest trees.

'Don't be too long,' Ryan calls after them.

'We won't,' Dayna calls back.

'Stop it, Day, I can walk by myself,' grumbles Pax, snatching his hand away from hers. 'I'm not a baby.'

'Don't fall behind then, we have to be quick.'

They move through the undergrowth until they are far enough away from the lorry for Dayna to feel unseen and unheard. She picks up a twig and pokes through the tall grass, checking for snakes and other unwelcome creepy-crawlies, just as Father has taught them. Satisfied it's safe, they relieve themselves. Dayna catches Pax watching her with interest and tells him sharply to turn around. He does, but says:

'I never knew you needed sanitary towels already. Is there blood in your pee, then? Can I see?'

Father has explained to Dayna (with a lot of stuttering and fumbling) what the menstruation cycle is, to prepare her. Pax wasn't part of the conversation, but he couldn't be got rid of.

'No, you can't see, don't be disgusting. Anyway, I don't need the towels yet, I only said that so he'd let me take my rucksack.'

'Why?'

'Just let me wee in peace, then I'll tell you.'

Pax giggles. He can; he thinks Ryan and Mart will help them, and Father will either get better by himself or will get better because of the vaccine. He thinks everything is as good as it can be. She wishes … But no, what good is it to wish?

She pulls up her pants and jeans, then tells Pax he can turn around now. And shut up and listen. There must be something in her expression. Pax shuts up, and listens. And his eyes grow wider and wider.

'What do you think?' Dayna asks him after she's finished. 'Who would you trust?'

Pax doesn't have to think about it: 'The boy in the cage.'

Dayna nods. 'Me too. But how can we be sure? The boy could be the dangerous one. They might have locked him up because of it. We might be throwing away the chance for the vaccine.'

'Only bad people would lock children in cages and give them black eyes,' says Pax. 'And you should never trust bad people.'

He's right. It's as simple as that.

'OK,' says Dayna. 'Then we have to get away. I think I know how to do it.'

'You took your time, didn't you?' says Ryan when Dayna returns to the lorry. 'We're on our second ciggie. Some things never change,' he mutters to Mart. 'Girls always need longer on the bog.'

He laughs, although Mart only snorts in acknowledgement. Dayna wonders how she ever could have liked him.

'Oi, where's the other one, then?'

Dayna steels herself. She doesn't know whether she's a good liar, but she thinks she is. She's good at pretending at any rate, in all those make-believe games she and Pax still sometimes play. And isn't pretending and lying almost the same thing?

'Pax is hurt,' she says, pretending. 'Not bad, but he can't really walk. He twisted his ankle in a rabbit hole. He cries when I try to hoist him up. Please, can one of you carry him to the lorry?'

The two men look annoyed, but not distrustful. The only question now is whether they will help. She's deliberately made the injury as harmless as possible. Nothing too inconvenient, just carry him to the lorry and he'll be all right.

Ryan throws down his cigarette with a sigh and grinds it into the dust. 'Fine,' he says, 'lead me to him. How far out?'

'Only about five minutes.'

'Jesus, five minutes? I told you not to go out far, didn't I? Fifty paces qualifies as not far …'

But he follows her. Mart watches them leave without a word. He takes another drag on his cigarette, then turns away. Dayna thinks that if it were up to him, he would decide to leave Pax behind. Maybe even leave her too if she complained. She wonders why the two men picked them up in the first place.

Pax is ready by the time Dayna and Ryan reach the small clearing. He's sitting in the centre, surrounded by the low-hanging branches of trees. It's difficult to make out the bent branch he's selected through all the thick green leaves. Dayna can, but she's looking for it. Ryan isn't. He steps forward, towards Pax, who is sitting up with an unconvincing expression of pain on his face.

'Jesus, can't leave you guys alone fo— ARGHHHH!'

His right foot is jerked upwards as the wiry branch snaps back, taking the paracord rope and Ryan's ankle with it. Pax scrambles out of the way fast as he can.

Rabbits and other smaller creatures would have been left dangling in the air, but Ryan does a strange sort of backflip and is hurled violently against a tree trunk, head and torso first. Dayna and Pax both wince at the thud. But there's no time to feel sorry or regretful. Dayna rushes towards Ryan, groaning and sprawled with his right leg sticking up at an odd angle, still attached to the rope. He's dazed, and she has to be quick before he realises what's happening.

She goes straight for his gun, fumbling it free from the holster. Then she backs away, holding the weapon, which is surprisingly heavy, in both her hands. She and Pax know how to use it in theory – Father has coached them in most things – but they have never fired one before. Uncle William's gun had no bullets left.

Ryan is beginning to come round. He twists to look at them. 'What the *fuck*? What the fuck are you two doing?!'

He reaches for his gun and finds it missing. 'You little SHITS!' he roars. He tries to push himself up and makes a grab for the rope around his ankle.

'Stop,' orders Dayna. 'I'll shoot you. I will.'

Ryan slumps down again: shoulders thumping against woodland ground, right foot dangling high over his body. He twists to one side to look at them, and in particular, to look at the nozzle of his gun in Dayna's hands.

'What the …' he pants weakly.

Dayna takes a step back, then another. Well out of Ryan's reach. 'OK, Pax,' she says. He trots up to her and she carefully passes the gun over to him.

'Is it too heavy for you?' she asks.

'No,' Pax says at once.

'Are you sure? No lying. It's important.'

'I'm not. All right, it is a bit heavy, but not too heavy. I'm a good shot, you know I am. As good as you.'

She knows he is, and she also knows that knives and slingshots are different from guns. There's a recoil, for one … But there's no time to argue. Too late to change the plan now.

'All right. Keep it for now. We have to hurry.'

'What are you doing? Come on, kids, it's all right.' Ryan has calmed down, is speaking as if his leg isn't suspended by a blue rope in mid-air while the rest of him is sprawled amongst weeds and earth. 'Just give it back. You could hurt yourselves. Just give it back and cut me loose. No hard feelings.'

'The safety's on,' says Dayna. She takes the gun, removes the safety catch, then hands it back to Pax. Pax points it at Ryan: 'Don't move, Ryan.'

'What the – what are you doing? We're *helping* you.'

'We found the caged boy,' says Dayna shortly. 'Take off that vest. Throw it here.'

'Do it,' warns Pax when Ryan hesitates. 'Or I'll shoot.'

Ryan considers him and seems to decide not to risk it. Instead, he opts for talking. 'The caged boy? That's got nothing to do with you. We didn't put you in cages, did we? We want to *help* you. He's a special case, nothing to do with you and your dad.'

All the while, he's wriggling his arms out of the vest, hampered by lying down the way he is. When he's finally free of it, he bunches it up and gives it a very awkward flick in Dayna's direction. The vest lands well within his range, and she doesn't move. One of Father's rules: Always keep your distance from dangerous creatures. Even if they look slow or hurt, they can still strike.

'Pick it up and throw it properly,' she says. 'I'm not going anywhere near you.'

'What are you afraid of?' he scoffs. 'You've got the gun.'

'Yeah, and my brother will shoot you with it if you don't do what I say.'

This time, the vest lands almost at her feet. She opens the right-hand pocket and retrieves a small ring of keys, perhaps six or eight. The lorry key is unmistakeable: bigger than the others, the end bit covered by thick rubber with two buttons. She thrusts the keys into her trouser pocket, burying them in as deep as she can. The vest she throws into the undergrowth. She doesn't need it any more.

'Turn your trouser pockets inside out,' she tells Ryan.

He does, muttering swear words under his breath, but all that falls out is a battered box of cigarettes. Good. Without a knife, it will take him a while to get free from the rope, even if he uses both his hands. Too risky to tie them up if she doesn't have to. He might well grab her, force her between himself and the gun, and that would be it.

'Come on,' she says to Pax. 'We have to move fast.'

Ryan's shouts follow them through the trees: 'You little shits! You've just ruined everything for yourselves. No sanctuary. No vaccine. You just killed your dad!'

They run and try to block out the words and their meaning. Lies, thinks Dayna. All lies. Good people don't beat and imprison kids. Soon, Ryan's curses are swallowed up in the dense leaves.

6

'Where're the other two?' asks Mart the moment Dayna is in earshot, as she walks towards him on the cracked and empty street. The lorry's door is open, and he's half sitting, half leaning against the passenger seat. By the look of cigarette butts on the ground, he seems to have smoked almost a whole packet. Dayna is intensely aware of the weight and slight bulge of the keys in her pocket.

'They're further back,' she says, gesturing vaguely behind her (the opposite side of where Pax is now). 'Ryan's carrying Pax, but I think Pax is too heavy. They're really slow.'

She'd hoped Mart might jog off in that direction to help his friend, but not really expected it. Mart just exhales irritably and checks his watch – a very strange thing to do, Dayna thinks. Who could possibly care what time it is?

At that moment, she spots Pax creeping out from behind a brick wall, holding the gun in both hands, heading towards Mart, whose back is turned to him. He's panting. She can see it even though she can't hear it: his mouth open, his cheeks wet and layered in sweat. She told him to wait, to get his breath back after his detour. He might ruin everything. Mart will hear him before he can get too close.

'Mart,' she says. 'Did you lie about the vaccine?'

Mart is alert at once. He doesn't go for his gun, but he stands upright and takes a step closer to her.

'Now why,' he asks, 'would you say that?'

'Because I think a vaccine ought to be given to a person straight away if they're sick.'

Mart snorts. 'You *think*, do you? Take it from me that we know.'

He makes to turn away, but Dayna says quickly: 'What are you gonna do with the animals?'

'What's with all the bloody questions? Just—'

And this is when Pax stumbles over something, weeds maybe or a tree root. He rights himself at once, but Mart hears and turns and sees Pax, and sees the gun. Pax stops where he is and points it right at Mart.

'Don't move, Mart,' he says. 'I'll shoot.'

Mart moves. He makes a grab at his own gun, and Pax fires. Both are knocked backwards, Pax from the recoil, Mart from the bullet.

Mart crashes on to the ground, six feet or so in front of Dayna. For the second time in fifteen minutes, which is also the second time in her life, Dayna finds herself reaching for a man's holstered gun. But Mart, unlike Ryan, has his wits about him. A big hairy hand grabs her by the arm and yanks it back hard. She screams and kicks out blindly, connecting with something flabby and soft. Mart grunts – 'Humpf!' – and Dayna, head reeling and eyes watering, sinks her teeth into the hand around her. It's a strange sort of distraction from the throbbing pain in her arm, but it's still disgusting: She can feel the hand's hair in her mouth, the salty taste of sweat and unwashed skin. And she can only hope that Pax will hurry up because she's only a girl and Mart is a man, even if he has been shot, and there's no way she's going to win this by herself.

'Get off my sister!' yells Pax's voice. Oh, thank you! Dayna opens her eyes (realising only now that they were closed) and sees Pax standing right in front of them, jabbing Ryan's gun into Mart's sweaty temple.

'Fuck,' pants Mart, and his grip relaxes. Dayna pushes herself into a sitting position and picks at Mart's holster with her good hand.

'Hurry up,' says Pax.

'I'm moving as fast as I can. My arm really hurts.'

She finally manages to tug the gun out, then scrambles up and away from Mart, still on the ground and not moving, just as Pax has told him. His left hand is sporting her red, circular bite mark. His right shoulder is bloody from where Pax's bullet hit him. Dayna turns away from him to take stock of her own injury. Gingerly, she flexes her fingers, then wrist, then arm – finding to her immense relief that she can do all these things. 'Not broken,' she tells Pax. Her voice sounds thin and wobbly in her ears. But she won't cry now, or ever, because tears make you blind, and then Pax would be all on his own against Mart.

'You think you can still get him if you take one step back?' she asks Pax.

'I got him from all that way over there,' he says.

'You didn't get him, not properly, or else he wouldn't be a problem now. But OK. Then take a step back. That way it's more difficult for him to jump you.'

'He's not going to jump me. I'd kill him.'

'Just do it.'

Pax does.

'Keep him there, I'm going to check on Father and the boy.'

'Is that what this is?' asks Mart. 'The bloody boy? What did you do to Ryan?'

'We killed him,' says Pax.

'Pax, don't talk to him!' Dayna unlocks the doors and peers into the back of the lorry. There Father is, lying at the far end, breathing, alive but not awake. She reaches out and lifts a corner of the tarp. The boy with the dreadlocks is still here too, his good eye very white and wide, his bad eye black and closed.

'We're leaving,' she tells him. 'I'll let you out of the cage soon as we're far enough away from them.'

She has the keys, and one of them must open the padlock on the cage door, but there's no time to lose. Ryan might have freed himself, might be on his way right now. Mart might have some other weapon hidden on his body.

Behind her, she hears Mart say: 'Shit, I can't believe this. Two kids. Ryan'd better be bloody dead, or I'll murder him myself. We had the boy, that's all we needed. *Shit.*'

They should kill Mart, but killing a human is very different from killing an animal and Dayna doesn't want to do it, and doesn't want Pax to do it either. But she has to be clever about this too.

She closes the back doors of the lorry and walks back to the other two.

'Shoot him in the leg,' she tells Pax.

'*What?*' Mart's cry is half-laugh, half-shout.

'He might try and get us before we're ready. I'd do it, but I can't, with this arm. Sorry.'

'It's OK,' says Pax. 'I can do it.'

Mart leaps at them then, but it's a clumsy leap with his injured shoulder, and he's too far away in any case. Pax fires the gun for a second time. Mart screams, and Dayna yells as Pax stumbles into her, and she falls to the ground. She looks up to see Mart writhing in the grass, clutching his arm, which is covered all over in a gobby dark red now. It's staining the grass red, too.

'I didn't mean to do that,' says Pax, sounding a little dazed. 'I got his arm again. Isn't that weird?'

'Good enough,' says Dayna. 'Come on, let's go.'

They leave Mart where he is and run to the lorry's front side. It's very painful and awkward, climbing in with her shoulder and upper arm on fire, but Dayna manages it. Pax follows closely behind and slams the door shut.

'Lock it,' says Dayna, pushing the knob down on her side too. Then she unslings her rucksack and takes in her surroundings. She and Pax are familiar with the interior of cars. In their games, Pax almost always wants to be a pilot or a driver. Now Pax is only a little boy, and he whispers: 'Are you sure we can? We don't know how.'

'Yes, we do,' says Dayna. 'Father taught us.'

But she knows what he means, and now that the impossible part of the plan is over and done with, the easy part is looking more and more difficult. They know how, but only in theory. Only in words.

'We have to change places,' she says. 'I can't steer anything with this arm.'

'But I can't drive,' wails Pax, as if *she* could.

'Yes, you can. You're the pilot, aren't you? Come on, we have to leave NOW.'

He struggles over her and takes his place behind the wheel. He can barely look over it to the windscreen.

'Put the key in,' says Dayna.

'I know that!' snaps Pax, and jams the car key into the small slot. He turns it, first to the left, and when that doesn't work, to the right. The engine growls to life like a big bear waking up after a long sleep. They both laugh in surprised relief. As easy as this?

Pax has to wriggle forward to the very edge of his seat to reach the pedals with his foot. He stamps on one of them, and the lorry hisses loudly but refuses to move.

'I broke it,' he cries; all trace of the boy who aimed a loaded gun at two men – and fired at one – has disappeared. 'Day, I'm sorry, I can't do it! We have to swap, I CAN'T—'

'Shut up, we missed something, that's all,' says Dayna, casting around. 'Cars don't break so easily. There!'

The gearstick, turned to the letter P. P for Park, she remembers Father saying. Which would make driving … She tries to thrust the stick down to D with her good hand, but it won't budge. Why? *Why?* She looks out of the window, but she can't see Mart from this angle. What is she missing?

'D is drive, isn't it?' asks Pax. 'Why won't it work? What do we do?'

'We try everything,' she says. 'Hit the pedals again, maybe it'll shift then. Not the one you did before though, the other one.'

'You do it, Day! It's too difficult to reach. I'll do the stick, you do the pedals.'

'What kind of pilot are you, anyway?'

But she kneels down in the narrow foot space and—

THUMP!

On Dayna's side, and she whirls round to see Ryan's livid face glaring at her through the window. He raises his hand again, and there is a big stone clutched in it.

'Where're the guns?' she shouts, searching the seats frantically. She can't remember what they did with the guns!

Her rucksack with her own weapons is way over by Pax and she can't—

THUMP! This time the window's glass turns white and fragmented. It's still there, but won't be for long.

'Day, do the pedals, quick!'

Dayna forces herself to turn her back on Ryan and his stone, just on the other side of the damaged pane of glass, and reaches out for the two pedals with her good arm. She hesitates, then chooses the one closest to her and presses down.

'I got it,' cries Pax from above her. 'I got it into drive, Day! The stick. But why aren't we moving?'

Dayna can feel the engine trembling under her hand, like it's only being held back by one thing. Slowly, she eases off the pedal and – yes! – the lorry jolts forward. Pax cheers, and the lorry jerks sharply to the left as he turns the wheel.

'Careful!' cries Dayna. 'You want to tip us over?'

'I'm driving! I'm driving!' yells Pax.

And that is when Ryan's stone hits the window for a third time – *CRASH* – and small shards of glass explode everywhere.

With no time to think or be frightened, Dayna hits the other pedal, what has to be the accelerator, with the palm of her hand, pushing down on it with the weight of her whole body. The lorry squeals and Pax yells, and now they're bumping along the potholed road at a speed that's almost unimaginable. From her position on the floor, Dayna can only see the blurry green shapes of trees whizz past Pax's window, there and gone in the blink of an eye. Ryan they leave behind, cursing them and God and maybe Mart as well.

'We did it!' yells Pax, his teeth rattling. 'We're so *fast!*'

Dayna manoeuvres herself up on to the driver's seat beside him, swapping her hand on the pedal for her foot. There's a big hole in the middle of the window and wind blasts in through it, whipping up their hair, roaring in their ears. And ahead of them: a broken road amidst weeds and grass and trees, winding and jumping like a snake. Pax spins the wheel, and they're thrown to the right as the lorry turns that way, two wheels sliding from paved road to grass and back to road.

'I'm a natural,' he laughs.

'Best put on the seat belt,' says Dayna. She's laughing too.

7

They drive – through roads and ditches and long-growing weeds – for a long time before they feel safe enough to stop. Then Dayna slams her foot down on the brake pedal, and the lorry jerks to a sudden halt as the engine protests, flinging them sharply to the windscreen until the safety belt catches them and jerks them just as sharply back. Then everything is silent and still. Dayna and Pax look at one another. Both are breathing hard, as if they had attached ropes to the lorry and pulled it all this way themselves, not only pressed a few pedals and spun the wheel.

'It worked,' Dayna finally says, and finds that she's very surprised.

'Yeah,' says Pax. And then: 'What now?'

Dayna chews her lower lip. 'We wait to see if Father wakes up,' she says. 'And we let the boy out of his cage.'

Father must have been tossed this way and that during the chaotic ride. He's not lying in the centre any more, but crumpled up and squashed against the tarp of the cages with all the animals on the other side. They hiss and whine and growl, clearly sensing that something big has happened. And someone is tap-tap-tapping again.

'His eyes are fluttering,' reports Pax excitedly. 'He might be waking. Father? Father?'

Dayna is still struggling into the back with her bad arm. Her heart jumps horribly at his words. 'Pax, get away,' she snaps. 'Waking could be bad.'

Pax ignores her. 'They're not pink any more, his eyes. I think it's OK. Oh, he's closed them again. But it's a good sign, right?'

Dayna has no idea. She knows only that they have to get the boy out of the cage quick, and leave this back space to Father, in case he turns. Which he won't. But might. 'Stay away from him,' she repeats. 'Help me with this.'

She grabs a fistful of the tarp and wrenches it off with all the might she can muster. The boy with the horrendous black eye stares up at her.

'Wow,' says Pax, walking over to join them: the boy in the cage, Dayna just in front of it.

'You're safe now,' Dayna tells him. She takes out Ryan's ring of keys and tries each key, one by one, on the cage's padlock.

'What if the key to that isn't there?' asks Pax, who is fingering his own left eye absently and staring at the boy.

'Where else would it be?' asks Dayna, and at that exact moment the key she has selected slips into the lock without resistance. She turns it and the padlock clatters to the floor. Pax flings open the cage door, and they each of them grab an arm of the not-caged-any-more boy and tug him out. His one eye flits from Dayna to Pax, and he makes strange noises in the back of his throat. He's trying to tell them something.

Dayna rummages in her rucksack and takes out her knife.

'Here,' she says to Pax, handing it to him. 'But be careful. Do his gag first, the knots look too tight.'

She usually wouldn't have trusted Pax to do something as precise as this, but her sore arm leaves her little choice … Pax surprises her, though, by being incredibly careful; slowly sliding the blade between gag and boy's cheek, moving it to and fro as gentle as can be. It takes a while, but when the boy's gag finally rips through, and he coughs and spits out a filthy cloth which has been wedged into his mouth besides, he hasn't got a mark on him. At least not from Pax.

'Where are we?' wheezes the boy. The pitch of his voice is exactly between Pax's and Father's. A child's and a man's both.

'In a lorry,' says Dayna, wondering if he has banged his head during the bumpy ride and lost track of things.

'No, where are we on the map? North or south? Which way were we going?'

'I don't know. We just drove to get away. And we did.'

Dayna thinks this boy could at least say thank you.

The boy shakes his head. 'Hurry up,' he snaps at Pax, who is in the middle of sawing through the plastic wire cutting into the boy's hands. 'We have to get out as quickly as possible. They might be coming if you drove us in the wrong direction. You should've let me out earlier.'

'They're not coming,' says Dayna, beginning to feel irritated. 'They can't ever catch up on foot, and we left them a good bit away.'

The boy looks at her as if she is being stupid. 'There are others,' he says. 'As soon as they find out what's going on, they'll track this lorry. Did you at least destroy their walkies?'

A hiccup of fear pops in Dayna's stomach. 'No,' she says.

The boy swears, like Ryan and Mart have sworn. 'Shit! How stupid are you?'

'Stupid enough to save you,' retorts Dayna, and it takes all her willpower not to shove the boy.

'You calling us stupid?' asks Pax indignantly. 'We're the ones who got the lorry. It was Day's plan, and it worked because I'm a good shot and a good pilot. I bet you wouldn't in a million years have got that lorry like we did.'

'Yeah?' says the boy, his voice mocking. 'And much good it'll do you when the others show up. Cut me loose, can't you? Stop wasting time. They'll already be on their way, and if you bozos went in the wrong direction, they could be here any moment!'

Pax cuts through the handcuffs, but sullenly, as if he isn't at all sure he wants to free this boy after all. Dayna isn't either. She glances at Father, and—

'Oh God, oh God.'

Father is awake. His bound hands and legs are flailing helplessly, his muzzled head swivelling this way and that, looking around at the cargo space in what can only be horror. His eyes are bleary and confused and scared, but not crazed. 'Oh God,' he wheezes. 'Oh my God.'

'Father!' They both rush to him. Dayna yanks Pax back just before impact. Father looks too frail and winded for even a hug. He focuses on Pax's face, on Dayna's. 'What …' he gasps. 'What …'

'You beat it,' laughs Pax. 'You beat the craze!'

'Hey, idiots,' says the boy. 'My feet are still tied. If you're too busy to help, then at least give me your knife. We gotta move.'

Pax ignores him, turning his attention to Father's restraints instead, so Dayna finds a smaller pocketknife and hands it to the boy, too happy to care about his rudeness. Behind her, her brother is talking and talking, telling Father all about the last night and early morning.

'Bout time,' grumbles the boy as he saws through the plastic rope. 'No chance you checked for trackers, is there?'

'What?' Dayna is hardly paying attention. Father is awake, alive, uncrazed. Everything else is secondary.

'God, I'll do it myself. You're useless, you know that?' The boy stands up, staggers, swears, and starts massaging his leg muscles.

'You're pretty disappointing,' Dayna tells him. 'You're the third new person I've met that I can remember, and you're pretty disappointing.'

The boy just grunts. Somehow, he manages to stumble to the open back doors. He pauses by one of the plastic boxes, reaches in, and pulls out a see-through pouch with a gas mask inside, which he slings over his shoulder by its loop. Then he climbs out. Dayna watches absently, wondering if he's leaving. She hopes not, at least not without explaining about some things. After that, she wouldn't mind him going.

She walks back to Father and Pax. Father (now unmuzzled and unbound) holds out his sweaty hand to her, and smiles, and whispers this: 'I am so proud of you.'

And this: 'Next time, don't be stupid.'

Dayna's momentary elation flips around and turns into something else entirely. 'I thought ...' she begins. 'Ryan said he had the vaccine—'

'There *is* no ... vaccine, Day. Not any more. Anyone who says ... anything else is lying.' Father has to pause after every couple of words to take another breath.

'Using the walkie-talkie was my idea,' mumbles Pax. She could hug him for saying it, although she knows it makes no difference: She's the eldest, she was in charge. Father must know too, but he doesn't point this out. He just smiles at them, a bleary smile that says: I can't believe it.

'Can we go back home now?' asks Pax.

Father coughs into his hands, shakes his head. He looks so tired. 'No. Not safe any more.'

'I'm sorry I was stupid,' she whispers.

Father squeezes her shoulder. 'Stupid in one way ... clever in another. We're all ... here, we're all still together. We can always find ... another Blue House.'

Something bangs against the back doors, and they all of them whirl around. It's the boy again, and he looks terrified. 'I can hear them,' he pants. 'Shit, I can hear them. They're coming!'

For a second, it looks like the boy will just run, into the trees and away, but he doesn't. Instead, he tells them to hurry up, be quick, come ON, as Dayna and Pax half carry, half walk Father out of the cargo space.

Once they're in the open, Dayna can hear the sound too, distant but there. Like wind or fast-moving water, only stranger; wrong somehow. Tyres on road, right out of the dead world's stories, and getting louder. Panic flares up inside her, but she reminds herself that Father is here, that Father will know.

'Let's drive, quick,' urges Pax. 'Day, you do the pedals again.'

'That won't bloody work, will it?' shouts the boy, taking a step towards the nearest trees. 'Come on, we have to go this way. Leave the lorry, there's an inbuilt GPS. I can't find it, I can't disable it, but it's there. That's what they're tracking. Come on, quick.'

Dayna doesn't understand *gee pee ess*, but Father groans, which must make what the boy is saying true. Doesn't matter. Both she and her brother are wearing their rucksacks again; they have their gear and weapons, they have

Father, and that is all they need. She begins leading Father towards the woods, but he pulls back.

'Come ON!' shouts the boy. 'COME ON, WE HAVE TO MOVE. NOW!'

Father is shaking his head. 'Too slow ... with me.'

He looks at Dayna, at Pax. 'I'll drive this a little ... further, get them away from here. I'll leave it at the next settlement ... much easier to hide. They won't ... find me. You go that way. Straight line.'

He nods to the south or south-east, the opposite direction from where the whoosh of approaching tyres is coming from.

'No,' moans Pax, and, 'We mustn't separate,' tries Dayna, but neither of them speaks with any great conviction. Father may be wheezing, but still his voice is firm and his eyes are hard, and it's clear he won't take no for an answer. It's the way he looked when he was teaching Dayna and Pax to swim or kill animals or gut fish or skin rabbits. No choice, he would say, you have no choice. Don't be soft. In this world, you don't survive if you're soft.

'Guys, I'm leaving without you if this takes much longer,' says the boy.

Pax tries to hug Father, but is pushed back. 'Go, now.'

Father knows, Dayna tells herself, swallowing the lump in her throat. Father will be all right. She grabs Pax's hand and tugs him away, towards the trees and the boy. Her eyes find Father's. She says: 'At the meeting point, then?'

Father nods. But he also says: 'If I'm not there by noon, leave.'

Then he turns his back on all of them and heads to the driver's cabin, slowly, like each step requires all of his strength and concentration. And Dayna turns the other way, pulling

Pax behind her, and she tries not to think of anything but the path ahead of them, and the meeting point.

'Take out your slingshot,' she tells Pax. 'You go last, OK? I'll go first. Straight line.'

'Straight line?' scoffs the boy. 'Let's just bloody run for all we're worth. Try to keep up with me.'

'You're in the middle,' says Dayna, handing him her wooden baseball bat. For herself, she chooses a tin can of pepper spray. She would have preferred her own slingshot, but that's a weapon for two good arms.

'Follow my lead. We can't leave them an obvious trail to track. And we have to be quiet in case of crazed.'

All these things should be obvious, but somehow the boy doesn't seem to know. A lot of different expressions flit past his face: annoyance, confusion, anger. At first, it looks as if he's going to argue, but then he just shrugs and says: 'OK, whatever. Let's just go. NOW.'

8

Dayna weaves and ducks and darts between trees and shrubs, and the others follow close behind. Twice she spots clumps of purple-pink Echidna fungus, and steers her troop around them in wide arcs. Some of the pulsating caps are bloated to their fullest; it wouldn't take much to trigger them. She can hear engines now, way back, and Pax's quiet tread, and the boy's much louder footfalls. One of the engines could be Father's, maybe, hopefully. It's been a little over two minutes since they left him, unless Dayna's counting is way off.

'What's this meeting point?' asks the boy.

'The next church we come across,' says Pax. 'There's always churches around, and they're easier to spot with their steeples. If we ever get separated in supply runs and such, that's where we meet. It only ever happened once though. We—'

'Shhh!' Dayna stops so suddenly that the boy walks right into her.

'Well, thanks for the warning,' he mutters.

'*Shhh*. Listen.'

No more engine noise. A second of silence filled only by insect chirping and their laboured breath, then – voices. Men's voices, shouting. Far too close.

'Oh shit.' The boy pushes past Dayna, jogs a couple of

paces, then turns back in exasperation when they don't follow. '*What?* Move it!'

'What're they doing so close?' whispers Pax. 'Father should've—'

There are two deafening reports: *BANG. BANG.* Dayna flinches each time, but otherwise is frozen, unable to move or think, and two minutes away from them, someone is bellowing in rage. More yells and grunts and thumps, and someone, *Father*, cries out in pain and someone else shouts: 'LEAVE HIM! LEAVE HIM FOR LYLE!'

'It's not your dad,' says the boy. 'Your dad must've shot one of them, with Ryan's gun, maybe? They won't shoot, they have to bring in people alive. It's not your dad, he wasn't shot.'

Not shot maybe, but caught and hurt and … (LEAVE HIM FOR LYLE!)

What to do? What to do?

'We have to leave,' urges the boy. 'You can't help him, they're bloody soldiers, aren't they?'

A rapid burst of gunfire, *BANGBANGBANGBANG*, and then the man who shouted before is shouting again, louder, or closer: 'ONE OF MY MEN DOWN, JASON! IF I CATCH YOU NOW, I'M NOT SURE WHAT I'LL DO!'

This snaps Dayna out of her numbness. He's coming, maybe all of them are. Even she could not prevent them from leaving some sort of trail through all the weeds and tall grass.

'OK, behind me again,' she tells the other two, and then starts sprinting. As soon as they get to a paved road, they'll be much harder to track. As soon as they're safe, she can think about what to do about Father.

But something is happening, something is in the air. And Dayna skids to a halt and now she hears it too, all around them. The gentle *pfft pfft pfft* noise that sounds like nothing but what it is: mushroom caps bursting open, to release their spores.

'Masks!' she yells, dropping the pepper spray so that both her hands, good and sore, can unknot the mask hanging from her trouser loop; vaguely aware of the boys doing the same. She holds in her breath, not daring to take even one last gulp of air. Already it is thickening in the oncoming mist; already it is tinged in pale rose pink. *Pfft pfft pfft* as more surrounding Echidna are triggered by the spores already set free. Frantic scrambling rustling fluttering everywhere, as animals try to get away fast as fast. A few leap or slither by close enough to see or even touch, there and gone with hardly a glance in the direction of three half-grown humans busy with their gas masks. It must have been those gunshots that hit the first cap. Or one of the pursuing men was careless with his step. Or they were just unlucky, and one of the Echidna reached spore-releasing maturity at this exact moment.

Dayna has named her mask Anteater like the knights from the dead world named their swords, because that's what it looks like to her, with its long snout ending in a filter and its big goggle eyes of glass. Once Anteater is unhooked, it takes less than five seconds to press him to her face, pull the flipped plastic straps over her head and gulp in the stale, filtered air. She checks on Pax, but he's fine, breathing through the filter of his own mask, named Kong because Pax always copies her best ideas. It's the boy (Jason?) who's having trouble, wildly trying to untangle his twisted straps, his cheeks puffed out with unexpelled air. Dayna, who can think more calmly because she can breathe, helps him straighten everything out and put on the mask, which is smaller than both Anteater or Kong, only covering mouth and nose. She bends down to retrieve the pepper spray, and the first bird falls from the sky with a little thud, not five paces away. It might be a robin, although it's difficult to tell through the pink hue. Its small body twitches and writhes on the dead leaves of the forest ground, and Dayna gestures for Pax to grab one of the boy's hands, takes the other, then pulls them onwards. Dangerous to wait even five seconds longer: The mist has become toxic enough to infect.

Hands linked, Dayna leads the others through the pink mist as quickly as she can while still being cautious. Dayna's right, stiff hand to Jason's left, Jason's baseball bat connecting him and Pax. Pax has exchanged the slingshot with his own bat, because the things that might come at them will appear suddenly and close. There are dark shapes everywhere, most stationary, some twitching, convulsing. All she can hear is her own breathing, magnified in the recesses of the mask.

Nothing has woken up yet …

The mist is so thick that she can only see her brother's outline. It's damp against the bare skin of her arms, and she can feel goosebumps erupting. They can't talk with their gas masks, but they only need a few commands, and these are clear enough even to Jason. A tug of the hand, the can pointed forwards, means: On, this way. The can raised: Stop.

Again concentrating hard on the way ahead, again trying not to think of what this sudden mist might mean for Father. At least now it will be almost impossible for the soldiers to see and follow their tracks.

They have left the forest behind, and are just entering a

dead village of some sort, when they hear the first crazed shriek. Jason jumps and tries to pull them to the nearest of the buildings, but Dayna shakes her head vigorously and keeps walking.

Lamp posts and broken-down cars loom up in front of her only a moment before she reaches them, and she has to swerve quickly. Houses are just indistinct shapes, the sun a small pinprick of white. Senseless to look for a church in this, especially with the newly crazed all around them, beginning to wake …

(next time, don't be stupid)

… and so, reluctantly, Dayna finally turns towards one of the shadow buildings. The moment it becomes clear what she's doing, Jason lets go of her hand and jogs past her to the front door. He turns the knob, and seems utterly taken aback when the door won't open. Dayna has already retrieved her lock pick from the rucksack. She goes through the various hooked skillets, only realising now that her hands are trembling, chooses one, then slides it into the keyway together with the loose pick from the special compartment. It takes a while of twisting and listening, but finally there is a click and—

From right behind her: a SHRIEK.

Dayna spins around just in time to see Pax's shadow swing out with his bat at something small and long and twitching. The thing (a ferret, maybe?) is up in a moment, about to launch itself at Pax, but now Dayna is ready, the can back in her hand, and she points its nozzle at the animal and releases pepper spray. The crazed ferret darts this way and that, trying to get out of the way, but Dayna moves with it, pressing down mercilessly until Pax seals the deal with another baseball bat blow, this time to the head. He turns to Dayna and gives her the thumbs-up sign, to show her that he wasn't bitten. Jason raises both his hands to his forehead. His own weapon, the baseball bat, is lying by his feet, useless.

Dayna gestures for him to pick it up and get a move on. One by one they slip through the door into the house, taking care not to let any mist seep in. Dayna and Pax do a quick sweep of the rooms, her taking the ground floor, him the one above, then meet back in the hallway, where Jason has slid into a crouch. Pax nods, and so does Dayna. No cracks, no windows left open. No crazed inside either.

Finally, they struggle out of their masks, gasping in the stale and rotting (but non-poisonous) air. After a moment's hesitation, Jason does the same.

'Jesus,' he says shakily. 'And what was wrong with the house I wanted to go to?'

Dayna ignores him, speaks only to Pax: 'Father will be fine. He has his mask, he will be fine.'

'But they caught him, didn't they?' whispers Pax. 'That was him yelling.'

'Maybe he managed to escape in the mist, like we did. Or they locked him into the cargo space again. Either way, he won't have breathed it in. And if he's caught, we'll free him, we'll save him. OK?'

Jason snorts, but she ploughs on: 'This is what we'll do: We wait here until the mist is gone, then we find the next church; maybe he's there. And if he isn't, we'll go back to the lorry. They can't drive anywhere now. They'd barely see where they were going, and anyway, they'd be way too loud. So they're stuck same as us.'

'Um, hello?' says Jason. 'Sorry, but are you mental? After the mist clears, the Hummingbirds will be all over the place.

If you think they snuffed it back there, you're dead wrong. They train for this sort of thing, they don't get caught out. What we have to do, soon as it's safe, is get the hell out of this area. Your dad ... I'm sorry, guys, I am, but it sounded like they got him. I dunno how you tricked Mart and Ryan, but that's not gonna cut it now. Your dad told you to leave, didn't he? If he didn't show up.'

'That's what we'll do,' says Dayna to Pax, as if there was no interruption. Because if Father really is lost, right after getting better all on his own, then it will be her fault. 'OK?' she asks.

'OK,' agrees Pax.

Only then does Dayna focus on the boy. 'Your name's Jason?' she asks. 'What that man shouted?'

Jason shrugs. 'So?'

'So: Tell us. About the soldiers. About the Hummingbirds. Why they beat you up and locked you up. Who Lyle is. We'll be stuck here until tomorrow at least. Tell us.'

Jason examines her through his one good eye. 'Fine,' he says. 'Because they've got your dad, I suppose you ought to know. Then you'll see there's no point. But I'm leaving soon as it's safe, just so you know. And I'm starving right now, haven't eaten for at least a day. Let's find some grub here first, then OK, fine. I'll tell you.'

There is no food in this house, just dusty framed photographs of a white-haired man and woman always smiling and always together, and empty cupboards. Instead of hoarding tin cans and bottles of water and rolls of toilet paper at the time of the Fall, this couple must have left in a packed car, hoping to find some place where they would sit out the craze in isolation, or with family further away. Father says many people did this, even though the authorities were telling everyone to stay at home and stay calm. He also says in most cases it didn't make a difference either way. So, no food here, but Dayna and Pax have a little in their rucksacks, and they snap open two cans of lentil soup, find bowls and spoons in the kitchen, and settle down to eat it cold.

And in a room with a dead television set, a sofa and moth-eaten crocheted blankets that must have once been as colourful as a rainbow, Jason licks the last lentils from his thumb and tells them about the Hummingbirds. Although he doesn't tell them much.

They're mainly scientists and the soldiers tasked to protect them, who live and work in a place they call the Station. They say they're on a mission to help humanity. They lure people there or take them by force. Because vaccines in the making have to be tested and retested until they're right, and for testing, you need people. And when those people die, you need more.

'So, there is no vaccine that actually works against the craze?' asks Dayna, just to be sure.

'Nope.'

'And who's Lyle?'

Jason shrugs. 'Just one of their doctors. There're others, but Lyle supervises most experiments.'

'And how do you know all this?'

'You think I'm making it up?'

'I just want to know.'

Jason is quiet for a while, frowning, like he's trying to work out how best to explain. Then he says: 'The Hummingbirds have deals with some people who live close by, food and services for safety. And the vaccine, if that ever happens. I was one of those people. Only the Hummingbirds went back on that deal, didn't they? Decided to make a human guinea pig out of me too, but I got away. And, well, then I got caught. They were greedy with you lot. They get rewards for bringing people in, especially infected people hanging on, like your father.'

(LEAVE HIM FOR LYLE!)

He sees Dayna's expression, and his voice softens somewhat. 'Don't beat yourself up. You couldn't have known. And you're not the only one who walked into their trap. I'm sorry about your dad, but ... well. There's nothing anyone can do about it. I'm gonna go sleep now.'

'What about your family?' asks Pax as Jason gets to his feet.

'Don't have one.'

He leaves the room without saying another word. They hear the stairs creak as he climbs them, and they hear old mattress springs of one of the upstairs beds creak as well, as he falls on to it.

'That's a scary story,' whispers Pax.

'Yeah,' agrees Dayna, and thinks: *Father.*

9

Exhausted, they go to sleep before the pale, mist-hidden sun has set. Dayna shares a double bed with Pax, after shaking the dust out of its blankets in the hallway. Pax wakes her in the middle of the night, sobbing and terrified, and at first, she doesn't know what to do. She ends up giving him Mother's photograph to hold, and although he can't see Mother in the gloom, this calms him. No need to ask what his bad dream was about. This time last night, she was talking to Ryan on the walkie-talkie, telling him exactly how to find their home. A couple of hours before that, Father hadn't even been bitten. How could so much go so wrong in only one day?

The next morning, the mist has thinned out enough to be almost gone, although the sounds of the crazed are everywhere. Dangertime, when the infected animals easily outnumber the uninfected. Father has told them the story of the original Echidna: a woman-non-woman from a place called Greece, who was known as the Mother of Monsters in the dead world. But even she couldn't have made as many monsters as the Echidna of Now.

Jason says there's no way he's going outside in dangertime, but when Dayna and Pax leave to find a church, he opts for joining them after all, rather than stay in the dead house, alone. The village church is cool and echoey and empty. Dayna tells Pax to stay here, with Jason, in case Father should come, while she goes back to the road where they left the lorry. She'll be careful and quiet and quick. Pax says it ought to be him because of her arm, and what happens if the soldiers grab her or something crazed gets her? They argue about it until she finally snaps: 'Look, I'm in charge when Father isn't here, you know that.'

'Aye aye, Sarge,' says Jason, giving her a mock salute. 'You do know you're being a total idiot, right?'

Pax giggles, then quickly stops when she glares at him.

'Swear you'll be back,' he says.

'I'll be back,' she agrees. 'With Father too, hopefully.'

But when she finally reaches the stretch of road where they left the stolen lorry, it's deserted. No lorry, no other Hummingbird vehicles, no soldiers, no Father. Just tyre tracks in the dirt. Just a dark stain of dried blood on the asphalt. Just a sole, dirty, once-white trainer she knows is Father's.

'I can't bloody believe it,' says Jason, back in the echoey church. 'They left. They actually gave up and left.' There is wonder in his voice; there is relief. Dayna wants to hit him.

'Did you check other churches, Day?' asks Pax.

'Couldn't find any others.' (And her voice sounds like that of another person entirely.) 'But his trainer … it's like they had him and dragged him and he tried to fight and kick and lost his trainer.'

(Her fault. All of it, her fault.)

Jason is hardly paying attention, too busy mumbling to himself: 'They must've wanted to get back to the Station. They must've thought sod it, we probably died in the mist anyway. Too risky, too much trouble to hang about. Shit,

I can't believe it. But if they were still here, they'd be out in that forest by now, looking for us, closing in. Or at least the trucks and lorry would still be there, no way would they drive anywhere in the mist. Must've left right when it started clearing—'

Dayna rounds on him: 'Will you SHUT UP? They TOOK Father!' – and she pushes Jason hard in the chest.

Jason looks so comically taken aback that she does it again.

'OK, OK, cool it.' Jason edges out of her immediate range. 'Look, I'm sorry about your dad, and I'm sorry we can't do anything. But we can't. At least we're still here and alive. That's what your dad wanted, for you to be safe. You don't honestly think he had a hope in hell of getting away from them in his condition? He knew that.'

Pax moans and hides his face behind his drawn-up knees. From behind them, he's muttering all the swear words he knows, most of them picked up in the last couple of hours.

Dayna takes a deep, shuddery breath. Then she says: 'We can follow him to the Station and get him out.'

'What?' says Jason, as if she is stretching his patience beyond endurance. 'Don't be thick. You'd—'

'Can we?' asks Pax, peering at her from behind his knees. 'Can we do that, Day?'

'Yeah,' she says. 'Yeah, course. Heroes in the old stories were always setting out on quests. Doing impossible things. Why shouldn't we be like that?'

'You *can't*,' groans Jason. 'Listen to you both, you think this is a bloody game.'

'I know it's not a game,' she snaps. 'It's our father. This is the only thing that makes sense to do.'

'Can we go now?' asks Pax. 'Right away?'

'Yes,' says Dayna. She turns to Jason: 'Are you coming too?'

'You're kidding, right? This is beyond stupid. It's bloody dangertime; at least wait until they've all quietened down.'

'We have to get to Father as soon as possible,' says Dayna (thinking of the man shout: LEAVE HIM! LEAVE HIM FOR LYLE!). 'And if we're quiet and quick, the crazed won't even see us. I got through to the road just fine. Crazed don't hide and wait, they always have to run, and they always run to the noise. We just have to be quiet, that's all. And alert.'

'Please come too, Jason,' says Pax. 'You don't want to stay here all by yourself. It'd be really lonely.'

'Thanks, mate, but I'm not suicidal.'

'Fine.' Dayna shrugs. 'Stay, then. We're leaving. Just tell us which way to the Station.'

This is just for show, on her part and his. Both of them know that he will come with them if he can't persuade them to stay. Without them, he wouldn't have put his mask on in time, he would have crashed through the undergrowth and alerted all kinds of unwelcome creatures, he wouldn't have got into the house, he would have been infected by that ferret. He might act like he knows it all, but he really, really doesn't.

Dayna takes out her compass and asks it again: 'Which way?'

N

W   **E**

S

Jason says south. And when the time comes to leave, he trudges after them.

PART 2
THE COURT

10

They walk in single file, their hands to their weapons. Dayna first, then Jason (carrying the rucksacks), with Pax bringing up the rear. Jason must know they've fobbed him off with the least essential task, but he acts as if he's in the middle because he's their leader, not their weakest link. He tells Dayna not to walk so fast because Pax is dropping behind; he tells Pax not to dawdle.

At first, they move in relative silence because this is the way you should be in dangerous areas: focused, prepared, quiet. But Jason hasn't been taught this, and by and by, his initial fear seeps away when nothing bad happens, and he starts chatting and joking around in whispers. Pax is reeled in, and after a while Dayna tires of telling them to shut up, as long as they keep their voices low and their eyes peeled. The boys whisper about the most delicious and most disgusting dead-world foods they ever ate, and the biggest crazed animals they ever saw, both of them exaggerating no end. Dayna's bad arm is throbbing after all the moving she made it do, and they have to stop for Pax to fasten a sling for her. In the distance, things are shrieking and snarling, but nothing comes their way.

The sun is still far away from touching the horizon when Dayna asks Pax, hopefully, whether he's getting tired. She knows he is. They all are, after being on the road and alert for hours. Her own feet twinge with every step, and there's a bad stitch in her side. She's actually been waiting for Jason to complain and make them stop in some village or other. He hasn't, even though he's plainly as exhausted as the other two. He seems to have decided that if Dayna and Pax can walk for this long, so can he.

Pax's jaw juts, and he glances at Jason before saying firmly: 'No. Not tired at all. Are you?'

She could kick him for not wanting to admit any weakness in front of the older boy. If it was only the two of them, he'd have begun whining long ago.

'I'm not either,' she lies. 'But maybe we should stop at the next village we come to, all the same. Give us enough daylight to look for supplies to restock. Then we can leave early in the morning.'

'All right,' says Jason, unconcernedly.

'All right,' echoes Pax, although he can't hide his relief as well as Jason.

It's been a long day. A day that has stretched over two nights and a hundred impossible things.

The place they find to rest is a once-upon-a-time inn nestled between trees, almost completely hidden by their leaves. There's a wooden sign hanging at a right angle over the front door: *The Green Man*, it reads in faded letters. It reminds Dayna of the illustrations in her old book of fairytales: a cottage belonging to a family of bears, to seven dwarfs, to a grandmother, to a witch.

They visit Dayna in her sleep that night, before turning into Father, captured and alone in a dark dungeon full of rats. She's looking down at him from an opening, and calls out: 'We're here! We'll get you out!' Father glances up, his whole face alight, like when he's about to tell one of his dead-world stories. But instead, he says: 'I told you not to take the radio. I told you to forget about the Hummingbirds.'

The next morning, Jason greets them with: 'You come to your senses yet?'

There's no right answer to this sort of question, so Dayna says nothing.

'In case I wasn't clear yesterday,' he continues, 'the Station has walls and soldiers crawling all over the place and those soldiers have guns.'

'I'll think of something,' she says.

'They won't expect us,' says Pax. 'They think we're dead from the mist or running. They'll never guess we're going right to where they are.'

'Only if they think we're being extremely thick,' mutters Jason.

They have a hurried and unappetising breakfast of tinned spaghetti with cold tomato sauce, pack their things and brush their teeth (Jason uses his finger and a splodge of their toothpaste), then set off again southwards. At least dangertime is over.

'Maybe we'll come back to live here after we save Father,' muses Pax. 'I'd like that.'

'Yeah, me too,' says Dayna. 'It was like a cottage in a fairytale, wasn't it?'

'Like the three bears.'

'I knew you'd say that. I think it's more like the one of the seven dwarfs because Snow White can rest there and is safe for a while, just like we were.'

Jason is staring at them, his expression half annoyed, half bewildered. The swelling of his eye, Dayna notices, has gone down enough for the white (which is also red) to be visible again. 'What the hell are you two on about?' he asks.

Because Jason, they learn, has never heard a single fairytale in his life. As soon as they realise this, both Dayna and Pax clamour to tell him their favourite ones, which makes the walking a lot easier somehow, even though everyone's feet have already started to hurt after yesterday's long trek: Little Red Riding Hood, the Witch in the Wardrobe, Cinderella. Though the most fitting of all is the legend of Sleeping Beauty, where a whole kingdom is under a spell. Sometimes Dayna still likes to pretend that the old world isn't dead after all, only asleep like that kingdom. And that someone can reawaken it all.

Jason is irritatingly dismissive of their wonderful, magical stories. 'What baby stuff,' he says. 'You don't actually believe it, do you?'

But Dayna isn't going to say whether she believes in them or not. As far as she's concerned, all the stories of the dead world are both equally true and untrue, each as fantastic and inconceivable as the next.

11

They pass a dead cow on the side of the road. Sometimes animals will die from the craze, like humans do, but mostly they recover. This cow was unlucky. Dayna feels sorry for it, but she's glad it's dead. Crazed cows can be very dangerous because they're so big, and can put on sudden bursts of speed. It looks horrible with its eyes bulging and its tongue lolling out, but the most horrible thing of all is the fuzz of purple fungus already spreading out from its mouth. All three of them stay well clear of the cow as they walk by. The baby sprouts of Echidna are too small now – there aren't any caps to step on yet and the spores still have to develop – but you never know.

'Hey, Jason, hey, Jason,' says Pax, trotting up to him eagerly. 'Did you know that Echidna isn't just the fungus or the Mother of Monsters, but also a cute little animal on the other side of the world? It's like a hedgehog-anteater, and it's the furthest away from a monster you can imagine, I've seen pictures in a book.'

It's obvious that he means to impress Jason with this fact, and just as obvious that Jason refuses to be impressed.

'Yeah, I know,' he says, shrugging, although he can't have done. Not even Father knew about the Australian hedgehog when Pax first told him.

No one says anything for a while, and then Jason speaks, and again Dayna is surprised by how easily she can read him. Now he wants to trump Pax's fact with one of his own: 'You know it's impossible to destroy those mushrooms, right?' he says in that maddeningly superior way of his. 'They tried burning and freezing and chemicals and whatever. They're virtually indestructible until they've completed their life cycles.'

'We know that,' says Dayna scornfully. 'Father told us he watched it on the news back then. On television. How they flew over some fungus field in helicopters with flamethrowers, and it was live TV, and he saw how all these spores were released into the air when the fire hit them. And the helicopters crashed. And then the man holding the camera must have breathed it in because he dropped the camera and the picture was gone.'

'I wish I could have seen that too,' says Pax wistfully.

'Don't be horrid,' says Dayna. 'Loads and loads of people died.'

'I know, but they would have died anyway, if I was watching or not. And I'd like to've seen helicopters.'

The day gets hotter and hotter as they walk, not just from above but below too, as the air closest to the ground begins to dance. Heat haze, Father calls it, and it's worse on asphalt because that absorbs the sun and gives it back. It becomes so bad that they leave the roads and head into the undergrowth, even though all the tangle of weeds and shrubs and bushes slow them down considerably, but at least there's shade. They have to be very careful though, of where they step, in case of the fungus, in case of crazed animals. They do hear some animals, but none of them have the craze.

Jason asks how they can be sure, but how can he *not* be? The rustles of movement are quick and light and sometimes wary, never frenzied or heavy. When Dayna tries to explain this, Jason interrupts her: 'Yeah, yeah,' he says. 'I know.' (Although he obviously doesn't.)

They make a pit stop by a gurgling stream and dangle their sore, blistered feet into the cool water. Jason's are worst of all, oozing pus. While he refills their water bottles, Dayna finds a box of matches in her rucksack and gets a small fire going – water should always be boiled before drinking. Pax walks a little way upstream with a hook, a bit of string and insect bait. It doesn't take too long before he comes back with two trout, one smallish, the other larger.

'Cool,' says Jason, forgetting to be aloof for a moment. 'Did your dad teach you how to do that?'

'Kind of, but Father's actually rubbish at all the outdoor stuff,' says Pax. 'He tells us how to do things, but he can't really show us himself.'

'He gets too tired,' explains Dayna. 'He doesn't like the heat. He usually guts the fish, though. Here, you do it, Pax.'

Pax slides a knife into the bigger trout's side and goes on: 'Father knows all the things he read about in books, but Day and me can hunt and fish a lot better than him.'

'Uncle William taught Father everything and us a bit,' says Dayna. 'Father taught us the rest. Uncle William was Father's friend, and he knew things like that. Father always says that we wouldn't have made it the first few years if Uncle William hadn't been there to help him.'

'Is he still around?' asks Jason, and he sounds excited. 'We could—'

Dayna cuts him off. 'No,' she says shortly. 'He's gone. Years and years ago. Went looking for his family and never came back. We think he died, or he would have come back. How much longer until we get to the Station?'

Jason just shrugs and mumbles: 'A while. Days, probably. Anyway, just because I know the right direction doesn't mean it'll be easy to find …'

Dayna nods slowly. A map would make things so much easier, but she doesn't know where they'd find any. Except at the Blue House, and those are all hand drawn by Father and just used for orientation. Real maps are rare because the last people of the dead world all had electronic ones on their phones and didn't need anything else. You can still find those phones everywhere, but they're all dead now, and useless.

It's somehow harder to get up and start walking again, even though it should be easier after their rest and with their bellies full. Landscapes merge into one another: wild corn, tall grass, trees again. Small hills, larger hills, and then— 'Oh, look!' cries Pax.

A streak of blue on the horizon. Bluer even than the sky. Stretching out from one side of the world to the other.

THE SEA.

It takes forever and ever to get to it, and for a long time, the water doesn't appear closer at all, as if it keeps shifting back as they move forward. But Pax uses his fingers to measure and prove their progress. First, the sea is so distant that from top to bottom it's only as thick as one of his fingers. Then two. Then, ages and ages, steps and steps later, three. And so on.

There are seagulls now, swooping about, screeching. Scary, if a cloud of mist should roll their way and infect them, but so beautiful and thrilling, Dayna hardly cares. The air already feels sharper.

The sea isn't just one colour, but lots of different ones: green and blue and grey, with white foam caused by the waves. Sometimes the waves form and break in the water, and sometimes they break on land, which is orange pebbles now. Dayna licks her lips and tastes salt. Pax is already wriggling out of his clothes. She shrugs off her heavy rucksack and follows suit. Her arm is almost healed now.

'Come on, guys, at least keep your underpants on,' mutters Jason.

'Er, why?' asks Dayna. 'We dry much quicker than clothes.'

Pax pulls off his underpants and throws them at Jason with a guffaw. Jason swears and ducks out of the way. Together, Pax and Dayna splash into the cool salty water, laughing like crazy people. They're actually in the sea. THE SEA.

Before Pax can, because she wants to be the first, Dayna dives into the water. She keeps her eyes open because she doesn't want to miss a single wonder, but this turns out to be a mistake. She has to emerge again, rubbing her stinging eyes and blinking hard. A second or two later, Pax appears too, doing the exact same thing.

Still standing on the beach, Jason laughs at them.

Dayna pushes a palm of water in his direction, and she's laughing too. It's dangerous to laugh when swimming, but she can't help it. At this exact moment, if she forgets what happened and what might still happen, everything is wonderful.

Jason strips too, although he keeps his underwear shorts on, and wades in gingerly.

'Come on,' calls Pax, beckoning.

'No thanks,' says Jason, sitting down close to the shore so that the waves lap up around his chest. 'I'm too tired to muck about swimming with you two clowns.'

Dayna is too, really, and her bad arm has started twinging again, so she stretches out in the water and floats, staring up into the sky, which is as blue as the blue door of their Blue House. Pax, incredibly, seems to have forgotten all about the long walk in the sun and his blisters and sore feet. He's splashing around like he does in the stream back home. If back home is still home—

'Hello-ooooh!'

A voice, shouting. A boy's voice. Or—

Dayna jerks to her side and there's salty water in her eyes, up her nostrils. She snorts and splutters, blinking at the blurry figures, one, two, three of them, approaching. Jason is on his feet now, wary but not running. Waiting to meet them, so they can't be Hummingbirds, or if they are, he doesn't know it. Pax is already striking out for the bank, so Dayna doesn't really have a choice. She follows.

And as soon as she's wiped the worst of the salt water out of her eyes, she can't help but gasp. It's three women. She can't remember ever seeing *one* before in real life. She knows she must have, but even so, she can't remember.

Dayna and Pax reach Jason almost at the exact same time, and together all three of them just stand there, staring at the women, who have come to a stop too, just ahead of the damp shadow made by the lapping waves. They all have very long hair, flowing far beyond their waists, not tangled at all but sleek and well-groomed. Two are wearing light-coloured dresses, the third a baggy white T-shirt and white knee-length trousers. They're barefoot. They look, to Dayna at least, beautiful and magical. In fact, the first coherent words that come to her are: wood nymphs.

It's almost as if they've read her mind because the woman in the white T-shirt, who is a little sturdier and a little older than the other two (maybe as old as Father) smiles and says: 'Well, what have we here? Three water babies.'

Her hair is blonde, while the others' is darker, and her face is warm and nice. Ryan's face was nice too, Dayna reminds herself. Careful ... Careful, yes, but somehow it is difficult to believe these women can be anything other than what they seem. They don't have guns, for one thing, just ordinary weapons the same as Dayna and Pax, to defend themselves against the crazed. And they're so pretty, so ... *female*.

Dayna has never needed to introduce herself properly in her life, but she's read and heard stories and knows how it's supposed to be done: 'Hello,' she says, 'how do you do?'

The light-haired woman laughs, delighted. She turns to her companions as if wanting them to join in on the joke, but they only offer her weak smiles that soon slip away again. Dayna feels her cheeks burn. Has she said something wrong?

'How do you do?' replies the woman, still chuckling. 'Who are you? It's been years since I've last seen children your age. Are you all alone?'

'I'm Pax,' says Pax brightly. His eyes flit from woman to woman, and he seems as wonderstruck by them as Dayna herself. 'And this is my sister, Dayna, and my friend Jason. And we're not alone. Not really, anyway. We've got Father.'

'Oh?' says the blonde woman. She makes a show of scanning the sea as if she thinks Father is swimming underwater and might bob up at any moment.

'He's not with us right now,' says Dayna. 'Hummingpeople have him.'

Beside her, she can feel Jason tense and then relax again when the blonde woman asks: 'Hummingpeople? And what are they?'

The voice she says this in makes it sound as if the hummingpeople are something amusing and not real, something out of a game.

'They're—' begins Dayna, but Jason is quicker.

'Just some bad people,' he says. 'Who are you?'

'Oh, we're the good people,' says the woman, and smiles.

12

The blonde woman's name is Rena, the younger women are called Claire and Liza. Rena, who does almost all the talking, tells them that they live in a seaside town with other people.

'Our group,' says Rena. 'All good people. We'll help you.'

'Help us find the Hummingbirds?' asks Dayna, her skin still pleasantly damp and salty under her dry clothes.

'Help you get to where you're going,' says Rena. 'We have maps, for one thing.'

Dayna's heart leaps. 'Really? *Paper* maps?'

Rena nods, beaming. 'And we know this area quite well, can show you which roads are safest and which should best be avoided. But now that you're here, you must stay a little, to rest and recuperate. Everyone will be so thrilled; we haven't had guests in such a long time, much less children! I could hardly believe it when me and the girls heard you laughing and splashing around like that. Claire here actually wanted to go back home, she was afraid you were ghosts!'

Claire bites her lip and looks down at her feet.

Pax cocks his head, trying to catch her eye. 'Ghosts aren't real any more, you know,' he informs her. 'Father says so. So there's no need to be frightened.'

Jason snorts. 'Says the boy who believes in fairytales.'

'Ghosts are the dead world,' says Dayna.

Rena laughs. 'Observant girl,' she says, and Dayna is pleased, even though she hasn't meant it to be funny. She only meant that all the stories and legends are just as true as anything else in the dead world, and just as gone.

'What are you three doing out here all alone?' Jason suddenly asks, addressing Rena.

'You're a careful one, aren't you?' she says, still smiling that warm smile of hers. 'The protector of your little gang?'

Pax snorts and Dayna has to clamp her lips together tight or she'll giggle.

Jason ignores them both, eyes fixed on Rena, and says: 'So?'

'We came to collect the crabs,' says Rena, gesturing to all their rucksacks. 'We have crates along the coastline, baited, and they swim in and get trapped. Every day or so we send someone to collect and rebait. Today it was our turn. Lucky us, eh?'

'Can you show us how to do that?' asks Pax, deeply interested. 'Me and Day know how to catch fish and animals in the woods, but not crabs. Can you teach us?'

'Of course, if you'll stay. For a bit.'

Pax glances at Dayna, who hesitates.

'You'll have to come anyway if you want one of our maps,' says Rena.

'All right,' says Dayna. After all, what possible reason could these women have to lie to them? It's clear they're not hummingpeople. 'Maybe we'll stay one night.'

Rena's smile widens. 'Oh, I'm so glad. You're going to love it! Absolutely love it.'

★

They follow the women along the coastline. Rena is holding a big chopping knife at the ready. Liza and Claire are silent, but their eyes swivel back and forth for any sign of danger. Their job must be lookout, like Rena's job must be protector. It's a little strange that they should have split up all these essential roles like this, but Dayna likes the idea. It means they think they'll stay together for always and always, so they can rely on each other. Father and even Uncle William (long ago) were all the time talking about preparing for the worst. And the worst is being left alone, all by yourself, with no one else to help you.

Rena asks about Father, and Mother too. When she learns that they've only recently met Jason, she asks about Jason's parents as well. Dayna answers everything truthfully (why would she lie?) but Jason clams up and gives only very vague answers if he gives them at all.

'Is your arm all right, sweetheart?' Rena asks Dayna, indicating the sling. Dayna likes being called sweetheart. It's what mothers call their children in stories. Maybe it's what *her* mother used to call her.

'Oh yeah,' she says. 'It's almost as good as new now, just got a bit sore because I was swimming. I'll probably get rid of the sling when we get going again. It wasn't broken or anything. Just yanked in a direction it wasn't supposed to be yanked.'

'Oh? And how did that happen?'

Beside her, Jason clears his throat loudly.

'I got it fighting one of the hummingpeople,' says Dayna proudly. He was a soldier and everything, but I fought him hand to hand, and I won. Kind of.'

Rena shakes her head, smiling. 'Ah-ah-ah,' she says in a sing-song voice. 'It's wicked to lie.'

'I'm not—'

'And you?' asks Rena, turning to Jason. 'What happened to your eye?'

'I walked into a door,' says Jason shortly.

Rena blinks, but before she can comment – 'Rena!'

It's Claire, shouting. Pointing.

A baby wild boar is charging at them from the overgrown road, grunting and snorting foam in its wake. Dayna and Pax both reach for their weapons, but before either of them can do any more, Rena's arm whips up and lunges. Something hurtles towards the approaching pig. At almost the exact same moment there's a terrible ear-piercing squeal. Then silence. The pig is sprawled on its side, Rena's knife sticking out right between its eyes.

'Phew,' sighs Rena. 'I thought all the possessed animals must have gone by now, but there's always some that take you unawares.'

'You were AMAZING,' shouts Pax.

'Yeah!' agrees Dayna. 'I can throw knives too, but nowhere near that fast. And then you hit it right between its eyes.'

'WHAM,' contributes Pax, smacking his palms together.

'Thank you, kids,' laughs Rena. 'All a matter of training.'

The three women walk to the boar and examine it to make sure it's dead. Dayna and Pax are about to follow, but Jason pulls them back.

'Listen, you two,' he says quietly. 'Be a bit more careful until you can be sure they're to be trusted, OK?'

'But why shouldn't they be?' asks Pax. Again Dayna thinks of Ryan, and again she pushes the thought away. Ryan is just one bad person; there are hundreds of stories about hundreds of good people.

'I'm not saying they shouldn't, I'm just saying we don't

know yet,' replies Jason irritably. 'And there you go, giving them your whole life story.'

'If I hadn't said that they wouldn't be helping us now, would they?' says Dayna. 'And why keep it a secret anyway? They're not hummingpeople.'

'Whatever,' grunts Jason. 'They don't know anything, so it's beside the point. But just be a bit more careful next time. And with people in their group.'

Dayna doesn't see what the harm is, but she's tired of arguing with him. 'Fine,' she says.

The women have taken out a blanket from one of their rucksacks and are rolling the dead boar up in it. Meat of crazed animals is tainted too, so why are they doing it?

'Also, I wanted to give you a heads-up,' continues Jason. Dayna reluctantly shifts her gaze from the women back to him.

'About what?' asks Pax.

'About me. If their group turns out to be all right, I think I'll stay on. Here.'

'But we need you to tell us where the Hummingbirds are,' says Dayna, outraged.

'You'll get a map soon, won't you? I can show you on that.'

'But ... don't you like us?' asks Pax in a little voice. 'I'm sorry if we were mean to you. I like you, anyway. You're cool.'

'*Cool*,' scoffs Dayna, looking at her brother. 'Since when do you say cool?'

'Shuttup. Since now.'

'God, don't be so pathetic,' says Jason. 'I said so from the start, didn't I, that it's a loony idea. Suicide. If this lot turns out all right, I'm staying. And I think you should stay too, both of you. You'll only get yourself killed or locked up if you go on with this crap rescue mission.'

'We won't!' hisses Dayna. 'And if we give up, Father's the one who'll be locked up and die for sure. We're going, no matter what you say or do. Aren't we, Pax?'

'Yeah. I'm no coward.'

'And I'm not either.'

'No, you're just a couple of idiots,' sneers Jason.

The women are trudging back to them, the bundled-up boar carried between Liza and Claire, who are each holding on to one end of the blanket.

'Well, that was exciting, wasn't it?' says Rena a little breathlessly. 'Now let's keep going, we're almost there.'

Neither Dayna nor Pax talks to Jason for the rest of the way.

They arrive at a seaside town, where houses get taller and more impressive. The tide is rising, and what's left of the wooden beach dividers (which are everywhere here, and covered in green slime) is mostly underwater. In the not-too-far-off distance, grass-topped stone cliffs stretch outwards towards the sea.

Pax nudges Dayna and points towards a lone brick tower on their left: 'Look, a castle! There used to be knights here.'

'It's the parish church, actually,' says Rena as they pass by. 'Sometimes we still use it for special services, but not too often. The outside is always exposed, and the larger the group, the greater the danger.'

As they walk down a broad road parallel to the shore, Dayna catches flurries of movement out of the corner of her eye. People half-hidden behind dead cars, peering at her and Pax and Jason curiously, following their little procession.

'Why d'you live this close to the sea?' asks Jason. 'Aren't you scared of floods?'

'We've lived here for years now,' replies Rena, 'and the water has never risen past the lower promenade. We're safe here because we're meant to stay. This way!'

She makes a sharp left, turning into a smaller road, steeply sloping upwards. The others follow, first Dayna and Pax, then Jason, and finally Claire and Liza, puffing at the rear with the dead boar between them.

There are even more people here, and they're closer. Men and women of all ages, although none of them are old enough to have white hair. When Dayna tries to meet their eyes, they let them fall hurriedly, shy, like Claire and Liza. Five, ten, maybe as many as fifteen people, all quietly curious.

Pax nudges Dayna. 'Look, Day. They're all wearing white.'

Now that he's pointed it out, it's obvious, and strangely beautiful. Everyone's clothes are pale or white, just like Rena's and Claire's and Liza's.

'It's to show that they all belong together,' says Dayna, and she wishes at that moment that she was standing along with the rest, wearing white too, belonging. With Pax, of course. And Father.

Rena points at a huge building up ahead, the biggest, bulkiest of the whole town, with a shape that reminds Dayna of a ship: a stepped profile and long, elegantly curved balconies, facing the sea. Like the *Titanic*, which was the largest passenger liner in the world and made famous because it sank. That's the way the dead world worked: bad things became famous because bad things were rare.

'See that?' says Rena. 'We call it the Court. That's where we all live, all together to keep safe. And there's heaps of space.'

At one of the many entrance doors stands a tall young man in a white T-shirt. He smiles at them but makes no comment. Beside him is an empty plastic box into which Rena lays her knife.

'We have a rule here,' she tells Dayna and the others. 'Everyone gives up their weapons before entering. This is supposed to be a safe space for all. You'll be able to take them again when you leave, of course.'

'OK,' says Pax, and puts his slingshot into the box too. Dayna hesitates.

'If you don't trust us, that's all right,' Rena tells her. 'But we won't be able to help you then, or even ask you in. We have to protect our people.'

'Makes sense, I suppose,' says Jason. He places his own bat into the box, even though he was the one who told them to be careful. And then told them he wanted to stay.

Dayna hesitates a moment longer, then throws in her own knife.

'The rucksacks too, I'm afraid,' says the young man apologetically. 'We just want to make sure everyone's safe.'

It must have taken ages and ages to get rid of all the skeletons and rot and creepers in all these rooms, but it must have been done because the Court is clean and smells like disinfectant. Pax has counted the storeys on their way and made it to thirteen, then fourteen, then thirteen again, depending on the count. The pale-dressed people have lost all pretence now and are following behind them on the black-and-white staircase as they mount step after step. Except for Claire and Liza, who have taken the boar around the building instead of inside it. Dayna is slightly uneasy about leaving their gear behind. She wonders if they made a mistake in coming here, but it was just too wondrous to resist. Anyway, they'll be on their way again come morning.

'Are all the rooms on the bottom floor taken?' asks Pax, wheezing.

Rena laughs. 'Of course not, we're just over sixty people. But I want to introduce you to Liam now. And he lives right at the very top. He enjoys the view.'

'Who?' gasps Dayna.

'You'll see.'

13

Liam is a man with piercing eyes and dark shoulder-length hair interspersed with grey strands, although he looks younger than Father, and his face is smooth and unlined. He's dressed in a white shirt and beige trousers, and his feet are bare. Dayna has time to take in his appearance in full because he doesn't acknowledge them at first. Rena has knocked and opened the door into this vast room of curved walls and chequered floors of black and white, in the middle of which Liam sits, cross-legged, with an open book in his lap. His hand is moving over the page with a pencil. Sketching. In front of him, a young woman is sprawled on the tiles, her long hair pooling all around her, her eyes closed, a serene smile on her lips. She isn't wearing white because she isn't wearing anything at all.

Rena motions for them to stop and closes the door behind them (making a shooing gesture to the pale-dressed followers in the stairwell). She stays there too, with her hands folded in front of her, waiting for Liam to notice. Liam doesn't turn, even though he must have heard them. He keeps on sketching and Dayna cranes her neck, trying to see, but the angle is wrong. So she looks at the windows instead, which show a panorama of the sea outside. It's as if they really are on a ship, in the middle of the ocean.

'Aren't you gonna say something?' hisses Pax to Rena. But she only puts a finger to her lips, smiling. Pax turns to Dayna. 'Why is that lady naked?'

'Shhh,' admonishes Rena in an undertone.

Jason is staring at the woman as if in a trance, which makes a giggle build up inside Dayna. She nudges Pax and nods towards Jason, and then they catch each other's eyes and it can't be helped, they start snorting helplessly.

'Children!' hisses Rena.

And that is when Liam finally looks up at them. And smiles. His teeth are crooked but very white.

'Children,' he says, in a very different way from Rena. 'Children. Now, Rena, where on earth did you find them?'

Rena seems to think it's all right to speak now, so she recounts their meeting.

Liam laughs at her reference to the naked water babies and winks at Dayna, whose stomach squirms, although she doesn't know why. He's being very friendly. Suddenly and for no reason she can see, she wishes the woman were wearing some clothes.

'Let's sit down at the table,' says Liam, jumping up from the floor with an agility that makes Dayna blink. 'Follow me, children.'

'What about her?' asks Jason, nodding towards the naked woman, who seems not to have moved a muscle during all this time. Not even to get a quick peek at them.

'Vera, dear,' says Liam, without looking at her, 'please stay exactly so, or we'll have to start all over again. I'll be back within the hour to finish up. I'm very sorry, but I have to entertain our young guests.'

'Sorry,' whispers Dayna as she passes by Vera. Vera keeps on smiling and says nothing.

Liam leads them out of the large, empty room through another with a lot of beautiful furniture, and then on to a wide balcony. The roof above casts a deep shadow, but it's still a lot hotter out here than it is indoors. Too hot for adults, Dayna would have thought, although up until recently, 'adults' to her has just meant Father. Liam, it seems, has no problem whatsoever with heat.

'I love the smell of salty air,' he says as if he's read her mind. 'So this is my favourite spot in the whole Court. It's worth sweating a little more for this, don't you think? Rena? Could you get us some refreshments, please?'

Liam sits at the head of a rectangular wooden table by the balcony wall and gestures for the others to join him. He watches them take their seats, and keeps on watching them after that, but says nothing until Rena reappears with glass bottles of different shapes and colours. The water in them is cooler than anything they have tasted on their journey, and they all drink greedily.

'And now,' says Liam, putting his own half-finished drink aside as soon as their bottles are empty, 'we will talk.'

Rena tips her head, almost as if she is bowing to Liam, then collects the bottles and goes back inside, closing the balcony door behind her.

'Let's start with your names,' says Liam.

'Dayna.'

'Pax.'

'... Jason.'

Liam repeats their names to himself slowly, trying out the taste of them in his mouth.

'And you know who I am, of course, because Rena told you. Do you also know *what* I am?'

He must see the confusion in their faces because he

continues almost straight away: 'I'm special, you see. I'm chosen.'

Liam pauses here, looking at them expectantly, as if this is all he needs to say for them to understand. Which it isn't, of course.

'Who chose you?' asks Pax just as Dayna says: 'For what?'

Liam chuckles indulgently. 'By God, our Lord and Father.'

This only makes it all the more confusing. 'But gods belong to the dead world, don't they?' asks Dayna. 'They don't exist any— *Ow!*'

Jason has just kicked her shin under the table.

Liam starts to laugh now. 'Oh, heathen children. I don't hold it against you; you only know what you're told. Yes, Dayna, God belongs to the old world, but also to our new world. He is the only constant, still trying to help us. He had to stop the old world before it destroyed everything, but even now he hasn't abandoned those of us who believe in good. He speaks to me. He chose me, the new Adam.'

Liam then begins to recount the story of Adam, the first man, and Eve, who was made of Adam's rib to become the first woman. Dayna already knows this story, but she lets it wash over her again, wondering whether Liam is playing a game with them. She knows about gods, the different kinds, the stories. Father never taught her and Pax outright, but he always answered their questions truthfully, and God, in their books and stories of the old world, is mentioned many times. But Father has always dismissed these things, saying they no longer apply to Now, and saying too that they caused a lot more trouble and grief than they were worth even in the times when they did. To Dayna and Pax, religion is the same as any other tale Father ever told, be it of giant apes or monster huntresses. They can't be real today, not like the Echidna are real, or the mist, or the craze.

When Liam has finished his tale, Pax asks the question on everyone's lips: 'But how can you be like Adam from the story? There've already been thousands and thousands of men. You can't be the first one.'

Liam's crooked teeth flash in a smile like he's been waiting for this exact question.

'I am the first of NEW men,' he says. 'The immune.'

In the old world, Mother was alive and was a doctor and researcher. In fact, she was one of the people who helped create the first vaccine, which turned out to be the last, as well as too late. But she studied the craze at its beginning. She told Father, and Father told them, which is why Dayna knows this to be true: No one is wholly immune to the Echidna.

Doesn't Liam know? Or is he really playing a game? The sort of make-believe game she and Pax used to play all the time and sometimes still do. About saving the world.

'You mean you got infected and didn't get the craze?' Pax asks Liam, just when Dayna has decided to keep peace and say nothing. 'That's not being immune, that's being more resilient. Father's more resilient too. He got bit by a crazed rat, but he got better again.'

Liam tilts his head to one side, considering Pax in an exaggerated way. 'No,' he says, 'that's not what I mean at all. Some infected people can recover from the illness, that's true. At least at the beginning. But I never *had* to fight. I never was infected. I *can't* be infected. Immune. That's why this place and these people are so special, and that's why I do hope you will stay on and be a part of this. The NEW new world will be reborn here, and nowhere else.'

'With you as Adam,' murmurs Jason, who looks as if he's eaten something he ought rather to have spat out.

'I take no pride in it,' says Liam, and this is obviously a lie. 'We all have our part to play if we want to save the world.'

He reaches out and strokes Dayna's cheek. Dayna isn't used to people touching her like this, but it must be normal here, so she forces herself not to pull away. Liam's hand is soft and oily. It smells sickly sweet, a little like flowers or fruit. Finally, it draws back, ruffling Pax's hair on its way to its owner's lap.

'Children,' he breathes. 'You are the truly good, the truly innocent. You belong here, with us.'

Dayna clears her throat, shakes her head. 'We have to go find Father,' she says. She wishes wishes wishes that she'd said no to Rena's invitation and moved on straight away. But then again, she had a reason for coming, didn't she?

'Maybe you could show us your maps now?' she asks. 'Rena said—'

'From what Rena told me, it seems like a fool's errand,' says Liam. 'If your father really has been infected and if he's being held captive by dangerous people, well … Your father wouldn't want you risking your lives for him. He's probably dead already.'

It's as if he's suddenly swung out and punched Dayna right in the stomach without any warning at all. Pax whimpers and Liam holds up his hands in apology.

'I'm sorry. I know it's harsh, but the truth often is. And if the truth will keep you children alive, then that's all the more reason to say it. You'll be much better off staying here. I know your father would agree. Please, will you think about it at least?'

NO, Dayna wants to shout, but she doesn't say a word. As

soon as she opens her mouth, she'll start crying, she knows she will.

Jason speaks for them, although that is exactly what he doesn't do: 'Yeah, we'll think about it,' he says.

'Oh dear, I think I've upset them,' says Liam. 'I'm sorry. I'm not used to talking to children. But please believe me, I am so glad you're here. And when you've had time to think about it, I'm sure you'll be glad too. To be part of something great. Adam and his Eves.'

And here Liam's eyes meet Dayna's. Just a glance, just the small quiver of a smile, but wrong, somehow. Hungry, somehow. She looks away, feeling hot and uncomfortable, not quite understanding why.

14

Rena reappears as if Liam has summoned her with his thoughts and tells them to follow her, she'll lead them to their room. Liam accompanies them as far as the wide-open room with his closed sketchbook and the naked lady, who is still in the exact same position as before with not a hair out of place. He gives them one last crooked-tooth smile before resuming his seat on the floor.

'We'll see each other at dinner time,' he says. 'Until then, feel right at home. And think about my offer.'

Rena leads them down the staircase, and they follow in single file like ducklings. Dayna feels dizzy from all the steps and turns, but that might just be because of all the new, uneasy thoughts floating inside her head. Father. Liam. The naked lady. Adam.

She must have followed the others into a room without having registered leaving the stairwell, because here they now are. The room has whitewashed walls, and they're clean and bright as if the job has only just been done. Two windows looking out to the sea, still a good way above-ground, and a large double bed with dark blue bed linen and three soft-looking pillows.

'This is our guest bedroom,' says Rena. 'Although we

haven't had any guests for such a long time, and never as young as you. Only a handful of toilets are in use here, you'll find one at the end of the hall. Use the bucket of seawater next to it to flush the waste down. I hope you won't mind sharing the bed, just for one night? Tomorrow we'll get your proper rooms ready, and then you'll have one each to yourself, won't that be fun?'

'We're not staying that long,' says Dayna quickly.

'You told Liam you'd think about it, didn't you? And once we've shown you around tomorrow, I'm sure I know what your decision is going to be. Now, I've got some things to take care of, but I'll be back in an hour to collect you for dinner. We all eat together in the old ballroom downstairs. There are so many windows, it's as if you're eating outdoors. I can't wait for you to see!'

'We're not gonna eat that crazed boar, are we?' asks Pax nervously.

'Don't be silly,' laughs Rena. 'We burn dead possessed at the offering ground outside. To prevent fungus from growing in their corpses, but more importantly, to cleanse their souls. Liz and Claire have probably held the ritual already.'

What is it with these people? wonders Dayna. They start off sounding quite sensible and suddenly, they're talking gibberish.

'Hang on,' Jason calls as Rena makes for the door. 'What about the kids' rucksacks? Where did you put them?'

Rena turns and smiles. Her teeth are straight and a bit brown, but somehow her smile reminds Dayna of Liam's. A clever smile. A cunning smile.

'Oh, you don't need to bother with that while you're here. You can have them again when you leave the building. I told you that was our rule. I'll try and find some clothes for you to wear soon, and a toiletry kit, so you're all set, aren't you? All right, kiddies, see you later!'

And with that, Rena leaves. As soon as she closes the door behind her, Dayna turns to Pax and says: 'Don't listen to them about Father. What do they know? He's still alive, OK? And we'll rescue him. Liam doesn't know what he's talking about.'

'No shit he doesn't,' agrees Jason in an undertone. He walks over to the bedroom door and peeks through before shutting it again. The hallway must be empty because he goes on: 'No one can be completely immune, not even animals. But if it *were* true ... oh man, wouldn't the Hummingbirds love to get a hold of him? He'd be like their holy grail.'

'But what if it *is* true?' asks Pax. 'About him being the New Adam. Why would he say he is if he isn't? I bet the others wanted proof.'

Jason snorts. 'You'll believe anything you're told, won't you? I don't really think God chose this guy to lead us all into a new, better world, no. This guy isn't as special as he likes to make out, but I think he actually believes he is. So we'd be smart not to tell him that to his face.'

'But why would God speak to him if he wasn't special?' asks Pax.

'Come on, Pax,' says Dayna. 'God's not real any more. Liam's just playing a make-believe game.'

Jason's confidence has restored her own. He nods at her now. 'Whether or not God is real is beside the point,' he says. 'Mad people from before used him to justify all kinds of crazy shit, and that's just what Liam's doing now.'

'He's mad?' asks Pax, impressed.

'Yeah, I think,' says Jason.

Dayna shakes her head. 'No, he just wants to save the

world. He's just playing a game he thinks is real. That's not mad, that's … wishful thinking, maybe?'

Jason grimaces. 'Not just thinking, is it? He's worked out a nice way to save the world. You heard him, right? Adam and *all* his Eves? Rebuild humanity with immune little Liams and Lilys? He's probably shagging all the women here, a different one each night.'

'What's shagging?' asks Pax. 'Funny word.'

'Oh my God, do I have to tell you everything?' demands Jason, clearly embarrassed. But he gives them a brief description.

'Oh, that's making babies,' says Pax, nodding. 'I know what that is. Everyone has to make babies that way.'

'But that's usually mothers and fathers, one each,' says Dayna. 'Not one man and a lot of different women.'

She's remembering the story of an eastern king who takes a different woman to his bed every night, only to kill them the following day. She's remembering Liam's eyes meeting hers, and quickly pushes the image away. Absently, she shrugs out of the sling, turning her arm this way and that. The hurt is almost gone.

'If that's what Liam's doing, wouldn't there be some kids around?' she asks. 'Everyone keeps saying that we're the first they've seen in ages.'

Jason shrugs. 'Maybe he's impotent.'

'What's that?'

'You really don't know anything, do you?'

'I know what shagging means,' says Pax, and bursts into gales of laughter.

Dayna elbows him. 'Shut up, Pax. It's not funny.'

'You shut up yourself. It *is* funny. It's a funny word. Shagging-shagging-shagging-shagging!'

'Shut UP!'

'If anyone's still interested,' Jason is saying, 'impotent means people who can't have any kids.'

'Are you still gonna stay here?' asks Dayna with a grin that feels forced.

'Ha-ha. I'm not into sex cults, thanks.'

'They want us *all* to stay,' says Pax, sobering right up in an instant. 'We kept on saying no, and they kept on saying, Oooh, you'll love it, you'll see.'

'You're right,' mutters Jason. 'We just have to be firm. Play along with their weird ideas, but be firm about leaving. Forget the maps, I don't think they even have any.'

'We gotta find out where our rucksacks are first,' says Dayna. 'We won't make it long out there without our gear.'

'Aye aye, Sarge,' says Jason, nudging Pax, who giggles. Dayna ignores them.

'Rena's good with the knife …'

'Yeah, but she's not about to hurt us, is she?' asks Jason. 'Remember, she's GOOD. They all are. They think they're the world's saviours, they're not about to kill kids.'

Jason is right, of course. Liam's people aren't dangerous like the Hummingbirds, like Mart and Ryan and the man who shouted to leave Father for Lyle, with their weapons and animal cages and laboratories. They're just wrapped up in their make-believe game. That's all it is. That's *all* it is, so there's no need to feel this uneasy.

'Piece of cake,' says Dayna because she wants to have the last word.

Although she's never eaten cake in her life.

15

The dinner hall is all windows and no corners, just as Rena described it. So around you are streets and trees and buildings, but mostly the wide, stretching, colour-changing sea. Gulls are still swooping every which way outside, but either the glass is thick or the people's murmuring is too loud for Dayna to hear their shrieks. So many people. Double the people who watched them come in, and then double that again. She tries to count while they follow Rena through the crowd, but everyone is staring at them and whispering, and it puts her off her numbers. It's like the village she sometimes dreamed of, the Hummingbird village back when that was just a woman's voice on her radio, telling her that she was welcome. She might have been tempted to stay with them after all if Liam hadn't talked about being chosen. If the naked lady hadn't been made to remain in that exact position on the floor all the time they were outside, smiling while she did it. If Liam hadn't looked at her in that strange, hungry way. But none of this matters because they have to rescue Father anyway, and once they've done that, Father will know what to do next and who to trust.

Rena is chatting away about the ballroom, which was once a fancy restaurant, then a nightclub, then offices, until a large-scale restoration was finally completed just before the Fall (which Rena calls Apocalypse). Dayna understands about half of everything she's saying.

The rectangular tables they are passing are arranged into a large U around massive pillars, with people sitting on the outside. At the far end of the ballroom is a small platform with little steps leading up and four tables placed sideways with chairs between them and the windows, so that this line completes the square but is simultaneously raised above all the others. Liam is sitting right in the centre of the platform table, drinking some red liquid out of his glass and watching them approach. Most of the other seats beside him are empty except for the one on the far left, in which a woman with closely cropped hair sits with a baby in her lap. The baby is wrapped in a white sheet which blends into the woman's white dress, so Dayna doesn't even realise what it is before she's almost upon the platform.

Breath and noise escape her, and it sounds like a short surprised laugh. 'Ha!'

'Oh, wow,' gasps Pax, and even Jason doesn't say anything sarcastic. They overtake Rena and crowd around the baby excitedly.

'It's so small,' whispers Pax. 'Look at the fingernails. Sooo tiny.'

The baby wriggles and its eyes move from one of them to the other, and its mouth opens into a toothless smile.

'Is it a girl or a boy?' Dayna asks the mother.

'A boy,' says the mother proudly. She's the only one of the white-clothed people who doesn't seem impressed by the new arrivals; she has eyes only for her son. For a second, it's as if she's Dayna and Pax's mother, holding either one of them, smiling down, so full of love and happiness.

'Hello, baby,' says Pax. He reaches out, but Rena pushes his hand away.

'No touching, please.' She says this pleasantly enough, but her movement was quick and precise, almost like a smack.

'What's his name?' asks Jason.

'He hasn't got a name yet,' whispers the mother. Her smile stumbles, then rights itself again.

'After the ceremony, we'll know,' says Rena. 'Now come along, children. The people here are as excited to see you as you are to see this baby.'

She ushers them along, past the empty chairs, past Liam, who winks at them, to three chairs at the far end. Dayna has just sunken into her seat – a beautiful wooden chair with a curved back and armrests – when Rena's hand grabs her arm and pulls her up again.

'Our people want to see you,' she whispers.

And so Dayna, Pax and Jason stand there and look at Liam's people below them, and Liam's people look right back. They are all different ages (though Dayna still can't spot anyone as young as her and the boys, or old enough to be wrinkled and grey) and their skin and hair have different shades, but they still all look the same because everyone is dressed in the same light colours. There are far more women than there are men, maybe twice as many. Dayna spots at least three different women with big, pregnant bellies. And a couple more who might just be beginning to show. Are these all Liam's Eves?

The whispers in the once-upon-a-time ballroom grow louder and louder until suddenly they're cut off. This happens because Liam has gotten to his feet.

'These three children have found us, and we have found them,' he says to the ballroom at large in a strong, clear voice. 'They are Dayna, and Pax, and Jason.' He points to them each in turn. 'They are welcome here, the first children from the outside we've seen in many, many years. They are welcome.'

And together, as of one giant echoing creature, his people chorus: 'Welcome!'

'Er, thanks?' says Pax.

Titters amongst the crowd, and Dayna feels herself relax a little.

'Now you can sit,' smiles Rena, sitting down herself on Liam's immediate right. The three sit down. There are empty plates and cutlery in front of them, but no food. This is carried in a minute later by more white-dressed people. They come in with big metal boxes from which steam escapes. These are placed, at intervals, on tables across the ballroom. People stand up with their plates and go to the boxes to dole out the food. They're very calm and ordered, no jostling or overtaking to get there first and claim the best bits. The pregnant women even stay seated while their neighbours carry their plates to the food boxes for them.

But when Dayna and the others make to stand up too, Rena tells them there's no need.

'Look,' she says, pointing. Two young men carrying one of the steaming metal boxes between them are mounting the stairs to the platform. They stop by the mother and her baby first and wait until she has ladled out the food on to her plate, then they move on to where Liam is sitting, ignoring the two empty places in between.

'Who's sitting there?' asks Dayna, leaning forward to speak to Rena over the two boys.

'Oh, they're often late.' Rena shrugs. 'Always some drama ... Ah, excellent.'

The food tray has arrived at their side of the table. In it, Dayna now sees, is some sort of red-and-white meat, a few potatoes and a purple vegetable that could be beetroot.

'Crab meat,' Rena informs them, and it's good! Nothing like Dayna has ever tasted before, and the flavour rubs off on the vegetables with it. It tastes like the sea.

'Stop stuffing your faces, you two,' hisses Jason at her and Pax. 'No one's started yet.'

And it's true, everyone is looking up at Liam, letting the food on their plates grow colder and colder as they wait. Reluctantly, Dayna lowers her fork. Pax does the same, although he manages one more furtive bite of crab meat.

Liam stands up again, smiling, and says in his loud, confident voice:

'Good bread
Good meat
Good God
Let's eat.'

Jason snorts, but turns it into a cough. None of Liam's people cracks a smile. In solemn voices, they repeat: 'Let's eat.'

'Amen,' says Liam.

'Amen,' they chorus.

Dayna is just scooping up the last morsels of food into her mouth when a hush settles over the whole ballroom. She looks up to see two people walking towards their platform: a tall woman and a little girl, much younger than Pax. The woman has very long straight black hair almost to her knees, and she looks beautiful, and very young. The little girl is holding her hand. Her hair is as black as the woman's (her mother? Her sister? Her mother, decides Dayna) but has been parted in two plaits. She's in what looks like a bridesmaid dress. Her mother's dress is white too, not just part white or light beige like most people's clothes, but all white. They are special, you can tell not just by the whiteness of what they're wearing but by how the people are reacting to them – turning as they pass by, pushing their chairs closer, holding out their hands, palms down, towards the little girl, without actually making contact. It's as if mother and daughter are radiating fires on a rare cold winter night. As if people want to be as close as possible to them, without quite daring to touch.

Mother and daughter seem oblivious to the clamour of people around them, but then the little girl spots Dayna and the others and points and makes a beeline for them, tugging her mother along too.

'Hello,' says the little girl, looking Dayna straight in the eye. 'Who are you? Where did you come from?'

'They're Dayna and Pax and Jason,' says Rena before Dayna can respond. 'We found them this afternoon and brought them here. You'd have known if you'd taken the trouble to be here on time.'

'Hi, guys,' the black-haired woman says to the kids, ignoring Rena completely. Her smile is different to Rena's or Liam's; not as knowing, but also not as happy. Up close, she looks even younger, maybe only a handful of years older than Jason.

'Where did you come from, then?'

'From the north,' says Dayna.

'And where're you going?'

'Who says they're going anywhere?' demands Rena.

'Yes, we are,' says Pax. 'We're going to the Hummingbirds. To rescue Father. We told you a HUNDRED times.'

'I'm Evie!' the little girl pipes up, tired of being ignored. 'It's spelt capital E, little v-i-e.'

'It's Eve, actually,' says Rena.

Beside her, Liam laughs and leans closer. 'Let her be Evie for now,' he says. 'She'll be Eve soon enough, when she's ready.'

Dayna doesn't make the connection straight away and is surprised at first, by the flash of feeling that streaks past the black-haired woman's face – too quick to tell what exactly it is, only that it's strong. Then, all at once, Dayna understands.

'Meet my daughter,' says Liam, 'proof that God still loves us.'

'Amen,' says Evie indifferently, then, to Dayna: 'You're a girl, like me.'

'I know I am,' says Dayna, who is beginning to feel light-headed and queasy.

'Yes,' says Liam fondly. 'The first child born with my immunity, but hopefully not the last.'

He raises his glass in the direction of the black-haired mother, toasting her. She inclines her head, a little sullenly, then turns back to Dayna and the boys.

'I'm Sachiko,' she says. 'And if you want to find your father, you'd better not stop here for too long.'

'Can you believe her?' gasps Rena, but Liam silences her with a raised hand.

'Sachiko, dear,' he says in a coaxing voice, 'sit down and eat before the food gets even colder. You're always a little sulky when hungry, aren't you now?'

Sachiko sighs and nods. 'Yes, I suppose I am. Come, Evie.'

'You're mine friend now,' Evie informs Dayna regally. 'The boys can be too. But you're mine special friend.'

Her mother takes her hand again and leads her around the platform to the two empty chairs at Liam's left. The woman with the baby nods amiably, but Sachiko passes her by as if she were air. Evie, however, pauses to stroke the baby's silky hair.

16

'The sooner we leave, the better,' whispers Jason.

They're back in their room, all alone. But who knows if anyone is in the rooms next to theirs, and listening. It's best to whisper.

'These people are nuts. That little girl's gonna be used as a breeding mare as soon as she's old enough to have kids! How sick is that?'

'What?' gasps Pax, shocked. 'When did he tell us? You sure?'

'He said she'd be Eve when she's ready. Like he calls himself the new Adam. Like the whole place is full of women he's impregnated. Didn't you see? If she really has the immunity like him, that would fit right into their little plan of saving the world, wouldn't it?'

'You said he was im-po-tent,' Pax reminds him.

'Well, I bloody know better now, don't I? Sorry, but are you really this thick?'

'Shut up, Jason,' mumbles Dayna. She's feeling sicker than ever. Children and the adult act of making babies shouldn't be connected … Is this what people are like now? Hummingbirds and new Adams? It's not as easy to see bad people as she thought it would be. Ryan was nice, and then she found Jason locked in that animal cage. But at least, after that, it was easy to tell the Hummingbirds were bad. These people are different. They smile and ignore what you say and act innocent and good. Open hostility Dayna could handle a lot better than this.

'Sachiko seemed nice, but she's staying,' she says now. 'She's staying with Evie, even when she told us to leave. Why doesn't *she* leave with Evie?'

'Because she's crazy like all the rest of them,' snaps Jason. 'She believes they really can save the world.'

'But I don't think she likes it here. She seems sad.'

'People don't have to like the bullshit they believe. They just have to believe. She probably thinks she's sacrificing her daughter to save the world. We are so not staying longer than we have to.'

'I'm not saying I want to stay, am I?' retorts Dayna. 'I want to take Evie with us. And Sachiko.'

'You're an even bigger idiot than I thought, then,' says Jason. 'What d'you think the crazy people would do if we took their miracle baby? Or the miracle-baby-producing mother? They'd hunt us down no matter where we went.'

'What about all the other babies?' asks Pax in a quiet voice. 'We ought to save them all, oughtn't we?'

Even Dayna can see that half a dozen pregnant women in the throngs of religious fervour will take a lot of persuading. And put it like that, so would Sachiko, wouldn't she, if she's stayed this long already? And Evie would never go without her mother.

She heaves a sigh, and it's as if all the hope for these people leaves her with it. 'Yeah,' she says to her brother. 'We ought. But I think Jason might not be completely, totally wrong about this after all. It'll be really hard to get them to *want* to leave.'

'Wow, did you actually say that I might be right?' asks Jason in mock gratitude.

'OK,' says Pax to Dayna. 'Then we just tell Father after we save him. And he'll know what to do about it. OK?'

'Yeah,' says Dayna. And thinks: How impossible is it going to be to save Father? As impossible as it would be to save Evie?

They pass a hot, uncomfortable night. The bed is just too narrow for the three of them and made all the warmer by their proximity. Dayna's light sleep is continually being interrupted by Pax's twitching feet or elbows, Jason's snuffling snores at the far end, not to mention the thoughts and worries dancing around her head, just out of reach. Evie in a wedding gown and Liam in a tux, bending down to kiss her. Watching them are Sachiko and the naked lady, who is laughing hysterically, laughing and laughing and unable to stop. And now Father is tearing down an empty street, running from a monster she can't see, and getting further and further away from her and Pax, for all that they try to keep up.

She is falling, falling – and is jerked out of her dreams to find herself on the very edge of the bed about to tumble right out of it. Beside her, the two boys grunt and stir in their sleep, and the patch of sky Dayna can see from the window is orange with the light of the rising sun.

She slides out of bed and pads to the bedroom door. It's locked.

Rena unlocks it an hour or so later, barging into their room with a bundle of towels in her arms and a cheerful, 'Good morning!'

'Good morning,' mimics Jason in a high voice. 'Why d'you lock us in?'

'Now, don't be rude,' reprimands Rena. 'The Court is a very big place, and we didn't want anyone getting lost on their way to the lavatory in the middle of the night, did we?'

'What, you'd rather we wet ourselves?'

'Speaking of which, all three of you do smell a little strong. So I've come to take you to have a bath.'

'Who's being rude now?' mutters Pax.

'We had a bath yesterday,' says Dayna. 'In the sea.'

'Well, you apparently didn't use soap or shampoo, and your fingernails are almost black with dirt. Didn't anyone ever show you how to wash properly?'

'Rude, rude, rude, rude, rude,' whispers Pax.

'Look, there's no point in our washing now,' says Dayna, irritated too. 'We're leaving today, and we'll only get dirty again. In fact, we were talking, and we think we'll go right—'

Rena shakes her head as if she is disappointed. 'Now look here, children. You've obviously been brought up like savages, but this isn't how we act in a civilised society, and the sooner you learn, the better. This is the way things are done, and will be done: When you are children and an adult tells you to do something, you do it. And when you are guests and your host tells you to do something, then you do it as well. And, honestly, do we really want to fall out over a bath?'

Dayna glances at the others, then swallows her anger with an effort. 'I suppose we don't,' she says.

She examines her grimy fingernails. They really could do with a wash.

★

Rena takes the boys to one bathroom, and Dayna across the corridor to another. The boys she leaves to their own devices, but to Dayna's annoyance, insists on staying with her.

'I'd rather wash by myself, thanks.'

'No need to be bashful. You weren't before, were you, little water baby?'

'I'm not bashful,' mutters Dayna, who suddenly is. She's swum naked with Pax all her life and thought nothing of it. But in the Court, nakedness is more complicated and more scary ...

The bathroom has a black-and-white tiled floor, like the one in Liam's rooms. The bathtub was white once, but its inside is a faint yellowy brown now, the water in it is as cool as that of the stream back home she's used to bathing in.

'How old are you, child?' asks Rena as Dayna peels off her clothes.

'What does it matter?' says Dayna curtly. She doesn't like the intense way the woman is examining her, especially her chest and the slight swelling of and around the nipples. Father said that was normal for growing girls, so she never gave it much thought. Until now.

'Have you started menstruating yet?' asks Rena. 'You know what I mean by that? Menstruation? Monthly bleeding?' (Dayna was right: nakedness in the Court is far, far more than just nakedness.)

'I know what it means,' she mutters, 'and I haven't.' She feels weirdly relieved by this fact. Maybe just because Rena obviously wanted a different answer.

Before any more questions come, she slides into the tub, eager to get this whole ordeal over and done with as quickly as possible. She submerges under the cold water, which, she discovers, has been taken directly from the sea.

When she resurfaces, Rena is kneeling beside her with a smile that is too wide and too bright.

'You wouldn't lie to me, would you?' she asks in a playful voice that makes goose pimples spring up on Dayna's flesh.

'No, why should I?' (And some part of her can guess if she'd let it. But she doesn't.)

'Absolutely no reason at all,' smiles Rena. From a plastic bottle, she squirts out a gob of fruity-smelling shampoo into the palm of her hand, then starts rubbing it into Dayna's wet hair.

'I can do that myself,' says Dayna.

Of course, Rena ignores her.

Dayna's clothes are gone when she is finally allowed to climb out of the tub, and worse still, her gas mask along with them. In their stead is a girl's light-beige summer dress and white underwear.

'Where're my things?'

'We're getting them washed,' says Rena. 'They were filthy.'

'What about the gas mask?'

'You won't need your gas mask indoors, will you? Now try this on and let's see if it fits.'

The dress is very simply cut, with ordinary straps and a knee-length hem. It fits all right, but Dayna doesn't like the feel of it one bit. She's not used to wearing dresses, and feels exposed and strange.

'Hmm,' says Rena, considering her. 'Your haircut spoils the effect a little, but otherwise you look quite pretty.'

Dayna rubs at her short hair self-consciously, making it stand on end, but Rena flattens it with a hairbrush so that it hangs down stiffly, not quite reaching her chin.

'A couple of months and it'll grow enough to make you look like a proper girl,' she says.

This isn't worth responding to, so Dayna makes no response.

They've even taken her shoes and left none to replace them with, so she has to walk barefoot as she trails down the stairs after Rena.

Breakfast in the ballroom proceeds much in the same manner as dinner has done, except that there is flatbread instead of crab stew. Jason and Pax (their hair damp like Dayna's) have both been forced into white clothes too, only theirs are the kind Dayna would have preferred: shorts and shirts. Pax giggles when he sees her dress but stops quickly when he sees her scowl. Both boys are barefoot as well, and Dayna wonders whether Liam's people took away their shoes to make it more difficult to run. Perhaps it's only another one of Liam's rules, as many people in the Court aren't wearing shoes either.

It doesn't take long for Evie to seek Dayna out.

'Hello, Dayna.'

'Hi.'

'Let's play a game?'

'No, thanks,' says Dayna, whose mind is on more important things (gas masks, gear, shoes, getting out out *out*). She makes a show of nibbling at her flatbread; she's read about bread but has never eaten it before and is a little disappointed by its neutral taste. 'Still having breakfast,' she says.

Evie obviously isn't used to people ignoring her. 'YES, I WANT TO PLAY!' she screams.

Dayna isn't used to people shouting into her ear. She shoves Evie away from her, and the little girl trips and falls on to her bottom. There is a sudden stunned silence, as if the whole ballroom has drawn in its breath and is holding it. Then Evie bursts into angry tears.

Rena swoops down and tries to comfort her while Dayna offers an unconvincing: '... sorry.'

'Way to go,' mutters Jason, just as Liam appears right at her side.

Dayna barely has time to register this when something strikes the side of her face with so much force that she is knocked from her chair and sent sprawling close to the sobbing Evie.

'Hey!' shouts Jason, but all Dayna can see is Liam's face inches away from her own. She can smell his breath, which is rank.

'You do not,' hisses Liam between his teeth, 'touch that child.'

He then hoists Evie up into his arms (Evie's howling intensifies) and sweeps down the stairs, past the tables and out of the ballroom.

'You've gone and done it now,' whispers Jason as he helps Dayna to her feet. 'You OK? That was a hell of a smack he gave you.'

'We don't use that word here, young man,' says Rena. 'Now sit down, both of you. And I hope that's the last of your foolishness. Eve is God's child, don't you see?'

A crybaby is what she is, thinks Dayna as she picks up her chair and sits down again. Her left cheek is throbbing something dreadful. Pax is staring at her with wide eyes. He looks ready to burst into tears himself.

'S'OK,' says Dayna.

'You're bleeding,' whispers Pax. 'If I'd had my bat, I would've whacked him over the head with it.'

Dayna reaches up and discovers something wet by her left nostril. She wipes the blood away with the back of her hand, scowling. Then she turns to Rena: 'We'll be leaving now if it's all the same to you. Can you tell us where our gear is?'

'Don't sulk,' is all Rena says.

'They'd really better be on their way soon,' says Sachiko. 'They're not used to children as small as Evie.'

'I am so,' fires up Dayna, who has just about had enough. 'What about Pax? I remember when he was little, and I don't see what everyone's making such a fuss about—'

'Be quiet, you idiot,' hisses Jason.

Dayna is. She can see now that Sachiko only wants to help them, and she can also see that Rena is seriously considering giving her a smack of her own.

17

In a former flat on the second floor, Liam's people have set up a food-processing station where harvested oat and wheat grain are separated from their stems and then pulverised in old coffee grinders. The fresh flour is then shaken into glass jars or plastic containers, ready for use or storage.

This is where they are brought after breakfast, and this is where Dayna is told to stay and help out.

'What about the others?' she asks.

'They'll be given different tasks,' says Rena. 'Everyone here has to do their bit. That's how a community works.'

'But we're not *part* of your community,' says Dayna. 'We're leaving today—'

'You've been our guests and slept in our beds and eaten our food,' replies Rena. 'You're right, until now you've only taken. Now it's time to give.'

Jason shoots Dayna a warning look. She grimaces. She knows very well that now is not the time to antagonise them. They can't go without their gas masks. She knows this, but she hates wasting all this time here while Father is imprisoned in some Hummingbird cell … and she hates feeling this trapped.

Rena leaves with the boys. A man who introduces himself as Alex takes Dayna to a large table where people are separating stems and grains, and shows her what to do. It's pernickety work, and frustrating too, as it goes on and on and the small pile of grain in her bowl hardly seems to grow at all. Dayna's fingertips soon hurt from all the picking, and she's sure Rena put her to work here as punishment; the other jobs can't be as tedious as this.

There are eight people working on the grains, and you would have thought that they'd be chatting or joking while they work, like she and Pax and Father always played word games or told stories while they were preparing dinner. But here everyone is silent and very focused on their task. Dayna does get some curious glances, but none of those make her uneasy in the way Liam did, which is a relief.

'Where are your cornfields?' she finally asks, simply to break the silence, which is unnerving her.

'About an hour's walk from here,' pants Alex, who has been cranking the coffee grinder handle in the same tireless rhythm for ages. 'It's about sixty acres, but we only use half that while the soil of the other half recovers.'

Dayna is impressed in spite of herself. They only grew vegetables at the Blue House. Father tried crops at various times, but they always withered away or were ruined in harsh rainstorms.

'How do you know how to do all this?' she asks.

'Well, you sort of learn by doing, don't you?' says a woman with a space between her front teeth, who is sitting opposite Dayna. 'Books about farming during the Middle Ages helped a lot too.'

'And don't forget Bob,' says Alex. 'He actually worked on a farm before the Apocalypse. He knew all the ins and outs.'

Dayna dismisses Bob but stores up books about Middle Ages farming in her mind for future reference. It's not a bad idea, she grudgingly admits. Depending on how easily found such books still are.

As her fellow workers seem quite happy to talk once prompted, she asks: 'How did you all end up here in the first place, anyway?'

'Liam found most of us,' says Alex. 'Before he was called to this place he wandered the land with his message, searching for followers. He's the chosen one, but we are the chosen people. He needs us to complete his destiny, and we need him. He gave us hope again, of a better world. Those of us of strong faith followed, and now here we are. Before we arrived, the Court had become home to savages, a place of sin and violence. We cleansed it and saved the innocent. Rena was one of them. They'd done terrible things to her and she was in a bad state, not just in body, but in mind. Liam saved her. He saved all of us, one way or another. Every year we send out messengers, trying to find more people. But it's so dangerous out there, some don't return at all, and those who do mostly return alone. People are fewer, and they've become harder and more cynical. They've lost their faith. We were all very happy when Rena brought you children here. Children have the purest faith of all.'

He speaks in a strange way, just like Liam sometimes does. A storytelling voice, not a real-life voice. But Alex believes this story, and so do the rest of them: They're nodding enthusiastically as they work. Two people even whisper: 'Amen.'

Dayna picks the oats in silence for a while, then asks: 'All those pregnant women here, are they all Liam's kids?'

No one answers, and she looks up to see they're all concentrating on their work, avoiding her eye, like this is a question that should not have been asked.

She's just about to apologise when Alex speaks. 'Yes,' he says quietly, and Dayna can't tell whether his tone is one of pride or shame, or both. 'All the children to be are our hope for the future. Little Eve is special, I'm sure you understand now. The very first to inherit Liam's immunity. She's God's sign that it could be done, and will be done.'

'Amen,' the others murmur, and now Dayna can hear what it is, and it's pride.

Liam's people take no food at midday as Dayna is used to, but work stolidly on in their allotted tasks. Under the pretence of going to the bathroom down the corridor, Dayna wanders around a little in the hopes of finding something useful. She doesn't know what that something could be, and doesn't find it in any case. Some doors on the second floor are locked, and others propped open to let window light into the winding corridor, but all those flats are empty and seemingly unused. From a window of one of these rooms, she can see a small group of people by the seaside with nets. It's hard to make out from that distance, but she thinks one of them is smaller than the others, and if so, it could be Pax. And if they let Pax out, they must have given him his gas mask …

On her return, Dayna asks Alex, as casually as she can, but he just shakes his head and says: 'There's no need to worry about that here, Dayna. We take care of each other, and when the time comes that you need it, it will be given to you.'

'What if I need it now?' asks Dayna.

'But you don't, do you? You're here, helping us.'

His head bobs up and down in a strange forceful nod to the beat of his cranking.

18

When Rena comes to pick Dayna up, she thinks she'll be taken to the ballroom for dinner (her stomach is rumbling), but instead, Rena walks up the stairs, not down. Rena may still be angry at Dayna for pushing Evie, or she may just be tired or preoccupied; either way, she doesn't say a word, and Dayna follows her example. Up and up they go, and Dayna is quite sure now where they're headed, and a sudden, inexplicable dread takes hold of her, but she can't see any way out of it, not without the others, not without the masks.

As she did before, Rena knocks on Liam's door, then opens it without waiting for an answer. And as he did before, Liam continues to sketch on the floor and takes no notice of them. His subject is a different woman today, in a different pose, but just as naked. In fact, Dayna realises with a jolt, it's Sachiko. Dayna looks away quickly, embarrassed, and her gaze falls on Pax and Jason, standing quietly in a corner. A great relief washes over her at the sight of them, although she isn't quite sure why. Pax smiles broadly, and even Jason seems glad to see her.

'I went fishing,' Pax whispers into her ear as soon as she's reached them. 'I caught a big one. But I didn't like being on my own with them, without you. If they hit me, I'd hit them back, but there'd be too many—'

'Hush, you two,' snaps Rena, still in the doorway.

'Is your cheek better?' breathes Pax, his voice so low now that Dayna can barely hear it.

She nods. She's itching to ask him if he saw where the gas masks are being stored, but that will have to wait until they're on their own again.

Liam takes his time, sketching for at least another ten minutes before finally turning and addressing them: 'How did you like the work?'

He waits, until it's clear none of them is going to answer, then says, 'You're not used to helping out in a community. But you'll learn. And you'll be the happier for it.'

Dayna steels herself to open her mouth, but Jason is faster: 'Look,' he says, 'we were happy to work for a day to repay you for the food and board, but we've got to move on now, like we said. We're meeting their father.'

'That's not what you said yesterday,' remarks Liam. 'You said their father was captured by some bad people, and, I'm sorry to have to remind you, we agreed that it would be pointless for you to go after him. You can't throw away your lives, not when they're needed here, for something great. Your father is dead, children. Even if he's still alive, he won't be for long, so you may as well think of him as gone already. It's harsh, but that's the way it is. Which is why what we're doing here is so important.'

This is too much for Pax. 'Father ISN'T dead!' he shouts at Liam. 'You don't know ANYTHING!'

Liam rises to his feet, slow enough to be threatening. Pax stands his ground, although angry tears have welled up in his eyes. Dayna gets ready to leap at Liam and scratch and bite if he should make any move to attack Pax, but Liam only stands there, looking down at them from his greater height.

'Yesterday you agreed with me,' says Liam, his tone like the calm before a dangerous, deadly thunderstorm. 'You asked whether you could stay here, and I said yes, of course. I said yes, but only if you took our mission seriously. You agreed. Didn't they, Rena?'

Speechless with indignation, they can only turn to her, gaping like dying fish tossed out of their stream and on to land. Rena nods. 'Yes, that's what was agreed upon,' she says without any sign of guilt.

'And now, after only one day of work here, you've decided you don't want to stay after all? Youth can be idle before it learns, but it will have to learn. I won't let you die out there just because you're too lazy to—'

'LIAR!' shouts Dayna. 'We never said that! We never wanted to stay, and I'm sick of going along with you. We're leaving!'

She grabs Pax by the hand and pulls him towards the door, fully prepared to knock Rena down if she won't get out of their way. She doesn't get out of their way. And all of a sudden there's a knife in her hand, maybe even the same one she felled the crazed boar with, and its blade is pointing right at them.

'You'd better calm down,' she says.

Jason is right beside Dayna and Pax. He says, 'She won't hurt us. There's no use in keeping us here if we're hurt or dead.'

Rena smiles thinly. Her eyes flick from one to the other to the third. Flick, flick, flick.

'Not true,' she says. 'It's the girl we need the most; you two boys are expendable. You think I'm lying? Try me and see which of you I slice up first.'

Her eyes settle on Pax. She isn't bluffing.

'OK,' says Dayna quickly. 'OK, we'll stop.'

'Stay put, please, Sachiko,' murmurs Liam, and Sachiko turns her head away from their group so that only her profile is visible again.

'Tell me,' Liam says to Dayna as if he's merely curious, 'were you really planning on leaving here without your gas masks or any weapons whatsoever? Did you honestly think that a good idea?'

He's right, and knows it. And so does she.

'What happens now?' she asks.

'Now? Now you behave and help out, like you promised you would. Although maybe a day or so to cool off would be more appropriate, what do you think, Rena?'

'I think they could all do with some cooling off,' she responds, and lets her knife arm fall to her side. 'Follow me, kiddos, and no more funny business, if you please.'

They're already in the hallway when Liam's voice calls after them: 'I *love* your new dress, Dayna!'

As they follow Rena (they always seem to be following Rena in this place), Dayna moves closer to Pax and whispers: 'Do you know where the gas masks are?'

But he shakes his head. 'Someone else brought them for me. It wasn't even Kong, it was some white flimsy mask you only put over your mouth and nose. And I never saw where they took them from.'

'Shit,' mutters Jason.

'They must be near the main entrance downstairs,' whispers Dayna, thinking. 'Somewhere easy to get to for everyone on their way out—'

'Stop talking, you three!' Rena calls cheerily over her shoulder.

She leads them out on to a short corridor with a once-red carpet, and although it's hard to tell (everything looks so similar here), Dayna thinks it's not the same floor as the one their room is on, but a little further up. Rena opens one of the doors and stands aside for Dayna to enter. As soon as she does, the door flies shut behind her and the lock turns with a little click. Only when she hears them shout from the other side of the door does Dayna realise that she's been separated from Pax and Jason.

19

Rena unlocks the door about an hour later, holding a bowl of steaming something, and two water bottles. With these, and the key, she wouldn't have a free hand to snatch up the knife if Dayna rushed her. Dayna imagines herself doing this, and how the bowl would clatter to the ground, and how Rena would scream in shock and how Dayna herself would tear down the corridor. It's a satisfying dream, but impossible now. When would it have been possible? This morning? The day before? They should never have abandoned their rucksacks. They should never have gone with the three women in the first place. Father was always so wary about strangers, and Dayna finally understands why. In the stories she knows, people are often helpful and kind, and the ones who aren't are usually easy to catch out. But these stories belong to the dead world. Now people are tricky: they smile and joke and make you feel safe. And then they pounce.

'It's a lovely apartment, isn't it?' says Rena, beaming at her as if their last confrontation never happened. 'We'll try and find some things for you, there's enough space, you ought to fill it up. Books, magazines … *make-up*! I could give you some *Cosmo* magazines, have you ever seen one? So many beautiful clothes. You could make collages of the outfits you like best and hang them up on the walls. Aren't you a lucky girl, a whole apartment all to yourself?'

Dayna is sitting on the sofa in the centre of the room, which smells musty and faintly of cigarette smoke. She's been wondering if she's the first person to sit on it since the time of the dead world. Every drawer has been emptied and there aren't any personal trinkets lying around at all, so Liam's people must have tidied the flat at some point. But there's a layer of dust over everything except for the bed, suggesting that it's been a long time since anyone lived here.

'Where're Pax and Jason?' she demands.

'They've each got an apartment of their own too. Like everyone here – there's enough to go around three times over, so there's no need to be stingy. Aren't you going to thank me for bringing supper?'

'Can I see them?'

'Of course, eventually. But not just yet. You all have to get used to your new surroundings. You're rather spoilt, ungrateful children, aren't you? Don't know how lucky you are, finding us to take care of you. You'll learn, hopefully.'

Dayna bites down hard on her lip, and manages to hold out for about five seconds before spitting: 'You're NOT taking care of us! You're LOCKING us up!'

'You'll be part of something great,' continues Rena as if she hasn't heard. 'Dayna, do you know what happens once you begin to menstruate?'

Dayna feels heat rush into her cheeks. 'You've already asked that,' she mutters, trying to sound defiant instead of ... what? (Embarrassed? Uneasy?) 'I'll bleed, once a month.'

'Down there,' says Rena, gesturing. (No, more than unease. Fear.) 'But do you know *what* that means?'

'It just means I'm getting older, that's all,' snaps Dayna. (Oh yes, fear.)

'It means you'll be ready,' says Rena, still in that same sweet, comforting voice. 'It means your body will be ready to do what it was born to do: to grow children of its own, inside it. Isn't that the most WONDERFUL thing?'

And Dayna's stomach writhes and twists as if to moan: 'No! I don't want that! Not inside *me*!'

'But you haven't started bleeding yet, have you, Dayna?'

Dayna shakes her head vehemently: 'No!' And even though this is true, it sounds like a lie. It sounds like a lie they won't believe, or won't care to have proved right or wrong.

Rena just nods, slowly. 'It's hard to tell sometimes,' she muses, 'when girls will start. You won't have to wait too much longer, I should think. You're around that age, and I have an intuition about these things. You must tell me when you begin to bleed, all right, Dayna? I'll get you sanitary towels. Yes?'

It's a very long and tense night for Dayna. She tosses and turns in her new bed while her brain grapples with one worry after the next. And these worries are far more substantial than the flighty things of last night. Pax, all alone in his room like she is and probably just as frightened. The sheer impossibility of their escape, because how can the three of them plan or communicate now or ever again? Gas masks and shoes and Rena's lightning reflexes. Father again, in his Hummingbird cell. And perhaps Father dead, because maybe Liam isn't as wrong about that as they want him to be. Sachiko, looking away. Little Evie, who'll be in big trouble as soon as her own menstruation begins – and Dayna has to stumble out of bed, to the toilet room, and heave her supper into the scrubbed white bowl.

When she can't push the dread away any longer, she worries about herself. She starts imagining the door being unlocked by Liam, his crooked teeth very white, glinting in the darkness like animal fangs, the way they only can in nightmares. 'You little liar,' he whispers. 'I can smell the blood on you and in you. I have an intuition about these things …'

And she stays awake for a long, long time, listening to the sound of waves breaking ashore outside and then being dragged back again, sucked back into the sea.

No one comes for Dayna the next day. She spends the morning searching through all the rooms and all the cupboards and chests of drawers (again, in case she missed something yesterday), and the spaces under the sofa and under the bed, but there is nothing to be found except dust and cobwebs. What was she expecting anyway? A key to the door? She walks over to it and jiggles the handle, just to be sure, then bangs against it.

'HELLO?! HE-LLO-OH! I'm still here, you've forgotten me!'

Still no one comes.

Dayna tries all the windows next and all of them are locked, as is the door to the balcony. Not that that way would be any use; she must be at least ten storeys aboveground. Heat from the blazing sun radiates from the windowpanes; her new hateful dress is already crinkled and damp from her sweat.

Dayna paces, she yells at the door, she watches the seagulls swoop and scream outside, she watches the gentle rhythm of the waves breaking on to what's left of the beach. She's hungry and apprehensive, and bored. She never knew you could be frightened and bored at the same time.

Finally, after hours and hours, Dayna can hear footsteps approaching in the corridor. She jumps up and hurries to the door, ready to start shouting if the person on the other side should pass it by. They don't. The lock clicks and the door swings open, revealing not Rena at all, but Sachiko. And Evie.

'I asked where you are at breakfast and Liam said here because you were naughty, and so I said I want to visit you,' sums up Evie all in one breath.

'We brought something to eat,' says Sachiko, holding up a bowl of brown mush. 'Porridge,' she adds, when Dayna sniffs at it suspiciously. 'Oats and water, and a little salt.'

The three of them sit around the bare table in what Dayna thinks of as the dead kitchen as she wolfs down her porridge. She doesn't much like the taste – it's too slimy, and in stories, people always eat it with sweet things like honey or sugar – but it's filling all the same, and she's hungry.

'Are Pax and Jason OK?' she asks between mouthfuls.

'Yes, everyone's OK,' says Sachiko. 'They're being kept in separate rooms, like you. You'll all be allowed out soon enough. Liam just wants to show you who's boss.'

Dayna looks Sachiko full in the eye. 'Do you know where our gas masks are?'

'Yeah, I do. But I can't tell you. I'm sorry, but I can't. He'd know, and he'd punish me.'

'Liam doesn't like people being naughty,' says Evie. 'I don't either because when Mummy's naughty, I'm not allowed to see her. We're not being naughty now, though. I asked and Liam said all right. Because you're mine friend.'

'*My* friend,' corrects Sachiko.

'My friend. Even though you pushed me. Mummy said friends sometimes push each other when they're playing, but that doesn't mean they don't like each other. I like you. Do you like me?'

'Yeah, I like you,' says Dayna. 'You're funny.'

'I'm the chosen child,' corrects Evie sternly, as if Dayna has missed a great point.

Dayna turns to Sachiko: 'You ought to come with us, then he can't punish you ever again. And then Evie doesn't have to be Eve later.'

'I WANT to be Eve,' says Evie.

'No, you don't,' says Dayna. '*You* don't want her to be, do you?' she asks, turning to the little girl's mother.

Sachiko sighs long and hard, like she's trying to press all the air out of her body. 'Of course I don't, of course not. But maybe … maybe that's the only way. For a new world.'

Dayna is silent for a moment, mulling this over. Then she says: 'If it is, I wouldn't want to live in it.'

Sachiko doesn't respond. Her eyes are fixed on the clasped hands in her lap. She looks very young. How old was she when she had Evie? Maybe not even as old as Jason is now.

'Stop talking,' Evie commands. 'You're making Mummy cry. I hate it when Mummy cries.'

'Sorry,' mumbles Dayna. 'What games do you play, Evie?'

It turns out that Evie hardly knows any fun games at all because she's not supposed to run around, as she might fall and hurt herself. They play I Spy together for a bit until Dayna gets bored and tries to initiate her into Hide-and-Seek. But—

'I'm not allowed,' says Evie, shaking her head sadly. 'Mummy used to play with me, but Liam said no.'

'Why? It's not rough, is it? You just find a hiding place and stay put.'

'Liam didn't like the idea of her hiding,' says Sachiko quietly. 'But Rena's not here to tell on us today, Evie. I think we could get away with it.'

'I can play?' breathes Evie, almost reverently.

'Just don't tell Liam, all right?'

'Yes! Can I hide first? Where can I hide?'

Evie isn't very good at the game, dithering over places to hide and always ending up following Dayna, even though there usually isn't enough space for two. And then she's overcome with fits of the giggles and has to stuff her little hands into her mouth to stifle the sound. Sachiko, who's It, manages to ignore the small grunts of glee or sticking out limbs for a long time before she finds them, purposefully overlooking them to give Evie pleasure (is this what mothers do?). It works and Evie is delighted.

'What a fun game,' she pants after an hour or so, worn out from all the laughing. 'This is mine absolutely favourite game of all time!'

'Do you want to try out being It for a change?' asks Dayna, feeling a little sorry for Sachiko.

'No.'

'Maybe I will, then.'

'NO! Mummy's too big to hide like we do. Do you want to hear a secret?'

'Hush, Evie,' says Sachiko. But Evie takes no notice.

'Mummy's going to have another baby! She'll be even bigger then, just like Kathleen and Patricia and Viv. Because the baby will grows in her tummy.'

'Will grow,' mumbles Sachiko absently.

Dayna looks at her and can tell by her expression that what Evie said is the truth.

'And Liam doesn't know yet because it's secret,' continues Evie.

Sachiko sighs and shrugs. 'Yeah, well, I thought he didn't. It doesn't show yet. But yesterday he wanted to sketch me. But you already know that, right?' she asks Dayna, with a small grimace. 'He usually only sketches us when we're pregnant. Every trimester. Rena must have checked my sanitary towels and seen there wasn't blood on them.'

'Rena's a old telltale,' says Evie.

'Yeah, she is.'

'But why did you want to keep it a secret?' asks Dayna. 'They're all going to see sooner or later.'

Sachiko shakes her head. 'I don't know,' she whispers. 'I wanted to keep it a secret for as long as possible, but I don't know why.'

'Mummy's afraid of the ceremony,' explains Evie.

'What ceremony?'

'Come on, Evie,' says Sachiko sharply. 'We have to go now or Rena will come looking for us.'

'That telltale,' mutters Evie, getting to her feet. Sachiko has to undo Evie's untidy plaits and use her fingers to comb her daughter's hair. Then she redoes the plaits, making them as neat as possible. Dayna watches, and there's a sadness in her, a strange longing.

'Bye-bye,' says Evie, as Sachiko opens the front door.

'Bye,' mumbles Dayna.

'I'm going to have to lock this door again,' says Sachiko. 'I'm sorry.'

'S'OK,' says Dayna, although it isn't.

'If they still don't let you out by tomorrow, we'll come by again.'

'Hmm.'

'And, Dayna? You don't have to worry about Liam right now, OK? He won't try to do anything until you start bleeding. I'm sure he won't.'

'OK,' agrees Dayna, her throat very dry. 'Sachiko? Can you maybe ask if I can have shorts to wear, like the boys? I don't like the dress.'

'I'll ask,' she agrees. 'See you soon and try not to worry too much.'

Then the door is shut behind them, and locked. Dayna listens to their receding footsteps.

She stays alone for the rest of the day until Rena comes in with her supper – fish stew – as the sky is just beginning to darken.

'You've been popular with little Eve, haven't you?' says Rena. 'What did you do today?'

Dayna shrugs. 'Nothing much.'

She can see this non-answer annoys Rena, who really seems curious, and annoying Rena gives her a vindictive sort of pleasure. She's longing to ask after Pax and Jason, and whether they'll all be let out the next day, and what about the books Rena talked about to help pass the time? But she manages to clench her teeth and say nothing at all. She doesn't want to give Rena the satisfaction.

'You're a lot quieter today than you were yesterday,' remarks Rena.

'No point in talking to you, is there?' says Dayna, pleased by this comeback. 'You only ever hear what you want to hear. You and Liam both.'

She half expects another slap and is ready to jump back if it should come, but Rena only smiles thinly as she turns to the door.

'Looks like you'll need to cool off a little longer,' she says. 'Another day should do the trick.'

'What?' Dayna can't help it, she rushes to the door just as it swings shut. 'HEY!' she calls, banging her fists against it. 'HEY! You can't lock me up a whole other day! You can't! I'll—'

She stops herself just in time. She doesn't want to shout it. She doesn't even want to think it.

(I'll go mad.)

20

In all the games she plays with Pax, Dayna is good at getting them out of imagined dangers (after first getting them in). But the dangers at the Court are real, and how can she get away when she knows nothing at all? Not where Pax and Jason are, not where their gear is. Not even when she'll ever be let out of this flat. As the night wears on, her plans of escape slip more and more into dreamlike fantasies. They often lead to killing Liam, which somehow breaks the strange spell he holds over his people. But then, at some point, the people start following *her* instead, calling her the chosen one, the God slayer, their new leader. She tries to run away, but they're tireless, loping after her in an endless procession of white. Rena is far behind, but she's faster than the others, weaving in and out of them, always gaining. And Dayna keeps glancing over her shoulder as she runs, and her eyes are drawn to Rena every time, and every time Rena is closer. And the crazed worship of the others isn't in Rena's eyes; instead there is only hatred and murder.

In the morning, Dayna wakes feeling ill and a little feverish. She wants to see Pax so badly. There's a strange light in the room, and she climbs out of bed to check the nearest window. A pink haze is hanging over the sea, still just translucent. No gulls are in sight, but they must still be there, on the streets and on the beach, their small bodies convulsing. Instead of their incessant screams, she can now hear, if she presses her ear to the window, dull clicking noises, wheezing and rattling. They've been infected. Even as she watches, the mist's hue becomes deeper and more opaque. The wind isn't too strong today, but the little there is, is moving the poisonous spores along more quickly than it would inland. If only …

Hurried footsteps are striding towards her. A jangle as the ring of keys slips through frantic fingers, falls to the ground, is scooped up again. A *bang* from outside and a second later the bedroom door flies open and Rena appears, without a bowl of food this time. She's out of breath, as if she ran up all the stairs as fast as she could.

'Come on,' she pants, snapping her fingers impatiently. 'You doubted Liam's power; well, now you'll see it in action.'

Dayna's insides lurch in sudden panic. 'I'm not going,' she says, backing away (even though, five minutes ago, leaving these stuffy rooms is what she wanted to do most). 'I'm not going to him.'

For a heartbeat, Rena simply looks bewildered. Then she snorts. 'Not *that*,' she says. 'This has nothing to do with you, self-centred girl. Hurry up, I'm not going to miss it because of you.'

On the staircase, they come across other people, all heading downward like they are. No one is speaking, but their excitement is evident. Something big is going to happen.

Dayna keeps an eye out for them, but can't see either Pax or Jason. But when they enter the ballroom (Rena painfully pulling her along through the crowd by her forearm now), there they are, standing together near the main entrance, looking for her as she was looking for them.

'Day!' yells Pax, already charging towards her. Dayna shakes her arm free of Rena and meets him halfway. They've never hugged each other much before, but they hug now, long and hard.

'You all right?' both ask, almost simultaneously, then laugh.

'Go on, you lot,' says Rena behind them. 'To the windows right at the front. And stop being so silly, you were only apart for a day. And in very clean and comfortable rooms as well.'

It's true what she's saying, but it's also a lie. How can the same thing be so frightening and sound so trivial?

'Were you two together?' Dayna asks Pax as they allow Rena to herd them in front of her towards the long windows.

'Only sort of. We were locked in different rooms, but the rooms are right next to each other, so I could hear Jason snore.'

'I don't snore,' says Jason. 'And Pax nearly drove me mad with all that knocking.'

'Jason doesn't know Morse code,' explains Pax. 'I was trying to teach him so we could talk properly. Were you all by yourself, Day?'

'Yeah,' says Dayna. 'It was really boring.' (But her voice wobbles a bit.)

'Did they hurt you?' Jason asks sharply.

Dayna shakes her head. The other two are looking at her anxiously, and she can't stand them thinking that. 'No, honest,' she says. 'It was … it was just horrid, not knowing what was going to happen and where you were.'

'I was scared too,' whispers Pax. 'Jason was too nice to

say just now, but I even cried. A little. But it wasn't too bad because I knew Jason was in the next room, even if he snores and doesn't know Morse code – What are we doing here?' he adds.

They've reached the windows, and Rena has positioned them at the very front of the crowd, so they have an uninhibited view of the gathering mist outside.

'Why are we looking at the mist?' demands Pax. 'How stupid.'

Rena is standing by the next window, looking out herself with an intent expression on her pale face. She doesn't appear to hear Pax through the crowd of people, which must be everyone they saw at dinner the first night and then some. People still aren't talking to each other, but a lot have begun to whisper what sounds like song verses or rhymes under their breaths. Only when she hears a stray 'Amen, amen' does Dayna understand that they're praying.

She doesn't know what's got them all so worked up, and momentarily she doesn't care. Best take advantage of these people's attention being on something other than them for a change.

She leans closer to the others and whispers: 'Listen, if we can get at our gas masks now, we could escape during dangertime. They'd be too afraid to follow, I bet.'

'Most people would,' mutters Jason. 'But OK, we got by before, didn't we? Only works if you know where the gas masks are, though. Do you?'

'No.'

'Great.'

'They have to be close to the outside doors—'

'I know, that's what you said before. But we won't have long to look, even if we can get away from this lot. Maybe we'll have to stay, just a little bit longer, until we find out where the gear is. And then use another mist wave as cover.'

Dayna knows this is the smart way to do it, but the thought of staying here, worrying about Liam and Rena, for another couple of days or even longer, makes her stomach cramp painfully.

'But we have to save—' begins Pax, then stops quickly when someone behind them squeals: 'Dayna!'

It's Evie beside Sachiko, behind them the woman with the buzz cut who is holding her baby boy. The crowd has parted to let them through to the very front, and Evie heads straight for Dayna. Sachiko and the other woman follow more slowly.

'You took your time,' Rena calls over to them.

Evie sticks her tongue out at her and turns to Dayna unconcernedly: 'Do you like ceremonies?' she asks.

'Er, what?' Dayna's gaze is stuck on Rena, who looks as if she'd like to give Evie a sharp smack. Instead, Rena addresses Sachiko: 'Are you incapable of teaching the child any manners? It's not becoming for Liam's daughter to act like this.'

'Oh, give it a rest, Rena, why don't you?' mutters Sachiko, not even glancing in her direction as she joins Evie and the others by their window. Her status as the mother of Evie must give her some protection over Rena – who turns back towards the window, muttering words under her breath that are most definitely not prayers.

'Mummy doesn't like the ceremonies,' says Evie. 'I think they're exciting. But they don't end good, I don't like that bit.'

'What—' begins Pax, but is cut short by Rena's excited shriek: 'Here he is! HERE he is! LOOK!'

They look, as she is looking, out through the window,

squinting into the clouds of pink mist. A man is standing there not three paces away, but on the outside, facing them. It's Liam, and – Dayna gasps as she sees – he isn't wearing a gas mask. He's breathing in the tainted air as if it were nothing, without any protection at all. He told the truth about that, at least. He really is immune.

The ballroom is above ground level, so he is standing on the concrete canopy that juts out below the windows. What a foolish thing to do in the mist ... Liam raises both his hands to the sky. Dayna doesn't know what this means, but it looks impressive and important. The people around and behind them must be of the same opinion because they start chanting in rhythm: a murmur at first, that swells and swells like an incoming wave: 'Chosen. Chosen. CHOSEN.'

Liam's arms must be aching now, but still he keeps them above his head, palms outstretched. His eyes are closed and there is a smile on his lips. He must hear what his followers are shouting through the glass; he must know how wonder-struck they are by what he can do.

'CHOSEN CHOSEN CHOSEN.'

Liam lowers his arms and opens his eyes. He's like a ghost in the thickening mist now, but he steps closer; closer and closer until he is almost touching the glass of the window behind which Dayna and the others are watching him.

'CHOSEN CHOSEN CHOSEN.'

He catches Dayna's eye briefly and winks (Look at what I can do. You didn't believe me, did you? But here I am), before nodding to someone behind her. She turns and sees silent tears streaming down Sachiko's cheeks. The crowd behind them parts, although they're louder than ever now

'CHOSEN CHOSEN CHOSEN.'

and little Evie makes her way through, towards the doors

at the end. She doesn't look back, and Sachiko, both hands in front of her mouth now, doesn't go with her.

'What's happening?' whispers Dayna.

No one takes any notice of her except for Jason, who says: 'Isn't it obvious? If she's got the immunity like Liam, then they'll want to show it off too.'

Dayna looks at Sachiko. But Sachiko's blurry gaze is fixed on the windows again. Liam has turned to his left, waiting.

'CHOSEN CHOSEN CHOSEN.'

And then a small figure seems to detach itself from the mist around it and become more solid as she approaches. Evie, without a gas mask just as Liam is, and just as immune to the deadly spores. Liam grabs her hand and parades her up and down past the three centre windows, back and forth. The crowd goes wild, screaming

'CHOSEN CHOSEN CHOSEN.'

and Dayna thinks: Please, don't fall. Not with Evie. There's a proud little smile on Evie's face, though she isn't looking at the people in the ballroom at all, but straight ahead. Except when they pass by Dayna and the others, when she gives Dayna a little wave. She doesn't look at her mother, and Dayna knows it's because she doesn't want to see her being so sad and afraid.

'What's the matter with you?' snaps Rena's voice over the CHOSEN CHOSEN CHOSEN. She's moved over to their window and is glaring at Sachiko: 'Haven't we done this often enough already for you to know that little Eve is perfectly safe? You're ruining the ceremony.'

Sachiko doesn't appear to hear her, but Rena continues: 'It's Lila's time to be afraid and hopeful, not yours. Or are you scared of what will happen to you when Liam has a new miracle mother besides you?'

A smart rap on the window makes Dayna jump and whirl back to it. Liam is right in front of them again, still holding Evie by her hand, but looking at someone else, someone just behind her.

'It's time,' says Rena.

The mother with the buzz cut lets out a long, shaky breath. A second ago, Dayna would have said that she seemed as elated as the people around her (she certainly Chosen-Chosen-Chosen-ed as enthusiastically as any of them), but suddenly, like one of those trick pictures from the past, that are two different things depending on how you see them, she seems absolutely terrified.

She hands her baby boy to Rena without a word, and Rena walks with him down the same parted way as Evie has done.

'CHOSEN CHOSEN CHOSEN.'

Ear-splittingly loud. Bodies are pressing into Dayna from behind, squeezing her against the glass, pinning her down, trapping her so that she has to watch; she has to see.

They can hear the baby's screams before they can see him through the mist. Rena is still holding him, one-armed, as she climbs on to the canopy from what must be a ladder. She's the only one out of the four people now outside who is protected by a face mask, a white nose-and-mouth one made of synthetic material. The baby screams and screams, sucking in more and more poisonous spores.

'Oh shit,' moans Jason's voice from somewhere to Dayna's left. 'Oh, *shit.*'

'Maybe it's all right,' whispers Pax.

But it isn't all right. As they watch, the little boy's screams turn into horrible, hacking coughs.

'He's not immune!' shouts Dayna. 'You have to take him back!'

But no one pays her the slightest bit of attention. Not even Sachiko, her hands still firmly over her mouth. Not even the baby's mother, who is shouting 'CHOSEN CHOSEN CHOSEN' like the rest of them through her sobs.

'Don't look!' Dayna tells Pax, pushing back against the throng of chanters to reach out and turn his head away from the window. She squeezes her own eyes shut so tightly that little stars erupt in front of her eyelids. She's holding Pax by his ears so he can't turn even if he wanted to, or else she would have stuffed her fingers into her ears to block out all the terrible sounds. Wheezing, rattling little coughs, so rumbling and high and tiny you can feel them tingling in your very flesh, then ebbing away into nothingness. And silence. **'CHOSEN CHOSEN CHO—'** cut off. A woman's long, shuddering, animal moan. And then silence again.

Minutes pass and no one speaks, and Dayna keeps her eyes shut and her grip firm on Pax's ears (she doesn't know why). And then a man's voice cuts through the quiet. Liam's. She opens her eyes and sees him by the entrance at the far end of the ballroom, next to Evie. Rena and the baby are nowhere in sight. Perhaps she's burying it before the animals begin to turn.

'It wasn't to be, friends,' says Liam. 'Our path is long and painful, but we shall be rewarded for our suffering and our sacrifices. Amen.'

'Amen,' they echo.

Liam doesn't speak to the mother whose baby he has just killed in front of them all, but turns and sweeps out of the ballroom. People begin trickling after him, slowly, as if in a trance, all their loud confidence evaporated. Everyone avoids Lila's gaze, and no one tries to comfort her except for Sachiko, who puts a hand on her shoulder.

Lila shakes it off forcefully, as if Sachiko wasn't meant to do this, then follows the others, head bent, face drained of all life.

'Does that happen every time a new baby is born?' asks Jason very quietly.

Sachiko nods, her eyes fixed on Evie, who is weaving through the crowd, heading their way.

'How many babies have survived it?'

Sachiko doesn't answer, and why should she when the answer is so obvious?

'Only one,' says Pax. 'Only Evie. How many—'

'Shut up, Pax,' hisses Dayna, who doesn't want to know the answer.

Evie arrives and allows her mother to bend down and hug her. Her muffled voice protrudes from Sachiko's left shoulder: 'I'm sad.'

They're the only ones left by the windows. Somehow they have been forgotten in the excitement and subsequent grief. This is their best chance, right now, before Liam remembers or Rena returns.

'Sachiko,' says Dayna urgently. 'Please, you have to tell us where the gas masks are. Please, we can get out *now*.'

The boys are silent, but their concentrated suspense is as palpable as if they had yelled: Yes yes yes! Please please please!

'You couldn't now,' whispers Sachiko. 'The animals will turn rabid soon ... become possessed. You couldn't until at least another day.'

'We *can*,' says Dayna. 'We've done it before. You have to be quiet, that's all. Quiet, slow, ready. Quick if something goes wrong. We won't get lost if we keep the sea to one side. Waves are loud. I'd rather chance it out there than in here. You can come with us. You don't want to stay here. It's sick what they do. You know it is.'

'Mummy?' mumbles Evie. 'What's going on?'

Sachiko looks at Dayna. 'I can't … I don't know how to survive out there, all alone. I've never been on my own.'

'*We* know how to survive,' says Pax. 'We're good at it, we got this far, didn't we?'

'And the only real trouble we've had is with people,' mutters Dayna.

Sachiko puts a hand on her stomach, bites her lip, looks at Evie. 'All right,' she says. 'All right. We'll come with you.'

21

Synthetic FFP2 masks are kept in a storage room on the first floor, and that's where Sachiko says their gas masks will have been put as well. The room is locked, but Sachiko shows them where the keys are – dangling from a nail in a broom closet close by. So painfully obvious, it's almost insulting. But then again, no one seems to *want* to escape here.

Dayna spots Anteater, Kong and Jason's unnamed gas mask at the bottom corner of the wall-to-wall rack straight away, conspicuous amidst the paper-thin synthetics. Sachiko retrieves two FFP2 masks from an open box for her and Evie.

'Does she even need one?' asks Pax.

Sachiko nods. 'I'm sure it can't be good for her, breathing in all those spores, even if she doesn't seem affected. Where did you find gas masks like these? They look government issue …'

'Where's our gear?' asks Dayna as her eyes frantically rove around the room, which only has masks. There's so little time, and they won't be able to survive without any weapons at all.

'There are rooms further on where we keep our tools and weapons,' says Sachiko. 'They must have been put there. I'll show you.'

Dayna bites her lip. At some point, very soon, someone will realise that they're missing and will come to investigate.

'I'll stand guard by the stairwell,' she says, making her mind up on the spur of the moment. In case someone comes.

Jason snorts. 'What're you gonna do *if* someone comes? Knock them out with a right hook? I'll stand guard while you lot collect your gear.'

Dayna shakes her head. 'No, it makes more sense for it to be me. You couldn't stop anyone armed either, you know you couldn't. And they'd hurt you. They won't hurt me, Rena said they won't because I'm to be another one of his Eves.'

'I'm Eve,' says Evie in a small voice. She doesn't understand what's going on, but she's picked up on everyone's tension and is clinging to Sachiko tightly.

'Just *go*,' hisses Dayna. 'We can't waste time arguing.'

'Where do we meet if anything happens?' asks Pax. 'The castle-church by the shore? The one we passed coming in?'

Dayna smiles. 'Yeah. I was just gonna say that.'

Jason shakes his head. 'You and your bloody churches.'

'Stop complaining and go, quick!'

They go. Sachiko strides ahead, surprisingly fast for someone toting a little girl, while the two boys follow behind at a trot; down the long corridor, into a room, out of sight.

Dayna takes a deep breath, then heads the other way, back to the stairwell. Then she stops as a thought hits her, and runs back to the mask room. She closes the door again and turns the key, still in the lock. Then she pulls the key out and dashes to the stairs. She has to keep it in her hand because she's wearing the hateful pocketless dress – oh, shoes! She hopes the others will remember the shoes.

The door to the stairwell bangs open and Rena strides through, looking livid. Dayna gasps and skids to a halt. She has the presence of mind to keep her fist holding the key closed.

'I thought you'd be here, you little brat,' snaps Rena. 'Taking advantage of our mourning to betray us first chance you get, eh? And I see you've found what you were looking for.'

She nods at Dayna's gas mask clutched in her free hand.

'That Japanese bitch told you where to go, didn't she?'

'No,' says Dayna, her mouth dry with nerves, her expression determinedly blank. 'I just looked. It wasn't hard to find.'

'Yeah, I bet it wasn't, not when she told you exactly where to go. Where're the boys?'

'Back in their rooms probably,' says Dayna. 'It's just me by myself.'

'Yeah, and that's why you only took one mask, isn't it?' sneers Rena. 'I'm not wasting my time playing Hide-and-Seek with you lot. They can't get away now, with the possessed outside, and they won't go in any case, not without you. Come on, give me the gas mask, and maybe I'll let it go at that.'

There's nothing else for it. Dayna holds out her mask, then pulls it back sharply just as Rena is about to take it. Rena totters, wrong-footed for the blink of an eye – and Dayna careers past her, heading for the stairs with her arms pumping, the mask straps in one hand and the now sweaty key in the other.

Rena is bellowing and thumping behind her, but Dayna is quick, and fear is making her quicker still. Sharp turn into the stairwell, a split second of indecision, and then up, up, up, Rena just behind her now.

Because she has to get Rena away from the entrance, or the others will never be able to slip out unnoticed. They must have heard Rena's screams of rage. And so must others. At any moment now, someone could be coming down the stairs from above, blocking her way ... Dayna wrenches open the next door she comes across and hurtles into the long, winding corridor behind it. Doors to either side, corners around which anything could be hiding. Please let this floor be empty. Please.

Down the zigzag corridor, doors whizzing past her in a blur, Rena's shouting, her own ragged breathing tearing into her throat and lungs, but no way is she going to slow down, even for a second. Even for the time it will take to glance behind her.

A door somewhere ahead bursts open and one of Liam's people comes rushing in from a side passage, a bulky man who might be Alex and might be someone else entirely. But with a little skip of her hammering heart, she sees a green sign attached to the ceiling above him. It says *Fire Exit*, and its white arrow is pointing to the passage he just came out of. Another staircase. Oh, thank you. She redoubles her speed. The man wasn't expecting this; he holds out his arms to grab her, but a second too late. She manages to dodge past him, banging into the wall to her right.

At the staircase now. Down this time, jumping two steps, three, four at once. Her knees pounding, but she's grinning too. Because she knows she can make it. The sounds of her pursuers are further off; the man must have gotten in Rena's way. Big black-on-gold numbers on each landing. *2* and then *1* and then *Ground*.

Almost there now. Almost there.

As she runs, Dayna tugs on her gas mask with a skill born

of hours and days of practice. The mask makes her vision blurred and breathing even more strenuous than it already is, but it also gives her a warm, protected feeling.

In the foyer: a black-and-white chequered floor, a glass-panelled door, then another, leading out.

'WHAT ARE YOU DOING, IDIOT GIRL?!' screams Rena from somewhere far away.

The door swings open and

'IT'S DEVIL HOUR, YOU'LL GET KILLED!'

Dayna runs out into the mist.

22

The world around her is hidden but loud, as newly crazed animals hiss and shriek and growl and scream. Out of sight of the Court, Dayna slows to a trot, then a walk, panting laboriously in her mask. She has to move carefully now, and as slowly as she can, which sounds easy but is very, very hard when all her instincts are yelling at her to run. But she can't risk running into a dustbin or across the path of a crazed gull. With no weapons, she's completely defenceless.

She's been heading away from the sea to get out of Reena's immediate range. Now she begins walking down the sloping roads, towards the gush of waves, as silent and invisible as a ghost on her bare feet. It's taking longer than it should because she keeps having to turn off course to avoid the newly crazed, but that's all right; if the sound of the sea guides her, she won't lose her way. She has to keep reminding herself that no one is following her, tiptoeing behind in the misty shadows. Her own breathing, magnified inside the mask, sounds very frightened.

If only she were with the others …

A commotion of animal noises erupts just ahead of her, and she freezes at once. Just in time. A bucking cat staggers out of the mist, its head twitching from side to side, snapping at the rat, which is scampering up and down its back, tearing into the cat's flesh with its little teeth and claws, squeaking frantically. It's unusual, but sometimes, the crazed also attack each other. The two animals careen past Dayna, too caught up in their frenzy to notice her, and are swallowed back up in the mist.

Dayna relaxes, takes a hasty step forwards and stumbles over the steep, uneven ground. She regains her balance almost immediately but can't prevent the little thud her right foot makes on the pavement. Just ahead of her, the unseen cat gives a sharp, strangled cry. Has it heard?

The key is still in Dayna's hand. It isn't too big, but it's old and heavy, and Dayna hurls it into the mist, towards that sound, with all the force she can muster. She hears it drop with an audible *clunk*, and then she hears the shrieks as both cat and rat seem to have momentarily forgotten each other and launch themselves at this new enemy. Dayna doesn't wait to find out what they'll do next.

She reaches the lapping water of the sea without further incident and starts walking westwards, concentrating on the misty shadows on her right so as not to pass by the church. The pebbles bruise her feet, but she feels safer down here; less exposed. She steps and pauses in time with the waves, to mask the noise. The salt water sloshes against her ankles and once a dead gull floats up against her and gives her goose pimples, but other than that, no creature crosses her path.

The church-castle looms up in front of a steep hill like a giant creature by the entrance of its cave. There must have been a small landslide at some point, or more than one, because hard bits of earth and stones surround the church, making the going difficult, especially for someone without shoes.

Two of the three big double doors are locked, but the third opens. Dayna slips through the door, taking care to close it behind her so that hardly any mist escapes inside. She's in a high-ceilinged, echoey hall with curved arches, wooden pews and a pulpit in the shape of a rowing boat bow. Dayna checks the long windows to make certain none of them are cracked or broken, then tugs off her mask and gulps in the cool church air gratefully.

'Pax?' she calls tentatively. Then again, a little louder: 'Pax?!'

A dozen Daynas join in, whispering 'Pax Pax Pax' all around her. But Pax doesn't answer. He isn't here.

Dayna waits and time passes and still the others don't come. She becomes steadily more and more certain that something bad has happened. She has to clutch her stomach and dig into it with her fingers to stop the squirming dread there flaring out of control.

It doesn't work.

Liam's people captured them.

Locked them up.

Hurt them.

They missed the church in the mist.

Are already miles and miles away.

She'll never find them again.

Crazed animals attacked them.

Infected them.

Killed them.

What should she do? Wait here? Go look for them? What should she DO?

A creak of rusty door hinges resounds through the church, and Dayna is on her feet in a moment, hardly daring to hope. A masked someone steps in and closes the door behind them at once. A large rucksack is on their back, and Dayna recognises it as her own. The person fiddles with straps and tugs the gas mask off their face, panting. It's Jason.

He spots her and his face breaks into a smile. 'Great, you made it too.'

'Where's Pax and the others?' she whispers.

The grin slips from Jason's face. 'You mean they're not here yet?'

They sit side by side on the pew closest to the entrance. It was warm outside in the mist, but it's cool in the stone church building, or else it feels cool. Dayna rubs her hands absently as Jason tells her what happened on their end:

'We got out all right. Thanks for that, by the way. Pax was pretty good at making everyone move slowly and stop the moment he heard a noise. But then this infected seagull whooshed past us, just by chance, and it saw us and made straight for us. We got all your guys' gear, did I say that? Pax killed the gull with his bat before it could do anything, but then … that made the little girl scream. And that made them come, seagulls all around us screaming bloody murder. Too many to fight all together, so we … we scattered. I knew I'd be useless at killing birds swooping down at me from the sky, so I just ran. Made enough noise for the gulls and any other infected animals to follow, but I'm fast and took all the turns I could, to make it harder for the birds to follow without smacking into buildings. Anyway, I found a house with an open door – I know how extremely lucky that was – and I waited there until things calmed down again. Then I came here. I … Look, was it wrong? Should I have stayed?'

'No,' says Dayna, and her voice sounds odd and far away. 'If a bunch of them attack like that, you're supposed to scatter. That's what Father always said.'

'Right. Good. Thanks, Sarge.' Jason lets out a shaky breath, then adds: 'And hey, it took me a while to find this place in the fog, and what with running off in a completely different direction. So we don't really have to worry yet.'

'Yes, that makes sense,' says Dayna. And worries.

Jason glances at her. 'While we wait, let's think of what to do next, as soon as they get here,' he says. 'So we won't waste any time.'

'We go on to the hummingpeople.'

'Yeah, but let's concentrate on getting away from the crazy cult first, OK? When we're safe, then we can think of the Hummingbirds again.'

'We might as well go in the right direction from the start, mightn't we?'

'I don't know what the right direction is from here. I need a map.'

Dayna grimaces, remembering Rena's false promise. 'Yeah, a map …'

'Let's just focus on getting away, OK?' says Jason. 'If we go along the shore, the way we came, they might find us. That's where Rena saw us first, and she might guess we'd go back there.'

'We'd have a head start.'

'Even so, I don't like it. We'd leave a trail, I suppose. They might be able to follow us like that. They will too, as soon as they find out that we've taken the little girl. They probably wouldn't have bothered for just us, but they will for her, big time.'

'She wanted to come.'

'No, she didn't. Her mother wanted to come.'

Dayna glares at him. 'You think we ought to have left them back there, don't you?'

'No,' says Jason at once. 'I'm just saying it'll be more difficult with them—'

'You're saying it's my fault, what happened with the gulls. Because if it was just you and Pax—'

'Don't be an idiot; how could it be your fault?'

Dayna isn't sure either, but she feels that somehow it is, all of it, her fault. And now Pax is lost. And so are Evie and Sachiko. They shouldn't have left on the spur of the moment. They should have waited until they had a proper plan. Her fault. Because she just couldn't stand the thought of staying locked up in that place for even a day longer …

'C'mon, stop it. You're being stupid,' mutters Jason, embarrassed. Dayna is hiccuping and choking, trying not to sob but sobbing anyway. Jason pats her on the back awkwardly. 'They'll be here soon,' he says. 'I'm sure, all right?'

He must have been lying because when, about ten minutes later, the church doors open and three people enter, he gasps: 'OH BLOODY HELL, I don't believe it! You're OK!'

Pax has only just managed to remove his gas mask when Dayna flings herself at him and hugs him tightly.

'Oh, you birdbrain, couldn't you've come earlier? I was *scared*.'

Pax is wriggling in her arms, and she lets him go. 'You—' she begins, then stops at the sight of his face.

'Day,' moans Pax. 'Day …'

'What—?'

And this is when Sachiko collapses on to the stone floor. Evie, who is maskless, shrieks, then begins to cry.

The others crowd around: Jason trying to shush Evie; Dayna and Pax rolling Sachiko on to her back. They unhook Sachiko's mask straps to make it easier for her to breathe.

'What's wrong with her?' asks Dayna. 'Was she bit?'

Pax shakes his head. 'She breathed in the spores,' he whispers. 'It was one of the gulls. It flew at her and started pecking at her. Tore through the mask's fabric before I could kill it. I didn't get there in time. I made Evie give Sachiko her mask, but I think it was too late … I'm sorry, Day.'

'Don't be stupid, it's not your fault.'

'She's right, you know,' Sachiko mumbles without opening her eyes. 'Not your fault. You killed the gull. You saved my life.'

'How much did you breathe in?' asks Dayna.

'A little,' says Sachiko, then rolls to her side and coughs. She coughs like it hurts her. Evie clings to her mother.

'Mummy Mummy Mummy Mummy' echoes through the church.

Jason and Pax turn to Dayna. The unspoken question hovers in the air: *What do we do?*

'I don't know,' says Dayna, who usually always, ALWAYS, has a plan. 'I don't know. I'm sorry. I'm *sorry*, it's all my fault.'

Sachiko has stopped coughing now. She props herself up and her hand gropes along the floor until it finds Dayna's. It's very cold, but somehow comforting.

'It's not your fault. Nobody's fault. I wanted to leave, I wanted Evie to leave. And I would've never been able to do it without you. Does anyone know how long I have left, before it takes me?'

Jason swallows, then speaks. 'It depends on the person.

And on how much you breathed in. Could be a couple of hours. Or even a couple of days. Animals turn a lot faster than people.'

'Maybe you won't turn at all,' says Pax. 'Like Father. Maybe you'll just get better.'

'So I'm safe for the moment?' Sachiko asks Jason. 'Are you sure?'

He nods.

'Then I have an idea.' She has to pause here and wait until another coughing fit passes her by. 'About how to get out. And we have to be quick. As soon as they realise Evie's missing, Liam will send people out to get her back, devil hour or no.'

It's windy, and the mist is getting thinner as they walk along the shore, heading westwards again, further away from the Court. As before and as always, Dayna is in the lead, her rucksack securely on her back again, her spray can gripped tightly in her hand. Behind her is Sachiko, whose arm is around Jason's bony shoulder, wearing Evie's mask over nose and mouth. Every now and then they have to stop until she regains her breath, but at least the crashing waves muffle her coughing. Evie is next, maskless. She's been instructed to close her eyes whenever something scary appears, and not, on any account, open her mouth. ('I know,' she replies sullenly. 'I know *now*. You should've said before.') She isn't used to walking though, and they have to lay in a lot of extra stops for her as well. Pax brings up the rear with his baseball bat at the ready.

It takes them over an hour to get to where they're heading, at a distance that shouldn't have been twenty minutes' walk on an ordinary day. But Dayna has keen eyes and manages to circumvent almost all danger. Those crazed animals they do run into are quickly dealt with by either the spray or the bat.

Finally, they reach the place Sachiko has in mind: rows upon rows of rotten wooden huts facing the sea, and boats. The boats are little and big, with cabins and without. Chipped, once-bright colours mingle with the green of algae.

These are the boats Liam's people use for fishing, Sachiko has explained back at the church. They've long since run out of petrol, but they have built masts and sewn sails for half a dozen of them. The wind is picking up, and a boat with a sail should get them a long way.

'Where's the Court?' demands Evie. 'I thought we're going back home. Why we here? I don't like these things, Mummy. I want to go HOME.'

Sachiko whispers reassurances into Evie's ear, then opens her arms and lets the little girl nestle against her chest while the others examine the six boats with masts.

Pax points to the largest, three times Jason's height, with a cabin and under deck. Dayna shakes her head firmly and mimes lifting the boat and collapsing. Too heavy. You'd need at least six grown-up people to drag it into the water. In fact, Dayna reckons as she looks around, the only boats that seem light enough are two rowing boats with rudimentary masts. She points to the slightly bigger one, with red peeling paint and three benches at the front, middle and back, which looks large enough for the five of them. There's even a battered lifebelt in the stern.

Together, she, Jason and Pax manage to push it into the choppy water. All the boats' folded sails are stowed in a nearby cabin, just as Sachiko said they'd be. Instead of just selecting one, Dayna bundles them all into her arms, three giant sheets of linen, and heads back to where Jason is restraining their bucking ship.

Sachiko nods when she sees that Dayna has brought all the sails. 'Good thinking,' she rasps.

She attaches one of the sails to the mast with the sureness of someone who has done this many times before, and—

'Look,' cries Evie, pointing in the direction of the Court, no bigger than a fingernail from here, but visible, as the mist is hardly even vapour now. An indistinct figure is in the distance, too far away to know whether it's heading in their direction or not; or whether it's standing or walking or running. A chill grips Dayna. She can guess what it's doing. She can guess who it is.

She motions to the others; a quick sweeping movement of her arm: GO. NOW!

She heaves Evie into the boat next to her mother (who immediately puts the lifebelt over her head), then flings the bundle of sails in after her. Without sails, Rena will never catch them. The boys are already pushing the boat further and further in, up to their waists now. Pax scrambles into the boat. Dayna splashes through the water and is helped in by Pax. She gestures to the oars in their sockets, and they both grab one and start rowing for all they're worth, in opposite directions. The boat lurches in a circle.

'Stop,' wheezes Sachiko, just as Jason clambers into the boat, dripping wet and shivering. Sachiko hoists the sail, which billows out the moment it's open and jerks the boat forwards, westwards with the wind.

Shivering in the sprays of seawater, and almost deaf from the blowing of the sharp gale, Dayna twists in her seat and waves to the figure in the distance. Pax joins in, and so do Jason (although he waves with only his middle fingers) and even little Evie, who seems to have forgotten all about wanting to go home for the present.

'It's Rena, isn't it?' she laughs. 'We've tricked her, the old telltale.'

Sachiko tears off her mask and coughs long and hard.

23

By midday, all the mist has either vanished or been left behind, revealing a deep blue, cloudless sky above. The sun, bouncing off the waves, is very strong, although no one notices at first amidst the wind and water spray, not to mention the thrill of their escape. It's Sachiko who instructs them to cover themselves in the spare sails or risk severe sunburns, just as it's Sachiko who shows them how to steer with the oars.

'We'll stay ... within sight of ... the coast,' she pants (she can do nothing but pant now). 'It's not rough, but you ... never know with this wind. Best stay close ... to land, it's a small boat. It could topple right ... over in a storm.'

'OK,' says Dayna. 'You ought to rest now. Close your eyes, we'll wake you if we can't cope.'

They're planning on sailing westwards for another hour or so, then hiding the boat and heading inland. That would make it difficult, if not impossible, for Liam's people to find them, and it would also mean (no one says this, though everyone is thinking it) that if Sachiko turns, they will be on land, able to run if they have to.

'Where we going?' whines Evie.

'We're going on an adventure,' says Dayna.

'I don't want to. I want to go home. I don't like it here.

It's rocky and I feel sick. And I'm scared birds will come again.'

'Why would you want to go back there?' asks Pax irritably. He isn't used to children younger than himself. 'They're all mad; why would *anyone* want to go back?'

'Because I'm chosen by God,' states Evie.

'No, you're not,' says Dayna. She's trying to be especially kind to Evie, but it's hard when she acts like she's their superior.

'I AM!'

'No, you're not,' says Pax.

'I AM I AM I AM—'

'Will you two stop winding her up?' Jason calls from the stern. 'She's only a little kid, she doesn't understand.'

'I DO!' shouts Evie, and then they all laugh, except for Evie, who sulks.

'Listen, Evie,' says Dayna after a bit, because Evie has to understand. 'I'll explain, OK? Are you listening?'

'No!' (But she is.)

'Liam was a bad person. He said he was good, but he wasn't. He wanted people to do things and if they wouldn't, he'd punish them. Like your mother. Remember? You said it yourself.'

Evie looks at Dayna pityingly. 'Liam is allowed. Liam is chosen. Like me.'

'People who are chosen ought to be nice, not horrible,' says Dayna. 'Did you *like* Liam?'

Evie shakes her head. 'I don't like how Mummy is with him.'

'How? Scared?'

Evie nods.

'There you go, then,' concludes Dayna, satisfied. 'That's

why we're leaving the Court. So your mother doesn't have to be afraid any more.'

'And when are we going back?' asks Evie.

Dayna groans. 'Never. Why would we want to go back and be scared again?'

'I wasn't scared.'

'Because you're an idiot,' says Pax helpfully. 'But you know?' he says, turning to Dayna, 'I wish … I wish we'd freed all of them. At least all the pregnant women. All their babies …'

Yes, thinks Dayna. That would have been nice. But not possible.

'We've been through this,' Jason shouts against the wind. 'There was no way we could have taken them all with us. Even if they wanted to come, which they didn't. They're all nuts.'

'I know,' mutters Pax. 'I know that. I'm just saying that I wished we could've. It feels wrong, us leaving all those babies to die. Not like it's supposed to be. In the dead world, they would've saved everyone.'

Dayna can't think of anything to say to this, but Jason scoffs. 'No, they wouldn't. They wouldn't have saved *any*one, only themselves. That's why today is like it is; because the dead world didn't care. Your idea of the dead world is only through their stories. Stories are just wishful thinking. You two are—'

He stops just in time to lean over and vomit into the sea.

'Ewww!' screeches Evie in delight.

The wind brings clouds, and then rain. The waves become bigger and harder to handle, buffeting their little boat from side to side.

Sachiko wakes and mumbles that it's time to land. She tells them how to lower the sail and steer towards the shore.

'Just a little longer,' begs Pax. 'It's getting fun—'

A particularly big wave breaks just ahead of them, spraying them all in cool salt water.

'Yeah, this is fun!' shouts Jason sarcastically. 'Especially for people who can't swim! Lower the sail, Pax, or I'll make sure you go under with me.'

'Scaredy-cat,' giggles Pax, but does as he is told.

'This isn't a real storm, is it, Mummy?' crows Evie. 'It's only choppy water. He,' she says, pointing to Jason, 'is scared of drownding in only choppy water!'

'Says the little girl wearing the only lifebelt,' mutters Jason.

They let the sea carry them ashore to a pebble beach and climb out of the boat on shaky feet, somehow not used to still ground any more. The waves seem much bigger and more violent on the shore, crashing down in quick and heavy succession.

Dayna and the boys help Evie and Sachiko out of the boat, then drag it behind the nearest hut so it won't be visible from the sea when Liam's people pass in their boats. Then Dayna and Jason hoist up Sachiko, who seems barely conscious now, each taking one of her limp arms over their shoulders, and Pax grabs Evie's hand, and together they turn their backs on the rough sea and head towards the maze of tall houses of whichever new town they've arrived at.

They decide to spend the night in a narrow vine-covered house with palm trees in its front garden. Everyone is suddenly very exhausted and hungry now that the excitement is over, and Dayna says that's not ideal for wandering through unknown territory during dangertime. Nobody points out that Sachiko's increasingly deteriorating condition would make this impossible in any case, but everyone is thinking it.

The five of them share the remnants of the tinned food that, thankfully, is still in Dayna's and Pax's rucksacks – so is everything else, including Mother's picture; Dayna checked first thing when they got to the house. Evie complains about it tasting horrid and cold, but everyone else feels better as soon as their stomachs are filled. Then Dayna and Pax choose a room for Sachiko and clear a space on the floor for dusty blankets and cushions.

'This is like the day Father was bit,' says Pax quietly.

'Don't think about that,' says Dayna. 'He got better, she might too.'

Sachiko is pleased they know how to handle someone who's been infected, and pleased by her new room, although she asks Pax to take the pillows and blankets outside and shake them free of dust. After Pax has staggered out with the pile in his hands, Sachiko turns to Dayna:

'No matter ... what ... happens, I'm ... glad I came ... with you,' she wheezes.

'Even if you die?' The question bursts out of Dayna before she can reel it in again.

'Maybe ... that's the ... price ... for Evie's safety.'

But that's wrong. What about Sachiko's safety? And what about the baby growing in her right now? Dayna doesn't say these things because Sachiko looks quite content, like she really means it about being glad. Maybe, in her state, she's forgotten about the baby to be, and if she has, Dayna will not be the one to remind her.

'I'll bring you more food in the morning,' she says. 'I'll knock so I'll know if it's safe.'

'Don't ... bring Evie ... tomorrow. I'll see ... her now, but that's ... the last time, unless I ... get better. Take ... care of her ... if I don't.'

Dayna hates the way Sachiko rattles and pants, and wishes she would just stop talking.

'I'll get Evie then, yeah?' she mumbles.

Sachiko nods. 'I can't ... stop you ... from ... searching for ... your father. But ... keep ... Evie safe ... Promise me.'

Dayna promises, even though she knows this might come back to haunt her. How can she promise something like that? All she can promise is to try.

'Thank ... you.'

Dayna stumbles out of the room quickly. It's too horribly unfair: Sachiko sick while Liam, who makes people have babies and then kills them, has the immunity. Sachiko about to die just when she is free at last?

Sachiko talks to Evie for a long time, and Evie listens sombrely. She doesn't cry or make a fuss, although she does look very sad and lost. Finally, she flings her arms around her mother and holds on tight. Dayna, watching from the hallway, wonders if her own mother ever got to say goodbye to her and Pax like that. Wishes Father had let them hug him before they parted. She would have taken that risk. Evie lets Dayna take her by the hand and gently pull her out of the room, and she lets Dayna close the door on Sachiko's pale face and tie the paracord rope around the knob. The rope's other end, she attaches to the front door, pulling it taut so that Sachiko is locked in.

'Did she explain it to you?' asks Dayna.

Evie nods.

'What did she say?'

'That maybe God will take her because she's tired. But I know she's sick, not tired. Because she breathed in the devil mist, and she isn't immune like me. Mummy says she stays with me afterwards, even if I can't see her or hear her, so it's OK, and I'm not supposed to be sad. And I have to do what you say because God sent you to rescue me and take me somewhere safe.'

Explaining the situation in terms the little girl can understand and accept is the clever thing to do. Even so, and even though she knows it's not true, the idea of a god of the dead world orchestrating all of this, simply so they could help Evie escape, makes Dayna feel shivery.

'I'm the chosen one,' says Evie, 'so everything is going to be all right.'

Evie is quiet and withdrawn for the rest of the afternoon. She stays in her corner and plays with a china dog figurine she's found on one of the shelves, and if anyone addresses her, she ignores them.

'Leave her alone,' Jason tells the other two. 'At least she isn't crying. I don't know what we'd do if she started crying and carrying on.'

'Does she know what's going on?' asks Pax. 'I mean, I'm glad that she isn't crying too, but if I were her, I'd be crying. It's not fair.'

'No, it's not,' says Dayna. 'But she doesn't really understand about things being fair or not. Sachiko told her it was all God's plan, and I think she believes that. Anyway, maybe Sachiko will be all right.'

'Well, it's no use in worrying about it before we know

for sure,' says Jason. 'Let's do something fun for a change, take our minds off things while we wait.'

'I'm too tired to run around,' says Pax, and yawns.

'There are games besides idiotic little kiddie games, you know,' says Jason. 'Look what I found in one of the drawers.'

He holds up a packet of playing cards. Both Dayna and Pax know from stories that people use them in games, but neither has ever played. It seems such a complicated affair, all those numbers and letters, and the strange little symbols in the corners. Jason goes through the cards, explaining one by one, although he quickly becomes impatient.

'What's wrong with you, it's *so* easy,' he complains. 'Just LISTEN.'

'You're just bad at explaining,' says Dayna.

'Off with your head!' giggles Pax. 'Remember, Day? That story about the girl in a strange land, with talking animals and such? The bad people were the playing cards, shouting: off with her head!'

'You two are off *your* heads,' mutters Jason as they fall about laughing. They laugh so hard it hurts, and whenever their giggles begin to subside, Pax catches Dayna's eye, or she catches his, and then they start rolling around all over again. It feels so good, after everything, to just be able to laugh.

They play Jason's card games for what's left of the afternoon and evening. They're quite fun, really (Pax says they're *cool*), and a good distraction from all the bad things that have happened and might still happen; are maybe happening right now, in the locked room, downstairs.

24

The next morning, Dayna heads downstairs with their very last food can while everyone else is still asleep. She's woken early from a nightmare she can no longer remember, and once awake, she finds it impossible to wait any longer without knowing. She can hear someone moving behind the locked door, pacing like a trapped animal, and breathing very fast and hard.

Oh no. Oh, it's not fair …

She knocks. She has to. 'Sachiko? Please—?'

Sachiko lets out a guttural scream and the door bangs as she flings her weight against the wood panelling from the other side. Dayna jumps back. It was a mistake to knock, and she knew it and did it anyway. The door opens a minuscule crack before the rope makes it slam shut again. Something left inside of Sachiko has worked out that she has to pull instead of push. Again. *SLAM. SLAM. SLAM.* How long will the rope last? Already Dayna sees the knot loosening. Her fault; she didn't tie it properly last night, her head too full of scary thoughts. *SLAM.* And the tin can drops on to the floor and rolls away as Dayna hurtles up the stairs to the others.

'Get up! Get up!' she shouts as she skids into the room with the double bed where they all spent the night, sending the pack of playing cards flying. Pax is awake already, and sitting bolt upright in the bed. He knows how to react fast in danger-situations, and scrambles to his feet at once, but Jason and Evie only grunt sleepily.

'Wake them, Pax!' Dayna tells him. Pax does, shaking first Jason and then Evie while Dayna darts around the room, collecting their rucksacks and weapons and gas masks.

From downstairs, there's a loud crash, followed by animal growling and baying.

'Quick, into the bathroom,' urges Dayna, grabbing Evie's hand with her free one and tugging her along the narrow hallway. The boys jostle behind them.

Bathrooms are often the safest rooms in any house as they usually have locks with keys in them, or bolts. The bathroom of this house has a bolt, and Dayna closes the door and slides it shut as soon as the last of her troop crowds in.

It's a very cramped room, and the four of them and the two rucksacks are squashed tightly against each other, the walls, the sink and a pale yellow bathtub. Evie whimpers: 'I don't like it. I want to stop.'

'Oh shit,' whispers Jason. 'She turned, didn't she?'

'Everyone shut up,' commands Dayna.

The thing that was once Sachiko is frantically blundering up the stairs. It hesitates on the upper landing, panting. If they can just stay quiet, it might decide they're not here and leave ...

Very, very slowly, Dayna cranes her neck to look at the others behind her, wide-eyed and frozen. She presses her forefinger against her lips, then gives them the thumbs up sign: Everything under control. As long as we keep quiet.

'Where's Mummy?' whispers Evie.

'*Shhh.*'

'WHERE'S MUM—' Pax clamps his hand against Evie's mouth, but it's too late. *BOOM.* The new Sachiko hurls itself against their door from outside. When the bolt doesn't give, she begins to scratch against the wood with her fingernails, all the while growling and shrieking. It's the most horrible sound Dayna has ever heard, and for a moment it fills her head and makes it impossible for her to think or move.

'MUMMY MUMMY MUMMY,' shrieks Evie, holding her fists against her ears.

'The window!' shouts Pax over all the noise.

The bathroom has only one square window above the bathtub. It's too small for an adult man, but even Jason ought to be able to squeeze himself through if he has to.

Pax is struggling with the lower window sash, but it won't budge. Who knows when it was last opened. Maybe as long as a world ago.

'Clear off, squirt,' says Jason. He steps into the bathtub and wrestles with the sash as well, managing to force it open as far as it goes. Both boys look out and Dayna pushes through to look out as well. It's not as bad as it could have been. Downwards isn't an option, as it's a high two-storey drop, but their window opens on to the side of the house, which is close to the squat, flat-roofed building next door. All you have to do is jump the gap (about as wide as Pax is tall), grab hold of the roof edge and pull yourself up and over. Easy.

'What?' demands Jason as Dayna outlines this plan. '*No* way.'

BOOM BOOM BOOM goes the door. *Scratch scratch scratch.*

'You want to wait here?' demands Dayna.

'Um, yeah, actually. She's tiny, she won't get in. But if one of us misses that jump—'

'Not *me*,' mutters Pax, because Jason is looking in his direction.

'It's, like, one and a half metres.'

'A bit less,' amends Dayna.

'*If*,' Jason ploughs on, ignoring them both, 'if one of us falls and breaks their leg or their neck down there, she'll twig and come racing down to meet them.'

'You,' clarifies Pax.

'Or HER.' Jason points to Evie, who is too busy crying to pay attention to their argument.

'She'll be fine, she's little,' says Dayna. 'We can tie our rope around her and pull her up that way. Me and Father used to do that with Pax before he was big enough. It's *easy*, Jason.'

BOOM BOOM BOOM

Scratch scratch scratch

Dayna has to get away from the noise; she can't stand it any longer.

'Look, you stay if you like,' she says to Jason. 'But we're leaving. Pax, you first.'

Pax nods and clambers, barefoot, on to the window ledge. He adjusts his position, leans through the window and begins to rock back and forth, which is the only momentum he can gather here. He counts as he does this, just as Father has taught them to do:

'One, two—'

Even Evie has stopped crying to watch Pax, open-mouthed.

'—three!'

Pax launches himself into the air and disappears from their sight. As one, the rest of them hurtle to the open window. Jason and Evie look down on to the weathered street. But Dayna looks up to the roof next door and waves to Pax, who waves back.

Dayna ducks back inside and grabs the rucksacks. 'Move it, you two,' she commands, pushing the others aside.

'Ready, Pax?'

'Yeah.'

Dayna swings one of the rucksacks by its strap and lets go just when it's level with the window. It soars through it and towards Pax in a high arch. He snatches it out of the air with an 'Umph!' and almost lets it drop.

'Careful!' shouts Dayna.

'I got it, didn't I?' Pax shouts back. 'As if you could do better. These things are heavy.'

'Ready for the second one?'

They repeat the procedure, right down to Pax almost, but not quite, letting the rucksack slip through his fingers.

'Now the rope,' calls Dayna.

'I know, I know …'

Pax takes a coil of paracord rope from one of the rucksacks, knots one end to give it more weight and lobs it towards Dayna. She isn't ready for it and fumbles her catch, and Pax jeers at her, delighted. He pulls the end up and throws it again, and this time she catches it.

'Come here, Evie, we're gonna tie you up so you can't fall.'

Evie scowls at Dayna through red, puffy eyes. She doesn't move.

'Is that Mummy?' she whispers, and points to the door.

Dayna is too full of adrenalin to think about what would be the best thing to answer. 'Yes,' she says. Then: 'No. Not any more. Sachiko's dead, and there's a monster in her body now.'

'Jesus,' mutters Jason. 'She's a little kid. Evie?'

With what looks like a tremendous effort, Evie tears her eyes away from Dayna and settles them on Jason.

'Your mum's OK now,' he tells her. 'Nothing can hurt her any more, but things can still hurt you. And she'd want you to come with us now, right?'

'God's plan,' mumbles Evie, and sniffs snot back up her nose. 'I know.'

'Well, come on then,' says Dayna. 'Let's get this rope on you or God'll look like an idiot for trusting us.'

Evie sniffs again but also manages a watery smile. She steps towards Dayna and allows her to tie the rope around her torso.

'Where we going?' she asks Dayna.

'To that roof where Pax is.'

'No, after that. I don't want to go back to Liam. Not without Mummy.'

'Why would we ever go back there?' asks Dayna. 'We just went to a lot of trouble getting out, didn't we?'

'Yes,' says Evie. 'But before, I said I want to go back. I don't now. Just so you know.'

'We're not taking you back,' repeats Dayna.

'But it's God's plan. And God likes Liam.'

'That's only what Liam says,' puts in Jason when Dayna doesn't answer. 'People who say God likes them are usually crazy. Personally, I think if God does exist, he couldn't give a toss about any of us.'

'He does give a toss for me,' says Evie indignantly. 'Because I'm the chosen one.'

'You're all set,' says Dayna, giving the knotted rope around Evie's chest one final tug. 'Now everyone shut up about God, please, I need to concentrate. I'm going to jump over, and me and Pax will pull Evie up. As soon as we're holding our end of the rope, you help her through the window, Jason. OK? OK.'

She clambers on to the window ledge, one-two-three, and leaps. It's an easy jump, but still her heart jolts at the moment of impact on to the roof edge. She's caught on to it in such a way that all she has to do is hoist herself up and over to where Pax is waiting with the rope in his hand.

'You looked funny doing that in the dress,' is how he greets her. 'I bet Jason and Evie could see your knickers— sorry, sorry, I take it back!'

Dayna gives him one last dirty look, then grabs a bit of the rope as well. From below them, Jason lifts Evie on to the window ledge.

'OK, hold tight to your end of the rope, Evie,' Dayna tells her, then she and Pax pull. Evie swings upwards, into their building with a small bump and a squeal. But she's not far below, and it doesn't take long until they're tugging her over the rim.

'Fun, right?' says Dayna encouragingly as she unknots the rope around the little girl.

'No,' says Evie, glowering.

A crash and loud swearing make all of them turn to see Jason's head, shoulders, arms and elbows over the roof edge, the rest of his body dangling below it.

'Oh shit oh shit oh shit,' he gasps.

Dayna and Pax rush forwards, but he manages to heave himself up and over without their help. He rolls on to the roof, gasping and swearing.

'We would've thrown you the rope if you'd waited a bit longer,' says Dayna.

'If you kids can do it without a rope, I can too,' pants Jason.

'We did it more elegantly,' says Dayna.

'And we were a lot quieter,' giggles Pax.

'I was quieter too,' says Evie. 'I was very, very quiet.'

25

Dayna smashes through a roof window and manoeuvres everyone inside, down, and on to the street without incident. Even down here, Sachiko's animal screaming from outside the bathroom door is audible. Evie sticks her fingers into her ears and trots after the others without a word or glance back. Pax, wearing his rucksack now, takes out his slingshot and Jason takes hold of one baseball bat. Dayna's arm has recovered enough for her own slingshot, which is her preferred weapon. She finds herself in the lead without any clear idea of where she is heading, only that it is away from the sea, where Liam's people will come from, and away from the thing that has taken over Sachiko.

After they've been walking for about ten minutes, they pass a sign almost entirely swallowed up by wispy plants. If you squint, you can just about make out a red-and-white train symbol.

'We might find a map there,' suggests Dayna without any great conviction. And so they go.

The train station has a glass ceiling, of which a number of tiles are smashed. Glass shards sparkle on the floor in the morning sun.

'Everyone stop,' commands Dayna. 'Not worth it, barefoot.'

They need to find shoes and socks soon, and also more

practical clothes. Dayna is itching to get out of the beige dress; all she found in their house yesterday was a couple of moth-eaten, too-large and way-too-warm jumpers and a lot of empty wardrobe space. But before they go clothes-hunting, it would be safer to move further away from the coast.

'There's a map, over there,' says Pax, pointing to a low billboard in the middle of the hall of glass. The display there really does look like a map.

Before Dayna can think of what to do, Pax is already dancing towards it: running and swerving and leaping on tiptoe, as if he's playing a complicated game.

'Stop, you idiot,' Dayna calls after him. 'Your feet'll get cut!'

Pax pretends to be out of earshot. He doesn't stop.

She turns to the others. 'He really is an idiot,' she says.

'It's only a map of this area,' Pax calls over to them, disappointed.

'What'd he expect?' mutters Jason. 'And watch the kid! She's going to go after him – stop her, Sarge!'

Dayna reaches forwards and yanks Evie back beside her. 'You could've done that too,' she tells Jason.

'You were closer than me,' he says, shrugging.

'Why are we stopping?' whines Evie. 'We have to go on moving. You're supposed to take me somewhere, but we're NOT moving.'

'Did your mother tell you that?' asks Dayna.

Evie scowls at her bare feet and doesn't answer. Tears are welling up in her eyes. Dayna doesn't know what to do or to say. What do you say to someone whose mother has just turned into a monster? Helplessly, she looks at Jason. He pulls a face and shrugs.

'Just leave her alone,' is his advice.

'Hey, guys,' calls Pax. He's moved away from the area map

and on to one of the long rectangular platforms. 'I found something! Better come here and take a look.'

'A map?' asks Dayna.

'It's better to show than to explain. Just come here. You can go around the glass easy, it's only in some places.'

'Oh, fine,' sighs Dayna. She turns to the other two. 'We'll go, but we're not stupid like Pax, so we'll walk *slowly* and look at the ground before we step on it. OK?'

Jason stands to attention and gives her a mock salute. Evie is still glaring at her toes.

'Hey, Evie,' says Dayna, 'want to have a piggyback ride? I bet Jason makes an excellent pig.'

A small, grudging smile twitches across Evie's lips. She sniffs, and it's gone again.

Pax, impatient, hops from one foot to the other while the others gingerly pick their way towards him. It's not just bits of glass they have to watch out for, but lost and forgotten things that are rubbish now, like scattered, mossy bags or aluminium drinking cans or rectangular boxes that used to be telephones and music players and maps all squeezed into one.

Father told them there was chaos at train stations and airports and motorways during the Fall, and that many people were killed by other people who didn't even have the craze yet, only the fear of the craze. Sometimes, Dayna will see Mother being stampeded to death by a horde of panicked, frightened people; drowning in a sea of squirming bodies. Bad people killed her, Father said, but somehow Dayna has still fixated on this as her death. She wishes she hadn't.

'About time,' grumbles Pax when the others reach him by a raised platform between two dug-out pits with train tracks and all manner of weeds at the bottom.

'Show us your feet,' orders Dayna. Pax rolls his eyes but turns and holds up first one leg, then the other. Dayna stoops to inspect the soles of his feet, which are grimy but miraculously uncut.

'How did you *do* that?' she asks, genuinely impressed.

'I just did,' says Pax. 'Without thinking. Day—'

'If you don't know how you did it, it was just dumb luck,' she says dismissively.

'We're here now, Evie,' coaxes Jason. 'Want to get down?'

Evie readjusts her grip around his neck and says: 'No.'

'My back's starting to hurt.'

'Huh, listen to the old man,' scoffs Dayna.

'*You* take her, then—'

'LOOK.' Pax's voice rings out clearly over their bickering. They look at him and then look to where he is pointing, which is one of the many signs with name places on them. This particular sign is just three paces away, on two posts stuck into the cement. In white letters on sun-bleached blue it reads: *Trains to London*.

Next to the word *London*, someone has spray-painted a bird in black. Its colour has long since faded in the sun too (white letters eating into the bird's body from below), but not so much as you wouldn't recognise it. Its stencilled wings and tail feathers are spread wide and its beak is touching the *L* of London.

A hummingbird.

Or: a Hummingbird.

Follow the Hummingbird.

    Repeat.

        Repeat.

           Repeat.

PART 3
THE ARCHIVE

26

Dayna and Pax know where London is on a map because Father taught them all the big places. They know it's nowhere near the coast at all, and that it's north from where they set out in the first place, even though Jason said south. Which means they've been walking in the wrong direction for days, getting further and further away instead of closer.

They round on Jason: 'You lied! You lied to us!'

He bends down and lets Evie slide from his back without looking at them. Then he straightens up and says: 'That could be any stencilled bird, done by anyone for any reason.'

'It's the exact same bird stencilled on to their van,' says Pax.

'You'd think they'd just tell everyone where they're based?' demands Jason. 'This is just some kind of false scent.'

Dayna takes out her little radio and tunes into the well-remembered frequency. The woman's voice is a lot weaker here and the crackling surrounding her much louder so that you have to concentrate to make out the words. But you can: *Come and be welcome. Follow the hummingbird. 51 degrees, 35 minutes, 53.88 seconds north, 0 degrees, 7 minutes, 10.92 seconds west. Repeat.*

Dayna thrusts the radio into Jason's face. 'Lot of trouble for a false scent, right? Seeing as no one would be looking for them in the first place if it wasn't for this. You said it yourself, they want people to test on.'

'Who're you gonna believe? Me or that random sign with the random bird?' Jason's voice is higher than usual, and he can't hold their gazes. He might as well be confessing outright.

'You're a liar,' snaps Dayna. 'You're lying right now, it's so obvious. You're a terrible liar.'

Jason snorts, shrugs. Gives up the pretence. 'If I'm such a terrible liar, how come it took you two so long to find ou— *UMPPH!*'

Evie yelps.

Pax has punched Jason – *UMPPH!* – right in his stomach, and Jason doubles over, wheezing and giggling as if this is the funniest thing that could have happened.

'You TRAITOR!' shouts Pax. 'You never wanted us to find Father!'

Jason, curled on the ground, dissolves into more feeble giggles. Like it's all one big joke. The only thing Dayna has in her hands is the radio, so that's what she hurls at him, as hard as she can.

'STOP laughing!' she yells.

It hits him on the shoulder and ricochets off, into one of the pits with a sickening *clang* as it bangs off a metal rail. It's broken now, she's sure of it. And it's all Jason's fault. ALL of it.

'Jesus, stop hitting me,' mutters Jason, but at least he isn't laughing any more. 'Sorry, I dunno why, I just couldn't help it. I know it's not funny.'

'Get up,' says Dayna.

Jason hoists himself into a sitting position. 'I think I'll stay right here, thanks. Don't want any other little kid punching me again.'

'Were you ever gonna tell us?' asks Pax. 'What if you'd stayed at the Court like you wanted in the beginning and me and Day left, were you gonna tell us then?'

Jason hesitates, then says: 'I'm not sure. It's not like I didn't want you to find your dad. It's just that I didn't want the Hummingbirds to get you. Because that's what'll happen in the end. If you find them. They'll take you too and keep you locked up and stick you full of needles until you die. That's what they do, all right?'

'Stop talking,' snaps Dayna. 'I don't care. We're leaving for London, me and Pax and Evie.'

Pax nods, but Evie doesn't make any sign that she's heard. She's watching them with wide eyes, her thumb in her mouth.

'You promised Sachiko to keep Evie safe,' says Jason. 'You're taking her to the one place where it's most dangerous for her. If they ever find out—'

'Shut up, I'm not listening to you any more. Let's go, you lot.'

Dayna hoists up her rucksack and jumps into the pit, next to the remains of her radio. She can feel hot fury pumping through her, radiating from her, that's how angry she is now.

'We'll just follow the tracks, they'll take us to London, like the sign says. Pax, help Evie down to where I am.'

Evie lets Pax guide her to the pit and lower her down, and she lets Dayna take her and pull her on to the train tracks.

'We'll need shoes soon if we're doing all that walking,' says Pax, climbing down himself.

'Next town we come to,' promises Dayna. 'What are *you* doing?'

Jason has jumped in after Pax. 'You need me,' he says. 'Soon as you get there you'll have to look out for other birds. I know where they'll be, and I know where the Station is.'

'So you'll lead us, like you did last time?' she jeers.

'If you really want to be so stupid, fine. But when we get to the Station, I'm not going near it, and neither is Evie. I'll wait with her, so if you don't come back, which you won't, she won't be all alone.'

'Since when do you care about anyone besides yourself?'

This touches a nerve: 'I DO care, or I wouldn't have tried to save you idiots from them, would I?'

'Saving your own skin, more like!' Dayna shouts back, outraged by him trying to justify his cowardice. 'You needed us to survive, and you didn't want to go back to the Hummingbirds. That's not saving us, that's saving yourself!'

'No more shouting!' shrieks Evie with her fingers in her ears and her eyes screwed up tight. 'NO MORE SHOUTING!'

'You're shouting loudest of all,' Pax points out. Then he catches Dayna's eye and they both snort, and just like that, Dayna feels better and more forgiving.

'Fine, come if you want,' she tells Jason. 'You'll probably be dead without us anyway. But that doesn't mean we're friends or anything. And if you lie to us again, I'll kill you. I mean it.'

'I won't, all right?' snaps Jason.

'Yeah, you sound like you're rea-aaally sorry,' says Pax sarcastically. 'Come on, Day. Let's get out of here. I'm sick of this place.'

So they set off, down the tracks, their old formation somewhat modified. Dayna first, as always, but then Evie, and then Pax. Three metres behind, Jason trails after them, holding his bat sullenly over one shoulder and not looking left or right or back but simply at his feet. Very unaware of his surroundings, which is stupid and dangerous. But Dayna is still too angry at him to give him advice.

27

Following the tracks is not as straightforward as Dayna hoped it would be. There are many tracks converging and diverging. They end up choosing the one closest to the north-west by the compass, which is where they think London should be from where they started at, but any one of those turns could have been wrong and sent them to another place entirely.

Everywhere looks the same: fields, woodland, clumps of pulsating Echidna, dead villages, dead train stations with faded paper schedules too weathered to decipher. But the dead world can always surprise you, and amidst all this sameness, they come across a chalk outline of a man etched into the grass slope of a hill, who Pax calls giant and Evie calls God. Who is taller than a house, and must have been magic, once. The younger kids are reluctant to leave him, but Dayna ushers them on. She wants to get further away from the coast. Yesterday, she felt so sure that they'd escaped. Now she can't quite shake the image of Rena creeping through the undergrowth in their wake, tracking them somehow ...

'Stop trying to act like Father,' mutters Pax. 'You're not him. Why can't we just look at the giant for a bit and rest our feet?'

'Someone has to act like him or it'll all fall apart,' says Dayna. 'Now come on.'

'That chalk matchstick man's not special anyway,' says Jason, who is carrying Evie on his back. 'Just a piece of artwork from before.'

Dayna ignores him.

The place they end up in is a very small village that seems to consist mainly of two parallel roads with only a scattering of houses, a supermarket and a petrol station. The tracks pass right by without taking any notice. The windows of the supermarket have been smashed, and its shelves are overturned and empty except for a few rats that scurry back into the shadows at their approach, but in one of the houses they find a larder stacked with supplies. And also full wardrobes. Whatever happened to the people here, they didn't have time to pack. Most likely, one of them got infected, then infected everyone else. The living-room window is a wide gaping hole of shattered glass, so that is how they must have left in their crazed state. Dayna wonders how far they got before their bodies gave up. She tries very hard not to think of Sachiko.

One of the people living here was a teenage boy, roughly around Jason's age, judging by the faded photographs stuck to his wall. The other was a younger girl. Most of her things are pink or frilly or have little flowers etched on to the hems or pockets. Dayna picks out a few clothes for Evie, even though they're too big for her. Anything would be better than that once-white bridesmaid dress that is now sporting dirt stains and grass stains and a rip down one side. It makes Dayna's skin crawl every time she looks at it, with the memory of Liam's wink and Rena's insinuations.

'I don't like it,' protests Evie as she glowers at her reflection in a dusty mirror. Dayna has forced her into a T-shirt with a pink star that is supposed to be tight-fitting, but drapes past Evie's knees.

'It's still like a dress,' says Dayna reasonably as she stuffs the other clothes into her rucksack – a purple cardigan for the cold and a handful of pants and socks that she and Evie will have to share.

'I like *mine* dress.'

'Well, your dress is dirty and smelly.'

'So are *you*.'

'That's why I'm gonna change too.'

Evie sticks her tongue out at Dayna, not in fun, but as if this is the most horrible thing she can think of doing. Dayna sticks hers out right back. She knows she should be more considerate to the girl, who has just lost her mother and has had her whole world turned upside down. And she does try, really she does. But Evie is just so difficult. Jason, to everyone's surprise, is the one who knows best how to handle her.

'That's pretty,' he says now, sticking his head round the door. He's already changed and is wearing a new old check shirt and shorts. 'Stars are special.'

'Really?' asks Evie as behind her, Dayna rolls her eyes.

'You bet.'

'You think it's prettier than mine white dress, Jason?'

'Sure, don't you?'

Evie twists her lips, thinking. 'Yes.'

Jason grins at Dayna, but she just looks back, stony-faced. 'I'm gonna find myself new clothes,' she says.

She crosses the landing to the once-upon-a-time teenage boy's bedroom, where Pax, dressed in a new purple T-shirt, is busy trying on trainers.

'Everything's way too big,' he complains.

'Course it is,' says Dayna. 'The girl's shoes are in the hallway downstairs.'

'I don't want to wear girls' shoes.'

'Why not, who cares?' asks Dayna, surprised. Pax has never been picky about clothes before. 'You're wearing her T-shirt, aren't you?'

'Yeah ... I'm not sure I want to after all. Jason says only girls wear purple. Maybe you should have it.'

'Forget stupid Jason. You *like* purple, you know you do. It'd be a bit too small for me anyway.'

'The clothes here would be a bit too big.'

'Better too big than too small. I'll grow into them. Why're you listening to Jason again, anyway?'

Pax shrugs. 'He looks sad whenever he thinks no one's watching. And he's being nice. I think he really is sorry.'

'If he is, why doesn't he just say it?' Dayna peels the hated beige dress off over her head and kicks it into a corner, where it lies like a shedded snakeskin.

'Urgh, finally,' she says, pulling on her selected T-shirt with a sigh of satisfaction. It's pale blue and shows a yellow comic boy with spiky hair spreading his arms out wide. A speech bubble issuing from his lips proclaims: *Don't have a cow, man!*

'Aw, if I'd seen that, I would've taken it,' says Pax.

'Yeah, but you didn't, did you?'

'What's it mean? Don't have a cow?'

'Maybe the boy here was a vegetarian,' suggests Dayna. 'I remember Father saying once that some people in the old world wouldn't eat meat because they felt bad for the animals. They were called vegetarians.'

'How weird,' says Pax. 'Didn't they grow weak and ill, just eating nuts and berries?'

'Nah. Not in the dead world. They had all kinds of food, they didn't need meat.'

All the teenage boy's trousers are too big for them, so Pax ends up with knee-length shorts with a flower patch on one side (which he tries and fails to tear off). Dayna is luckier; she finds roomy jeans covered in useful pockets, ending only a few inches over her ankle.

'Can't we swap?' asks Pax.

'Nope.'

Into her new pockets, she distributes lock pick, compass and slingshot, as well as a few preselected stones she's picked up from around the tracks. If someone should take her rucksack again, she'll still have her most important things. As an afterthought, she also slides Mother's picture into her back pocket.

'Come on,' she says, 'let's go check out which of the shoes fit best. They're mostly trainers, I saw, good for walking.'

They spend the night in separate rooms, except for Evie, who is put with Dayna, although she wants to be put with Jason.

'You'll see him again in the morning,' mutters Dayna. 'Now go to sleep.'

Because it's the two of them, they're in the big double bed which used to be the parents' bedroom. Pax is in the girl's room, snoring softly, Jason in the boy's.

'Is Mummy dead now?'

'Yeah,' says Dayna, wondering if this is true. 'But that's a good thing. The monsters won't hurt her any more.'

'And she'll watch over me, like she said? Together with God?'

'She'll always watch over you. So you don't have to be sad, OK?'

'I know. I'm not very much sad. Only a little bit. Sometimes a little bit more, sometimes not sad at all. Is Mummy watching me right now?'

'Yes. She wants you to go to sleep.'

'How do you know? Can you see her?'

Dayna sighs. Even though her world lives in the shadow of the dead world, always, she's never believed in ghosts. Father made sure of that. He didn't want her and Pax to be frightened by all the signs of death and decay surrounding them. And it worked. But, oh, how nice it would be, to know, not to pretend, not even to hope, but to *know*, as Evie does (or thinks she does) that her mother watches over her. To Dayna such things belong to the magical past, where anything was possible, not to Now.

'Dayna?'

'Go to sleep, I'm sick of answering questions.'

'Hello, Mummy. Goodnight, Mummy, sleep tight, don't let the beddie bugs bite. Why are you angry with Jason, Dayna?'

'Urgh. Go to sleep.'

'I'm not sleepy yet. I like Jason. Don't be angry with him.'

'He lied to us. And his lies brought us to Liam.'

'He brought you to Liam and to Mummy and me. He's part of God's plan.'

'Did Jason tell you that?'

'No. I know things. Lots of things happens for a reason, even if we don't understand right away. So don't be angry with Jason. Yes?'

'I'm sleeping, I can't hear you.'

'You're not sleeping. You're talking.'

'I talk in my sleep.'

★

When Dayna does finally drift off, she dreams of Sachiko. A crazed Sachiko with bloodshot eyes and wild hair and a twitching body. Chasing her, on all fours like some giant crab with human limbs, scuttling as fast as fast towards where Dayna is rooted to the ground, unable to move. Grass growing up her ankles, twisting around and around, trapping her. She slashes at the grass blades with her pocketknife, quick, quick, and then she's sawed through enough and is free and runs. Right into Liam, who wraps his arms tight around her, tight enough to squeeze the very breath from her body and—

'Day,' whispers Pax, and she wakes with a start.

'Bad dream?' asks Jason. Dayna blinks in the gloom. Shadows all around her, including the two boys, the night sky outside the window is still as black as ever.

'What're you doing here?' she gasps. She can still feel Liam's grip on her arms. She can still see the Sachiko-crab.

'Someone's here,' whispers Pax. 'Outside.'

28

'Liam?' says Evie in a small voice that makes everyone jump. She's curled up next to Dayna as if fast asleep. But her eyes are open.

'Is it?' asks Dayna.

'I don't think so,' says Pax. 'They came in a car. You can see them through the window. We just have to be quiet.'

Dayna pushes the sheets away and slides off the bed. 'You stay here, Evie,' she says. But Evie ignores her and jumps down as well.

'Evie, I said stay.'

'I want to see too. I want to know it's not Liam.'

Dayna turns to Jason. 'Tell her to stay.'

'Evie, stay, you're too loud,' he says.

'Am not.' Evie ignores both of them and marches over to the window, where Pax already is.

'Jesus, does that kid ever listen?' grumbles Jason as he and Dayna follow.

Jason looks over Pax's head, and Dayna over Evie's. The street outside is not as dark as she first supposed. It's a cloudless night with a bright, almost completely full moon and many, many stars. By their soft light, they can see a car parked right in front of the old petrol station on the other side of the road, only a few houses away from theirs. It's covered in painted symbols and letters, and although it's too dark for Dayna to make them out properly, she can tell that none of them are a hummingbird. Inside the car is light – a torch – and two, maybe three people.

Evie lets out a sigh of relief. 'Not Liam,' she says with satisfaction. 'Liam only has boats, not cars. All our cars won't go.'

'When did they come?' Dayna asks Pax.

'Just now. I'm getting better at hearing noises in my sleep, aren't I?'

He's right. Before, he would have slept through anything. Before, she would have been the one to hear the car, to wake him. It makes her uneasy that she hadn't heard its engine. Things have gotten mixed up now: Pax is more alert, and Dayna more easily sucked in by nightmares ...

'I woke Jason and then we came here. They haven't moved since. Just sitting there. Maybe they're trying to work out where to go.'

'Let's ask them to take us in the car,' says Evie. 'Take us to London.'

'No,' Dayna and Jason say at the exact same moment.

'Shhh,' admonishes Pax, his eyes still on the car.

'Why not?' demands Evie. 'They can help us.'

But Dayna has learned her lesson about strangers. 'We can't just assume people are nice,' she says. 'Everyone we met so far, they always say they want to help us, but they never do. They just make things worse.'

'Mummy helped you.'

Dayna sees the Sachiko-crab again and suppresses a shudder. Yes, she thinks. And look where it got her.

'Your mother was the only one out of really really loads,' she says. 'That's not good odds.'

'And I'm helping you,' says Evie stubbornly.

'Fair point,' says Jason. It's too dark to see his face properly, but Dayna can tell by his voice that he's grinning. 'How about we change the Sarge's generalisation to: All the *adults* we meet are untrustworthy. That doesn't include you, and not even your mum because she was only a bit older than me.'

A rush of sudden and unbidden anger flares up inside Dayna's chest. 'You do know that I'm counting *you* in the people we couldn't trust, don't you?'

'Hey, that's not fair—'

'They're getting out,' hisses Pax. 'Shut up, everyone!'

Car doors slam through the silence of the night, first one and then two. Whoever these people are, they're either very brave or very stupid. Sounds this loud attract the crazed. It's two men, Dayna thinks, squinting through the silvery gloom. They're only shadows, but big and broad-shouldered. One of them is bare-chested, and his pale torso glimmers like a ghost in the dead world's stories. He's the one who leans against the car while the other man, who is as thick as a tree trunk and holding a large canister, approaches the pumps. That's where petrol used to come out, Dayna knows, like water sometimes will still come out of taps. But mostly the petrol is either gone since the great rush of the Fall or all gummed up from the years of stagnation. Even if it wasn't, there's no way to get it from the pumps without electricity. The big man examines one of the hoses with nozzles, says something, then turns to the cars parked in the station. He opens a small hand-sized door – the hole where the car used to feed on petrol – in the back of the nearest car and slides something inside it. A rope. Or a big straw because he then puts the other end of it into his mouth.

Pax has to stifle a giggle. 'What's he doing?'

'He's sucking it, to get the petrol going,' says Jason in an isn't-it-obvious voice. 'How d'you think most people get petrol nowadays?'

'I dunno,' says Pax. 'Father said all the petrol is useless now. Fermented or something.'

'Degraded, you mean, but it can still work. Additives in the newer kind had it actually reach a pretty decent shelf life just before the Fall. What did you think the Hummingbird lorry ran on? Love?'

'Shut it, Jason,' snaps Dayna. 'Stop trying to make out you're so clever and we're so stupid. We didn't need cars or petrol, so we didn't need to know those things, did we? I'm glad we didn't, that sucking trick looks revolting.'

'Seems to work though,' says Pax. 'Look at his face!'

Outside, the man has just spat a mouthful of liquid on to the asphalt. It's gushing from the tube too, and he quickly directs the stream to the opening of his canister. When the flow dries up, he tips the salvaged petrol into the feeding hole of his own car before moving on to the other vehicles.

'I bet he's gonna be sick before he reaches the last,' says Pax cheerfully.

'Nah, he must be used to it by now,' says Jason. 'But I'll take the bet. What're we betting for?'

'I don't want him to be sick,' says Evie. '*I* bet he won't be sick.'

'How about the winner gets to call the loser *loser* all day tomorrow?'

'Look!' whispers Dayna. 'Look at the car!'

On the side facing the road, not the two men, one of the car doors is being opened very, very slowly. Neither of the men notices. The big one is too far away, and the other is on the other side of the car, watching his friend. Dayna sees a hand, a head, a body, as the person manages to slip out and crouch by the car's wheels.

'It's a woman,' whispers Jason.

Long, straggly hair is falling across her face, hiding it from view. Dayna thinks she may be barefoot, but it's difficult to be sure at that distance and with the poor light. She crawls to the end of the car, hesitates.

'She's making a run for it,' whispers Pax.

'She's thinking about it,' whispers Dayna.

As soon as she leaves the shadow of the car, the woman will be out in the open, and the men will see her. And so she hesitates.

'Is she their prisoner?' asks Pax. 'Why would they keep her prisoner? What do they want from her?'

'What d'you think they want from her?' returns Jason.

Like Liam, thinks Dayna. Shagging. But why? She doesn't understand why. Do they like it? Do they like doing these things?

'Run, lady,' whispers Evie, whose nose is flattened against the window. 'Run, run, run.'

And it's as if the woman has heard because it is at this precise moment that she moves, like a stone released from a slingshot, sudden and quick and sure. And loud. Too loud. One of the men shouts, and now both of them are tearing after her. The woman shoots past their house and out of their sight. The men gallop past too, first the one with the bare chest, then the big man, puffing and grunting.

'She'll make it,' whispers Pax excitedly.

'Yes yes yes,' squeals Evie, and has to be shushed.

But then someone screams. It could be a crazed animal, but Dayna knows it's not. They come back into sight two minutes later, the woman between the men. She's limping now, and the big man has his hand twisted in her hair and is tugging at her whenever she slows down. Evie begins to cry and Jason pulls her away from the window and tries to comfort her, and when that doesn't work, he holds his hand to her mouth to stifle the sounds. The bare-chested man stops abruptly.

Dayna ducks quick as quick and pulls Pax with her, heart hammering in her ears. Jason freezes where he is, his hand still firmly over Evie's mouth, although she must have sensed the danger too because she's stopped squirming. Male voices from outside, deep and hoarse. Dayna closes her eyes.

It was nothing, she wills them. An owl, a rat, the wind. Go away, go away.

And then the woman speaks, a defeated-sounding murmur which is followed by a sharp slap and laughter. And footsteps, as the three of them move on. Inside the dark room, Dayna and the others breathe again.

Pax straightens up on his knees and peers out of the window.

'Pax, don't,' hisses Dayna.

'It's OK, they're by the car now. They're moving past it, to the house next to the petrol station.'

Dayna gets up too and is just in time to see one of the men throw something through a ground-floor window. She winces at the loud smash of glass. Something shrieks again, but this time it's not the woman but a bird, a crazed bird, judging by the jerky way it flaps its wings, drops, rises again, making its wonky way towards the three adults and the noise.

'I hope it kills them,' says Dayna bitterly.

Two explosions.
BANG. BANG.
And more laughter.

Dayna, who has flung herself down like the others, gets to her feet again to peep through the window. The man with the bare chest is slinging his rifle over his back; it must have been there all the time, only she missed it in the dark. The big man pushes the woman through the jagged glass hole of the window and climbs in himself. The rifle man picks his way in after them more gingerly. And then the street is empty again, except for the dead crow, sprawled just in front of the men's car, its broken wings splayed like those of the Hummingbird symbol.

29

'We should save her,' says Pax.

'Excuse me?' says Jason.

'We should save that woman. Shouldn't we, Day?'

'And what d'you think would be the best way to do that?' asks Jason, his voice heavy with sarcasm. 'Do you want to chuck stones at those blokes with your toy slingshot?'

'You can kill animals with slingshots,' says Pax. 'You can bore through their throats, you can take eyes out. Would be the same with people if you aim right.'

'Yeah,' says Jason. 'And they don't dodge. And they don't aim a bloody rifle at you while you're busy with the slingshot. Yeah, that sounds like it ought to work. Great idea!'

'I don't care what you say,' Pax shoots back at him. 'You're a coward. You don't have to do anything. Day and me will save her by ourselves. Won't we, Day?'

Dayna looks at her brother, and knows he's afraid, and knows he means what he says all the same. She wants so badly to say yes. Yes, of course, we'll save her. Yes, we're the heroes, aren't we?

But she also knows what those men are doing to that woman (maybe doing it now, right this minute). And she knows that if they get caught, the men will shoot them dead. Or keep them too, like they keep the woman. Like Liam wanted to do. And that thought is so horrible that it's almost too much to bear.

'No,' she says quietly. 'We can't save her. We'll only end up getting killed ourselves.'

Pax is stunned. As if she's just punched him in the stomach, out of the blue. 'Yeah, we can,' he says. 'We can save her.'

'No, we can't. We're only kids. And they've got a rifle.'

'That didn't matter with Ryan and Mart, did it? We stopped those two. We saved Father and Jason. Because we're the heroes.'

Dayna wants to hide her face away from them all. But instead, she keeps her voice dull and steady: 'We didn't save Father in the end, did we? And we didn't save Sachiko.'

Were they lucky with Ryan and Mart? Or was it because she believed it could be done? If it is the former, that isn't any good. Because luck always runs out in the end. And if it is the latter, that's even worse. Dayna has stopped believing she can do anything. She's become afraid. It's a terrible feeling. Maybe the worst feeling in the world.

'We can't, Pax,' she whispers. 'I wish we could, but we can't.'

Pax is silent for such a long time that she thinks he isn't speaking to her any more. Then he asks: 'What about Father?'

There is challenge in his voice, and Dayna isn't prepared for how much this hurts. Does he really believe she could just abandon Father?

'Course we're still saving him,' she says. And thinks: If we can.

'You see, mate?' says Jason to Pax. 'Even if I'm a coward, you know the Sarge isn't.' (Yes, I am, thinks Dayna. I am now, even if I wasn't before.) 'And if she says we can't save that woman, then we can't. It's one thing to be brave, another to be stupid.'

'You saying I'm stupid?' Pax fires up at him.

'No, because you're not going to do anything stupid, are you?'

Pax turns his back to them all to glare at the window.

Jason says: 'What do we do now, though? Do we stay here and just hope they leave tomorrow?'

'They're likely to search the houses tomorrow,' says Dayna, trying very hard to sound like her normal self. 'Scavenging. We ought to be long gone by then.'

'So we leave now?' asks Jason.

Evie whimpers. 'I'm tired. I don't want to leave now. In the dark.'

'It *is* a lot more dangerous outside at night-time,' concedes Dayna. 'We wouldn't see things coming at us, and we'd make a lot more noise. Better to make noise bumping into things than to use a torch, though. That draws the crazed from further away.'

'But could we do it?' asks Jason.

Dayna shrugs. 'Yeah. Probably. And better than staying here where those men might find us.'

'I don't want to,' whines Evie. 'I don't I don't I don't.'

Pax turns from the window with a defiant look in his eye as he says: 'Let's steal their car.'

He scowls at Dayna and then at Jason, waiting for them to contradict him again. Dayna almost does. If trying to save the woman might get them killed, then attempting to steal the men's car is surely the next worst thing ... But she bites her lip and holds back until the first wave of sudden fear has washed her by. Then she says: 'We'd need a car key, and they're sure to've taken it with them.'

'We don't need the key,' says Jason slowly. 'I could hot-wire it.'

Dayna looks at him. 'Hot-wire?'

'You know, make the engine start without a key. You have to twist cables together, I've done it a couple of times. Someone taught me.'

'Who?' asks Pax.

'Why, d'you reckon you'd know them?'

Dayna is chewing her lip. 'You sure you can do that? How long would it take?'

'I'm sure. Maybe two minutes if the car's right. Doesn't work with the more modern ones – modern by old-world standards, I mean. But this one looks older anyway. People nowadays prefer older ones if they can get them. Straightforward mechanics, and way easier to tinker with if anything needs fixing.'

'Well, can't we just do that?' asks Dayna. 'Take another old car, not theirs?'

Jason shakes his head. 'I wish. But car batteries that haven't been used since the Fall would be completely drained now, totally useless. Even if you do find some with a bit of juice left, they'd have to be restarted, and I dunno how to do that. And that's without worrying about whether or not they have petrol. If we're doing it at all, it'll have to be this car. What do you think?'

Jason is talking to her, not to anyone else. He seems to think that Pax's idea is a good one, but won't say it before she does. It's part of his campaign to make peace, she knows, but she still appreciates it.

'… OK. Let's do it.' (Because she can't be more afraid than Jason. This will be her new rule.)

'Yes!' says Pax, punching the air.

'Yes, yes!' Evie repeats, imitating the punch. 'I never was in a car that goes.'

'Everyone, pack your things,' commands Dayna. 'And, Jason, see if you can find a rucksack or bag for yourself. We'll wait another hour or so. They should be asleep by then.'

The almost-full moon is high and bright over their heads as they creep, single file, towards the car in front of the petrol station, flitting from shadow to shadow like ghosts. First Dayna (of course). Then Jason, pulling Evie along with him. Lastly, Pax. The windows of the men's chosen house are black and have been black for a while before Dayna gave the OK to move.

One-two-three, Dayna counts in her head as she dashes silently from a low front-yard wall to an overgrown hedge. From the hedge to a car with flat tyres. From the car to another wall.

Uncle William's rule, which Father took up: a maximum of three seconds' exposure in dangerous territory, and chances are fairly good that you won't be seen by monsters.

One-two-three. Jason and Evie take closer to four-five seconds. But at least they're quiet. All of them wear their scavenged shoes around their necks, tied by their laces or straps – if you don't want to be heard, bare feet are best.

One-two-three again, Pax knows how it's done.

If they're lucky, both men (and the woman too) are sound asleep. If not, the men will take turns in keeping watch over the woman. Dayna thinks this is likely. She doesn't believe they will keep an eye on the car as well, but you have to consider all possibilities. This would be the worst one.

Dayna reaches the car they plan on stealing. Cautiously,

she lifts her head to peer through its grimy windows and towards the house to the right of the petrol station. Still no sign of movement. Good.

One-two-three; Pax is there.

Four-five, and so are Jason and Evie.

'What's wrong with you,' hisses Dayna. 'Don't all go together.'

'Evie wouldn't move, so I went first to show her it's fine,' whispers Pax. 'Not my fault they didn't wait.'

Jason cranes his neck to look at the house on the other side of the car, just as Dayna has done. 'No one noticed anyway,' he says.

'I don't like this game any more,' mumbles Evie. 'I don't like being outside in the dark. Let's go back.'

'You should've waited,' says Dayna.

'So-rry.' Jason clasps his hands in an exaggerated way. 'Please don't write me up, I'll do fifty push-ups, Sarge, but please don't write me up!'

'I don't know what you're on about, but you're not funny, and you can just shut up,' hisses Dayna. She glares at Pax, who has just snorted.

'Let's just get on with this, shall we?' says Jason, as if Dayna is the one wasting everyone's time. 'OK, Sarge?' Now that they need him again, he's a lot more cocky and sure of himself. 'Let's see if – aha!'

He's just tried the front door on the driver's side, and it has clicked open instantaneously. He slips in and starts twiddling at something under the steering wheel with the screwdriver from Dayna's pocketknife.

Pax moves in closer and holds up the wind-up torch so that Jason can see what he's doing. This is the dangerous bit. Dayna takes another uneasy look at the house. Still nothing.

Would they be able to see the light in the car if they looked out of their window?

'I want to go back,' Evie moans again.

'Shhh.'

Evie sticks her tongue out at Dayna and then flops on to the ground with a little thud, crossing both arms and legs tightly.

'How much longer?' she asks Jason.

'Getting there,' he mutters, his face hidden under the steering wheel. 'I think.'

'You *think*?'

'This isn't as easy as it looks, you know.'

'I never thought it was,' hisses Dayna. 'That's why I asked you if you were sure you could do it, didn't I? And you said no problem. You said two minutes—'

'Just let me concentrate, OK, Sarge?'

'Stop calling me that!'

'Day, just let him try,' whispers Pax.

Dayna glares at them both, then checks the house again. The seconds drag. And the fear inside her mounts. It's all she can do not to call it off and just run, just get away.

'I hate you,' states Evie. 'All of you. All of you ignore me. I want Mummy. Mummyyyyyyy …'

'Shhh!' Dayna squints through the car windows, but the house stays as black and silent as ever. 'Shhh,' she repeats, but more gently this time. 'Look, how about you already get into the back seat so we're all set when Jason finally manages to start the car? Just don't cry, OK? We'll all be in big trouble if you cry.'

'I know,' says Evie sullenly. 'I know that. You told me. I'm not stupid. And I wasn't crying.'

Dayna opens the back door and begins piling in their

rucksacks. Again she checks the house. Again nothing to be seen. She pushes in the last rucksack, her own, then turns to Evie: 'Now you.'

Evie clambers in just as the car's dashboard lights up. Dayna's heart leaps as Pax whirls around excitedly, but Jason mutters: 'Light, Pax. I'm not done yet.'

Pax swings the torch back to the exposed wires. Dayna edges closer to get a better look. In the dashboard, the petrol needle has just sprung up to indicate a half-full tank, and

vroooOOOOOOOM!

So loud, like a roaring monster. Was the Hummingbird lorry this loud?

'Score!' (Jason, his gleeful whisper also partly a yell.)

'Whoo-hooo!' (Pax.)

He has actually done it. Jason has actually awakened this car to life. It's quivering and alive, and something smelly is coming from a small tube at its end.

The house still looks like it's sleeping, but how can she be sure about that? Any second now, the door will burst open, and the men will come rushing out. Especially the bare-chested man frightens her; he was so *fast*.

'Quick, we have to move. Now. Pax, get into the back with Evie.'

Dayna scrambles over the driver's seat, and Jason shoves in just behind her. He reaches out and closes the door as softly as he can – just as Pax slams the back door behind him, loud enough to wake even the deepest sleeper.

'Pax,' moans Dayna. 'You idiot!'

'Sorry! Sorry! I didn't think—'

'Jason, go! NOW.'

'Aye aye,' mutters Jason.

And the car slides into movement, slowly, gracefully,

nothing like the hard jolt Pax and Dayna managed with the lorry, which seems like months or years ago. The house is still dark and unchanged; can they really not have heard?

They move down the road slowly, quietly, almost at walking pace, and Dayna is suddenly filled with horrible visions of the men materialising out of the darkness—

'Everyone, lock your doors,' she orders. Pax does both his and Evie's sides at once, eager to make up for his mistake from before. Dayna pushes down the little knob on her own side – and there the bare-chested man is, inches away, staring at her from the other side of the glass. Dayna draws in breath to scream – and then he's gone. Her imagination, that's all. Or (worse, somehow) her fear, so strong now that it's taking over the rest of her senses. Heart hammering, head swimming, she leans over to Jason's side and pushes the knob down as well.

They're coming up to the end of the road, and the moonlit street behind them is still devoid of anything alive. Only her fear …

'Left or right, Sarge?' asks Jason.

'Doesn't matter,' says Dayna, and finds that she has barely any breath left in her. 'Let's just get out of here.'

'Left,' says Pax at random.

'No, right,' says Evie earnestly, as if she actually *knows*.

Jason swerves to the right. 'Best follow the voice of God, eh?'

'Don't humour her,' mutters Dayna. 'She'll believe it …'

Jason pushes a thin lever by the side of the steering wheel upwards, and lights flare up on either side of the car's front snout, illuminating a stretch of cracked road ahead of them in a puddle of yellow-orange brightness. Pax whoops again, a little louder this time.

Relief is slowly swirling around Dayna as the realisation that they're safe sinks in.

Safe safe safe.

At least for now. But with the relief comes something else, sticky and unpleasant. 'Can't you go a little faster?' she asks.

'Give us one more street, then they definitely shouldn't hear,' says Jason. 'Although they're probably deaf anyway, if they didn't even wake with Pax slamming the door like a moron.'

'Shuttup,' mutters Pax. 'Day?' She twists around in her seat to look at him. His face is suddenly serious. 'If you say we couldn't have helped her, I'm gonna believe you. As long as you don't ever say that about Father.'

'Pax, I already—'

'I know. I just wish ... I hate that we had to leave her. It's not fair.'

'Pax ...'

'S'OK. I'm OK.'

'You better be,' says Jason. 'The great car pirate of southern England.'

Pax smiles. 'That was cool, wasn't it?'

'So cool.'

Dayna turns away from them to look out of the window, at the silvery-grey leafy shadows passing them by. They took the car but left the woman behind. How horrible that sounds. How unlike any of the heroes in the old world's tales. They just left her. Because of Dayna.

Whatever would have happened, good or bad, hasn't happened because of her. And even the knowledge that this is in all probability a lucky thing doesn't console her now. Because what if ... ? What if they *would* have been able to save her? Like they saved Jason. Like they saved Evie.

I'm becoming a coward, thinks Dayna. I'm not a hero any more, just a scared girl. Liam made a coward out of me, and there's no going back. I can try and fight it, and I suppose I'll have to if I want to save Father, but that won't change being scared.

I'll be scared now for the rest of my life.

30

It's an hour later, and the two men and their prisoner are far, far behind. In the back seat, Evie's and Pax's heads loll over their fastened seat belts, both of them asleep even through all the car's bumping and stopping and starting on the damaged winding roads. In the front, Jason's whole attention is focused on the way ahead – a couple of times already they've come across fallen trees blocking the road and were forced to dodge on to uneven fields or reverse altogether and find a different path. Dayna, sitting in the passenger seat now, has an open street atlas on her lap and is trying to find the names of the places they pass with the help of the index and her wind-up torch.

The atlas is frayed around the edges, its paper a little sticky by the years of greasy fingers handling it. It's one of the miraculous finds they made in the glove compartment. The other is a handgun without bullets, which is now in Dayna's rucksack. Other things they've found in the car – smelly socks, dirty underclothing, old cigarette butts – are less appealing and soon dumped at the side of a road.

The paper landscape of small roads and settlements and words blur, come into focus, blur again. Dayna's eyes are drooping. She tries blinking hard and squinting, and that works for about half a minute before everything swims out of focus once more.

'Maybe we should stop for the night,' she admits.

Jason shrugs. 'I'm so full of adrenalin, I can keep going for at least another hour.'

'Well, I can't.'

'I can manage by myself for an hour.'

'No, you can't. You could turn the car right around and drive somewhere else. Or you could get lost.'

Jason doesn't take his eyes off the road, but his voice is sharp when he replies: 'Can you stop treating me like shit, please? I said I was sorry, I'm leading you to the bloody place. What more can I do?'

Dayna glares at him, even though he won't see. 'You didn't. You didn't say you were sorry, not once.'

'Well, maybe because I was trying to save your lives,' says Jason. 'Why should I be sorry for that?'

'I'm sorry I ever told Ryan where to find us, even though I was trying to save Father's life,' retorts Dayna. 'I'm still sorry for it. And I'm sorry about what happened to Sachiko, even though I was trying to save hu-uhh—'

Dayna has to stop here because her words have suddenly turned into ugly, hiccuping sobs. She draws up her knees and presses her face against them because she doesn't want to wake the others, and she doesn't want Jason to see, and, most of all, she doesn't want to be so weak.

She stays in this position long after the sobs have all been squeezed out, arms wound tight around her knees, hot eyes pressed against them. She's too exhausted to think coherently, can't really pinpoint what it is exactly that is making her feel so miserable now; there are so many things, and in all likelihood, it is a combination of all of them: Father's capture, Sachiko's turning, Jason's betrayal. Her fault, her cowardice. The woman she left behind. The creeping fear that they won't be able to rescue Father after all …

'Hey, Sarge? I'm sorry too.'

Dayna doesn't respond. A finger pokes her in the shoulder, and she flinches, badly. 'Don't *do* that,' she mutters through a blocked nose. And: 'Watch the road.'

'I just stopped the car. Did you hear me? I'm really sorry for lying to you. And I'm sorry we ended up at the Court because of me. I told myself it was to save you, but … shit, I just never thought I'd be this useless on my own.'

His voice is higher than usual, different altogether, and Dayna realises an amazing thing: 'You sound as if you're nearly crying.'

'Shut up, I'm trying … to apologise.'

Dayna has to snort at this, even though the snort is small and watery. 'I think you just ruined it again,' she says.

'Yeah, maybe. Those two back there are definitely asleep, right?'

Dayna turns to check. 'Yeah.'

'Good. Wouldn't do for them to wake up and see us crying like two toddlers, would it? Would ruin my image.'

'No, it wouldn't,' says Dayna and, incredibly, she feels like smiling. 'But it would mine.'

'Hmm.' Jason shrugs. 'So now that I've said sorry properly, with tears and everything, can we call it a truce?'

'You also told me to shut up.'

'Shut up. We good?'

Jason holds out his fist to her, a strange gesture Dayna has never seen before. She studies the fist warily. It's too dark to see his face, but she can hear the eye roll in his voice as he says: 'You're supposed to bump my fist with yours.'

'What does that mean?'

'It's like a handshake. Only cooler.'

'Like we made a deal?'

'Yeah, sort of. So you're not gonna keep me hanging, are you, Sarge? Come on, are we good?'

Dayna forms a fist and bumps his knuckles with her own. It feels strong and important.

'Yeah,' she says. 'I suppose we're good. Because you cried.'

'I only *almost* cried. And I really am sorry.'

'I know. Because you almost cried.'

'Ha-ha. I think I'll get some shut-eye after all. Apologising to you is pretty draining.'

Dayna hesitates, then says: 'Anyway, only an idiot would think he was useless if he could start cars without the key, and knew about gee pee ess and Hummingbirds.'

'You calling me an idiot, idiot?' Jason sounds both surprised and pleased.

It's a calm night, the only nearby sounds the quiet rustling of nocturnal creatures in the undergrowth, or the whispers of leaves in a not-quite-wind. The howls and shrieks of the crazed are only in the distance, so far away they could be in a dream. Soon Jason is asleep, his breathing as slow and rhythmical as that of Pax's and Evie's.

But Dayna stays awake for a long time afterwards, watching the bright stars through the windscreen, thinking about the woman they left behind. And what will become of her.

Car travel is not without its problems, they realise the next day, if the sun is out and blazing. Even with all the windows rolled down it is like slowly being cooked over a campfire – and they have to make many stops, not just to restock on water or do their business, but to breathe.

They pass no more giants or gods or men carved into the earth. Instead, they pass meadows and hills and forests and streams and farmhouses and hamlets and towns. They pass a herd of deer fleeing from something, and, not long after, they pass a crazed dog with tangled fur and stubby little legs who charges at their car with its head and knocks itself into a stupor and the car nearly into a ditch. Finally, they leave the winding roads in favour of a much broader one with white lines painted on it and signs on metal bridges with the names of places, and one of these places is *LONDON*.

'We'll have to go right into the city,' says Jason. 'Find another one of the sprayed hummingbirds. I know the Station is in North London, but not how to get there from here. The car atlas is no good, it just shows the main roads. I'd need a map. Or a hummingbird.'

'What about where you lived?' asks Dayna. 'Would you know where the Station was in relation to that?'

Jason looks uncomfortable. 'Not really,' he mutters. 'Look, it'll be easier if we just go into London and find a train station. If their sign was all the way back in that seaside town, it'll definitely be in London. They *wanted* people to find them. To walk into their trap. Morons, like us.'

'We're not walking into a trap,' says Dayna, who is trying very hard to believe this. 'We'll be ready for them and we'll be careful. And we'll sneak up and check things out without them even knowing we're there, and we'll make a proper plan.'

'If you say so.' Jason shrugs. 'You'll have to be extremely careful doing that though. A large area around the Station has drone surveillance.'

'I'm always extremely careful.'

'I'm sorta glad that we have to go to London,' pipes up Pax from the back seat. 'I always wanted to see it.'

'Yeah, me too,' says Dayna quietly. It's true, London is connected to the lost world like no other place. This is where the parliament was and the queens and kings and where all important things happened, and this is where so many people from the Before used to live, people she only knows from stories, made up and true, all of them real and not real at the same time. This is also where she and Pax and Father and Mother lived, a very, very long time ago. Before the dead world was dead. So yes, she wants to see London. But now she's also thinking about other people, living people, bad people, who may have had the same idea. Who may still be in—

'London!' cries Evie suddenly. 'I see London!' She points, not straight ahead, but to her right.

Shadowy shapes loom up in the distance like mountains, like giants. Tall, elongated, strange. Buildings and towers. Man-made.

London.

31

The brick houses around them still look ordinary and small and overgrown when the car suddenly huffs and sputters and wheezes. Jason slows down immediately and stops the engine.

'What's wrong?' asks Dayna.

'Looks like we're finally out of petrol. Thirty minutes longer, and it would've taken us right into the city.'

'Hey, don't blame Betsy,' says Pax. For some unknown reason, he has given the car this name as if it is another member of their party. 'She brought us all the way to London – we *are* in London, we passed the sign—'

'Looks more like a suburb of London,' mutters Jason.

Pax ignores this. '*All* the way to London,' he repeats. 'And you're moaning about her breaking down before we reach a train station? We'd have been walking all this way if it weren't for her. And me, because it was my idea to take her, wasn't it? I bet any other car would've run out of petrol long ago, but she kept on going until she knew we were there and – and – and … you ought to thank her!'

'What is it with you?' demands Jason, looking at Dayna for support. 'It's a bloody car, not a person. *I* was the one who did all the driving.'

'You did the steering,' corrects Pax. He strokes the car's door fondly and says: 'Thanks, Betsy.'

Evie copies him immediately: 'Thanks very much, Betsy. Mummy says thank you too.'

Evie has been good all day – not well-behaved, but fairly cheerful – and she hasn't cried once, although sometimes she will look up into the sky and stare at something no one else can see. She seems to have decided to believe wholeheartedly that Sachiko is watching over her. There are worse things to believe.

Dayna grins, and more to annoy Jason than to please Pax, she reaches up to touch the roof and says: 'Thanks, Betsy.'

They walk north in their familiar procession, weapons at the ready. The streets here don't look too different to the ones Dayna still calls home in her head, way back by the Blue House: brick or whitewashed houses and street lights and rusty cars covered in creepers; grass and weeds poking out through cracks in the pavement; small, unseen animals scurrying away in their wake, larger ones staring at them with bristling fur and bared teeth. The only difference is that the roads here go on and on and on.

They come to a tangle of shrubs and trees and dry fields that must have once been a park. Now it's an oasis amidst the hot asphalt streets, and Dayna leads her troop on through its dappled shades without a moment's hesitation. There's a large pond topped with algae and surrounded by mosquitoes and dragonflies and other insects. They're almost out of water and Dayna would love to refill their bottles, but the stagnant water looks nasty and like it might make them sick, even after boiling. She explains this to Evie, who is clamouring for a drink.

'I'll starve,' complains Evie.

'No, you'll die of thirst,' says Pax helpfully. 'And then you'll starve because we haven't got any food left either.'

Dayna flushes. The house yesterday had so many food cans, and no one had thought to pack any of them. Herself included. Her mind was on those men, on the woman. 'We'll find a house with a good supply,' she promises. 'Otherwise, I'll catch a rabbit; I saw two here already.'

'Can't you catch it now?' asks Evie.

'Water first,' says Dayna, handing Evie her bottle. 'Here, take mine. But save some—'

Evie gulps down everything in two quick seconds.

'Great,' says Dayna. 'No wonder you lot are thirsty if you don't ration your stuff.'

'We're in the largest city in Britain,' says Jason, and yawns. 'We'll find something. Let's just get back to the streets.'

Dayna has actually planned on walking for another hour at least before making a big stop, but she can see that this isn't going to work if half her troop is thirsty and hungry. 'Fine,' she says. 'But next time, ration it properly.'

'Yes, Sergeant,' trills Jason, saluting smartly, which makes Pax and Evie giggle. Dayna scowls at them all, particularly at Pax (that traitor!), then sets off again. The others follow in their old formation, still grinning.

'Sarge,' says Jason quietly, catching up to her, 'just so you know, we'd better stay away from East London altogether. Everywhere else should be fine.'

'Why—'

'A playground!' yells Pax excitedly, pointing towards something through the leaves: a clearing of weeds and wild flowers, rusty swings and slides and weathered ropes. And suddenly, everyone's forgotten about being thirsty and hungry and hot.

Pax shrugs off his rucksack and sprints towards some tall structure made out of poles and intertwining ropes. Dayna has never seen such a thing before, and neither has Pax, but he knows what to do and scales up the nearest rope like a squirrel. Evie is staring, wide-eyed, at the dusty steps leading up to the slide.

'I want to do that,' she informs the other two.

'Well, go on then,' says Dayna.

Evie turns back to the slide and advances warily.

'She's never seen a slide before, I bet,' says Jason. He slings down his own rucksack and follows Evie. Left alone, Dayna looks around, drinking everything in. She knows playgrounds, or a playground, from back home, but this is much larger, with more equipment.

Something snaps and Pax cries out as he hurtles downwards. He flails wildly in the air and just manages to grasp another rope, giggling like a lunatic as he pulls himself up to safety.

'Phew,' he laughs.

'Get off that thing!' commands Dayna.

'S'OK,' Pax calls back, then ignores her and continues climbing.

Dayna hesitates, then shrugs off her own rucksack. Why should she be the only one who isn't having fun? She runs to the swings and then she is up in the air, the rusty linked chains creaking wildly, as she flies and falls and flies again. And an amazing thing happens: the knot in her stomach loosens. It's like she's back at the Blue House, and all her worries and fears have faded into almost nothingness, as long as she doesn't look at them too closely. She can't stay this way, of course, has to keep on going, save Father, make good. But just a little longer …

It is from the swing, perhaps ten or fifteen minutes later, that Dayna sees the approaching caravan.

32

It's an old van, the colour of dried grass, towed by two horses. The van's motor and bonnet have been removed, and over the hollow place they left behind there is a wooden plank with deckchair cushions, and on this sits the driver, holding the reins loosely in his hand. He's wearing a wide-brimmed straw hat over shoulder-length dirty-blond hair. It hides his face in shadow, but he must have seen them because he's steering the horses right towards the playground. A rifle is slung across his back.

Dayna's new trainers skid to a halt in the weed-infested dirt under the swings.

'Pax!' she shouts, her fingers already closing around the handle of her slingshot. 'Jason! Evie!'

They understand the urgency of her tone because they come at once, even Evie.

'Get behind me, Evie,' Dayna tells her. 'And don't say anything about being immune, OK? You have to keep it a secret, especially here.'

Pax positions himself to her left, his own slingshot in his hand, while Jason snatches the bat from the pile of abandoned rucksacks, then jogs back to join them. And so they stand, in a crooked line by the swings, fingering their weapons nervously. When the caravan is close enough for the driver to be in shouting distance, Dayna raises her slingshot and draws back the pouch with the small stone inside it, as far as it will go. She aims at the stranger's head, then holds.

'Stop right there!' she orders. 'Or I'll shoot.'

She's scared, but her body knows what to do and her hands don't tremble and her aim is straight.

The driver stops the caravan, about ten paces from the playground. But instead of turning back, he climbs down, slowly, to face them. And suddenly a dog is by his side, big, with pointed ears and bared teeth and bristling fur. If it were a little bigger, and grey instead of brown, it would look almost exactly like a wolf. Its growl is low but powerful. Dayna feels it in the back of her teeth.

'Pax,' she says, hoping her voice sounds strong and confident. 'You aim at the dog.'

'OK,' he says.

'If it comes, it'll be fast.'

'I know that.'

'Oh shit,' mutters Jason. 'You mean the only thing stopping us being mauled to death is Pax's slingshot?'

'And mine,' says Dayna.

This is when the driver speaks: 'Hey, everyone calm down. No one's mauling anyone to death.'

It's a female voice, not a man's at all. The driver is a woman. As if to confirm this, she pushes up the rim of the straw hat so that her facial features, clearly feminine, are visible. Makes no difference. Women can be dangerous too.

The woman lays a hand on the bristling hump of the dog's back, and he sits at once, although his eyes remain fixed on the kids. The woman is wearing a white shirt over a T-shirt, and canvas trousers with a lot of pockets in them, neither of which makes Dayna feel at ease: the shirt reminds her of Liam's followers, and the trousers of Mart and Ryan. She could be from the Court, come to track Evie down and take her back. She could be one of the Hummingbirds.

'Evie,' says Dayna without taking her eyes off the woman and her dog. 'Evie, do you recognise her?'

'What?' asks Evie in a small, high voice.

'The woman, do you know her? Is she one of Liam's people?'

'I don't know any Liam,' the woman calls over to them.

'I wasn't talking to you,' says Dayna. 'Well, Evie?'

'I don't know her.'

'Look at her face.'

'I am. I don't know her. But that dog looks like a hellhound.'

'You had dogs at the Court?' asks Jason.

'No-ooo,' says Evie impatiently. 'Hellhounds from hell.'

'Ha!' exclaims the woman, a sound between a laugh and a bark. 'Dog's a mongrel,' she tells them. 'Predominantly border collie and German shepherd.'

'She's not one of the Hummingbirds either,' says Jason.

'How do you know?' asks Pax. 'You can't have seen all of them.'

'I know, OK? She isn't one of them.'

'I'm not,' confirms the woman. 'Whatever that is. Look, I'll leave you alone again in a minute, but maybe you could do me a favour first?'

Dayna doesn't lower her slingshot. 'Probably not,' she says. 'What is it?'

'You're a tough one, aren't you? I'd like to take your picture. Just as you are, weapons raised, in front of the playground.'

Dayna isn't sure what she's been expecting, but it wasn't this. 'What?'

'You mean you have a photographic camera?' asks Pax, thrilled. 'One that still works?!'

'I have,' says the woman. 'And only the digital cameras have stopped working. The older stuff, the analogue stuff, I mean, works just as fine as always. For now, at least. It's in my bag. I'll get it if you let me, and show it to you.'

'Yeah!' says Pax immediately.

'Slowly,' warns Dayna. She doesn't dare take her eyes off the woman to check, but she's pretty sure Pax has lowered his slingshot. At least the dog has stopped growling now.

Pax is all for going straight up to the woman, but Dayna calls him back. 'If you're gonna stay here longer, you need to tie up that dog,' she tells the woman.

The woman considers her, then nods. 'All right, that seems fair.'

Dayna makes Jason throw over a coil of their own rope because she knows it's strong, and she watches carefully as the woman ties the loops – one around the dog's neck, one around a nearby tree – and knots it, to make sure the knots aren't trick knots, and are tight enough.

'Toss the rifle to us,' Dayna tells her as soon as the dog is tied up. 'You can have it back when you leave.'

But the woman shakes her head. 'I don't think so,' she says. 'Not unless you toss all your weapons too. Look, tough girl, all I want to do is take a picture. My dog's tied up, he's no threat. I'm not either, but I'd prefer to still be able to protect myself if it comes to that. You're four and I'm on my own. You understand?'

Dayna hesitates, then nods. She's never considered the possibility that other people might see *them* as threats. It makes her feel strong; in charge. Also, she would very much like to have her picture taken.

'All right then,' she says.

'Why do you want to take our picture?' asks Jason, and he sounds ... what? Suspicious?

'Because it would be a good picture,' replies the woman. 'You kids will represent the new generation. Children of Now. I collect pictures, you see. Mostly from the past.'

'Why?' asks Pax.

'Because someone has to, or at some point all that history will vanish as soon as there's no one left to remember.'

'If there's no one left to remember, why bother?' asks Jason.

The woman shrugs. 'For those who'll come, for future generations, if there should ever be such a thing. For any alien race, maybe? Frankly, I'd do it even if I knew the world was going to implode in ten years' time. It makes me feel ... useful. Ha. Sane?'

'But what's the point?' persists Jason.

'If you don't know, I can't explain,' says the woman. Out of her shoulder bag, she takes a small black box with a protruding lens that glints as it catches the sun. 'Now, are you ready for your picture?'

She advances, her gait a little uneven, and Dayna sees that she's walking with a slight limp. Which is good for them. Safe. They are told to budge up so that they all fit into the frame. Then the woman raises the little box to her eyes, adjusts one of its knobs and presses a button. There's a barely audible click, then nothing.

'Is that it?' asks Pax.

'That's it.'

'Can we see?'

'I'm afraid not. You're captured on film now, but the film has to be developed first. I'm hoping to find some developing fluids in London, actually.'

'You mean we won't ever get to see our picture?' demands Pax. Dayna too feels as if the woman has tricked them in some way.

'If you give me your address, I could mail you a print,' says the woman, then smiles at their confused faces. 'Sorry, couldn't resist.'

'Ha-ha,' says Jason. 'Everyone thinks they're a comedian.'

The woman considers them for a moment, then says: 'Tell you what, I'll make it up to you. I'll treat you to lunch – if you don't mind ten-year-old baked bean cans.'

'Ooooh, yes!' says Pax. 'I'm starving!'

'Have you got water?' asks Jason. 'We've run out.'

'Yes, I have enough.'

Pax and Jason both look at Dayna. 'All right,' she says. 'But we could've gotten something by ourselves in another hour.'

'I'm not so sure about that,' says the woman. 'All the houses I've checked here so far have been completely cleaned out. It looks like systematic raiding parties.'

'I could have caught a rabbit,' says Dayna defensively.

'Of course, I do beg your pardon … If we're sharing my lunch, maybe you would allow me another picture? Of you?'

'Why? You already have one.'

'Because I like your *Simpsons* T-shirt. Another connection to the past, and your arms were in the way in the first photo.'

'Me too!' pipes up Evie, who seems to have decided that she likes this woman in spite of the hellhound. 'You need to take a picture of me because I'm—'

'Shhh!' hisses Dayna, elbowing her. 'Secret, remember?'

She turns to the woman. 'What's *Simpsons*?'

'The Simpsons were a cartoon family on TV,' the woman explains. 'They were hilarious and very popular. Hence the T-shirt. That's the boy on your shirt, Bart Simpson. He was always full of pranks.'

'And he didn't eat cows,' adds Pax.

For a second, the woman looks completely mystified. Then she bursts out laughing.

33

The woman's name is Jean. The dog's name is Dog. Pax says that's not a proper name, but Jean says she hasn't much imagination, and she's had a dog called Dog even when the dead world was still alive. Dog is her first dog's puppy. The original Dog was the reason Jean survived the Fall because she (a girl dog) was fierce and protective, and she hunted down animals, like hares or foxes, and brought them to Jean for food. Dog's previous owner was a hunter, who must have taught her how to do that.

'What happened to her?' asks Pax. 'Did she die?'

'She got infected,' says Jean. 'She killed two people and three of her pups. I had to kill her.'

'It's very difficult to kill crazed dogs,' says Dayna.

The corners of Jean's mouth twitch. 'Are you trying to catch me out in a lie? It was luck on my part. She was distracted by the pups. It was still a very hard thing to do. In more ways than one.'

She's sitting by Dog, who is still tied up. The kids are, at Dayna's insistence, grouped a little further away. A small campfire crackles between them, under a pot in which tomato sauce is beginning to bubble.

'I think they're done,' says Pax, who has been watching the pot the entire time.

Jean gets to her feet, a little awkwardly, and doles out portions into tin bowls. There aren't enough to go around, so she refills the empty bean cans as well.

'What happened to your leg?' asks Pax as he rummages for spoons in his rucksack. (Dayna keeps her eyes on Jean the entire time.)

'Something tore a chunk out of it. A long time ago.'

Jean passes out the bowls, then eases herself back into her sitting position. Dog watches the steaming bowls intently, even though Jean gave him uncooked baked beans – and a whole can of them – not ten minutes before. The baked beans are hot and full of flavour. Pax wolfs them down so fast that he burns his tongue and has to gulp down water before continuing. The other three eat almost as quickly, and everyone licks the bowls clean afterwards.

'Hungry, were you?' asks Jean with raised eyebrows.

'We ran out of supplies,' says Dayna. 'We'll get more soon enough.'

Jean nods absently. 'Would you like to see some of the pictures in my archive?'

An archive, it turns out, is a place where collected things are kept safe. Jean's archive is in the back of the old van. It's much smaller than the Hummingbird lorry and instead of cages, cabinets with doors take up the entire right-hand side. On the other side is a very thin, rolled-up mattress and a cardboard box full of tinned foods; another with gear similar to the things in Dayna's and Pax's rucksacks. They don't take up much space, though.

Jean shows the kids how the cabinets have been screwed into the van's wall so that they won't topple over, then she opens the lowest one for them to see. Inside are mostly old shoeboxes, and in these are loose bits of paper and postcards and photographs. All have numbers written on the back – 'For the index,' explains Jean, 'to make it easier to find if I'm looking for anything specific. You can look at them but don't muddle them up, or I won't be able to find anything any more. I'd rather the little girl doesn't touch them, I'm not sure she understands.'

'I DO,' says Evie indignantly. 'I'm careful!' And she fingers through the pictures with such elaborate care that Jean doesn't stop her.

The photographs are mainly of things: a mobile telephone with a cracked glass front; tall, angular stones in a row; a paperback book with a mouse-nibbled cover, the words *The Tempest* just barely recognisable.

The other pictures must be from the dead world when it was still living. There are pictures of paintings: a teeming street in vibrant colours; a strange, spotted landscape; a distorted man who could be a ghost, open-mouthed, screaming. And photographs on thick cardboard postcards: crowds of people in some city square, on a beach, sitting on raised seats that stretch out in all directions. Buildings in the dark, all lit up, not just the windows, but signs in front of them and around them. A man and a woman kissing on a crowded black-and-white street. An old woman with white curly hair and a purple jacket and skirt, waving and smiling to a crowd.

Beside the numbers on the back are handwritten titles: Football match (2010s), *The Scream* (E. Munch, 1893), celebration Trafalgar Square (1945, VE day).

So many windows into the dead world. Dayna had known it was full, but not as full as this.

'I would have loved to actually take a few more tangible things,' says Jean. 'Not just pictures of paintings but the paintings themselves, for example. But one has to be realistic. Basically, it comes down to space, which I don't have a lot of. Sometimes I take a history or art book, but usually, I just tear out the pictures I want and leave the rest behind. I'm pleased by your enthusiasm. I don't often get a chance to show the archive to people.'

'How long have you been doing this?' asks Jason.

'Not that long, actually. I've been toying with the idea for a while, and started the collection a few years ago, in Cornwall, which is where I spent most of the time after the Collapse. But I couldn't walk any long distances, not on this leg. It was the horses that made that possible. A traveller sold them to me. He'd been part of a group, but everyone else had died, so he had too many horses. Cost me most of my stashed medical supplies, but worth the price. We set off about three months ago. From Cornwall to Stonehenge, then down along the southern coast, and now up to London. I'm planning on collecting pictures from the whole island, if I can make it. Waiting spore mists out sets us back, of course, but that's true of everyone, and there's no hurry.'

'Don't you get lonely?' asks Pax.

Jean shrugs. 'Not really, no. I have Dog, and I was never much of a people person, even before all this. I've been in a couple of groups since the Collapse, but none of them has worked out. Some disintegrate, some go bad.'

'Not ours,' says Dayna.

'Then you're lucky.'

'We have a photograph too,' Pax tells Jean. 'Of Mother. Show her, Day.'

Dayna shoots him a dirty look. 'Not now,' she mutters because Mother's picture is special and private.

'Aw, come on,' says Jason. 'I want to see your mum too.'

'*No.*'

'Mine Mummy's up there,' Evie informs Jean, pointing to the archive's roof. 'She watches over me and won't let anything bad happen. I don't need a picture because I can see her if I close mine eyes. And when I sleep.'

'Oh,' says Jean, hesitantly. 'That's nice.'

'Evie's sorted herself out pretty fast,' mutters Jason to Dayna. 'Coping mechanism, I suppose. I hope it holds, but I don't think it will …'

Dayna doesn't know what a coping mechanism is, but if it makes you believe that your dead mother is still watching over you, makes you even hear the things she might say to you, then Dayna wishes she had some of that as well. It would be nice.

'OK, guys,' Jean is saying, 'give the pictures back, they shouldn't be handled too much. But if there's anything specific you'd like to see, I can check if I have it.'

'Do you know King Kong, the eighth wonder of the world?' asks Pax as he and the others reluctantly hand back the pictures.

Jean blinks. 'I do. I'm surprised you do.'

'Father told me about him. Have you got a picture?'

'Just a sec.' Jean places all the pictures back into the cardboard box, checking the numbers on the back to make sure they're in the right order, then takes out a small notebook.

'This is my index,' she explains. 'Whenever I add a new picture to my collection, I mark it here. King Kong is a film character, so he would be under "entertainment". Which is this notebook. I have a different one for each category.'

Someone is tugging at Dayna's arm. She turns to find Evie. 'What?'

Evie holds out a photograph. Not a postcard or magazine print, but a real photograph. On it is a building that looks like a ship. The Court.

Jean, busy flipping through her index notebook, hasn't noticed. Dayna holds up the photo so that the others can see.

'Everybody out,' she hisses.

Pax and Jason glance at each other, but they do as she says. So does Evie. Dayna is last. She knocks into the box of tin cans on her way out.

'What's going on?' asks Jean. 'What are you doing?'

'You said you didn't know Liam!' shouts Dayna. Her heart is pushing hard against her chest. It wants her to run. Dog jerks up and begins to growl, but he's too far away and still tied up.

'I don't,' says Jean. She sounds utterly bewildered. Like she really has no idea what is going on. But maybe she's just a very good liar.

'What about this?' Dayna thrusts the photograph at her feet, then, quick as a flash, takes out her slingshot and the stone and aims right at Jean. Dog barks, loud and sharp.

'Sarge, hang on,' mutters Jason, 'Evie's never seen her before.'

'Day?' squeaks Pax, sounding alarmed.

'I'm not going to shoot her, just make sure she doesn't grab the rifle,' replies Dayna. 'Well?'

Jean has picked up the photograph. 'It's Marine Court,' she says. 'St Leonards-on-Sea, in Sussex. I don't know what that has to do with—'

'It's where they live. Liam's people,' says Dayna.

'Calm down, OK?' says Jean. 'I don't know any Liam. I was passing on my way to Hastings Old Town, and I liked the building, so I stopped and took a photo. That's all.'

'Sarge, it makes sense,' says Jason. 'She's not one of them. How'd she get all those pictures? And the dog? There weren't any dogs there. Evie never saw her before.'

'If she was passing, they would have come down to get her,' says Dayna. 'Like they got us. Why didn't they? What if she's one of their scouts? They have scouts, Jason, to find more Eves for him. They told me. What if that's why Evie's never seen her? Maybe the pictures are just her cover. A way to get people to trust her.'

Dog is straining against the rope, jumping, barking.

'I don't know what you're talking about,' says Jean, calm as calm. 'But you can just leave, can't you? Just go your way and I'll go mine. I don't care about you, or Liam, or any of that. I just want to collect pictures. So leave. I won't follow you.'

'We should go,' whispers Jason. 'The dog's making too much noise. Things might be coming.'

Dayna nods. She hates being this afraid. She hates not being able to trust people.

'Get the gear,' she tells the others. 'I'll stay here and watch her. Go to the main street. I'll run after you as soon as you're there.'

'She's not gonna come after us, Sarge,' says Jason softly. 'Not with that limp.'

'She might set the dog loose.'

Jean makes a noise between a sigh and a snort. 'Of course I wouldn't do that.'

'Just go, Jason. I'll be right behind. Take my rucksack too.'

'Liam must be a nasty piece of work if you're this afraid of him, tough girl,' says Jean as the others set off.

There seems little point in denying this, but Dayna does it anyway. 'I'm not afraid.'

Then, after a moment's hesitation: 'I'm sorry if you're not one of them. But I'm not taking the risk.'

'All because of one photograph?'

'If you were that close to them, they would have seen you. They would have come out to get you.'

Jean shrugs. 'They were probably afraid of Dog. Dog and the rifle keep away most unpleasant things. Sometimes the way you present yourself is enough to scare people off. That's why I keep my hat low, so people won't see straight away that I'm a woman.'

Dayna bites her lip. It's plausible, especially, the bit about the hat. If Liam's people had seen a man with a dog, they might not have bothered. Not if he had a rifle. For a woman, they might have taken the risk … But how is she to know? She trusted Rena on that first day on the beach. She trusted Ryan and Mart.

'I just don't want to risk it, you know?' she repeats.

'It's fine. You've given me the chance to show off my collection, which I appreciate. And you're not planning to rob me, as far as I can tell.'

The others have reached the main road, just visible behind the trees' thick branches. Pax is waving at Dayna.

'I have to go,' says Dayna. She hesitates, then adds: 'If you come across people calling themselves the Hummingbirds, don't trust them and don't go with them.'

Jean nods. 'All right. Thank you. And I won't be trusting any Liams either, I can tell you that.'

Dayna lowers her slingshot. 'It was … it was nice to see the pictures. I really hope you're who you say you are, and I hope you'll find loads more pictures for your archive.'

'Thank you,' says Jean again. 'You take care now. I won't

untie Dog until you're out of sight, and I'll leave him on the rope for a while longer until he calms down.'

Dayna nods, then she turns and races through the tall, dry grass, towards Pax and the others.

No one speaks as they walk away from the park. Dayna knows Pax and Jason both think she overreacted, that Jean is who she says she is. She's beginning to think so herself.

'I just … I didn't want to risk it,' Dayna finally says into the silence.

Jason looks up at the sky instead of at her. 'It's clouding over,' he comments. 'Might be a storm later.'

'She was nice,' says Evie. 'I don't think the dog was a hell-hound. He's not barking now.'

'Either way we should be moving,' says Dayna. 'We're here for Father.'

'You know,' says Jason, his eyes still on the clouds, 'she didn't ask us a single thing about ourselves. Not even what we were doing here or where we were going. She didn't really care about any of that, I think. She only cared about the pictures.'

'I wish I coulda seen that King Kong,' mutters Pax morosely.

They walk on in relative silence, for the next hour or so. The streets go on and on, but the skyscrapers in the distance don't seem to be getting any closer. Like the city is under a magic spell, safe from intruders.

'I'm thirsty,' announces Evie.

'It'll rain soon,' says Dayna. 'We can set up a water trap then. Let's just try to get further in before it starts.'

'Jean had water,' says Pax, unnecessarily.

'Shhh,' hisses Dayna.

'Shush yourself. It's all your fault, Day. She wasn't—'

'*Shhh!* Look.'

She points to it, not twenty paces away, half-hidden behind a rusty car. It's nibbling at the wild grass curling up through the cracks in the pavement. A doe, and she looks beautiful.

'I'll kill her,' says Dayna, as she slowly, slowly, takes out her slingshot. The doe, oblivious, continues to graze.

'What?' demands Evie, outraged. 'No! Don't kill her, I'm not hungry!'

'We just ate,' says Jason. 'We don't need—'

'We'll get hungry again,' says Pax. 'Soon.'

Dayna draws the rubber band back as far as it will stretch, closes one eye. Aims—

'I DON'T WANT YOU TO KILL HER!' screams Evie. She leaps forwards, yelling: 'RUN RUN RUN!'

The doe jerks up and darts away and is gone before Dayna has even taken her next breath.

She groans in exasperation and rounds on Evie: 'You can't just—'

'*Day.*' Pax's sharp whisper is urgent, and it makes her shut up at once. Now she can hear them too: footsteps. Someone is coming.

34

It's three men, and they look like monsters. Not crazed, just scary. The hollows around their eyes are black, and there are black vertical lines over their lips, as if they were sewn shut at some point, then cut open again. Two of the men's heads are shaved, but the third has long, scraggly hair hanging down past his shoulders. They're dressed in different mismatched clothes, not uniforms, so they aren't Hummingbird soldiers but something else.

Dayna watches as the three men stride down the road, past her hiding place, further down the street, towards the spot where the kids were just before they fled. The two bald men are dragging a dead animal behind them, its throat slit, leaving a trail of its blood on the asphalt in their wake. At first, Dayna thinks it's their doe, but then she sees the animal is a horse. Its eyes are open and bulging and a milky pink.

What are these men doing with a dead crazed horse?

Then one of the men, the one with the long hair, makes Dayna jump badly: 'HELLO-OHH!' he bellows in a sing-song voice, revolving slowly on the spot. 'Anyone here?! Come out, come out, wherever you are!'

Dayna creeps backwards, out of sight. They heard Evie yell. They know that at least one child is out here, somewhere.

'Last chance!' the man's voice yells. 'Last chance before we come to look for you!'

Then, quieter, to the others: 'Looks like we've got ourselves a game of hide-and-seek.' He sounds excited. Gleeful. 'Leave that here, we can pick it up later. Oh yes yes YES! This is turning out to be a GREAT day!'

'Same terms as always?' another man asks.

'Winner gets a week, participants split the reward. Game over by sundown.'

'Good by me.'

'Me too.'

'Aaaaaaaand ... GO!'

Banging, smashing not five houses further up the road, intermingled with the men's whoops and laughter. And Dayna, horrified by the quick turn of events, runs back to the stairs where the others are crouching in the shadows. They've hidden in a concrete building with a red circle above the entrance, cut in two by a narrow blue rectangle. The building looks small, but the word on the blue rectangle says UNDERGROUND, which was why Dayna chose it. And the stairs do seem to go down for a very long way; you can feel the vast space, even though you can't see much of it in the darkness.

'It's three of them,' Dayna tells the others. 'They're smashing up houses, can you hear them? Looking for us. But like it's a game. We have to leave. Now.'

'Oh shit oh shit oh shit,' whines Jason. 'It's one bloody thing after the other. They weren't supposed to be *here*.'

'Where are they, Day?' asks Pax. 'Where do we go?'

Dayna points below, where the steps are swallowed up by shadows. 'Underground.'

She knows that there used to be underground train

tracks in London. Tunnels like mole burrows. Connecting all places.

Jason gapes at her. 'You can't be serious? You want to go there, where we'd be trapped? There's no place to hide if they come after us down there.'

'They won't. They heard Evie. They think we're kids. Or at least one of us is.'

'We *are*,' hisses Jason, sounding panicky.

'Yeah, but they wouldn't think we'd go down there.'

'They wouldn't think at all! They don't think straight, they're crazy!'

'I'm not going down in the dark,' whimpers Evie, close to tears.

'Wouldn't we be faster on the street?' asks Pax. 'If it's only three of them—'

'Shut up, all of you,' orders Dayna, feeling panicky herself now. 'Any second, one of them might come here to look. We go down *now*, and we hold hands, and no one says a word. We walk slow and quiet. No arguing, there isn't time.'

She pulls on her rucksack and grabs Pax's sweaty hand. 'I'll go first. Jason, you go last. A hand squeeze means stop, OK? You pass it on to the next person.'

Pax grabs Evie's hand. Evie's gropes for Jason's.

'Two squeezes mean go again.'

A loud crash of glass that must be the building right next to theirs. Jason takes Evie's hand.

Dayna nods. 'OK. One step at a time. Both feet have to be on the same step before you go on, OK? And don't be scared of the dark, Evie. We've got torches, and we'll turn them on as soon as we're somewhere they can't see us.'

She takes a step down, and then another, and another.

Pax follows, one step behind. And then Evie, and then Jason.

    Step.

        Step.

            Step.

It's getting darker and darker and then, suddenly, there's nothing, only blackness.

Don't be scared of the dark.

Don't be scared of the dark.

Easy to say. But this isn't dark. This is blindness. Dayna is blind. They've all gone blind.

    Step.

        Step.

            Step.

She wants to squeeze Pax's hand to reassure him, but if she does that, he'll take it for a signal to stop. The steps are just a little too steep. Dayna knows that they used to move in the old world – carry people up and down without them having to do a thing. They used to be alive and magic. Now they're just dead and cumbersome and feel wrong.

The stairs are endless. They go on and on, down and down. There are no turns. And then she hears it. Heavy footsteps far away, far above. Excited panting. If he'd been quieter, she would have missed it. Dayna squeezes Pax's hand and he stops immediately. He must have squeezed Evie's hand, and she Jason's, because they all fall still. She can hear their frightened breathing behind her, can feel Pax's hot breath on the nape of her neck. Oh please, she thinks, be quiet. He mustn't hear.

'HELLOOO!' a man's voice bellows. Pax's hand twitches in Dayna's. A small whimper escapes Evie but luckily it is lost in the echo: 'HELLOOO-OOOH-OOOH-OOH-ooh-ooh.'

The man laughs in delight. And shrieks again: 'ANY KIDDIES HEREEEEEA? HEEA-heea-heaa?'

He's mad, thinks Dayna. Crazy, as Jason said. Jason ... why did he say that? As if he knew who they were. If the man shines a torch beam down, will it reach them? Maybe she was wrong to make them stop. They should have used the echo as cover to get further away ...

But there is no light from above, not even any sound.

Has he left with the echo?

Is he listening?

Dayna stays put, and the others do too. How long?

Outside, the other men (or maybe all three of them again?) are still whooping and demolishing.

Dayna counts to sixty. And then she counts again.

And then she squeezes Pax's hand twice, and they set off once more. Step by step. Even if he was listening, maybe he wouldn't hear their shuffling.

The sounds above become more and more distant. The air becomes thicker, and hotter. Pax's hand squeezes Dayna's, once, and she stops, alarmed. His breath tickles her ear as he whispers into it: 'Evie's scared we're going down to hell.'

Dayna rolls her eyes, although none of them can see that, of course. 'We're going to the underground train tracks,' she breathes in Pax's general direction. 'City people used to go there all the time. Not hell.'

She hears Pax relate the message, so quietly she can't make out the words, even though he's right behind her. Then, two seconds later, he squeezes her hand again, twice this time.

Dayna's knees are sore and trembly when they finally, finally reach the bottom. She hoped her eyes might have adjusted to the dark just a little, but she's still as blind as ever. She stretches out her free hand and waves it in front of her, shuffling forwards and pulling the others after her. She can hear tiny patters darting around them. Rats, probably. If a crazed rat gets them in here, before she manages to turn on the torch, they are finished …

Her hand knocks into something solid and cold. A wall. Good. With this to guide her, she can quicken her pace. Along the tiled wall, which curves into a different direction. Down a slope; are they far enough away yet? Can they turn on—

Dayna steps into thin air and tumbles forwards. Pax tries to wrench her back, but only half succeeds. She stumbles down even more invisible steps, then finally loses her footing and crashes hard. Loudly. It can't have been far, but everything hurts. Bright spots flare up in the darkness, and she panics, thinking it's the men with torches, come to get them. And then the spots vanish. And then there's an even brighter light as Pax turns on his torch.

'Day?' He rushes to where she's sprawled, maybe ten or twenty steps below him. What is the point of having only a few steps after those thousands and thousands? Who would have expected it?

Jason and Evie are there too, all crowded around her as if she has just done something brave rather than stupid.

'You OK?' whispers Pax.

'Anything broken?' asks Jason, vaguely wiggling her arms.

'Ow, stop that,' snaps Dayna. Or she wants to snap, but her voice has gone shaky. She has to screw up her eyes against the new brightness. 'I'm fine. Just got the wind knocked out of me.'

'I said this place is bad,' whispers Evie.

'You think they could've heard?' asks Dayna. 'Pax, turn the light off.'

'No, leave it on,' says Jason. 'We've turned at least one corner, they won't be able to see any light from up top.'

'If they come down—'

'They won't. They're making way too much noise to hear anything. And we're too far away in any case.'

'And I don't think they have torches,' puts in Pax. 'Or that man would have turned on his torch when he was on the top of the stairs. So it was a good idea to come down, Day. They won't want to go down here, without torches.'

Jason and Pax help Dayna to her feet.

'I can walk,' she tells them, annoyed.

'Sor-reee,' says Jason. 'Only trying to be nice. I won't, in future.'

'Wow, look at this place,' says Pax. He moves the torch beam all around this giant man-made cave. Two long tunnels disappearing into shadow and an inwards-curving outer wall. Benches and boards, lines drawn on the ground, black screens.

'Down here,' says Dayna, and Pax points his torch down into one of the pits to either side. A flurry of movement as rats scatter, revealing the dull gleam of train tracks.

'I'm not going into that,' says Evie at once. 'Not where there's rats. Rats are bad.'

'Don't I know it,' mutters Dayna, thinking of the crazed rat that bit Father.

'Tough luck, because you have to go,' Pax tells Evie. 'We all do.'

'I won't. I'll stay here and then go back up when the men are gone.'

'All by yourself?' jeers Pax. 'In the dark?'

'Pax, light up that board over there,' says Dayna. 'To your left.'

Pax swings the light over to it and they all four study the complicated map right in the centre of the platform, consisting of different coloured lines and names.

'Well, they could've made that more simple,' comments Pax. 'How're you supposed to find anything here?'

'We have to be somewhere here,' says Dayna, indicating the bottom of the map. 'That's south, and we're in the south-most part of London. And we want to get to a train station.'

'It's sooo many,' marvels Pax. 'Which one would we need, Jason?'

Jason clears his throat. 'We'll figure that out later, let's just get away from the Undead first, OK?'

'The what?' says Dayna at once. 'I knew it! I knew you knew them.'

'Later, OK? Look, try and find Clapham North. That's where we are.'

'How d'you know?' she asks suspiciously.

'Jesus. Because I seem to be the only one who read the sign when we came in.'

'It said: Underground.'

'The other sign.'

'Found it!' says Pax, pointing to a small indication close to the bottom. 'Here. It's connected to a black line.'

'OK, cool,' says Jason as he traces the line upwards. 'That's cool. We can get right to the city centre if we follow it. And then further north too.'

'Which way?' asks Pax. 'There're two directions, aren't there? How do we know which is which?'

'It'll say somewhere,' says Jason, looking around. 'They

used to write down everything here, didn't they? Even mind the gap.'

Dayna reaches into her pocket. 'Or we just use the compass,' she says, shrugging.

A minute later, all four of them are in the pit under the sign: *NORTHBOUND* ('Told you,' says Jason), and walking in a straight line. Dayna in the lead, her slingshot temporarily exchanged for the baseball bat. Jason right behind, carrying Evie piggyback while she carries his rucksack and holds the torch, illuminating the way ahead in an eerie half-light with long black shadows. Pax last with his own bat at the ready. Rats scurry out of their way, squeaking angrily, but nothing attacks them.

Dayna finds, to her relief, that she isn't afraid. Rats are dangerous, and crazed rats would be more dangerous still. But these are dangers she knows how to handle, and what to look out for. In narrow, confined places like this, they'd hear the craze coming from a long way away. Dayna can handle that. But not those men.

'Who are they?' she demands, giving Jason a quick glare before turning back to the shadows ahead. 'And why didn't you warn us?'

35

'I don't really know them,' says Jason. 'But I know *of* them. Did you see their faces?'

'Yes.'

'Black circles around their eyes? Jagged lines over their lips?' supplies Jason.

'Yeah.'

'Then it's them, all right. They call themselves the Undead. Those markings you saw? They paint that on themselves; they're supposed to look like a skull. You know, like the hollow sockets and the grinning teeth. I didn't think they'd be this far south. They hang around East London mostly. The old airport. Canary Wharf, the Isle of Dogs.'

'You say those things like we ought to know what they are,' says Pax. 'What about the important bit: Are they Hummingbirds?'

'No. But some of them used to be Hummingbird soldiers who deserted. They've got a deal with the Hummingbirds, though. They ... if they come across people, they take them to the Station. For the tests. They're also supposed to bring food and stuff, but they haven't in ages. And the people they do bring, they ... rob them before, have their fun with them sometimes. They've been promised the vaccine as soon as it's developed, so they leave the Hummingbirds alone. And the Hummingbirds leave them alone because they're like a sort of small army at their doorstep. They don't have firearms, at least as far as I know, but they've got other weapons, and they're pretty violent. I don't think they really believe in the vaccine any more, or even care so much. They're like … I dunno. Some must be OK, but the way I've heard it, a lot of them think this is the best thing that's ever happened. Like they're free now, everyone can do what they want as long as they're stronger than the other person. But they wouldn't say no to a vaccine, so they do kinda help the Hummingbirds.'

'Why didn't you tell us all this before?' presses Dayna.

'I was going to. Soon. Remember? In the park, before Jean came, I was about to tell you, but then you all went nuts because of the playground. And then I sort of forgot. I didn't think it was that important, anyway. I thought they were only in East London.'

Some rats are following them, Dayna notices. Keeping their distance, but following them all the same. Would they attack, even without the craze? Would they do such a thing?

'How many are there of these Undead?' she asks.

'Maybe thirty or forty,' says Jason. 'Mostly men, some women too.'

Dayna is thinking of Jean and her archive. 'You said they sometimes have fun with people they catch. Fun how?'

'Well, you know … rape.' He mutters this in an undertone, as if Evie, on Jason's back, can't hear every word.

'What's rape?' demands Evie.

'*Shhh.*' Dayna hasn't heard the word before either, but the way Jason says it makes her think of the woman in the car who tried to run and was dragged back. Of Evie's bridesmaid dress, of Liam opening the bedroom door in her nightmare with his crooked-tooth grin.

She can guess what it means. And she hates it.

'There's other stuff too, apparently,' continues Jason. 'I only know what I heard. Might be total bullshit, but the way they went on today … I mean, they hear a little girl yell something, and they go totally berserk. Like it's the best game ever, finding this little kid. I heard they sometimes take people's weapons and give them a head start and then go out after them. That they call it hunting. Stuff like that. But I don't think even they would do that sort of thing to kids.'

'You should have warned Jean,' says Dayna. 'She's heading right into the city.'

'I was *going* to. I really was. I wanted to tell her after we'd finished with the pictures. But then … well.'

Dayna's stomach squeezes tight. Because of her. Because she made them leave so suddenly.

'What if they find Jean and Dog and the horses?' asks Evie anxiously. 'Will they hurt them? What's rape?'

The dead horse flashes in front of Dayna's eyes. It was a dark brown though, and she's almost certain the archive horses were grey and chestnut.

'They're nowhere near Jean,' says Jason.

'She's going into the city,' whispers Dayna. (Her fault.) 'They might find her.'

'I think Jean can handle a couple of them just fine,' says Jason, and maybe he really does, and maybe he only wants to. 'She's got a rifle. And the dog. Look, guys, there's nothing we can do. She can take care of herself, and they probably won't even find her in the first place, OK?'

And Pax says: 'She can't run, with her hurt leg.'

★

They can't run either, in the dark. They walk, and walk, and walk. Along the tracks, past underground stations as black as everything else, among rats. When Pax's torch dims, dims, goes out, Dayna turns on hers. In the second or so of darkness, the rats have come disconcertingly close. They scatter as soon as light flares up again, squeaking and squealing and jumping over each other. From then on, it's much more difficult, but still they keep on walking. Pax begins to recharge his depleted torch (*shumm-shumm-shumm*), but Dayna tells him to stop the noise and concentrate on the shadows. Even Evie is walking now because Jason can't manage her weight any longer. But she walks with her eyes firmly shut, her hand in Jason's, and whenever she feels something brush against her leg, she *shrieks*.

'SHHH!' the others hiss, but it's no good, she does it every time. And a dozen little girls shriek all around them, in the echoey tunnel. Too far under the ground, hopefully, to be heard from above.

'Let's go up.'

'Three more stops, OK?'

'They can't be here, we must've been walking for over an hour.'

'Just two more stops.'

'Sarge, we need light and air.'

'One more stop.'

'I WANT OUT!'

'Fine! Fine! Next stop, we leave.'

And they do.

And step out into a new world.

36

All around them are buildings and towers and structures made of concrete and glass and metal and iron. There are trees and bushes and weeds too, of course, and creepers and ivy are snaking up these things like they do everywhere else, trying to take them back, but it seems like nature will have a long way to go. Some buildings are so tall, you have to tilt your head back as far as possible, and still you can't see the top. It's like the people of the dead world wanted to reach right up to the clouds.

They move through these giants silently, even though Jason says it's very unlikely that the Undead would be here. But it's the buildings themselves, and the abandoned red buses and stranded cars, rusting on the road. It's the towers with the criss-cross structures, shaped like the number seven, with swaying, creaking bits of metal dangling from them; cranes, Pax says, which were used to build things (even more things!). It's the faded posters on the walls, their faces and letters smeared unrecognisable. It's the hundreds and hundreds of small dots on the pavement, marks of chewing gums spat out decades and lifetimes ago, and trodden on, and forgotten all about. It's the gigantic wheel towering above the broad grey river, which Jason says was called the London Eye.

'Why?' asks Pax, and Jason explains that when you got into one of the glass cabins and rode to the top, you were supposed to see the whole city, north and east and south and west.

Because of all these things, all these signs of so many past lives lived, the old world, at the moment, seems more sleeping than dead. And so they are quiet, mostly. Maybe, thinks Dayna, I believe in ghosts after all. If ghosts do exist, they would exist here.

A jagged streak of light illuminates the dark sky just as they're crossing the river on one of the many, many bridges. Evie shrieks. Pax tells her to shut up. Jason tells Pax to shut up, she's only little. And Dayna counts: One-two-three-four-five-six—

Thunder rumbles like a growling monster, poised just over the ghost city: loud and threatening. Hungry.

'We have to find cover,' Dayna calls to the others.

They move quicker, away from the water, away from that streak of lightning in the east. The buildings around them are tall again, taller than any trees, tall enough to draw bolts of lightning ten times over. They have to find cover, yes, but there's no need to panic and rush things and become careless. They have time, and Dayna sizes up the entrances as they pass and wonders which would be the best shelter.

'Let's go inside,' whimpers Evie. 'Before the lightning comes.'

'We're safe as long as there's tall buildings around us,' says Dayna. 'Lightning always hits the tallest thing around.'

'No we're not! Lightning is God and he can always find you!'

'I thought you were supposed to be on God's side,' says Jason, although he's glancing at the dark clouds himself, nervous. 'Mind you, Sarge, it's not a given that lightning will only hit the tall stuff. It doesn't always stick to the rules.'

'Anyway, I *am* on God's side,' says Evie. 'But Liam is too. And Liam doesn't like you. I'm chosen, so I won't die. But you might. Liam talks to God, not me. Liam might tell God to kill you. I don't think Mummy can stop God, even from up in the sky.'

'Oh, you're worried about us?' asks Jason.

'Don't sound so pleased about it!' complains Pax. 'Tell her it isn't true … It isn't, is it?'

'Don't be stupid,' Dayna and Jason say simultaneously, and then laugh. And Pax laughs too, and Evie begins to cry and says wicked people who don't believe die all the time, and so Jason has to try and calm her down and explain that Liam is a liar.

Dayna feels a raindrop on the bare skin of her arm, then another on the bridge of her nose. And then it all comes crashing down, all at once, as if the clouds have suddenly decided to let go of everything they're holding *now*. And rain is everywhere, hammering against glass windows and tin roofs and pavements and walls. Against clumps of Echidna fungus winding their way up a nearby building. Rain is not one of the triggers to set spores loose, but the danger of this happening in heavy downpours is never far from your mind. They run, holding hands, heads bent low, blind and deaf to everything but the rush and thud of water.

Dayna fancies that she might hear Evie shrieking, something that could be: 'See? SEE?!' But if so, it's drowned in the rain.

They find shelter in a grand building made out of once-white stone, with faces and forms carved around its many windows. And inside: painted eyes everywhere, staring at you in the torchlight. It's a whole place just for painted portraits, like Jean's picture archive, but these are only of people. The older kids are fascinated, but Evie shrieks that she wants to LEAVE!, and she won't stop howling, not for Jason's comforting nor Pax's ridicule. On their way out, Dayna glimpses a picture of a smiling woman with exposed breasts that are almost as white as her painted open shirt, and with a sudden chill, she understands, and redoubles her strides, all too keen to leave this place as well. Only when they're back in the storm does Evie quiet down again, sniffling.

'It was the paintings,' Dayna explains to the others, giving Evie a one-armed hug. 'Reminded her of Liam painting all his Eves …'

Five minutes later, they come across another grand building and enter it because Dayna is choosing, and she chooses only the interesting ones. This building turns out to be a theatre, with a vast black space which has frayed red seats all lined up next to one another and descending a slope. Dayna knows about theatre and knows that at the bottom of it will be the stage, but it's too dark to see, and the room is far too big for their torchlight to reach its end. Outside, daylight is fading, and so this is where they decide to stay. In that part of the theatre that has windows and plush-covered seats and little round tables, Pax discovers a small room stacked with glass water bottles and tiny salted pretzels in plastic bags. Not enough to feel properly full, but nice all the same.

Dayna and Pax go down into the vast room with a torch and weapons, and at the very back they find the stage. And on that stage, amazingly, waiting for them: three children's beds. With dusty pillows and sheets and blankets. There are costumes hanging on a rack, with names in plastic wrappers attached to them.

'It's *Peter Pan*,' says Dayna, laughing because Father has told them this tale often. About a boy who could fly and fight and stay young for always. Peter Pan was here! In this theatre.

She beams her torch around and sure enough: There are loose-hanging ropes, which make you soar over the stage in wide arcs if you take a running leap, and if someone is holding the other end. Dayna goes first, with Pax holding, and then they swap, both of them laughing now. But then Pax announces that he wants to go on and on, the entire *night*, which breaks the spell, reminds Dayna, without warning, of where they are. So close. Only one sleep away from the Station, from Father, maybe.

And she says: 'No. Gotta rest before tomorrow. We'll sleep upstairs, out of the dark. Help me with the bedding, we'll take it up to the others.'

Pax glowers at her. 'I wish you'd stop worrying. Why d'you have to make things so difficult when they're not? We saved Father once already, and we'll save him again. We're the heroes, remember?'

37

Another nightmare, always nightmares now. And Dayna is crouching in an animal cage, and opposite her cage is another, with Father inside, she knows it, only she can't see because a man in a white coat is kneeling in front of it, blocking her view. She knows who this is too, Lyle, of course—

(LEAVE HIM FOR LYLE!)

But then he turns, and he has the Undead markings, and his face is Liam's.

Pax is shaking her. 'Day. Day.'

'Hmmm,' murmurs Dayna, trying to push him away. It's morning, and the storm has passed. She can see sunlight behind her closed eyelids; red and bright.

'*Day.*'

'What?'

'That dog. Hear him?'

And she does, the moment he points it out. A dog, somewhere in the distance, barking angrily.

'It can't get us here,' says Dayna.

Awake now, she pushes herself up into a sitting position, rubbing the sleep from her eyes. Beside her, Evie mumbles, 'Shhh,' and burrows further into the blanket.

'What're you two on about?' yawns Jason, rolling over on the floor so that his back is facing them. 'It'd be nice if I could get one decent night's sleep without being interrupted.'

'It's morning,' says Dayna.

'It's Dog,' says Pax.

'I told you, it can't get—'

'No, it's DOG. Jean's dog. That's him barking.'

'Is Jean back?' mumbles Evie.

'I think she's in trouble,' says Pax. 'Something loud woke me …'

Dayna listens to the barking again. 'That could be any dog,' she says.

Pax shakes his head. 'It's Jean's dog,' he says stoutly. 'I know. He sounded just like that when he was barking yesterday.'

'Because all dogs sound alike,' snaps Jason, fully awake now.

Dayna looks at her brother. 'You sure?' she asks.

He nods, and from outside, there's a high-pitched yelp.

The dog stops barking.

'Shit,' says Jason. 'Can't we have one day when nothing happens?'

Pax looks at Dayna. 'We have to make sure Jean and Dog are all right. Please, Day.'

'Are you *insane*?' demands Jason. 'If it *is* them, the Undead have got them. There's nothing we can do, haven't you been listening? These people are really dangerous, you honestly don't want to be seen by them.'

'What about Jean?' persists Pax. 'What about the archive?'

'We're not even sure we can trust her, remember?' Jason shoots back.

'Yeah, we are! I know you thought so too. You're just scared. *Day.*'

And Dayna can only look back at him, helplessly. She wants to say: Leave them. She wants to say: Save them.

'They'll just take her to the Hummingbirds,' says Jason. 'That's where we're going anyway, isn't it?'

'They'll hurt her before! You said. They'll have fun with her. And she can't *run*.'

'Sarge, tell him. Tell him it's a stupid—'

'We did what you wanted at the petrol station, now let's do what I want. Please, Day!'

'Shut up! Let me think.' Dayna jams her fingers into her ears. What to do? What to do? Disjointed thoughts brush past her, linger, are gone. About Jean; one of Liam's people, not one of his people, collector of the past, who has a rifle and a dog, who could be fine, outnumbered, hurt, dead. Dog isn't barking any more. What will happen to the archive? What will happen to *them*? The Undead look like monsters. She's so scared. As scared as she was when she left behind the woman who tried to get away. When she wanted to be safe. When she took the car but left the woman …

In the end, it's this that decides it for Dayna. Because this is the worst thing she's ever done. No matter how scared she is, she doesn't want to feel that kind of shame ever, ever again.

'We go there to make sure she's all right,' she says. Pax and Jason stop their whispered argument at once. Pax whoops and Jason swears.

'If they catch us—' begins Jason.

'They'll give us to the Hummingbirds,' Dayna finishes for him. 'That's where we were headed all along.'

'Let's hope that's about all they do …'

Dayna forces herself to shrug. 'They haven't got us yet.'

'*Shit*,' hisses Jason. 'I hate you so much right now.'

'You can stay behind,' says Pax.

'No, I can't, can I?' he snaps. 'Bloody hell. You better come up with a decent plan, Sarge. As long as you leave Evie well out of it.'

People are jeering; laughing, but in a cruel way that Dayna had never realised was possible. She and Jason follow the sounds, skirting around buildings and cars and shrubs until they reach a pavement clearing. They're not far from the museum with all the paintings, of course they're not, just where the archive *would* go. Hidden behind a gigantic statue of black-stone lions, they peer out on to the scene, and this is what they see:

Four men and one woman, each with drawn weapons (axe, baseball bats, one sledgehammer), grouped around the horses and the van that is the picture archive.

Another two men sprawled on the ground. One looks asleep, the other torn apart. Blood everywhere.

Dog lying there too, on his side. Unmoving.

Jean's outline just about visible behind her attackers, by the van. Not standing, but on the ground.

And a few paces away from them, to the right: a human leg in a green trainer.

The world tilts and spins until someone nudges her. Jason. 'It's not a real leg,' he whispers. 'It's a prosthetic. Plastic. Hers, probably; that's why she limped.'

'I knew that,' Dayna whispers back, although she didn't. The dizziness is subsiding again, the world righting itself.

'You still want to do this?' whispers Jason.

(No.) 'Yes.'

She takes a deep breath, then nods. 'OK, let's go.'

Heart thumping in her ears her throat her whole body,

Dayna walks out from behind the statues and towards the van with Jason close beside her, holding the gun. The gun they found in their stolen car. The gun without bullets.

Dayna's first draft of the plan was to go out alone with the gun, but Jason squashed it, saying that people weren't going to take a young girl seriously, that they might take the risk and jump her. The only way for this to work was if they believed that the handgun was loaded, and that the person holding it was capable of pulling the trigger.

'Bluffing is about presentation,' he said. 'And I present a bigger threat to them than you would.'

So instead of the gun, Dayna is holding her taut and raised slingshot. Which she fires, straight at the back of the shaved head of the closest man. Father taught her to always act first and decisively. Show monsters that you're not afraid from the very beginning. Show them that you're a threat. Back then, monsters were just the crazed, or hungry, vicious animals like wild dogs. Only now does she realise that Father must have been training them to fight other monsters too.

A surprised cry escapes the man as he is knocked to the ground. He does not get up.

That gets their attention. They all whirl around, axe and hammer and bats at the ready – and freeze when they see the gun Jason is pointing at them. Not even the man who has the loop of Jean's rifle slung across one shoulder moves, but when he does, he will be the real threat. Pax was supposed to have— *CRACK*. The man screams as he drops his weapons, drops to his knees, clutching his left eye socket. Pax is a good shot, even at a distance.

'We've got you surrounded!' shouts Dayna (lie). 'And we've got a gun with fifteen rounds left' (lie). 'We don't like to waste the bullets' (true), 'but we will if we have to' (lie).

The Undead flick their eyes to a man with waist-length scraggly black hair, who is standing right in front of Jean. Flick, back to the gun. Dayna recognises him from yesterday, by the underground station. He looks at Dayna, and he looks at Jason, and then he laughs. He laughs so hard he has to bend double, leaning on his bat for support. The bat has been driven through with long, pointy nails.

'What the … ?' he wheezes.

Both of his companions start grinning too, although neither of them moves, and neither of them takes their black-rimmed eyes away from the gun in Jason's hands. Behind them, Jean's two horses paw the ground nervously.

Dayna would like very much to shoot the laughing man with her slingshot just to make him stop (she has five stones in her pocket and a new one in the sling), but it's a lot harder to do, to shoot a man, if you can see his face. And then the man stops laughing of his own accord, as suddenly as he began: He takes a deep breath, and with it he instantly becomes serious.

He straightens up.

He looks at Dayna and Jason.

He says, calm and unsmiling: 'What the fuck is this?'

Dayna can feel her hands begin to shake, she can't help it. They'll ruin the pretence (be calm), they'll fumble any shot she takes (BE CALM). She concentrates on her breathing, in through the nose, out through the mouth. The trembling stops. The fear stays.

Pretend, she wills herself. Pretend you're still brave.

Dayna nods to where Jean is slumped against one of the front wheels of her picture archive. There's blood matted in her hair, dark against dirty blonde. Her lower right trouser leg is flat and crumpled and empty. Her face:

dazed bewilderment, as she stares at Dayna, and stares at Jason.

'She's with us,' says Dayna.

Dayna lays out the terms: 'We're going to go to the caravan and get on and drive off. You lot are going to stand over there, by those lions, that statue. You're going to drop your weapons and stay there until we've left. Or me or one of my friends will shoot you. We've got this gun with fifteen rounds. And we've got slingshots, not just me, but the others too. I won't say how many, but you know it's true. One of them got that man in the eye.' Dayna points to the man who is still on his knees, cursing and moaning. The hands pressed to his face are red with blood.

'Your friend doesn't speak for himself?' asks the long-haired man.

'I do the talking,' replies Dayna without looking at Jason, hoping his expression won't betray them. 'He does the shooting. He's good at it.'

'Where'd you come from?' asks the man. 'A kiddie brigade, is it? Did I hear one of your party squealing yesterday?'

'I'm not telling you anything,' says Dayna. 'Drop your weapons now.'

They don't. Dayna has half expected this and has already briefed Pax. She lifts her slingshot in the signal they agreed to. Two stones come whistling out of the undergrowth where Pax is hiding with Evie, one after the other. The long-haired man is quick, though. He manages to get his bat up in time to deflect the stone meant for him. His friend isn't so fast, and there's another loud, sickening crack. The sledgehammer thuds to the ground as the man crumples beside it.

'You little SHITS!' screams the Undead woman, outraged.

'It's only two of you left now,' says Dayna. Her voice is a little shaky, so she has to stop for a second. Calm down calm down *calm down*. When she speaks again, she sounds more in control: 'Drop your weapons. You might dodge another stone, but you can't do that with bullets. My friend will start shooting with his gun next.' (lie-lie-lie-lie-LIE)

The woman drops her axe, although her expression makes it plain that given half a chance, she would whisk it up and come sprinting straight towards them. The long-haired man gives Dayna one last appraising look, then tosses his bat carelessly in their direction too. It clatters on the weed-strewn ground and rolls almost up to Jason's new trainers.

'Like playing games?' he asks Dayna quietly. 'All kiddies like games. I can't wait until *we* get a chance to play.'

'No thanks,' says Dayna. She's feeling giddy and lightheaded and has to remind herself to keep her slingshot trained on him. (Almost there now, almost there.) 'Go to the lion statue NOW. Go on.'

Jason and Dayna circle towards Jean and the archive, keeping in step with the two remaining Undead who are moving towards the statue. It's like a strange dance. Or a horrible game. Sweat glistens on the skin of the Undead and makes their face paint trickle down in black lines. The man's eyes never leave them, and Dayna is worried that he could crack any second and make a break straight towards them, no matter the gun or slingshots.

She grabs Jean's rifle the moment she's close enough – the man with the bloody eye takes little notice of her or anything else – but Jean, speaking for the first time, whispers: 'There's no more bullets. I used them all up.'

So Dayna has no choice but to slip the rifle's loop

through her shoulder and revert to the slingshot. She was counting on that rifle, but that would also explain why the Undead didn't open fire with it at their appearance. Maybe this is better after all.

Now comes the most risky part: in order to help Jean, one of them will have to put aside their weapon, and that will have to be Dayna because the useless gun is the only thing that's really keeping them at bay.

'Don't let them out of your sight,' she tells Jason as she offers Jean her hand. Jean takes it and pulls herself up.

'I can't believe you just did that,' she says.

'I can't believe it either,' says Jason in an undertone. 'I honestly, honestly can't.'

'Shut up, they'll hear,' hisses Dayna. She wants to give Jean a boost, but Jean says:

'It's all right, I can do the rest.' She turns and finds a hand-hold in the van and hoists herself up and on to the deckchair cushions of her driver's seat in one fluid movement.

'What about Dog?'

'I'll get your leg,' mumbles Dayna, and dashes out to retrieve it. She has to pass Dog on her way there, and again on her way back. She has to make certain, even though she knows what she'll find. She puts a hand on the animal's body. It's warm. It's completely still. All the life inside has vanished. Dayna jerks her hand away and hurries back to the others, clutching Jean's leg (so real-looking, with its skin-like coating) to her chest.

'What about Dog?' repeats Jean, accepting the synthetic leg Dayna gives her without even looking at it. Looking at Dog. And then at Dayna.

Dayna just shakes her head. Jean draws in a sharp breath and lets it out in a little moan.

'Oh no no no no no no no.'

'We gotta go,' says Dayna. She climbs on to the driver's seat, then turns. 'Jason, come on. Give me the gun—'

'No, give *me* the gun,' says Jean. There's a scary look in her eyes and a hardness in her mouth that wasn't there a second ago. 'We should kill them anyway, or they'll come after us.'

Jason shakes his head. 'They'll come after us no matter what,' he says. 'There are more of them. Loads more. We ought to leave, now. Sarge, tell her to leave.'

'Come on, Jean,' says Dayna. 'We have to go. Maybe others are already on their way here. Tell your horses to move.'

Jean is staring at Dog's body. She makes no sign of having heard. Jason hands the gun to Dayna as he clambers on to join them. And in one quick motion, Jean has wrenched it from Dayna and is pointing it right at the two Undead people by the statue, who both flinch.

'No!' shouts Dayna.

'Don't!' shouts Jason.

Both try to grab the gun, but too late—

Click. Click. Click it goes as it fires nothing, air.

'What the—' begins Jean, frowning at the barrel.

'GO!' screams Dayna. 'GO GO GO!'

'SHIT SHIT SHIT!' Jason takes up the reins and throws them up and down, up and down, without any effect at all. The horses whinny and toss, but they won't move.

And the Undead are running now, straight towards them, murder in their eyes. And excitement too. Pax gets one of them with a stone, and they fall, tripping up the other—

'GO GO GO!'

And Jean finally pulls herself together. She tears the reins from Jason's grip and whips them smartly. Dayna doesn't know what she's done differently from Jason's harried attempts, but it works; the horses rear into sudden movement, trotting then galloping then careering down the cracked London pavement at the speed of animals fleeing the craze. And the caravan-archive is being dragged and bumped and battered after them, and Dayna and Jason have to cling to each other and to the bucking seat or risk being hurled off.

'That way!' shouts Dayna to Jean, pointing. 'That way, we have to get the others!'

Jean obeys immediately, and Dayna is knocked into Jason as the caravan turns a sharp right.

'Shit shit shit shit shit!' gasps Jason, his head and torso angled dangerously over the ground whizzing past.

Jean's hand shoots out and grips his wrist and wrenches him back into safety.

'Stop swearing, we're fine,' she pants. 'I can't *believe* we're fine. I can't believe you did all that with an unloaded gun!'

'That way!' shouts Dayna.

'Oh no, really? That's just taking us back ...' But Jean follows Dayna's instructions. Dayna spots them immediately, Pax dragging little Evie along by the hand, both out of breath and covered in small scratches from the thicket. Neither is carrying the rucksacks that were left with them. Pax waves and smiles as if there was no doubt in his mind at all that Dayna would find him.

'Stop!' yells Dayna into Jean's ear. 'They're here!'

This time it's Dayna who almost gets flung overboard at the sudden halt. Jean makes a grab for the back of her T-shirt. 'You *said* stop. Oh my God, I can't believe ... I ... The others had better get into the back with the pictures, the cabin's full of boxes. Tell them—'

Pax and Evie don't have to be told; they are already in the process of doing just that.

'Close the doors properly,' Jean calls out, 'and DON'T touch the pictures!' Then she starts the horses galloping again.

'Do we have any idea of where we're going?' she calls through the wind in all their ears.

'Out,' says Jason at once. 'Out of London. They'll be looking for us now, it's not safe to stay.'

'I've completely lost my bearings. Which way *is* out?'

'West,' says Jason. 'We can't go east and we sure as hell can't go north. Go west!'

'For God's sake! Where *is* west? Left or right or straight ahead?'

Dayna checks the sun up above, already hot and only getting hotter. 'Left,' she yells – and then, to Jason: 'We did it! I can't believe we did it!'

'I can't hear you through this wind,' Jason yells back. 'Oh shit, what a morning!'

38

London is big. The two horses are tiring now, sweat glistening on their backs, and still there's no open countryside, but buildings left and right and ahead and behind, much lower than before, yes, but never ever-ending. Jean decides that the horses need a rest, and says she's pretty sure that no one's following them.

'I'm very sure,' says Dayna. 'And I was watching, I would've seen.'

She jumps from the van before it's properly stopped moving and races to open the back doors. And there Pax and Evie are, and then Pax flings himself at her and talks talks talks all the while, breathless and excited: 'That was AMAZING what we did! AMAZING! You were so brave walking up to them like that, and I was good too, wasn't I? I got almost everyone I aimed at, even that lady when they came charging—'

Dayna has spent the last half-hour trying not to think about the man her stone hit right at the beginning. The man whose back was turned. She knows she had to do it, she had to eliminate threats and make the others take her and Jason seriously. But still …

'You were great, Pax,' she tells her brother. He can't have seen or properly taken in the rifle carrier's eye wound, or he'd be acting differently now. She's glad of that, at least.

'Yeah, you saved our skins back there,' says Jason, who has joined them. 'Especially when they were coming at us, shit, I was so scared I could've wet myself! I would've done too, but I took a piss right before we left. Didn't want to die with smelly, wet trousers.'

They all laugh at that, and then Evie proclaims 'I DID wet myself!' and then they all laugh harder than ever, especially Evie, who seems pleased that she's set them all off. And Dayna's sides hurt and she's unable to stop and it's wonderful. Pax is rolling on the ground, cackling uncontrollably, and Evie is dancing, holding her voluminous T-shirt up so everyone can see her damp underwear, and Jason is bent double, shaking and spluttering. This is good, thinks Dayna. And why should she feel bad about a maybe-dead Undead man, who would have tried to kill all of them anyway, given half the chance? All four of them are still here, and that's the important thing. And they saved Jean. Who is limping up to them now, her false leg back where it should be.

'What's so funny over here?' she asks. Her eyes flick to the interior of the picture archive first, miraculously unruffled and undamaged through all of this, and only then do they settle on the kids.

'She ...' wheezes Pax, and then dissolves into giggles.

'I ...' attempts Evie.

'It's stupid,' says Jason, still grinning. 'I suppose we all just needed a laugh.'

'No, it IS funny,' says Pax, finally calming down. 'Evie can be funny. Only it wouldn't be funny now if we explained. You OK, then?'

'Yes,' says Jean. 'Thank you.'

She doesn't look OK, though. She looks shaken and thoughtful.

'I'm sorry I almost blew it for you, for all of us,' she says. 'I just never thought you'd come in there with an unloaded gun. And I also wasn't thinking at all. God, I don't know what I'll do without Dog. He's been with me through all of this ...'

She sighs, then looks around at them all. 'I'm so ... Thank you, for helping me back there. It was very brave and kind. But –' her gaze settles on Dayna – 'it was stupid, too. Especially with an unloaded gun.'

'I dunno what you're complaining about,' mutters Pax. 'We did it for you.'

'I know,' says Jean. 'That's my point, can't you see? Why would you risk your lives for me? You hardly know me. You didn't even *trust* me the last time we met.'

'Because they were bad people,' Pax says simply. 'And you're not. That's why.'

Jean looks at Dayna, who doesn't speak, and then at Jason, who shrugs. 'You don't have to tell *me*,' he says. 'I know it was stupid. I told them not to, but they wouldn't listen. And I wasn't gonna let them walk into all that on their own, was I? Plus, Dayna's plans usually seem to work. And it worked now.'

And Jean says: 'You can't always play the hero. You'll get yourselves killed.'

'We're not playing,' says Pax indignantly. 'We *are* heroes. We saved Jason, and then we saved Evie, and now we saved you. And we're gonna save Father too, so there.'

Dayna says: 'We'd best be moving again. OK?'

'Give the horses ten more minutes to catch their breath,' says Jean. 'Why does your dad need saving?'

Jason takes Evie's hand and pulls her to a house with a

smashed-in window. 'Come on, let's see if they've got any underwear that could fit you.'

'Careful,' warns Dayna, but Jason is. He takes the empty rifle (holding it like a bat) and he listens at the window before climbing through. Not long after, he has unlocked the front door for Evie.

As soon as they're out of earshot, Jean says: 'Well?'

It's Pax who explains when Dayna won't, and Dayna, listening through an outsider's ears, realises just how impossible it all sounds. Before Jean can make any comment, Dayna cuts in: 'I know what you're gonna say but it's none of your business, it's *our* business. And we're not taking Evie. Not even Jason; he'll look after Evie. But it's Father, *our* father. We *have* to try.'

'Try,' repeats Jean. 'I'm sorry to say this, but it sounds like your dad is probably—'

Pax clamps his hands to his ears and Dayna says: 'Shut UP. It's NONE of your business. OK?'

There's a long, uncomfortable silence. Then: 'I'm sorry,' says Jean quietly. 'I shouldn't have said that. You're absolutely right. It's none of my business. I don't know what's the matter with me, anyway. I never get involved. I just collect my pictures … I won't say any more on the subject, I promise.'

Dayna considers her; a rather small woman, thin and wiry, in dusty, shapeless clothes and an artificial leg. She says: 'Has your archive got a map?'

Jason marks an X on Jean's map of London (finally: a real map, not just lines of roads), to the north-east of where they are, then draws a larger circle around it.

'That's the Station,' he says. 'And the area around it is full of patrols, sometimes drones. If we're doing this, we need to find a base as close as possible, but still outside the circle. Wouldn't hurt to get a car working or something, to have a quick getaway if we need it.'

'We've got the archive,' says Pax.

'Ha!' exclaims Jean. Then: 'Um, hang on. This is cultural heritage, a pictorial documentation of the old world. It's not a getaway vehicle—'

'It can be both,' says Pax, but Jean is shaking her head.

'This is crazy. I know I can't stop you, but you're not dragging me into it. I'm not risking the archive. Or my life, for that matter. I'm sorry, but I'm not. This is exactly why— I may be in your debt, but that doesn't mean I have to throw everything away. If you're really set on this, I'll take you up a little further, nowhere near that circle, mind. But then I'm off. I'm not hanging about for soldiers or psychos or whatever else is crawling around here to destroy it all.'

Her eyes meet Dayna's. 'I'm sorry,' she says quietly.

Dayna forces herself to shrug. She knew Jean would say this, so why does she feel disappointed?

The archive horses take them to a place where brick buildings merge with leaves. Jean halts the van by a flood-swollen stream so that the exhausted horses can drink their fill. She checks the map over Dayna's shoulder and says: 'Circle of doom's coming up. Looks like this is as far as I go, guys.'

Dayna nods. The X is about an index finger's length away from them on the paper.

Jean closes the faded rainbow-striped umbrella that's been keeping the worst of the sun away, then swings down to the ground, favouring her left leg. Dayna hops off too, and helps Evie down just as Jason and Pax emerge from the back, their sweaty T-shirts glued to their chests.

'It's baking in there,' complains Jason.

'Yes, well,' says Jean. 'Not really ideal for conservation purposes, but I can't think of any way around that.'

She opens the van's front door and takes a cardboard box full of canned food out of the space where, in the Before, a driver would have once sat behind the steering wheel.

'Here,' she says, pressing it into Jason's hands. 'Fifty fifty if what's in them is still edible. See how you get on.'

'Wait a minute,' protests Pax. 'I want to see King Kong first, you promised!'

So Jean takes them into her archive and finds every picture they ask for, if she has it. Pax is awed at the sight of the giant gorilla on the top of a high building, with red aeroplanes flying all around him like mosquitoes just like in the story. Dayna asks for the wizard boy with the lightning scar and Bart Simpson and, best of all!, Dana Scully! And Jean has them all. Dayna has never seen her namesake before, and she studies the cut-out magazine picture of the red-haired woman closely, trying to imprint every detail into her mind so that she'll never forget. Next to her, in the picture, is a man who must be her partner in the fight against the monsters. He believes in monsters. She doesn't, but she fights them anyway. Jason and Evie don't know what pictures to ask for, so Jean shows them a photograph she took of Dog as a puppy and a piece of paper with lots of drawings of an ugly boy with knobbly knees and a red-and-black striped jumper, and a postcard of a giant blue eye with clouds floating in it.

It's the best thing ever, the archive. It's like magic.

And we saved it, thinks Dayna.

'Can we keep a picture?' asks Pax. 'Just one each?'

The others all look up hopefully, but Jean shakes her head. 'I'm sorry, but it wouldn't be much of an archive if I started giving things away, would it? What if there's another little boy somewhere down the line who wants to see King Kong, and I'll have to tell him, sorry, but I gave the last one away?'

'That doesn't sound very likely,' mumbles Pax.

'You'd just lose it anyway,' says Jason.

'I wouldn't.'

'You lost all our stuff.'

'I DIDN'T—'

'He *didn't*,' says Dayna quickly because Pax is looking unusually flushed. 'You know it's not his fault – they had to get out fast, didn't they?'

'I know,' says Jason, 'I was only joking, mate.'

Pax just shrugs.

'I like the one with Dog best,' says Evie. 'Can I have him?'

Jean is watching them with a funny expression on her face. 'You're sure about this?' she asks. 'I mean, are you really sure you want to go to these Hummingbirds?'

'Course I don't want to,' says Dayna. 'But I have to. And you said you wouldn't bring it up any more.'

Jean takes all their pictures (Evie surrenders the Dog photo reluctantly) and slides them into a box at random. 'Yes,' she sighs, 'I suppose I did.'

'Aren't you gonna sort them?' asks Pax.

'I'll do it later. I want to be moving again.'

She closes the doors of the archive, turns to them. 'Well. Thank you, for my life. For the archive. I hope it all works out for you. As London's out, I think I'll head to Oxford next. In case … well. I don't think we'll be seeing each other again, either way.'

She takes all their hands in turn, not really shaking, just holding and squeezing. When she reaches Dayna, she says: 'Thanks for saving Mr Smith. The state I was in, I would have left him behind.'

Dayna frowns. 'Who?'

Jean bends down and raps against her prosthetic leg. 'Have you ever heard the joke about the man with the wooden leg named Smith? Ha! Why on earth would you have? Never mind. Take care of everyone. And be careful, all right?'

Then she walks over to her driver's seat and pulls herself up. 'Bye, tough kids,' she says. 'I wish …' But she never finishes the sentence. She gives them one last nod, one last wave, then flicks the horses' reins.

They watch the archive becoming smaller and smaller until it is swallowed up by the leaves of low-hanging branches. Dayna is the first to turn away.

39

They choose a house, make sure it's empty and sealed, open the first of Jean's tin cans, and recoil at the green mouldering mess inside. Dayna reaches for another, but Pax announces: 'Nah, I need to do something after all that sitting. I'll catch us some fish. The stream goes right through this garden.'

'Take Evie with you,' says Jason, with a meaningful glance in Dayna's direction, and is met with protests from both sides:

'What? She'll scare them away!'

'I don't want to watch him kill fishes!'

'Just take her,' says Dayna, giving Pax a little nod so that he can see it's important.

'Well?' she says as soon as they're alone.

'Well,' says Jason, and groans. Next to two mugs with stains of brown tea from a world ago, there is a hardcover book on this kitchen table, with a long title Dayna doesn't understand. Jason pulls it towards him, opens it and tears out the very first page, which is blank.

'What're you doing?'

Jason takes a pencil lying by the last shopping list the person who used to live here ever wrote. Then he begins to sketch what looks like different squares on the torn-out paper.

'OK,' he says, his eyes fixed on what he's doing. 'I could just give you this without telling you how I know, but you'd never accept that, would you? You'd want to know everything, or you wouldn't be able to trust it. So I'll get it over with now.'

'But what *are* you doing?'

'First rule,' says Jason, 'don't interrupt me. And don't freak out again like before. I wasn't lying this time, not really. I just didn't tell you everything because it's none of your business.'

'Go on, then!' urges Dayna, when he doesn't.

Jason adds another square to the paper. 'I said I lived close to the Station, right?'

'You hardly said anything at all about that.'

'Yeah, cos I'm not good at making stuff up, and I didn't want to tell the truth. So, here goes. I grew up at the Station.'

'… Oh,' says Dayna: a breath of expelled air, nothing more. She opens her mouth, then shuts it again.

'I was … my father is a scientist. He works there. He's actually one of the top scientists. All the doctors and scientists were allowed to take their families to the Station. My dad took me and my mum when everything went to hell, but my mum got sick pretty early on and died. I was six. That's not so young, but I still don't remember anything from before. Only the Station. It seemed normal to me. There were other kids, a bit more right at the beginning, but some left and some died. In the end, we were five kids in all, although the others were a lot older. It was nice. Comfy. Nothing like out here, stuck back in the Middle Ages. Running water, *warm* water, electricity for lights and fridges … good food. There's a deal with this farm family—'

Experiments, thinks Dayna, and only when Jason answers does she realise she's spoken aloud.

'I didn't know about that, did I? Not when I was younger. All I knew was that my dad and the others were looking for a cure. And that they would save the world, and I was proud to be connected to that. About a year ago, Dad decided I was old enough to know what was going on. We went into the restricted area. It was horrible. All I was expecting was high-tech science labs, but there was this long corridor with prison cells. They have glass doors instead of bars and there are proper beds and desks and bookshelves and even pictures on the walls, but they're still prison cells because the people inside are locked in. The ones I saw didn't know that, though. The ones that were awake waved at Dad when he passed, then went back to reading or whatever. Dad waved back and smiled. He said that all of these people had been given a different dose of their current vaccine, and I was like, oh wow! You mean you already found a cure? And he said no, of course not, they'd already developed loads of potential cures, but nothing was working yet, which was why they were stuck on the human trial stage. He was smiling at the people like he was their best friend, and then he said to me that he seriously doubted that any one of them would survive, but that every new failure was a step in the right direction, or something like that. Then he said: Don't worry, they can't hear me through the glass. It's soundproof.

'And it really was because in the second-to-last cell was a woman who was crying and yelling so much she was red in the face, but I could hardly hear anything. And the other patients – that's what Dad called them – they definitely couldn't hear. They were right next to her cell and smiling and thinking everything was more than great, and they'd lucked out finding these doctors with the cure, and there she was, screaming and screaming and crying, and they didn't know. Dad said to me that she was one of the patients who knew that they still had a long way to go with the vaccine, and that was the first time I twigged that people were being held there against their will. Not the smiling ones; they'd been found by our recon soldiers and told about this vaccine and believed it, but if they suddenly got second thoughts, you could bet that they wouldn't be let out either. You know what the principle of making a vaccine is? It's trying to find some substance of the disease that's harmless to put into the body so that it can produce antibodies so that the actual, dangerous disease won't take hold. Only problem is, they haven't found any part of the Echidna that is harmless. Get it?'

'No,' says Dayna, whose head is hurting.

'Whatever. Doesn't matter. Anyway, all the so-called patients wind up dead eventually. If it's not the experimental vaccines, it's other stuff – like sometimes the doctors will actually infect them with the pink rabies so that they can study how it affects the body or how it differs from infected animals. Shit like that. It's messed up. But they all say it's for the greater good. And I just couldn't stand it after a while, just knowing that that was what they were doing. It was driving me nuts, making me sick. I started dreaming that I was the one locked in the cells and that Dad was on the other side nodding and smiling, but I knew he was going to do something horrible to me. I had that dream a lot. Still do sometimes … I started avoiding people and just staying in my bedroom the whole time. It was miserable. I kept on thinking about those locked-up people. And honestly? That nightmare? It wasn't just a nightmare. I started getting afraid that my dad really would use me as one of his guinea pigs as soon as they didn't have anyone any more. It was like he hated me. Because I think it's wrong, what he and Dr Lyle and the others are doing, and he thinks it's so right. He thinks it's his life's mission … Often there'd be weeks without anyone in those cells at all; it's not like there's that many people left, right? One morning I just cracked, I think. I woke up from that nightmare again, and it was a really bad one, and I suddenly knew I had to get out, or I'd go mad. So I did.'

Jason glances at Dayna, then looks down at his half-finished sketch again. He's stopped drawing. Dayna is chewing her lip. Finally, she says: 'You could just walk out of there?'

Jason snorts. 'Trust you to keep your priorities straight. Yeah, I could just walk out. But that was because I was the Eggman's son. They all knew who I was, didn't they?'

'The Eggman?'

Jason shrugs. 'That's what everyone calls him. He's got a bald head, like an egg.'

'Tell me how you got out,' persists Dayna. 'It's important for now.'

'Fine, but it won't help you much. I wasn't allowed out of the compound, but I just told them my dad had said I had to, to toughen me up. I said he wanted me to go hunting. And the soldiers at the gate—'

'There're soldiers at the gate? Like guards? All the time?'

'Yeah. And they let me pass straight away. Weren't even the tiniest bit suspicious. I took one of their vans. Ended up a write-off after Mart ran me off the road. I was heading to the south coast. If I'd made it, I would've followed it westwards. Cornwall seemed pretty far away from the Station.

But that wasn't on the cards. They caught up to me the next day, Ryan and Mart. They were on a recon and happened to be closest, but there must've been at least three others in the area. I didn't know about the GPS trackers in all the Hummingbird vehicles, but that's how they found me, once people'd worked out I wasn't coming back. I was so slow, kept on being turned around by fallen trees and stuff. I'm surprised they didn't catch up sooner. It was a pretty pathetic getaway, all in all. Shit, the soldiers must've really hated that, being sent out to bring back a runaway kid. You saw the way Ryan beat me up, right?'

'Wouldn't your father have punished them?' asks Dayna. She thinks of Jason when she first saw him: the closed eyelid that looked more like a plum than an eye, it was so purple and black and swollen; the bruises.

Jason shakes his head, shrugs. 'Ryan also made a show of taking the detour to pick up you and your dad. To make the trip worth it, he said. And then, when the mist came, and your dad had shot someone, good old Sir just couldn't be bothered any more.'

'Who?'

'The sergeant. I call him Sir in my head, yes sir, no sir, may I lick your boots, sir? That was him shouting, right before the Echidna was triggered.

(LEAVE HIM FOR LYLE!)

'Probably told Dad that I'd died in the mist. Probably assumed I had. Fair assumption, really ... Sarge?'

'What?'

Jason is looking nervous. 'Your plan, for getting your dad out ... there's one way that might work. You know that, right? But you're not gonna do it, are you?'

'What?' repeats Dayna, mystified. Then: 'You talking

about a swap? You for our father? I was actually just thinking about that.'

Jason opens his mouth, clearly horrified—

'No, no! Not for real. Are you stupid? We're not gonna betray you!' Dayna is indignant – does he really think this? 'No, but there has to be some way we can use this to trick them ... maybe a prisoner exchange and then ambush them?'

'You're joking, right? The Hummingbirds have proper guns, not like the Undead. You're not gonna get anywhere with your slingshots.' Jason's voice sounds weak with relief. Which makes Dayna irritated.

'How can you even think I'd sell you out?!' she demands.

'Sorry.'

'Yeah, you'd better be. And maybe not an ambush, but maybe I cut a dreadlock as proof I've got you prisoner, and will only let you go as soon as they give me Father?'

'Now there's an idea where nothing could go wrong.'

'Shut up. I'll think about it. But I bet I can find something good, now that I know. You should've told me before. Did you really not trust us?'

Jason doesn't say anything for a long long time, and when he finally speaks it's in a small, strangled voice, as if he's trying very hard not to cry. 'I just ... I didn't want to be one of the Hummingbirds. I didn't want my father to be the Eggman.'

Dayna hugs him, even though it feels strange and awkward. Because he needs it.

'Doesn't matter,' she says. 'You're *our* family now.'

40

Dayna watches over Jason's shoulder as he finishes his drawing. The torn-out page fills up with interconnected squares, long and squat and big and little. Two of these, one on top of the other. A layout. With scrawled words to label the different rooms. It takes Dayna a while to decipher these, but when she finally works them out –

Canteen
Sleeping quarters
Rec room

– excitement flares up inside her. It's all here.

Lab 1
Lab 2
patient rooms/holding cells

'Oh, Jason,' she whispers. 'This is perfect.'

'Yeah? I dunno what help it's gonna be. You'd have to get in first. Look here –' He flips over the page and draws a rough sketch – a square surrounded by a bigger square. 'This is the outer wall. And there are guards, 24/7. You'd never be able to get in without anyone seeing. A bit of bad luck and the drones might spot you before you've even reached the gate anyway. They've got thermal imaging.'

'I can dodge drones, easy. You mean people on patrol, right?'

Jason sighs in a very exaggerated way. 'No, I mean *drones*. They're like, um … sort of like big metal insects. That can fly. They have cameras and their operators can see through the cameras. They can also see body heat. No hiding from that if you're in the open.'

'Spy flies,' mutters Dayna.

'The Hummingbirds have three that still work, and they use them to secure the Station. Make sure nothing bad comes too close. I do realise that you and Pax aren't gonna qualify as anything bad, at least to them, but you'd be two fresh guinea pigs, wouldn't you? Before Mart and Ryan picked you up, I actually didn't think they'd be shitty enough to use kids too, but well. Seems like I was a bit too optimistic about the human race in general, cos here we are … And *done*.'

He hands her the finished Station layout.

'Knock yourself out coming up with a plan for this. There used to be more entry points, but most of the outer doors have been sealed off now. Bricked shut.'

Just then, the front door bangs open with unnecessary force. Both Dayna and Jason jump up out of their chairs, Dayna already reaching for her slingshot – but it's only Pax and Evie.

'You done talking about stuff we're not supposed to hear?' asks Pax crossly.

He's holding four dead trout by their scaly tails. Evie is pointedly standing as far away from him as she can.

★

They build a small campfire in the overgrown garden, made up entirely of the tiniest twigs so that it is near to smokeless. The trout are hot and tangy and delicious; even Evie wolfs her share down, after Jason fillets it for her. The back of this wild garden has become a riverbed, and Dayna finds a pot in the kitchen, fills it up and puts it on the fire to boil for fresh drinking water.

When Jason and Evie move away to wash their hands in the river, Pax leans in to his sister and whispers: 'So? You are gonna tell me what he said, right?'

'Just some more scary stories about the Station.' Dayna shrugs. 'You don't want to know, at least not now. And he told me ... doesn't matter. Jason thinks it does, but it doesn't, not any more. I'll explain later.'

'What do we do now? Do we go straight to the Station?'

'No. Jason drew me a map. I'll have to think about it before we do anything.'

'OK. I can't believe Father is so close. We will save him, OK? You said before we'll *try*, but we *will* do it. He'll be so happy to see us, Day. He won't have been expecting it at all, and then: BAM! There we are. He'll be so happy, he'll forget to be angry that we broke the rule.'

'I broke it, not you,' says Dayna. 'I was in charge. I was so stupid. Father warned and warned us against strangers, and I still trusted Ryan straight away.'

'The walkie-talkie was my idea, Day. If I hadn't said that—'

'You only wanted to help Father.'

'So did you. If it's not my fault, it's not your fault, either. OK? Don't be sad. Father will understand.'

'OK,' says Dayna. She knows he's right; one way or another, Father will understand. If they can only get to him ...

Pax nods, satisfied. 'Cool,' he says, and she has to laugh.

'And after it's over,' he goes on, 'we'll find a new Blue House somewhere. Us three like always, and Jason and Evie too. And we'll set up traps all around it so that no one can sneak up on us. You know what, Day? I think the warning traps at the old Blue House were meant for bad people just as much as for crazed.'

Dayna's mind has been so focused on what is ahead that she has not thought back at all, except to long for what is lost. But now that she does, what Pax is saying makes sense. Hide and wait for my signal, Father used to tell them whenever one of those traps was triggered. Did wanderers ever stumble across them, only to be scared away by Father? She doesn't like the idea of him lying to her and Pax, even if it was only to protect them.

Pax pokes at the fire with a stick for a while, then says: 'Day? Was Mother in your rucksack? Is she lost now?'

Dayna smiles. 'No, she's in my pocket. You want to hold the photo?'

'Not now, my fingers are all greasy. But I'm glad she's still here.'

After all the fish has been eaten, and the water boiled and divided up into their plastic drinking bottles to cool down, Pax and Evie fling off their clothes and splash into the sluggish stream, and Jason sprints in after them to yank Evie into a shallow part. Dayna rolls up her trousers and wades in up to her knees, savouring the cool wet too.

'Come on in, Day,' calls Pax, bobbing up and down in the water.

Dayna thinks of Rena and the bathtub, of Liam painting the naked Sachiko, and shakes her head firmly. 'Not now,' she says.

Jason, who has stripped to his shorts and is wading in himself, pauses to look at her. 'Court's long behind us,' he says. 'But just leave your stuff on, if you'd rather. Clothes dry quickly in this heat.'

'What's the Court got to do with anything?' asks Pax.

'Nothing, that's my point.' Jason pushes a jet of water in Pax's direction with the palm of his hand. Pax retaliates immediately, delighted.

'You're too loud,' says Dayna. 'You'll attract the crazed, and then you won't even hear them come.'

'OK, OK, no more splashing, guys,' says Jason. 'But seriously, Sarge. Try to have some fun, OK? You do realise this might be the last peaceful afternoon we have before it all goes to shit?'

'Yeah,' says Dayna, turning back to the house. 'Which is why I'm going inside to try to work out a plan, exactly so that won't happen.'

Evie calls after her: 'You have to use me in the plan too! I'm chosen, I can help best!'

So while the others splash and play outside, Dayna goes back inside and sits at the table in front of Jason's layout, and tries to think. But instead of plans and ideas, there's a question in her head, an endless whisper like the repeat-repeat-repeat Hummingbird lie on the radio: What if we can't? What if we can't? What if we can't?

No other choice, Dayna tells herself. No other way.

And Evie SCREAMS.

And before that scream is finished, people begin shouting. And those voices are strangers' voices, adult voices, dangerous voices. And they are loud. And they are close.

Dayna's chair topples over as she jumps to her feet.

Through the glass door leading to the garden, she sees maybe six, maybe eight strangers in sweat-stained vests and faded army trousers. One of them is holding Evie by her skinny left arm. All of them are holding handguns or rifles, trained on Jason, trained on *Pax*. The boys are half in, half out of the water. They're naked or as good as; no clothes, no weapons. No warning, either. Dayna never knew adults could be as silent as this. Although now they're loud, yelling at the boys to COME ON, COME THE FUCK ON!

Jason is shouting too, at them: 'Just take me, leave them they're only kids *leave them alone you shits*,' until one of the men backhands him violently and he stumbles to his knees with a splash. Dayna needs a plan. Quick. *Now.* She tries to think, but fear freezes her brain. All she can do is watch the soldiers and Evie and Jason and Pax, in plain sight, just on the other side of this glass door, not ten paces away should any one of them bother to turn around and look.

And then a woman soldier does just that, and her eyes meet Dayna's, and Jason, nose gushing blood, bellows: 'GET OUT OF HERE!'

And Dayna thrusts the door handle down into the lock position, and turns, and runs.

PART 4
THE STATION

41

Run.
  Run.
    RUN.

Swerve around the kitchen table
  down the hallway
  turn the knob
  through the door
  out

Behind her: a brief spurt of gunfire, an explosion of glass.

She's already vaulting over the rotting gate, making for the trees and shrubs on the other side of the street. Pax and Jason and Evie are caught, and she is running in the wrong direction. But what can she do, with only herself and a slingshot against all those guns and all that noise?

Leaves swishing around her. Thin branches scratching her arms, her face. Whizzing past.

Are the Hummingbirds behind her? She can't hear anything except for the thud of her feet, her own ragged panting.

She's weaving and ducking, darting through holes in the leaves that look only just big enough for her and no one else – and spots the telltale purple-pink only just in time to skid to a halt right in front of it.

The Echidna is spread over and around what looks like a dead cat; its mushroom caps are small but already pulsing with spores. Dayna, wheezing now, bent double, stares at the fungus and thinks wildly: If they come, I'll trigger it. And hold my breath until I've tugged on Anteater.

But no one comes. She's alone.

She closes her eyes, listens hard. Not even adults who can sneak as quietly as these soldiers would be able to move through this wood without a noise. She hears no noise, except for the creatures that belong here. And … far away, the slamming of vehicle doors, followed by the growl of engines. The sound fades almost at once, but still she knows what it means. Pax and Jason and Evie are in a Hummingbird van and the van is on its way to the Station. If there was something to be done, she should have done it already. But she ran. Slipped away, or was allowed to slip away, because they couldn't be bothered. Not now that they have Jason. And two more people to—

(NO. Don't think about that. Think about what you will do. That's why you ran like a hare, so you could be free to *do* something.)

But do what? Do what? And how did the soldiers even find them, supposedly safe on the outside of that circle? What did she miss?

Doesn't matter now. What does she *have*? Her slingshot, her lock pick, her compass, Mother's photograph, in all her various trouser pockets. The crumpled Station layout in her hand. Anteater hanging from his loop. A buzzing in her head. Nothing else. No one else.

She needs to get out of here in case they send people

back to look for her. She needs to find someplace to think. There's a hollowness inside her. It's been there ever since Father was taken, but it's so much bigger now. The buzzing drones on and on. Maybe not in her head, after all.

She glances up, expecting to see a hornets' nest, and spots a black shape in the air above her, partially hidden by tree leaves. Immediately, she ducks down and creeps along a rabbit trail to a part of the wood that is denser. She can't see the sky at all now, but still she hears the thing buzzing. It's following her.

Spy fly.

It can see body heat, Jason said, only she wasn't really paying attention. Too busy being excited about the layout he was drawing. She took in the information and stowed it away for later, for her plan, not for now. Is this how they were discovered? The spy fly saw the heat of their fire, the one they took such pains over to make small and smokeless? It seems likely. How could she have missed that?

She begins to trot.

The park-forest blends back into buildings and cars and street lights. As soon as Dayna steps on to the road, she looks up again, and there it is, the spy fly. Hovering over her, as high up as a three-storey building. A small cube with four spinning propellers. Its buzzing sounds like a hundred angry insects.

Dayna's slingshot is already in her hand, the stone in the pouch, the band drawn back as far as it will go. She fires, and hits one of the propellers, which stops spinning. The spy fly's hovering becomes jagged falling, as the rest of its propellers try to keep it airborne. She aims again, and there is a loud *SNAP*, and her stone bounces harmlessly off the cracked pavement. Dayna stares in horror at the broken rubber band of her slingshot. It took Uncle William weeks before he found the right sort in a hardware store. Father would help them replace the bands whenever they needed replacing. There is still a good supply, back at the Blue House. Nothing here. No one here.

The drone touches down on the street, near the stone that was meant to break it. Dayna slides her now-useless slingshot back into her pocket, feeling sick. Then she walks over to the drone – the size of a large rat under all its propellers – and stomps on it.

At first, Dayna doesn't know where it is that she's going, only that she needs to find somewhere far far away from everything, where she can think undisturbed. She stays clear of areas that are too overgrown. It wouldn't do anyone any good if some crazed animal took her unawares and infected her. She tries not to think about how vulnerable she is out here, without any weapons except for a dull-bladed paring knife she scavenged from a kitchen along the way.

The road, she soon realises, is the road that Jean passed through earlier. It's easy to spot the signs if you know what you're looking for. Bent weeds that must have been crushed under the archive's tyres and righted themselves up again, occasional horse droppings. Dayna follows this trail simply because her friend has already taken it. Also, this way, she can tell herself that she has a specific destination. It's all pretend. She knows very well that there's no chance of catching up to Jean, who is travelling with horses and has a good head start. Even if Dayna found another map and trekked all the way to Oxford, the one place she knows Jean wanted to go to, the chances are still very slim that she'd actually find her. And if she did, what then? Jean would just tell her not to be stupid, and give up on Father, and give up on Pax, and Jason and Evie.

But still, there is something comforting in Jean's route, which is why Dayna sticks to it.

It takes her through small villages and more wild fields, and Dayna knows she will have to stop soon and start thinking, but she's afraid of doing that in case she shouldn't find the solution. So she keeps on walking away from the Station, and keeps on telling herself: The next village. I'll stop in the next.

And then she does stop.

In a small village road with weeds pushing up through the tarmac lies a dead horse with its neck torn wide open and flies buzzing around it.

Dayna edges around the horse, her stomach roiling. The van's tracks are red skid marks until they fade into the street. Dayna is too exhausted to run outright, but she jogs as best she can, following the trail.

'Jean?' she calls. She knows this is very, very stupid. The Undead could be lurking. Or the Hummingbirds, or other monsters. But she can't help herself. 'Jean? JEAN?!'

She turns into a lane dense with trees and shrubs crowding in from the sides, and there the archive is, in the middle of the road. Without horses, without driver. Abandoned, dead looking.

'JEAN?!'

Three houses down the road, a door is flung open, and a one-legged woman hops out into its overgrown driveway, leaning on the barrel of a rifle for support.

She stares at Dayna.

Dayna stares at her. Then she rushes forwards.

42

Dayna holds on to Jean for a long time, and only when she lets go does she realise that she's shaking. And then that she's sobbing too.

'What happened?' Jean keeps asking. 'What happened? What happened?'

Dayna tries to answer, but she can't form words any more, only gulps and whimpers. Jean steers her back into the house. It's difficult for her without her prosthetic leg, and it seems to take a long time until they're in an unfamiliar hallway and Jean closes the front door behind them.

'In here,' says Jean. Then: 'Sit down. Here.'

They sit, side by side, on a dusty, mouse-nibbled sofa, and still Dayna can't stop shaking and sobbing. Jean says nothing more, just holds her tight, and waits.

Finally, Dayna manages to calm down. 'You're a good hugger,' she says thickly as she wipes snot from her nose with the back of her arm. Better than Father. Much better than Pax.

'Well, men are often useless in these situations,' says Jean.

'Hmm.'

'How did you find me, tough girl?'

Dayna shrugs. 'I followed your tracks. And the horse poo.

I didn't think I'd actually catch up to you, though. Are both horses dead?'

'No, just the one. Attacked by an infected fox ... But the other mare panicked. I had to cut her loose, or who knows where she would have dragged the archive to. Probably into the nearest ditch. As it is, it's totally exposed now, and I can't do a thing about it until I find a car that will still work, which could take a while. I'm glad you found me, although I hope the Undead aren't as good trackers ... Now tell me: What happened?'

'It all went wrong,' whispers Dayna.

'Yes, I can see. But how wrong exactly?'

Dayna takes a deep, shuddering breath and tells her exactly how wrong. When she's done, Jean hugs her again. It feels strange to be hugged, and embarrassing, and safe.

'Oh, what a bloody mess,' mutters Jean.

Dayna pulls away to look at her. 'Jean,' she says, 'you have to help me save them.'

'Ha!'

'It'll be so much easier if it's two of us and not one. And you owe us.'

Jean shakes her head. 'I owed you before too, and you didn't ask me to do this. You know what I think of it. It's stupid. Impossible. *Pointless.* Please, you're a clever girl. Think about it. I'll help you in this way: I'll take you with me on the archive, and I'll tell you that there is *nothing* you could have done.'

'You owe us,' Dayna repeats doggedly. 'I didn't ask before because I had Pax and Jason to help. But now it's only me. And I need you.'

Jean is shaking her head. 'I'm unarmed and outnumbered,' she says gently, as if this might soften the blow.

'I can't help you. And even if I could, I have to think of the archive. And even if I didn't, I'm not ready to die for something that hasn't got a chance of succeeding. Please, just stick with me, then no one else has to die.'

'Pax and Evie and Jason will have to die. If we don't do something.'

'I'm sorry. I am. But it's too late for them. We can't do *anything*.'

'You owe us.'

'Will you stop saying that? I never asked ... I never wanted you to help me back then! And yeah, maybe I do owe you, but I'm not just going to throw my life away – my life's work, just for some hare-brained child's fantasy. I'm sorry, but I won't do it.'

'You owe us.'

'You sound like a broken record. But I don't suppose you even know what that is. I owe you, yes. That's why I'm trying to help you. Stay with me; that's the only thing you can do now, to live your life. They'd want that. Wouldn't you want that if it were Pax who'd escaped instead of you?'

Dayna hesitates. 'Maybe. But I'd still know he wouldn't leave me even if I wanted him to.'

'Oh, you stubborn girl! Do what you want. You will anyway, it's not like I can stop you. Just, please, think about it. OK?'

'That's what I wanted to do,' says Dayna. 'I'll think about it, and if I come up with something that could maybe work, will you help me then?'

'I don't—'

'If it makes a difference? If you think it would work? Because you wouldn't be throwing everything away, you'd just be helping us. You. Owe. Us. You keep on talking about the archive, but you wouldn't even have the archive any more if it wasn't for us.'

Jean hides her face in her hands and breathes in and out very loudly. 'All right,' she finally says, her voice muffled. 'All right. This is the deal: If you can come up with an idea that has even a fifty per cent chance of actually succeeding, then, all right. I will help you.'

She takes her hands from her face and looks directly at Dayna. 'I think that extremely unlikely, though. If you don't find a way, you must agree to at least think about coming with me to Oxford. That's the deal.'

Dayna shakes her head. 'No, the deal is: I come up with a good idea, you help me. I come up with a bad idea, you don't help me. That's all.'

'Fuck – sorry.' And suddenly Jean is laughing, a little wildly, but laughing. 'Oh, listen to me, apologising for swearing. Almost as if you were an ordinary kid. OK! OK. You win.'

Jean, wearing Mr Smith the prosthetic again, goes outside in search of a working car that will replace her lost horses. And Dayna spreads Jason's layout and another one of Jean's maps out on to the moth-eaten living-room carpet and begins studying them.

The whisper comes back (What if I can't? What if I can't?), but it's far weaker now and easily pushed aside. Because all the bad things have already happened, she can't make them much worse. And ideas are what she's good at, aren't they? Ever since the first story she invented for herself and Pax to play at, years and years ago, and kept on tweaking and elaborating. They were the heroes in those games, and in the end, they always won. Now she'd settle for just being someone who isn't caught.

Jean returns when the sky outside is orange and pink and the sun is on the verge of disappearing for the night. She's limping worse than ever and looks sweaty and exhausted, but also pleased.

'I found a car,' she announces. 'Well, the battery's capable of starting anyway. Looks like it was only abandoned recently, months maybe. Extremely lucky find. Whether or not it actually runs, I'll see in the morning. I'm not going out after nightfall if it can be avoided.'

'That's great,' says Dayna from her position on the floor. 'That means we have a good getaway option.' She tries not to think of what it means for the people who came in the car. Who might have been following a stencilled hummingbird …

'It means the archive won't be stranded here,' corrects Jean. She falls on to the sofa with a satisfied 'Umph', then starts easing Mr Smith from her lower leg.

'Did you walk very far?' asks Dayna, propping herself up on her elbows to watch. It's very strange, seeing someone take off part of their leg. Mr Smith has clearly been knocked about a bit over the years, but he still looks so *lifelike*. 'Why didn't you just drive the car back?'

'No petrol,' says Jean. 'Maybe the driver just ran out, although I'm assuming that either the psychos or your Hummingbird friends scavenged it. None of the other cars I checked had any, either. I've got half a canister in the archive. I'm not sure how far that can take us, it's not as fresh as it once was, but getting well and clear out of London shouldn't be a problem. And yes, it was far. For me, anyway. It took me over an hour just to walk back. It gets harder the more I walk. Mr Smith isn't exactly the best fit any more. If the old world hadn't gone up in flames, I would have replaced him with a better model long ago. Mmm ... something soft and comfy. Maybe with useless little gadgets. A pedometer, maybe. Yes, a pedometer.'

She makes an odd noise, somewhere between a laugh and a sigh. But when she lays Mr Smith down on the floor, she's very gentle, almost as if he were a living thing after all. Her right leg ends somewhat below the knee, in an inflamed and bruised stump.

Dayna winces. 'That looks like it hurts,' she says.

'Too much walking, that's all.' Jean shrugs. 'The swelling will go down soon enough.' She uses a bit of sleeve to dab at the sweat on her stump. 'Forget the pedometer; inbuilt ventilation is what I'd really go for in this heat. Seeing as I'm dreaming anyway.'

'Where did you find Mr Smith in the first place?' asks Dayna, as Jean begins to massage what is left of her leg. 'Couldn't you just go back there and get something that fits better?'

'Ha,' says Jean, her short bark of a laugh. 'I was consulted by specialists at a rehabilitation centre. This was before the Collapse, fortunately. No chance now. They have to be custom-made or they're no good.'

'Oh. I thought you were attacked by a crazed animal or something. Earlier you said—'

Jean raises a hand to stop her. 'I know. That's what I tell people when they ask. It sounds more impressive, more on par with the image of a survivor. What actually happened is that I was in a car accident when I was in my early twenties. I used to think that that would be the most horrific event in my life by a long stretch. Ha.'

Dayna turns back to the map. Turns back to Jean.

'So, in the morning we see if the car you found works?'

'Yes. And if it does, we'll harness it to the archive. Harness ... I can't think of the right word. I'm too tired. Why don't you go to the archive and take your pick of the cans? How's your master plan coming along?'

Dayna gets to her feet, and stretches, and yawns. 'I think I've got it now,' she says. 'I'll tell you after dinner. And Jean ... what's a pedometer?'

Dinner is porridge and tomato soup, rounded off with fresh apples Dayna scavenged from a tree in their temporary front yard. After what happened with the spy fly, they don't risk a fire outside. Nothing out of tin cans has much taste if it's not warmed up, but the apples are crisp and sweet. Pax would have loved them.

Maybe she'll be with him this time tomorrow, and maybe she won't ever see him again; Dayna won't let herself examine the what-ifs because she'll only wind herself up even more. She has a plan, and she'll either succeed or fail, but she will try.

She explains her plan to Jean as soon as they've eaten their fill and drawn the dusty curtains, and lit up a candle. Its flame makes shadows dance and Jean's face flicker. Doubt, surprise, amusement, unease. Flick flick flick. She listens to Dayna and doesn't interrupt once until Dayna has finished. Then she closes her eyes and leans her head back until it touches the wall behind her, and swears.

'Bloody hell. That actually does sound like a fifty per cent chance. I should have set the bar higher. Seventy at least.' She opens her eyes again, looks at Dayna. 'You're going to get us killed. Or save your friends. Whichever, could be either one. Did you really just think of all of this today?'

Dayna nods. 'See, Jason drew a layout—'

'Yes, yes. I see.' Jean blows up her cheeks and exhales loudly. Then she says: 'This is even more far-fetched than how you saved me from those psychos. Which almost got every one of us killed.'

Dayna shrugs. She's hurt, but she knows she shouldn't be. 'Fine, don't help me, then,' she mutters. 'I can do it myself.'

'Ha,' says Jean. 'And how would you do that? This won't work without me.'

'I made a backup plan,' says Dayna. 'Because I thought you might break your promise.'

'I didn't say that. What's your backup plan?'

'Same as the other one, only I let myself be caught for real.'

Jean groans. 'Oh, God. I'll have to go with you.'

'You don't. I just said.'

'Oh yeah I do. Your so-called backup plan is bollocks, in case you hadn't noticed. Anyway. I did say fifty per cent success rate. You seem to have taken me by my word.'

'You will?' asks Dayna. 'You'll help me? Really?'

'Yes. I must be mad, but yes. Really.'

Relief floods through Dayna like warm water. She hasn't realised before how much she was banking on Jean to be there, with her.

'Thanks.' It's all she can think of to say, even though it doesn't seem nearly enough.

Jean smiles weakly. 'I owe you, don't I?'

43

Dayna is restless that night, her thoughts on tomorrow; getting nervous now. Getting more and more scared. Impossible to stay still, let alone sleep. Finally, she gives up and rolls out of her unfamiliar bed with the faded football patterns on the sheets; a dead boy's room. Dead boy from a dead world.

She wanders down the stairs with a vague idea of poring over the map again, and there is Jean's outline perched on the window seat, her forehead pressed against the glass. She turns briefly when Dayna enters the room, then turns back again.

'Couldn't sleep either, eh?'

'No. What're you doing?' Dayna hoists herself up next to Jean and peers out. Nothing but night and shadows and the endless stars.

'So many of them,' says Jean. 'The longer you look, the more you see ... Did you know, before all this, people living in big cities, like London, couldn't see them at all? Light pollution. Well, no, I'm exaggerating, I think. It's so hard to remember some things. One does tend to exaggerate. We could see some stars. But never like this.'

They're both silent then, each lost in her own thoughts, lost in the stars. And Dayna's thoughts are of Mother.

'My mother was named after the night sky,' she tells Jean now. 'She was called Belinda, which is one of Uranus's moons. And Uranus is one of the planets revolving around this world, both old and new. All its moons are named after people and spirits in stories, and the original Belinda was a woman who had a lock of her hair stolen, and it turned into stars.'

'Oh,' says Jean. 'Right.'

'My mother isn't in the Station, in case you're wondering,' says Dayna. 'She's dead.'

'Yes,' says Jean. 'I thought she probably would be.'

'Why?'

'Oh, just because most people are nowadays …'

'Is all your family dead, Jean?'

'As far as I know.'

'You must miss them.'

'Yes. Sometimes.'

Dayna nods. 'I miss my mother too. Even though I don't remember her. But I still know her, through Father's stories. Do you want to see her picture? I have her photograph. It's from the old world. I was thinking … maybe we could put her in your archive. Not to keep. But in case things go wrong. I'd rather have her in the archive than in the Station. When we get back, I'll take her again. Would that be all right?'

'That's probably a good idea,' says Jean. 'Even though I was hoping for a little more confidence in your battle plan on your side. Let's see your mum, then.'

Dayna reaches into her left knee pocket and pulls out her mother. She smiles at her, and Mother smiles back in return. She passes her to Jean, and Jean does the right thing. She smiles as well.

'How did you save Mr Dreadlocks and the little girl?' asks Jean, as she holds the photograph and looks into Mother's eyes. 'Didn't your brother say that's what you did? You saved them? Like you saved me?'

'Yeah, I suppose we did,' says Dayna. 'Why?'

'Oh, I was just trying to reassure myself that you have a good track record when it comes to saving people. Can you tell me how you did it?'

Yes, Dayna can. And she does. But to do so, she has to explain other things too, things that make her cheeks burn. How Ryan and Mart found them in the first place. How it was at the Court, and why Evie and Sachiko needed saving.

Jean says Liam sounds like a right creep, and it's good they got Evie out. She also says that Dayna has a good head on her shoulders.

'You're trying to make me feel better about tomorrow, aren't you?' says Dayna.

Jean laughs. 'No, I'm trying to make *myself* feel better about tomorrow. And it's working a little. Isn't it working for you?'

Dayna shrugs. 'Dunno. Maybe. I'm still really, really scared.'

'Scared is good. Just means that you're not stupid,' says Jean. Know the consequences, know the risks. You're scared, but you want to do it anyway? Don't think of yourself as scared, Dayna. Think of yourself as brave.'

'You called me stupid before.'

'I know. I'm full of contradictions, aren't I? With this plan, you're only fifty per cent stupid.'

'Ha-ha,' says Dayna, Jason-like.

'Hundred per cent brave.'

Dayna pulls back from the cool windowpane to look at

Jean; a face in shadows, turned to her. How much simpler things seem if you have someone older you can confide in, someone to explain them to you. She'd forgotten.

'I never thought of that. I never thought you have to be scared to be brave … But if I'm brave, then so are you. You're scared too, right?'

'Ha. I am absolutely terrified. So, yes, maybe you're right. Maybe that makes me brave too, a little. Probably it's just my ego trying to keep up with you.'

'Your what?'

'Never mind. Come on, brave girl. We've talked for long enough. Let's get back to bed. Big day tomorrow. Big plans.'

44

The Station is gigantic and grand and looks nothing like what its name suggests. Dayna has seen pictures of palaces in books, and the Station reminds her of a shabby version of these: at the very top of a steep incline, with glass roofs and long windows and patterned brick walls still visible under the creepers. All except for an antenna tower at one of the outer complexes, stretching up like the sky-reaching buildings in the inner city. This must be where the Hummingbird message comes from. The one that started everything.

'Poor Ally Pally,' whispers Jean. 'Like a fortress.'

She means the array of rusty panels set up all around the Station on its hill, and a gate with closed doors facing the road. A Hummingbird soldier stands straight-backed in front of it, alert, his hands on his weapon. Because he's watching them approach, Dayna and Jean.

In too deep to go back and rethink. The thought from this morning, yesterday night. Doubly true now.

'Here we go,' mutters Jean. 'I must be mad.'

'Thanks for being mad,' says Dayna.

'Shh, he shouldn't see you talking to me.'

Jean looks like a different person with her coal-ringed eyes and the lines drawn across her lips. Dayna has snatched many glances back at her during their way here, and still she can't get used to it. How easy it is to become one of the Undead.

Their paved road cuts through a jungle of trees and undergrowth, obscuring everything but the Station dead ahead. They pass an old road sign, over which a stencilled hummingbird has been sprayed in black paint. Under it the lie: *SAFE ZONE*.

(Be brave, Dayna tells herself. Be brave.)

She resists the urge to pat the Tupperware box, tucked deep into her largest trouser pocket.

'Halt, that's far enough!' calls the soldier, advancing. He's young, red-haired, lanky. Dressed as Ryan and Mart were, in a sweat-stained vest and canvas trousers. Small peels of skin are flaking off his nose and cheeks, the remnants of a sunburn that make him look more intimidating than he'd otherwise be.

'Another kid? We picked up three others yesterday. Where'd you find her?'

'In the city,' says Jean, and Dayna is relieved to hear, not the slightest tremor in her voice. Jean is out of Dayna's line of sight, poking the barrel of the unloaded rifle into her back for effect; one of the Undead, bringing yet another captive to the Station.

The sunburned soldier bends down so that his face is all that Dayna can see. 'Those other kids, they something to do with you?' he demands.

Dayna shrugs, her heartbeat urgent in her ears.

'You look scared,' says the soldier, trying a lopsided grin. 'Because of her? Don't worry, your friends are safe, and now you are too. We help people, that's all we do here. We've got scientists here, people trying to find a cure. Don't worry about her, that bunch isn't allowed on the compound. You're safe now.'

He grabs hold of Dayna's wrist with his hand and starts to tug her towards the gate.

'Not so fast,' says Jean. 'I'll need a reward for that one.'

The soldier snorts. 'We've got a deal with the Undead, in case you've forgotten. You're not entitled to a reward.'

'I am for that one,' says Jean, nodding at Dayna. She's good at playing. Maybe anyone would be good if they knew that they'd be dead otherwise.

'Oh yeah?' asks the soldier, in mock sincerity. 'What's so special about her, then?'

'She's immune,' says Jean. 'I saw it. She's what those doctors up there would call the Holy Grail.'

'Immune? How? What did you see?' Under his scorn, there's something else. Excitement? His fingers close down harder around Dayna's wrist.

'She was bitten by an infected animal. She didn't so much as catch a fever. Shrugged it off like it was nothing.'

'Might not have been infected.'

'Oh yes, it was. It bit two other people from my group. Both of them are dead now.'

(Jean, improvising. This wasn't part of Dayna's story. It makes her nervous.)

'Where's this bite, then?'

They've foreseen this, and Jean doesn't hesitate. She points to Dayna's ankle, where Dayna herself has opened up an old scratch wound only this morning. The soldier squints at it.

'That doesn't look like a bite,' he says.

'Well, what can I say? It is,' says Jean. 'I'm not expecting you to believe me without any proof. Test her, you'll see.

But I'm coming with you to make sure I get what she's worth.'

'You're really saying she's immune?' There's definitely excitement in his voice now, and greed too.

And so the soldier lets Dayna and Jean through the gate, and comes through himself, into the compound of the Station. He's not completely careless: He asks Jean for her weapon, and Jean hands the unloaded rifle over at once, setting him at his ease.

The three of them walk up the remainder of the hill. There are only a couple of soldiers outside the building, playing cards, smoking. They look up when the red-haired soldier passes with Jean and Dayna in tow, mildly curious, faintly wary of Jean in her Undead guise, but nothing more. There's a truce, after all, and everyone knows that breaking it would be far too risky. Only one challenges them:

'Oi, Private Carrot! You're on guard duty!'

The private's pallid cheeks flush instantly as the others snigger. They're a lot older than he is, and it strikes Dayna that their red-haired soldier can't be a proper one at all. He's only a few years older than Jason, which would make him far too young at the time of the Fall. Perhaps he's one of the doctors' children who has to be made use of.

'Important business,' the soldier-boy says. 'One of you can keep lookout. Or no one. Nothing ever happens anyway.'

'What business? You want a quick shag with the corpse before you send her on her way?'

'Come on, *go*,' the boy hisses to Jean and Dayna, urging them past the antenna tower as the older men laugh and catcall after them. Through the chipped entrance doors, into a vast hall under a roof of glass, an odd, brightly coloured patterned floor that clashes with the stone pillars. There are sandy marks of a hundred footprints criss-crossing everywhere, but no one in sight. Dayna can hear a buzz of voices coming from somewhere close by, though, purposeful footsteps in the distance. Not since the Court has she been anywhere with this many people all in one place. And look how that turned out …

'This way,' says the young soldier, motioning to the left. He's not holding his weapon (or the useless rifle, slung across his back now), but his hand is hovering close to it, and he makes sure Jean is in front of him the whole time. His eyes keep darting to Dayna as well; she can feel them, watching. Maybe this isn't going to be as straightforward as they'd hoped.

Through a door where the glass roof ends and a staircase and shadows begin. Down a corridor (still no one in sight), until they come to another door, thick and heavy. Dayna knows from Jason's layout where this leads to, and she's ready for it. A narrow aisle, on its left: sturdy doors and big window-walls of heavy glass, reaching from floor to high ceiling. Inside: identical rooms. A neatly made bed, a box-wardrobe, a picture print on the wall. A beach in one room. A sunset over a big city. Green and pink lights in a night sky. Dayna's eyes search these places urgently, but all of them are empty.

Except for the very last.

Where they stop.

45

The first thing Dayna sees is Evie, sitting on a bed, legs dangling. The second thing she sees is no Pax, and no Father. And no Jason, either. Instead of them: a man in a shabby white coat, crouching in front of the bed, his back to the door because he's turned to Evie, talking. His head is completely bald (Eggman, thinks Dayna with a sharp intake of breath), not a bristle of hair in sight. What he's saying they can't hear through the thick glass, but Evie, watching him intently, biting her lower lip, doesn't look frightened at all.

Carrot raises his fist to knock against the window wall – then hesitates, uncertain whether or not to interrupt. Dayna catches Jean's eye: as good a chance as they could have hoped for. Jean doesn't hesitate. She's quicker than anyone would have thought she could be with her limp. She moves in on Carrot – flash – a knife suddenly in her hand. From her sleeve, from nowhere at all. Carrot has just enough time to draw his handgun when Dayna meets him from the other side. She has no weapons because they expected her to be searched. But she has her teeth, and the soldier-boy SCREAMS. It's just like the time when she bit Mart, only it's different too. The boy's hand is dry and cold and hairless, nothing at all like Mart's fleshy hand, but just as revolting. She wants to gag, but instead she holds on tight as he flails and bucks under her teeth, trying to shake her off, sobbing, swearing. And then all of a sudden, a great stillness settles over him, and Jean's voice is saying: 'It's OK now, Dayna. I've got him. You can let go.'

She does, spitting his blood out on to the white tiles of the corridor, wiping her mouth. They haven't even started yet, and already she feels sick and trembly. But she won't show it. (Be brave.) She takes a deep breath and straightens up. Jean is pressing Carrot's gun right into the side of his head. His eyes are wide, and his breath is coming out in quick little gasps. He looks younger than ever.

'Sorry about this,' Jean says to him pleasantly. 'We're just here to pick up a few people, then we'll be on our way. No one has to get hurt.'

On the other side of the glass wall, Evie is jumping up and down, waving and calling something Dayna can't make out. She must have caught the flurry of movement outside, or else Carrot's scream was loud enough to penetrate even these walls. The doctor is backing away, as far as he can, from the door.

'Give me the rifle,' Dayna says to the soldier. He unslings it awkwardly and hands it to her. It's long and cumbersome (and useless) and she would much rather have the gun, but it would be a risk, swapping.

Jean's knife is on the ground, somehow ended up there in the struggle, so Dayna bends and picks it up.

'Now open the door,' she tells the soldier, pointing.

'It … it doesn't need a key,' he says. 'Not from outside. You can open it like any other door.'

'You do it anyway.'

He glances at Jean, unsure. Jean shrugs. 'Don't look at me, the girl's running this show. Better do what she wants.'

So he does and the door swings open and suddenly Evie's arms are around Dayna and she's laughing, not hurt at all.

'Ohhh, I'm so glad you're here too!'

Dayna hugs the little girl back, but over the top of Evie's head, she's staring at the doctor at the far end of the room, who is staring at her. Like a trapped rabbit with nowhere left to run. Like a snake, readying itself to strike.

'Jean?' asks Dayna without turning.

'I've got him,' says Jean's voice from the door. Soldier Carrot stumbles forwards. Past Dayna and Evie, coming to an uncertain halt in front of the doctor. 'I've got both of them,' says Jean. 'But let's hurry anyway, yes?'

Dayna disentangles herself from Evie. 'You OK?' she asks.

Evie gives her an isn't-it-obvious? look. 'Yes,' she says.

'OK. Good. Do you know where the others are?'

'They're here. With their families. If I'm good, they'll visit me.' Evie turns to the doctor. 'You promised.'

'I promised,' he repeats. His eyes have shifted to Jean and her gun now.

'What the hell do you think you're doing?' he asks, obviously shaken even when he's pretending not to be. His skin is light, but there is unmistakeable Jason in his features. 'We have a truce with you people, a mutual agreement. What do you think will happen now? To your gang?'

Jean exhales a little laugh. 'I thought it would have been obvious by now. I'm not with them, I'm with the kids. Hi, Evie.'

'Hi, Jean,' says Evie. 'Jean, you're scaring them. Don't scare them, they're nice. They're the good people. They're trying to save us.'

'No, they're not.' Dayna straightens up and glares at the doctor. 'You tell me, then. Where're the other prisoners?'

He turns to Carrot in feigned disbelief, turns back to Dayna. Adopts a soothing voice, which can't hide his distress. 'We're … we're scientists, not wardens, young lady. We're doctors. No one's holding anyone against their will here. Ask little Evie. Evie, you want to stay and help us, don't you?'

'Yes,' says Evie at once. 'Dayna, they're GOOD.'

'They're liars. Last chance, Eggman. Tell me where they are!' (A terrible fear, bubbling up inside her. If not here, then where? Unless nowhere at all …)

'Everyone's fine,' says the doctor. 'Everyone's safe. There's been a misunderstanding. We're on your side. You're welcome to stay too—'

'If that's true, you won't mind us collecting our friends then, will you?' says Jean. 'That's all we came here to do.'

'Of course,' says the doctor at once, his teeth flashing as he smiles. 'Of course you can. This isn't a prison. But ask them. Ask them if they want to leave. I don't think they do.'

'I DON'T,' insists Evie. 'I can *help* them. I can save the world with them. I'm the saviour, that's how it's supposed to be! That's why we came!'

'We don't have time for this,' says Jean. 'Which one, tough girl?'

Dayna looks at the soldier and looks at the doctor. 'Him,' she says, pointing. 'In the leg.'

The encouraging smile slips from the Eggman's face. 'What? No! Nonononono, what are you *doing*?'

Jean is pointing the gun at his upper thigh.

'NO!' screams Evie. 'No, Jean, you mustn't! Don't hurt him!'

'Evie, shut up,' hisses Dayna, elbowing her out of the way. She's aiming the useless rifle at the soldier to keep him in check. Unnecessary, because the boy looks a sickly white, freckles standing out in a rash, like he might be ready to faint dead away at any second. The Eggman's eyes are white too, wide and terrified.

'No, no, no,' he whispers. Only a rabbit now, not a trace of the snake left.

'Tell us, then,' says Jean. 'Stop wasting time.'

'All right. I will. Just don't … Jesus, don't shoot … barbarians …' (In between gasps, wheezing.)

'Well, go on then,' snaps Dayna.

'The little boy's in Dr Lyle's room. It's—'

'Don't tell us, show us,' says Jean, nodding him in the direction of the door. 'Your guard had best stay here, he's looking a little peaky. I probably am too … For Christ's sake,' she mutters to Dayna. 'You said they'd all be here. That's the only reason this qualified as a fifty per cent chance, and now look at it. They're sprinkled all over the building, it'll be a miracle if we get out of this.'

She turns to the Eggman. 'How far—?'

But Dayna has a more urgent question. 'What about Father?' she asks. 'You got him days and days ago. And what about Jason? Where're they?'

The Eggman is shaking his head. 'No,' he says. 'No. You are NOT taking my son.'

'I am if he wants to go,' says Dayna.

'Dayna—'

'And what about Father? Where's—'

'*Dayna*,' hisses Jean. 'Where's the kid?'

It takes Dayna a second to understand which kid she means. The door still open. Four people still inside the room, eyes trained on each other. No one looking at Evie at all. No one noticing as she slipped out.

★

Evie is scampering down the corridor. She's at the heavy door. She's pulling and heaving and dragging it open.

'Evie, you idiot! Stop!'

Dayna, whisper-shouting, as she hurtles after the little girl. She reaches her at the door. She yanks her back and Evie shrieks: 'I WON'T GO I WON'T GO I WON'T I WON'T I *WON'T*!'

Flailing in Dayna's arms, wriggling and twisting. Dayna clamps her hand on to Evie's mouth and is promptly bitten for her effort.

'Ow! Stop it, you'll get us all killed!'

'I CAN'T LEAVE,' howls Evie. 'I have to HELP THEM! I'M THE SAVIOUR!'

'You're *not*. Stop parroting Liam—'

The heavy door flings open with such force that it ricochets off the wall. Men's voices, shouting, and Evie is suddenly gone and Dayna's right cheek is pressed against floor or wall, she can't tell which, and her head is throbbing and there's something warm and wet on her face and Evie is screaming: 'DON'T HURT HER!'

Then she's dragged upright again and a thick vine of a forearm is slung across her neck, digging in. Hard to breathe. Her fingers strain blindly towards her pockets, find only the knife, which she manages to pull up by its very tip. But something bashes against her hand, and she lets go. The knife clatters to the ground and a brown boot kicks it forward and when Dayna looks up, there Jean is at the end of the corridor, with the Eggman in front of her as a human shield, the gun pointed towards his throat now. The Carrot she must have locked into Evie's room.

'Let her go,' demands Jean. 'Let both of them go!'

Too far away and too dim to see her expression. Her voice

is loud. Her words are shaking. If only Dayna had given her the Tupperware box; their secret weapon ... Again she tries to reach for it, again her hand is knocked aside.

'Let her GO!' shouts Jean.

'No,' says a new voice (behind her, above her) and it belongs to the man who is holding Dayna's neck in a death grip. Dayna recognises it instantly, even though she's only ever heard it once before. It comes back to her sometimes, when she's worrying about Father and what they'll do to him and what they've already done.

'*You* let him go, or I'll break this girl's neck,' says Sir. He doesn't shout. He says, calm as calm. 'I don't like to do it, but I will. You know I will.'

'What do you think I'll do to this one?' asks Jean. 'Just let us go. No one has to get hurt.'

'Oh, I disagree.' Sir is smiling. Dayna can hear it. 'Only question is, how many, and how much. You can kill him if you like. And then what? You kill him, you die. And this girl dies. You surrender, and you both survive.'

'For God's sake, Murray!' whines the Eggman.

'Don't do it,' rasps Dayna. 'He's their head scientist. They need him. They're not gonna risk—'

Sir's grip tightens around her neck. A boa constrictor of hairy man arm squeezing, squeezing the air right out of her. And Dayna can't speak any more. She can't even ... even ...

Sounds are criss-crossing. And she can't unravel the words or tell who is shouting saying threatening what. And suddenly she's coughing and rasping and *breathing* again. And falling. And all she can think is: Not on to the box, not on to the box. She twists. A blinding pain. Bright spots. Darkness.

46

She wakes in a room of olden times.

A large bed. Soft. Deep blue covers; a clean, fresh, good smell. A blurry shelf full of books. A closed door, not like the one in Evie's cell, no glass or food letter box, just an ordinary door with a door handle. A desk with papers in neat stacks on it, and a picture frame with a photograph. Four little blobs, a family.

Her hand jerks to her trouser pocket and comes in contact with only skin. She's in her underpants. The cartoon T-shirt Jean admired is gone too, replaced by an unfamiliar adult shirt. It's white, which makes Dayna think of the Court, and shudder.

And then next to her someone says her name, and she turns and there is Pax, right there, his head propped up by a pillow, his smile stretching long and happy over his face.

'Oh, Pax!' croaks Dayna (why is her throat so raw?) and flings her arms around him, breathing in his wild, familiar Pax scent. 'I thought … I was … you weren't in the cells.'

'I knew you'd come,' says Pax. 'I told them you'd come. Day, let go, your hair's tickling me. It's gonna be OK now.'

But it isn't. Because Dayna has been caught. And it hurts her to speak or swallow, and there's an unknown, throbbing pain behind her eyes and the room is swaying and then stationary and then swaying again. And because she has been caught. The Tupperware box is gone, and even if it wasn't, it's useless if she's locked up in here. The plan is useless now, and she might as well have been captured along with the others for all the good that she's done. At least then she wouldn't have dragged Jean into it too.

'D'you know if Jean's OK?' she asks Pax.

'Jean?' he repeats, confused.

'She helped me get here. We got in together … what about Jason? Do you know where he is?'

Pax shakes his head. 'I didn't really notice stuff when I got here. Not much. I bit one of the soldiers when he was pushing me into the van. I almost got away like you did, but then someone whacked me on the head, so hard I actually went to sleep. I still feel a bit funny now. Dizzy, you know. They're both OK, though. Evie and Jason. She said.'

'Who said?'

'And, Day! Father's OK too! He's sick, but they're making him better.'

Excitement quivers through her. Dies again.

'Did you actually see him, or did they just say?' she asks.

'I didn't see him because he's ill, but—'

'Then we don't know it's true. They're all liars here.'

'No, they're not. Day, the best thing happened! The best thing in the world!'

His fingers are digging into her wrists; his eyes look feverish. Is this still the after-effects of a blow to the head, or have they given him something? Some experimental drug or vaccine or whatever it is they give to the people they catch? She tries to shake him off.

'Not now. I have to think. D'you know where we are in

relation to the cells?' (But what's the use? How will she ever get out now, let alone get all the others out too?)

'But—'

'Shhh!'

She hasn't registered the footsteps until they come to a halt. Someone is on the other side of the door. A metal scraping sound, a click. The door opens and in steps a woman in a white coat similar to the one the Eggman was wearing, and just as frayed around the sleeves. A lab coat from way back. A doctor's coat. She freezes when she sees Dayna, and Dayna, on the very verge of leaping up and sprinting to the now-open door, falls back against the pillow. And stares.

Her eyes are more tired and her face is thinner and her hair is tied up into a bun and not open and wavy. But Dayna knows every inch of this woman's features, would recognise her anywhere. Impossible. But here she is.

'Do you know who I am?' whispers the woman.

Dayna gapes.

Dayna nods.

And Mother strides forwards and swoops downwards and hugs and hugs her.

She whispers: 'Oh, my baby girl.'

She whispers: 'Just look at you. Look at you.'

She whispers: 'I thought I'd never see you again.'

And Dayna holds tight and squeezes back and can't believe it, can't dare believe it. 'Mother,' she whispers. 'Mother, Mother.' Sprung to life from that old photograph, from her and Pax's imaginings. Here.

Here …

Father's tale, Jason's story. LEAVE HIM FOR LYLE!

Dayna squirms away from Mother. Looks at her. The

best thing. The worst thing. Asks: 'You … you're here? With them?'

'You make it sound like we're the enemy,' says Mother. She's smiling. She reaches out and brushes a strand of hair out of Dayna's eye, her fingers pausing to rub against some gauze material on the side of her temple, which Dayna only notices now.

'Murray did that, bloody Neanderthal,' mutters Mother. 'You mustn't judge us by the soldiers, Dayna, they're a law unto themselves. Or by Jason's stories. The boy's troubled. I'm not saying he meant to lie to you, but he has a very vivid imagination.'

Dayna looks at Pax, and Pax nods encouragingly. She glares at him and turns back to Mother.

'We thought you were dead.'

'I thought *you* were dead,' replies Mother, smiling, smiling.

'You were here all along? At the Station?'

'I was here all along.' She takes Dayna's hand in her left one and Pax's in her right and squeezes them both. She feels warm and safe and like mothers are described in stories. No wonder Pax wants to trust her. Dayna does too, but how can she?

'Tell me,' says Dayna.

Mother laughs, but her laugh cracks and almost breaks. 'Straight to the point, Dayna? Oh, I can't wait to get to know you properly.'

She surveys Dayna with a thoughtful expression on her face. Then she nods. 'All right, I'll tell you if you'd like to know. And I can see that we're not going to get anywhere until I do, are we? All right, kids –' she squeezes both their hands again – 'I'll tell you a story.'

Pax grins and leans back on his pillow and closes his eyes,

a position he used to take up whenever Father told them a tale. Dayna does not smile and does not relax and does not take her eyes off Mother.

Mother gives Dayna a knowing look, a twitch of her lips, then begins:

'I was a biomedical scientist before, specialising in vaccine research. Quite well-known in my field. So I was recruited for the Hummingbird Project. Do you know why we call ourselves Hummingbirds? No, of course you don't. They're small, beautiful birds, native to the Americas. They symbolise healing, amongst other things. So there you are. Our purpose was, and is, to heal.'

(the cages, Jason's beaten-up face, the deal with the Undead)

'The project was conceived before anyone had ever heard of the pink rabies,' says Mother, 'but other pandemics and epidemics had come and gone, and the government wanted a ... let's call it a security net to ensure the continuation of the human race, if I can be that blunt. If the worst should come to the worst. Which it did.

'Quite honestly, I never for a moment believed that Project Hummingbird would be launched. I lived my life, met your father, had you two. I'd just resumed my job at the Laboratory of Medical Sciences after my maternity leave when the first reports of the mist reached us from the United States. Then the first fungus was sighted in mainland Europe, not a week after the great fire catastrophe in Maine. This was when the Americans tried to destroy the Echidna with fire and only released an explosion of spores with a force and scope akin to an atom bomb. My thesis is that this was a deciding factor in the speed of proliferation, but that the spores would have spread anyway, given time.

The very same night I got the call. All of us recruited to Project Hummingbird did. We were to pack our bags – no more than one per person – and meet at the agreed rendezvous point at four a.m. the next morning. We were to tell no one or risk starting a panic. It was terrifying.'

'And you just left us?' asks Dayna, indignant. 'Father thought you were dead! They tell you not to say anything, and you don't? Just like that?'

Pax opens his eyes.

'No,' says Mother softly. 'I didn't leave you, Dayna. I would never have done that. I would never have gone if they'd asked me to do that. We could take our immediate families with us. And I did. I took you with me. I took your father with me. All four of us left London with the Hummingbirds.'

47

Father gave them Mother's photograph and said that was all that was left. Said she was dead, shook his head whenever they asked how, said it made him too sad. Said the Blue House was their first and only home after the Fall. Said so many things. Told so many tales. Did Mother end up being just another one of his stories?

'We lived *here*?' gasps Dayna (Father lied), just as Pax says: 'All of us went HERE?' (Father *lied*.)

'Of course you don't remember,' says Mother, 'you were so young. We didn't come here straight away, we went to a safe house right outside London. It had mobile lab equipment and food and resources, but it was never meant to be permanent. Just a place to wait out the storm. And what a storm it was. The soldiers sent out scouts, and they'd report all manner of terrible things. Looting, riots, people trying to get away in a panic, their cars blocking each other's way out. Everyone had gone crazy. Your father wanted to go back to London to get his mother from the care home, but I stopped him. He wouldn't have stood a chance, and the next day the first real spore mist hit London and, well, you can imagine. The bigger the infected population, the greater the carnage. We stopped sending out scouts and just holed up where we were. There were fifty scientists recruited, but only about half that amount showed up at the rendezvous. It was all very hectic and short notice, and many people wanted to join later, but they never made it. Then more left after the first big wave had passed, to find other family members or friends, and none came back, not one.'

There is a small name tag on the left side of Mother's white coat. It reads: *B. Lyle, M.D.* (Father told them of Belinda, but never of Lyle.) And again Dayna hears Sir's bellowed threat: LEAVE HIM FOR LYLE! Whatever else this is, whatever else she wants to be true, Mother is Lyle, and Lyle is the Station, and the Station is danger.

'In the end, we were only eleven scientists left,' says Mother, 'and those families we'd brought along. And thirty soldiers to guard us. The surprising thing, at least to me: the discipline of the soldiers. Not one, not even the youngest of them, left their posts. And they hadn't been able to bring any family at all. Oh, we've had desertions since then, mainly to that lunatic group in East London, but not as many as you'd think … Well. Anyway. We stayed at the safe house a while, but we knew we couldn't do any actual work there. Scouts were sent out again, but all the places that would have been of any use to us, clinics, universities, hospitals, had been smashed up and looted. People trying to get their hands on a vaccine that was non-existent. Just an urban legend, this supposed vaccine. We had nothing. We hadn't even begun.'

'That's not true,' says Dayna, who has been ready for the lies; hoping they wouldn't come, knowing they would. 'We had old vaccine at the Blue House. Father said—'

'Your *father*,' repeats Mother with a derisive snort. 'He stole that from the Station when he left. It was an early experimental version. More importantly, he stole you two.'

But Dayna won't think of that, not now. She says: 'That

vaccine worked. You can't have made it here or you wouldn't need to look any further.'

'We were very close in the beginning, yes,' says Mother. 'It didn't have a particularly high success rate, but even so, something to build on. We almost had it. But we weren't fast enough, and it slipped away again. The pink rabies pathogen has mutated dozens, maybe even hundreds of times since the Fall. By that I mean it changes its basic genetic structure. It evolves, if you will, to survive better, spread quicker. Thrive. Which is what makes finding a cure so difficult: something that will incorporate the basic elements of the fungus, something that remains constant no matter how often it mutates. And we haven't got the sophisticated technology of the past, sadly. We have to make do. But let me explain in the right order. Let me get on with the story.

'We settled on Alexandra Palace, mainly because it was large and fairly undamaged and not at all far from our safe house. Transporting all the heavy equipment was a major obstacle, and so its proximity really decided it for us.'

'Did the kings and queens of England used to live here?' asks Pax.

Mother smiles and ruffles his hair. Like a mother in a story from the dead world. Like a mother in the new world too, apparently. Pax beams, and Dayna thinks again: This is my mother. She's alive. She's here.

And thinks, again: Here means the Station. Here means don't trust her.

'No, this wasn't a real palace, more like a palace for the people. They used to host entertainment here, concerts, ceremonies, broadcasts, that sort of thing.'

'Broadcasts ...' repeats Dayna. 'You mean with radio?'

'I think so. But mostly television.'

'That's why there's a metal tower here,' says Dayna. 'That's how the Hummingbird message is sent out.'

'Clever girl.' Mother reaches out and it looks like she's about to mess up Dayna's hair too, but Dayna flinches to the side and Mother withdraws her hand.

'Well,' she resumes, her cheeks a little pink now, 'we had a lot of remodelling to do. But they'd given us most of the necessary materials, and what we didn't have, scouts collected from the city. So strange, you can't imagine. This huge city, so empty now. Not entirely, of course. Small gangs were roaming the streets, some people were holed up in their flats. The gangs died or moved on or became the Undead. The others … well, if we could persuade them, they'd come to the Station and they'd help us. Some did, others didn't. Those who didn't come to us were killed by the gangs or the pink rabies, or they left for other parts of the country to find their families. Those who came helped us build what it is today. We have warm water and basic electricity via solar panels on the roofs – do you know what that is? Solar energy? It's when—'

'Doesn't matter,' interrupts Dayna.

'Yeah, it does,' says Pax. 'But you don't have to explain, I already know all about solar energy. Power from the sunbeams.'

'Pax, shut. Up.' Dayna turns to Mother. 'You keep on saying *we*. But you didn't all decide together, did you? A big group like that needs a leader. Who's your leader here? And are they in charge of the soldiers too?'

'Straight to the point again,' says Mother. 'I think I know what you're getting at. Yes, there is a hierarchy, but it doesn't just come down to one person. Dr Peters and I are the senior members of the medical department; Sergeant

Murray is in charge of the soldiers. Decisions are made by a number of people. The scientists and soldiers don't always see eye to eye, that's true. Soldiers think we lack discipline, and we don't like their trained brutality.' She nods towards the bandage on Dayna's forehead. 'On the other hand, we know they're essential to our survival. There is no way we would have made it these past years without them. They bring food and supplies; they keep away bad people and the infected. And they know that, in the long run, we're essential to the world's survival. We're the only ones who stand a chance of finding a cure.'

Dayna swallows painfully, her throat on fire. She says: 'So, you're one of the people who decided to do human experiments?'

Mother sighs. 'I already know Jason has been filling your head with stories. I explained this to Pax earlier. I'll explain it to you, if you'll listen.'

'OK,' says Dayna. 'But first, if you're in charge, you have to tell people not to hurt Jean or Evie or Father.'

'Dayna, no one is going to hurt your friends.'

'It's all right, Day,' says Pax. 'She already told everyone.'

Dayna rounds on him. 'Do you honestly think Jason made it all up? They have a deal with the Undead, they just *took* Father! They came with their spy flies and took you!'

'I'll answer for Pax,' says Mother. 'I'll tell you exactly what I told him. The first thing is, there were never any human experiments. The word *experiment* implies we have no data. We have data. We have years of study on infected animals. Trials? Certainly. And I'll be the first to admit that none of these trials have been successful. But each failure brings us a step closer to our goal. And all of those trials are made with the patient's consent. You'd be surprised by how many people are willing to risk their lives for this.'

Yeah, thinks Dayna. I would.

'What about Ryan and Mart picking up Father and Pax and me?' she demands. 'We never gave consent. We never knew. They said they had vaccine to help Father.'

'Your father was infected,' says Mother quietly. 'It was the only chance he had. Our trial vaccines or nothing at all.'

'He had nothing, and he got better,' says Dayna, so angry she can hardly bring the words out. 'He got better, and those soldiers still took him. And he wouldn't have wanted to go, not in a million years. He wouldn't've just left us behind!' Whatever else he lied about, this at least she is certain of.

'The soldiers weren't to know that, Dayna,' says Mother. 'He was still sick when they took him with them, he still needed help. They wanted to take you too, but you'd disappeared, and the mist … they reported that you'd died. Not an assumption, a fact. Jason and the man's kids, caught in the mist, maskless, they said. The bastards didn't … I thought you were dead. Ever since I found out it was your father they brought in, it was like I'd lost you all over again.'

She reaches out again, and this time Dayna leans into her, she can't help it. Tears in Mother's eyes now, and Dayna's thoughts are whirling, thinking back, trying to find a hole in this story. The only hole is Jason; Jason who said to go south when they should have gone north. The only hole is Father; the teller of tales, who lied about the most important thing ever. And Mother's words sound so true. She wants them so badly to be true. Like Pax, like Evie. Like Liam's people, clapping and chanting when he's killing little babies because he told them he was a god.

Dayna pulls back, and she feels cold and hard inside. And

she says: 'I don't believe you.' And she says: 'Where's Father? Because if he's not well, that's proof. He got better by himself, and if the soldiers didn't see that, then you would have. If what you say is true, you'd have no reason to do the experiments on him, and he wouldn't want them done anyway. If he's sick, that makes you a liar. I want to see him. WHERE is he?'

'I didn't know,' snaps Mother, finally raising her voice, finally on the defensive. 'It wasn't me! It was Peters. I didn't know. I would never have— Even after everything he did. I wouldn't …'

She closes her eyes, sucks in air, exhales slowly. Opens them. 'All right, Dayna,' she whispers. 'I didn't want to do this now, not when everything is still so new and overwhelming for you. We still have to get to know each other, and I didn't want to start with … This is a complex … a difficult … But all right. There is no patient's consent. I lied. To protect you. Jason wasn't ready to know, and clearly, you're not either. It's hard enough to find people, let alone people who are willing to put their lives on the line for something as abstract as the future of mankind. Look, these trials. They may seem unfair, but this isn't a fairytale. We're living in a post-apocalyptic world. If we want to survive this, and I'm talking about humanity in general, we'll have to make sacrifices. Generations of vaccine developers have faced such dilemmas throughout modern history. Take the moral high ground and spare a handful of people. And doom millions to their death. Make the tough call, the *right* call, and that handful of people will save those millions of future lives.

'I'm not being callous. Every time another patient dies, I come in here and I lock the door and I cry. But I keep on going because it's either this or it's oblivion. It's as simple as that. We're the last chance civilisation has.'

She grips Dayna's arm. She grips Pax's.

'But listen to me: I will never, ever let anything happen to you. And I would never have let anything happen to your father. I love you. I love you so much.'

She's telling the truth. And perhaps this is the hardest thing of all.

'Father knew all along, didn't he?' says Dayna quietly. 'That's why he left. He couldn't stand it, what you're doing.'

Mother sighs. 'Yes, that's right. He overreacted. And he just left. He took you away from me, just like that. In the dead of night. I woke up the next day and all three of you were gone. Oh, how I've hated him for that. I sent out men to find you, but he'd had a head start. And he'd convinced some soldier to help him. They took a van and sabotaged the others.'

'Uncle William,' whispers Pax, sounding close to tears.

'He wasn't your uncle. And you were gone. What sort of man does that? Takes children away from their mother? And, Pax, you were so young! Too young to be without your mother; he could have killed you! I thought he had. I thought you must have died somewhere out there … all of you, dead.'

She pulls them both towards her and holds them tight and doesn't say anything for a while. There's a lump in Dayna's throat when her mother lets go of her again, her eyes red and moist.

'Some people don't have what it takes,' says Mother quietly. 'Your father didn't. I can't blame him for that, although I'll never forgive him for taking you away. At least he looked after you. At least you're here now, and alive.

We'll start over, the three of us. I'm so glad we're together again.'

'What about Father?' whispers Pax.

Mother opens her mouth, then closes it. For the first time, she looks afraid. Dayna's insides twist.

'Is he alive?' asks Dayna.

Mother hesitates.

'Is he dead?'

Mother nods.

'I'm so sorry. I didn't know how to tell you ... I found out too late. Peters didn't recognise him. I stopped the treatment as soon as I saw, but ... but it was too late.'

Pax emits a high, wounded-animal wail. Mother locks him into her arms and kisses the top of his head as he sobs and sobs against her shoulder. Dayna just sits there, stunned and unmoving and unseeing.

All of it, all the walking and running and driving and planning and horror and fear, all for nothing.

48

Mother stays with them, holding them, for a long time, and Dayna can't think. And then someone knocks, and Mother murmurs something and leaves, locking the door behind her, and still Dayna can't think. A distant rumble of thunder outside. The first drops of rain hit the windows, stream down like tears. In the very distance: the shadowy outlines of London's sky towers.

Think. Think. THINK.

Dayna closes her eyes and tries to block out Pax's snuffles beside her, and tries to focus.

(Father)

No. Not on that. What good will that do?

Priorities?

Get out.

Get out?

Leave Mother.

But does she really want to do that?

Yes.

Don't know.

YES.

Dayna loves Mother because she is Mother. But Mother is also a Hummingbird doctor. Mother has explained why what she is doing is good. But so did Liam. The fine line between heroes and monsters.

Dayna opens her eyes. Takes a deep breath. In. Out.

She turns to Pax. 'Stop crying,' she says. 'We can cry later. When we're out of here. We can be sad then. But we have to be clever now.'

Pax looks at her, his eyes glistening, his chin jutting. 'I'm not going,' he croaks. His voice is wet with tears but stubborn. 'I'm staying here.'

'With the people who killed Father? Who beat up Jason and locked him in a cage?'

'With Mother,' says Pax simply. 'And I think … maybe she's right? They're just trying to find a way to save the world. Once they develop the proper vaccine, they'll have saved the world.'

Dayna reaches out and – '*Ow!*' – punches her brother's left shoulder. 'And once Liam has a hundred Evies, he might have saved the world too,' she hisses. 'But before he gets a hundred Evies, he'll have killed a hundred million nameless babies in the mist. Does that make him a hero?'

Pax rubs his shoulder and says nothing.

'And you do know what Mother and those other doctors will do, don't you? The very first thing? Remember when Jason said that the Hummingbirds would kill to get their hands on someone immune like Evie? They'll cut her up and try and find out how exactly she's immune and everyone else isn't. They'll kill her. Do you want them to kill her?'

'No! But they won't. Mother said. She'll stop them.'

Dayna mulls this over. 'I don't think she will if she believes doing it will help their vaccine. But even if she does, Evie can never be safe here, can't you see?'

'You don't trust anyone any more!' shouts Pax, desperate, furious.

'I *do*.' And Dayna is equally desperate, for him to understand. 'I trust people who deserve it. I trust you and Jason and Jean. I don't trust Evie so much because she's a stupid little idiot, but that's not her fault because Liam brainwashed her.'

'You didn't trust Jean, first time we saw her!' Pax hurls at her. 'And you didn't trust Jason after the Court.'

'Yeah, and I did trust Ryan and Mart, and I did trust Rena. And see where that got us?'

'I don't CARE about that! I care about Mother! I never had a mother before, Day. Outside of stories. I want to keep her.' (He's pleading now, begging her.)

'I want to keep her too,' says Dayna quietly. 'I want to keep the story Mother. From before. That's who I want to keep. And I don't want to stay here and be part of this.'

'They're doing something good,' whispers Pax, unconvinced but trying so hard to believe it.

'Only if they get it right,' says Dayna. 'Until then, they're doing something bad.'

We're the good people, said Rena.

We're the good people, said Liam.

We're the good people, said Mother.

Pax lets go of a long, shuddery breath. He doesn't speak for over a minute, and he doesn't look at Dayna at all, but out through the rain-blurred window.

'OK,' he finally says in a small, small voice. 'I know all that, really. I just thought … they know more than us, don't they? Adults. I thought if Mother said it was good, then it had to be, and maybe I was just too little to understand. I thought …'

'Yeah,' says Dayna. 'I know. But here's the thing, right? Most adults, they don't seem to *know* what's good and what isn't.'

'Maybe we ought to explain,' says Pax. 'Maybe if we explain it to her, Mother might come with us? Maybe she'll help us get out?'

'Maybe,' says Dayna. But she doesn't believe it.

Pax's plan is to convince Mother to leave the Station with them and Evie and Jason and Jean. Dayna's private plan is to jump Mother while she's distracted with Pax and wrestle the key from her and escape and lock her into the room.

But when the door does finally open again, Mother is not alone. She's with a soldier – and Dayna recognises the peeling sunburn and fiery hair of Private Carrot, whose right hand is now bandaged. Both he and Mother are carrying trays of food. Carrot eyes Dayna suspiciously, and she knows he will be ready for her this time. She stays put.

'We've brought some food from the cafeteria,' announces Mother. 'You must be hungry.' They put the trays on to the desk side by side, pushing away notebooks to make space. Carrot's eyes keep on swivelling to Dayna.

'You ought to be careful around her, Dr Lyle,' he says. 'Little savage, that one. Almost bit me to the bone.'

'She did grow up without a mother,' says Mother, smiling. 'Thanks for your help, Kevin. You can go now.'

'Sergeant Murray says I have to stay. To make sure they behave themselves.'

'Kevin, they're my children. They won't hurt me.'

Kevin shrugs. 'Sarge's order.'

Mother breathes out irritably. 'Oh, fine. But stand right over there, by the door, will you? So that we at least have the illusion of privacy.'

Kevin hesitates. 'Mind if I take a chair?'

'You're the one who wanted to be a soldier, Kevin. Soldiers stand to attention, don't they? Go on.'

Kevin goes on, his cheeks blushing red, to the door. Once there, he meets Dayna's gaze and grimaces, like his humiliation is all her fault.

'Now, come here, come here,' Mother says to them. 'Tuck in.'

Under different circumstances, the food would have been delicious. Salted smoked venison and boiled potatoes and carrots from a nearby farm, so much fresher and richer than the diet of canned foods they have mainly been living on for the past ten days. But after all that has happened and is happening, Dayna is too tense to be hungry. She forces down as much as she can, though, telling herself that she has to keep her strength up. Even Pax, who is usually greedy as a crazed cat, seems to be chewing more than he's swallowing.

When she feels her stomach protesting, Dayna lays down her knife and fork and pushes her plate away. She looks at Mother and says: 'We want to see Jason.'

Mother shakes her head indulgently. 'I'm afraid Jason is being punished for running away and giving his father so much worry. He's under room arrest.'

'But—'

'I'm sorry, but it's not my decision. It's what Dr Peters wants. His father. I'm sure you can see him in a couple of days. What a strange coincidence that you found each other on the outside. Jason must have taken almost the same route as your father and that soldier did all those years ago …'

'Then I want to see Jean and Evie.'

'We let them go, Dayna. Just like you wanted. The little girl knew the woman, so we thought it would be safe enough for her.'

Dayna blinks, taken aback. This is such a blatant lie that she can't believe Mother would tell it.

'You let them go? What, just now?'

'Yes.'

(Pax, squirming in his seat, hoping, hoping this is true.)

'And why didn't they say goodbye to us?'

Mother smiles sadly. 'Your friend just wanted to get out as soon as possible. I'm sorry.'

'You're lying.'

'Day,' says Pax. 'Maybe she isn't ...'

Dayna rounds on him. 'Stop being so stupid – of course she's lying! They wouldn't just give up Evie. And Jean wouldn't just leave without us.'

'How long have you known this woman, Dayna?' asks Mother, still calm and composed, still smiling. 'I'm betting you met her around here, didn't you? So not long at all. What do you really know about her?'

'More than I know about you,' snaps Dayna.

'Told you she was a savage,' mutters Kevin from the door.

Mother ignores him and ignores Dayna. 'As for Evie,' she says, 'it did take some convincing, you're right. But we have Evie's blood and saliva samples, and they're useful enough to begin with. And I'm more important to the success of the programme than even an immune girl is, so at the end of the day, the others do as I tell them to do. And you two are more important to me. I know you might not be able to trust me right now, especially you, Dayna. But I want to change that. Letting the little girl go is the first step.'

Under the table, Pax nudges Dayna. He believes it. He's hoping again. He's dreaming again. Idiot.

49

Mother says they both need a wash and leads them to a small adjoining shower room. Dayna knows what showers are, of course, but showers are part of the dead world and don't work any more. Only this one does. Multiple thin streams of water splatter downwards like a miniature rainstorm that fogs up the glass walls around her because the water is *hot*. Hot water, like sorcery.

Mother rubs Dayna's hair with a towel when she comes out in the scuffed bathrobe she was given, with such tenderness that it hurts. Pax is in the shower now, the door closed, singing one of his nameless songs. Mother hums along, looking so happy. This hurts too.

Kevin is sent off to find some old children's clothes in the storeroom. He looks reluctant, but leaves. Maybe he's decided that Dayna won't attempt an escape if all she's wearing is a dressing gown. Mother picks up Dayna's discarded white blouse and puts it into a wicker laundry basket in a corner, and Dayna's heart skips a beat.

For the first time she realises that her old clothes might still be in the room.

'It'll be picked up later,' says Mother, noticing Dayna watching it.

'OK,' says Dayna, trying to sound indifferent.

★

When Pax is done with the shower, Mother goes in to make sure he's turned everything off. Which is when Dayna darts to the wicker basket. And yes! In with crinkled shirts and underthings of Mother's are Pax and Dayna's clothes. Most importantly: the trousers with all the pockets. She almost laughs out loud when her fingers make contact with the rubber edges of the Tupperware box, still there, still sealed. But now she hears the others coming and is forced to rush back, her fingers still tingling with the brush of canvas material. Mother returns, with Pax by her side, flushed and grinning, his towel trailing behind him like a cape.

'The water's so HOT,' he informs her, as if she wasn't in there right before him.

Dayna nods absently, and thinks: If someone picks up the laundry, then it's all over.

Just then, the door opens for Kevin, carrying a cardboard box full of clothes. Mother takes out checked pyjamas and says they can sort through the rest in the morning. Pax gets dressed right there in the room, but Dayna hugs her dressing gown to herself and mumbles: 'I'll get changed later.' Mother doesn't seem to notice; she's busy pouring out steaming camomile tea from a thermos into three mugs.

'Mother? What's gonna happen to us now?' asks Pax.

She smiles at him fondly, handing him a mug. 'Now we all stay together, Pax. You stay here with me. I'll teach you things. You're both very clever and adaptable, I can see that already. You'll learn about biology and medicine, and when you grow up, you'll be able to help our world – don't frown at me like that, Dayna. I've already explained. Sadly, in this new world, we only have a choice of doing nothing or doing something hard that will result in something good.'

Dayna takes a sip of the tea and it scalds her tongue. Then do nothing, she thinks, but she doesn't say it out loud. There's no point in arguing with people who are so convinced that they are in the right.

But Pax still hasn't learned this yet. 'Mother, we met a man called Liam by the sea,' he begins, using the exact same argument Dayna used on him not half an hour ago.

Pax tells Mother about Liam and what Liam does, and how Liam says he is saving the world. Mother smiles at first, and then her smile freezes.

'Liam was immune?' she asks. 'Like Evie?'

'Yeah,' says Pax.

'Still is,' says Dayna. 'So if you want someone to cut up, go to the south coast and get Liam. But leave Evie alone.'

'She's already let Evie go,' Pax reminds her. 'And she's not cutting up anyone any more. Right, Mother? You get it, right? Some things are too bad to ever be good. Right?'

'Oh, children,' exhales Mother. She sits on the bed, between them. Her left arm goes around Pax's shoulders, her right arm around Dayna's.

She feels so safe.

She isn't safe at all.

'We're nothing like Liam. You can't possibly compare a scientific research facility, officially appointed by the very last government this country had, to some pseudo-religious cult. If Evie is the only immune child he's fathered in all this time, then obviously his plan isn't going to work. But ours is. It's based on science; it's controlled. Even your father knew it. He ran away, but not before helping himself to vials of experimental vaccine. The hypocrite. You said before that the vaccine worked, Dayna. You could only know that if ... well, if you had to use it. Which of you was infected? Which of you did we save, with that early trial version?'

Dayna stiffens, says nothing. What is there to say? Little Pax would have died if not for the vaccine Father stole, Mother made, people died for. Mother nods. She knows she has won this argument. How can something be right and at the same time so wrong?

'You said girls.'

Dayna looks up, meets Mother's eyes. They're brown with flecks of green, the exact same shade as Pax's. And her own.

'What?'

'I just ... You said this Liam took women *and* girls to be his ... well, breeders.'

Her insides are squirming. 'Yeah. So?'

'He didn't ... he didn't do anything to you, did he?'

'No,' mutters Dayna, her cheeks burning.

'Yeah, he did,' says Pax. 'He locked us all into separate rooms. And he made us stay there for two days!'

Mother looks so alarmed that Dayna takes pity on her: 'Yeah, but he never *did* anything. I was scared that he would, but he didn't. I'm not old enough for that. For having babies. So he left me alone.'

Mother pulls Dayna into a sudden tight embrace, and it's all Dayna can do not to hug back, although she really, really wants to now. Her mother, holding her. She smells of faint soap and warm skin and love. If only it wasn't here.

(Don't trust her don't trust her don't you dare trust her!)

'How did you end up there?' asks Mother. 'How did you get away?'

Pax trusts her. He tells her everything, their whole journey from the house with the blue door to the Court to

London, to the Station. By the time he has finished, the sky outside is black and Kevin is snoozing in a chair he has covertly slipped into, and Mother's eyes are bright with wonder. She hugs them both and tells them they are brave and clever and resourceful. She tells them that she is proud of them beyond words.

And then she tells them all the danger is over now because they're here, with her, with solar energy and walls and guards and warm water. Nothing bad can get to them now, not Liam's people or the Undead or the crazed.

Not long after that, they lie down, all three of them on Mother's bed. Her in the middle, between them, so warm; Kevin banished to stand guard outside the door. Pax gives Dayna one last pleading look before closing his eyes. Don't let's give up on her just yet, it says.

Dayna decides to wait until Mother is asleep, then wake Pax, grab her trousers and get out. If Kevin is still awake, she will just have to use the box and hope for the best. She can't wait much longer; who knows what these people might be doing to Evie and Jean. She decides this, but something is wrong, blurred, heavy. And once she closes her eyes, she can no longer open them.

50

If she dreams, she can't remember, that's how far away she goes, and when she wakes, the sky outside is not black any more, but grey. It's still raining. Mother is sitting at her desk, studying paper notes and nursing a mug of what smells like the instant coffee Father loves. Used to love.

'You put something in our tea,' accuses Dayna. She shakes her head, trying to get rid of the grogginess. Beside her, Pax is rubbing his eyes and yawning.

'Just something to help you sleep,' says Mother. 'I always take it. Keeps away nightmares. I thought that wouldn't be such a bad thing for you, considering.'

The casual way Mother says this, as if it's the most normal thing in the world, to drug people before bedtime. Maybe it is, here. Maybe that's the secret to living at the Station and doing the things they do and telling themselves they're good.

Mother ignores Dayna's scowl. 'Come have some breakfast, you two. Kevin brought us toast.'

They're just finishing up when there's a knock on the door, and it's Jason's father, who casts a nervous, wary look at Dayna, and whispers something into Mother's ear. Behind him, Kevin is lurking in the hallway, looking bored and sleepy.

'I'll have to leave you on your own for a little,' Mother tells Dayna and Pax, slipping into her white coat, becoming once more a Hummingbird doctor. She smiles, says she'll try not to take too long, and closes the door behind her. The lock clicks, and they're alone.

NOW, thinks Dayna, and suddenly all her tiredness is gone. She jumps up and strides to the door, as silent as a cat on her bare feet. She presses her ear against its smooth, cool surface and listens: The footsteps of the three adults – and Dayna is almost certain it's all three of them – are moving away.

'What're you doing?' asks Pax as Dayna walks to the laundry basket. She tips over its contents and starts to rummage through the discarded clothes on the floor, looking for her trousers. How amazingly lucky that no one has searched its many pockets after she was captured. Or if someone did, this someone must have dismissed the small blue Tupperware box of what looks like mould from the outside, and they must have thought no harm could come from the five thin FFP2 masks, and they must not have looked thoroughly enough and simply missed the compact lock pick which has slid into the narrow space between protruding canvas lining and inner trouser leg as if it was conscious and knew that it had to hide.

'Get dressed,' orders Dayna, already halfway through wriggling into her own beloved trousers. 'We're leaving.'

'But what about—'

'Just do it, all right? First, we get out. Then we think about what to do about Mother. She's not in any danger here, *she's* the danger. But Evie is. And Jean.' There are two sets of trainers in the cardboard box of old children's clothes, and both look roughly the right size for them. She takes the slightly larger pair.

'Mother said they let them go,' mutters Pax, half-heartedly moving clothes aside with his toe.

'I know what she said. I don't believe her.'

'Well, I do.'

'Do you want to stay here?' snaps Dayna. 'She as good as told us they wouldn't stop experimenting on people. They think it's the good thing to do, they'll never, ever stop!'

'I don't know!' Pax looks furious. He looks close to tears. And he pushes Dayna so hard that she almost falls over. 'I don't know, OK? I don't know what to do!'

'That's why you just listen to me,' says Dayna, trying to sound calm and soothing. Like someone who knows for a fact that everything will be all right. 'I know what to do, I'm the eldest. So all you have to do is listen to me. And I say get dressed. Come *on*.'

She pulls her yellow cartoon boy T-shirt (grass-stained and dirt-stained and a little musty-smelling) over her head, ignoring the selection of shirts Private Kevin has brought. Then she locks eyes with Pax, a staring competition like one they've had a hundred times in the past, and not like that at all. Because this is important. Finally, giving her one last scowl, he bends down and picks up a random pair of shorts.

As soon as she's satisfied that Pax is (grudgingly) obeying her, Dayna turns her attention to the door.

It's an easy pick, doesn't even take her a minute.

Dayna peeks outside. A high-ceilinged hallway with doors to either side. No one in sight. According to Jason, there are six doctors, twenty-two soldiers, three technicians, one caretaker, one cook, and five family members of the doctors on the premises. Thirty-eight people in all, and this is a big place, a palace. It should be possible, shouldn't it, to move through it without coming across anyone? Unless there are patrols. Unless all the activity is centred around this particular part of the building ... Best not to think about that. If someone does come, she will be ready for them.

She closes the door again, hands Pax an FFP2 mask to loop around his arm, because Kong is gone, like Anteater, vanished somewhere into the recesses of the Station. But better that they took the gas masks and left the trousers.

'I want to write Mother a note,' says Pax. 'So she won't worry.'

'We don't have time—'

But Pax ignores her, already heading towards the desk. Curious in spite of herself, Dayna watches as Pax flips through one of the notebooks, past scrawled and illegible writing and numbers and equations, until he finds only white. On to this, he writes his message for Mother.

'You want to sign too?' he asks Dayna when he's done.

She looks over his shoulder. In his very best handwriting (and this from the boy who hated all writing lessons), her brother has printed this:

Dear Mother,
dont be sad. We love you, but we dont like the Station.
We'll be OK in the world, dont worry. Its not so bad, just wild.
We'll come back for you if you want to com too.
Pax

Dayna takes the pen and adds a *Maybe* in front of the last sentence. Then she signs as well:

Pax
Dayna

And now it's time to go. Into the empty hallway, the row of doors. Dayna sees how to find Jason as soon as theirs closes behind them, revealing a handwritten sign:

B. Lyle, M.D.

Another trick of the old world. All the doors are named, and the names correspond to the people who live behind them. How helpful. But what's the Eggman's real name? Dayna has heard it, she knows she has, but can't remember ...

They pass label after label, some blank, some with unfamiliar names, Dayna's heart pounding against her ribcage all the while until—

L. Peters, M.D.

Yes. That was it.

But now Dayna hesitates. She's assumed up until now that if Mother is gone, working, then the Eggman, who has taken her, will be gone too. But what if that's not the case? What if he's inside this room?

'Well, come on,' says Pax impatiently.

But come on what? How can she make sure Jason is in there and not warn anyone else who might be there too? She has to be clever. She has to—

'*Jason?*' hisses Pax through the keyhole. He keeps his voice low, but still Dayna winces.

'Jason, you there?'

At first, there's nothing. And then, from inside, a sudden scrambling noise. Dayna jumps back, pulling Pax with her by the scruff of his T-shirt neck. The Eggman's there, she thinks. A soldier's there, maybe even Sir, keeping an eye on Jason.

But the door doesn't open at all. Instead, a familiar voice from its other side whispers: 'Pax? Pax, is that you, mate?'

Pax runs back towards the door. 'Yes! Yes, it's me!'

There's a strangled little whoop from inside. 'Yes! YES! I knew they'd underestimate you! You've got some balls!'

Dayna steps forwards too. 'Are you alone in there?' she asks.

A pause, then: 'Sarge?'

Dayna rolls her eyes at Pax. 'Yeah, it's me. You're alone?'

Another pause, then an exhaled: 'Ha. Yeah, I'm alone. They're all in the observation room, most of the soldiers too. All of them as excited as little kids on their birthdays. No prizes for guessing why … Shit. How did you—?'

'I'm getting you out. Pax, you stand guard.'

'I should've guessed,' Jason's voice is saying through the door as she begins to work on it with the lock pick. 'That you were here too. Should've guessed. You're one resourceful kid.'

'Do I have balls too?'

'Uh, yeah. More than any of us.'

'What's that mean, anyway?'

Jason laughs. 'Means that you're brave.'

Well, thinks Dayna, it's easier to be brave if you're not in any real danger. 'You know about our mother?' she asks.

'Dr Lyle,' says Jason. 'I still can't bloody believe it, it's too crazy! But actually, it isn't at all. Your gas masks, you calling the purple fungus Echidna … it was the docs here who came up with that name. Your mum, actually. I was so thick not to make the connection before. They didn't know at first. They put Pax into the cells along with Evie, thought he was just a nobody I'd picked up. Both of them. And then Evie starts boasting about how she's special the minute

Dr Lyle spins her spiel about them saving the world. And then she spots Pax and stares at him like she knows him but doesn't know where from. But Pax knew right away. Dunno how.'

'We have a photograph of her,' Dayna reminds him. She twists the pick, but she's being too hasty; the lock is still locked. 'How d'you know all that? You were in the cell with them?'

'Yeah, they put us all in one at first. They do that sometimes if they bring in a group of people. To keep them calm. When the tests begin, they separate them but say it's only for a few hours, and most people go along with it. With me, I think they wanted to scare me. Make me think that I'd be a test subject too after all the trouble I'd caused. It worked, I actually did think that. Anyway, Pax is in the bed, they knocked him out bringing him in, and he still isn't all there, and he looks at Dr Lyle, and he says: Mother. But not really surprised, just happy. Like he thought it was part of a dream. Kilburn laughed. He's another doc. But Dr Lyle, she just stared. And then she had soldiers come in and take Pax out of the room. She went with them, and Kilburn was like, hey, what's going on? After that, I was taken here. Shit, this is so weird. You two are Lyle's kids.'

'Do you remember us? From when we used to live here?'

'Nah, too long ago. I remember kids younger than me that were there and gone, but no faces. But the older kids sometimes talked about this soldier and Lyle's husband running away together. But they never mentioned children. They made it out to be more of a love story.'

'Hmm.'

'Not easy, is it? Having one of them as your parent?'

'No,' whispers Dayna.

'My dad's a piece of cowardly shit, but Dr Lyle was always nice. Must be hard for her to be so nice. And still do what she does.'

Dayna concentrates on the lock and doesn't respond.

'How'd you get here, Sarge? Did they catch you too?'

'I came in here with Jean. We wanted to rescue you.'

'No shit, really?!'

Finally, the click.

'Yeah, really. Didn't all go according to plan, though.'

She swings the door open, and here Jason is, wearing a white T-shirt and black floppy trousers that look like night things, with a fresh bruise on his left cheek, swollen and purple, with all his dreadlocks cut off. He's almost bald now, except for a thin layer of hair, and his head looks far too small for his shoulders.

Jason grins and gives a little shrug. 'Don't stare.'

'Why did they—'

'I'm a soldier in training now. No dreads allowed. Hey, Pax.'

Pax has abandoned his lookout to come flying towards Jason.

'You look different,' is his verdict.

Jason holds out his right hand and lets Pax slap it. 'Good to see you too. What's the plan, Sarge?'

'To get Jean and Evie. And then get out,' says Dayna. 'Assuming you still want to.'

'Want to what?' asks Jason, bending down now as he pulls on trainers. They're not the shoes he's taken from the family's house, but white and clean-looking. Not new (what is new?), but fairly unused. 'Get out? Of course I want to get out. Why wouldn't I?'

'That makes you the first one here,' says Dayna, shooting

Pax a dirty look. 'Evie's the reason me and Jean got caught in the first place because she wants to stay and save the world. And Pax wants to stay with Mother.'

'I don't!' says Pax quickly. 'I'm here, aren't I? Stop telling him lies, Day!'

'It's OK, mate,' says Jason. 'Anyone would be thrown off a bit if they found out their mother was here.'

'Not me,' lies Dayna.

'Yeah, well, you're Sarge, aren't you? What's the plan to get the others out, anyway? You do have one, right?'

'Yeah, I have one. Sort of.'

Jason nudges Pax: 'Knew she had one.' Turns to Dayna: 'All right,' he says, in a resigned sort of tone. 'Let's hear it, then.'

51

The observation room is not a room at all but a great hall sinking into the ground. There are rows upon curved rows of shabby, battered seats, and even though some seats and some rows have been taken out like rotten teeth, there are still so many of them. Most are empty, but at the very far end of the auditorium, shadows sit, and those shadows are hummingpeople.

There are no windows, but there is scaffolding high above everything, and on this electric lights are attached, all their beams trained towards the same place: a giant glass cube at the very end and at the very bottom of the hall. And in this cube: Jean, her face washed clean of her Undead disguise, her jaw set, her hands tied to the armrests of the metal chair she is sitting in. And in this cube with her: Evie, in a little girl's blue summer dress with spaghetti straps, casting anxious glances at Jean. Both of them have some sort of band wrapped around their upper arms, connected to a wire, connected to a small screen with blinking numbers and wavy lines glowing in it.

Observation room. Observation cube.

Dayna knew that Mother was lying, knew it all along. And still ... and still ...

In front of the cube, white coats are milling, talking to

each other or taking notes or reading notes. Five, six, seven, eight, counts Dayna. All doctors present, and two who must be doctor-children who have been awarded the lab coats also. More people sprawled in the front seats, and Dayna thinks she recognises Mart's thick arms, one of them in a sling. A low hum of conversation. Until one crisp voice cuts above all others and a woman steps on to the low platform, right in front of the cube and Jean and Evie in it, and turns to address the hall at large.

'You've all earned your right to witness this,' calls Mother, 'but bear in mind that this isn't a show purely for your entertainment—'

A man's voice shouts something about it being the right venue, accompanied by whoops and laughter from the shadows.

Mother purses her lips and waits until the noise has abated. 'Thank you for demonstrating exactly what I don't want to see once we begin,' she says. Her voice carries all the way back to where Dayna, Pax and Jason are crouching, on the dark balcony.

'This is a highly important experiment, perhaps the most important since this project was launched. But you already know this, or you wouldn't be here now.'

More whoops and cheers from the shadows in the audience (twenty-two soldiers, three technicians, one caretaker, one cook, and five doctor relations – are they all here, excepting the current guards outside?). This time, Mother smiles along too.

'She lied,' mumbles Pax, more to himself than anyone else. 'She lied about letting them go. I believed her. She just lied …'

'I know,' whispers Dayna, moving slightly so that her

shoulder nudges his. 'And it's horrible and it hurts and it's not fair. But that's all for later, OK? Afterwards.'

'Now, I'll walk you through the very basics of what we're doing,' Mother is saying. 'But, as I've said, as soon as we begin, we need absolute silence, or Murray here will begin ejecting observers.'

She turns and gives first Jean and then Evie a nod. 'And I'll also explain it for the better comprehension of our two courageous volunteers.'

Jean snorts. She's trying to look tough, but what she actually looks is scared. Evie begins to chew her lower lip.

'Young Evie here is immune to the pink rabies, and, by her own statement, has been so all her life, which means that this immunity has so far held its own against all mutations. I can't verify whether or not the latter is true, but I can – and did – verify that Evie here really is not affected by the pathogen.'

'Go get into position,' Dayna whispers to Jason. He nods and slips off into the darkness.

'Which means young Evie is our starting point and our ultimate goal. We have to understand what her body does differently from ours. A cursory examination hasn't given us any definite results, but now we have a second volunteer, we can delve deeper. We have a control group, albeit a group of one, to establish how this special little girl's body reacts differently to the pathogen than 99.99 per cent of other humans'.'

And Dayna's right hand, reaching into her pocket for the Tupperware box, hesitates. If she does this, Mother might die.

'We'll administer increasing doses of the pathogen to both patients, then take blood, saliva, lung and finally brain tissue samples to study and compare. We already know that the fungus comes into contact with all of these, but as it's mutated since our last biopsies, we have to be certain of an uncorrupted comparison – which is why your contribution –' turning to Jean – 'is so vital.'

'They'll be safe, won't they?' whispers Pax.

'Yes, I think so.'

'You *think*?'

'Jason says the cube has a venting system with a filter. So yeah, it should be fine, OK?'

'I DON'T WANT YOU TO HURT HER!' screams a shrill little voice. Evie's. She's banging both her fists against the cube's glass until Mother turns to look at her. She crouches down to Evie's level, almost nose to nose, with a slab of glass dividing them. She says something that Dayna can't hear, but she can guess. More lies, more justification. Evie looks like she's about to burst into tears.

Mother turns back to the white coats. 'I assume this is obvious, seeing as where we are, but I'll say it anyway. As soon as the patients have been given the doses, and for each subsequent dose, up to and including the time the pathogen takes the woman over, make sure you make a note of everything. I want every muscle twitch, every spasm recorded. I want to know the extent and speed of sclera discolouration, if there's a dilation of the pupils, myoclonus of the limbs, seizing, perspiration, *anything*. Yes? Keep an eye on the vitals on the monitors too, even if they're recording.'

(Here it comes ...)

'The first dose the patients will receive is so low that there is only a slim risk of being turned. Dr Peters, if you please.'

The Eggman opens a glass door at the right-hand side of the cube and steps into it with a syringe. Dayna had thought, had hoped, it would be Mother, but she stays right where she is. Outside. Observing. In the open.

Doesn't matter, Dayna tells herself. If everything goes according to plan, if they just listen …

Evie whimpers as the Eggman injects the craze into her upper arm. A great cheer rises up from the front row seats, despite Mother's warning. Mother doesn't turn. None of the white coats do.

'No visible reaction at all,' says Mother, sounding satisfied. Sounding eager.

(But what if they *won't* listen?)

The Eggman has reached Jean now. He takes out a second syringe.

'What are you waiting for?' urges Pax.

And Jean hooks her left leg around the Eggman's and jerks sharply to the side, throwing him off his feet and on to the ground with a startled THUMP.

Dayna has to do it. She HAS to.

The hummingpeople in the auditorium are howling with laughter, catcalling.

'For goodness' sake!' snaps Mother. 'Murray—'

Jean throws herself – body and chair – on to the Eggman, pressing him into the ground, preventing him from getting up. He's squealing, thrashing like a fish out of water.

'Evie!' yells Jean. 'Quick! Untie me!'

Evie, staring, horrified, rooted to the spot.

Sir, sprinting to the platform.

'Hurry, Evie!'

'Hurry, Day!'

'STOP!!'

Dayna doesn't recognise her own voice, it's so shrill and loud. It reverberates through the hall. It cuts through the jeering shouting squealing pandemonium by the stage. Every head she can see turns. Every head she can see stares. Sir comes to a halt five paces away from the cube. Jean looks up, the Eggman stops wriggling and does the same.

Dayna has risen to her feet, Pax beside her. Two small shadows on the balcony.

'Dayna? Pax?' says Mother. Then she screams: 'NO! Put that down, you imbecile! They're my *children*!'

Someone unseen by Dayna has aimed a weapon at her. They lower it again at Mother's words. Dayna's heart pulsing in her throat, her ears, her breath. This close to death, and she didn't even realise. (Be *brave*.)

'What do you think you're doing?' Mother yells at them. 'Come down here at once!'

'We're warning you,' shouts Dayna. Both she and Pax are wearing their masks, and it must be this, rather than anything else, that makes the hummingpeople hesitate. Dayna is finally opening the Tupperware box for all to see.

'We've got an Echidna here,' she shouts before anyone else tries to intervene. 'So you better not shoot. If you hit it, it'll release the spores.'

She raises the plastic container with its deadly occupant high over her head. Now that the lid has been removed, the mushroom caps are rising, stretching, pulsing. Dayna and Jean dug it out of the earth with their hands the day before, slow as slow, wearing masks, Jean muttering all the while: 'This is crazy, this is crazy.' Even in the relative gloom of the balconies, the purple-pink colour is unmistakeable.

'Fuck!' exclaims a young male voice that might even belong to Private Carrot.

The hummingpeople are stirring, uncertain whether to attack or flee or laugh. Some, those few who have brought gas masks with them, are frantically fumbling with the straps. Others bellow that the kid is bluffing.

'I'm not,' says Dayna. 'If you do anything, if you try and stop us, you'll see I'm not. Should have checked my trousers properly, shouldn't you?' Her eyes find Sir (masked now, but just as trapped as the others if he wants them to survive), before flicking back to Mother. 'Should have taken me seriously.'

'You wouldn't,' says Mother. 'Not with them—' She points to Jean and Evie, silent and staring.

Dayna forces herself to shrug. 'They're in a glass box,' she says. 'You're not.'

Jean mutters something to Evie, and a second later Evie is scurrying to the door of the cube. She drags her metal chair to its handle and positions it. But she doesn't get the angle right. If someone wanted to come in, they still could. But the hummingpeople don't seem to know this. Evie's action confirms to them that there is real danger. A great hush falls over the auditorium; a collective holding of breath. It would be funny, if it wasn't also terrifying.

Dayna licks her dry lips. 'All right,' she says. 'Anyone with weapons: drop them. Then I want all of you to go to the right side of that stage. And just wait, and do nothing. If you do nothing, we won't either. If you try to stop us in any way, we'll trigger it. Jason will give Jean and Evie masks in a second, so don't think I won't do it. I don't care about you, any of you.'

(staring at Mother, Mother staring right back)

Dayna carefully passes the Tupperware box over to Pax and takes a lighter from her pocket. It's from the Eggman's room. Echidna can be triggered in so many ways, but this will show them all how much she means what she says. She holds it, unlit, close to the pulsating mushroom caps, her thumb on its button.

'Go on then,' Dayna tells the crowd below her. This will work, she tells herself. It worked with the Undead, didn't it? Until they discovered the bluff. She isn't bluffing now.

Some people stumble into movement, hesitant, dazed. Their heads swivel this way and that, searching for someone who knows what to do, returning, always, to the lighter in Dayna's hand, the Echidna in Pax's. Mother stays where she is, maybe in defiance, maybe just lost.

'They're doing it,' whispers Pax, his voice all trembly. 'It's—'

A white-coat makes a sudden break for the nearest door on the left, his tails flying. A catalyst, and now others are tearing after him, pushing, shoving each other, scuffling and grunting.

No no no

'STOP!' Dayna screams after the runners, but they don't listen or don't hear. And now she will have to trigger the fungus, she'll have to do it or risk being attacked from all sides (stairs leading up to the balcony from left and right and behind them). She'll have to do it, but Mother hasn't moved, is there, right *there*.

'Mother, get out!' she yells. 'I'm gonna have to release the spores!' She takes a step away from Pax and the Echidna, hesitates for a heartbeat, then presses down the lighter button. The flame is instantaneous, and bright, and unpredictable. She can see Mother flinch even at this distance.

More hummingpeople break away, tripping over seats, their own feet, each other, in their haste to reach the exits.

Still not Mother.

Come on, Dayna wills her. The flame in her hand begins to tremble as Dayna herself begins to shake. 'Please, just GO.'

'Day, people're coming up the back stairs,' hisses Pax. 'I can hear them. They're coming here.'

Out of time. Out of options.

'I have to do it!' (Her eyes are hot and wet, the mask suffocating her.) 'Please, just get out! I'm doing it NOW.'

And then she does.

52

Flame and fungus collide.
    A pink explosion.
        Shrieks.
           Blindness.

Everything is white and grey and tinged with pink. Thicker than Dayna has ever known in this enclosed space. She can't even see the hand in front of her own eyes. She can hear, though; sounds both loud and somehow hushed. In the distance: people yelling and screaming and knocking into things. A bang as the balcony door is flung open – a short flash of outside light framed in the doorway before the mist takes it for its own. More screaming, closer now. The heavy, frantic thudding of people's escaping feet. Dayna lets go of the lighter and reaches into nothingness until she finds Pax's small, sweaty hand.

There's no time to waste. FFP2 masks are adequate, but they're nowhere near as efficient as proper gas masks. Best not test them for too long. With one hand tugging Pax behind her, the other on the line of frayed velvet chairs, the wall, the doorframe, the banister, Dayna leads them both downwards. Step by step, down the invisible stairs as fast as she can without being careless; as slow as she can without being exposed.

No one stops them. No one even tries. They could be alone in the mist, were it not for all the muffled sounds around them. Not just of people trying to escape, but also spluttering and choking. The unlucky, the caught. Far away. Dayna's stomach twists in a rush of sadness and guilt, even though she did warn them, and even though they gave her no other choice. There's no saving them now. In a few hours they will be crazed, or dead. She did that.

But they did it too.

Jason must have reached the cube by now, with the masks for the others. Dayna and Pax were to meet them all on the outside, but she sees now that this was a mistake. Anything could happen between now and then, a million reasons why they could miss each other in the mist and the rain, with most of the hummingpeople unscathed and at large. She sees herself waiting, and them not coming, and it becoming more risky by the second, and what will she do then? She won't leave without them. So instead of heading outside, she turns again, Pax's hand in hers, and feels her way to the theatre auditorium doors she and the boys slunk by earlier. Finds them, steps in.

Her fingers trail along the flaky wall, as they walk on, straight ahead to where the cube should be. Halfway through, Pax stumbles over something, and then Dayna knocks into an overturned table; evidence of the hummingpeople's frenzied flight. The sounds of (running) (dying) people are further away now, not in the auditorium, and Dayna hopes with all her might that Mother has managed to escape after all.

Her eyes are stinging in the mist. She rubs them with her free hand. They're watering too.

Her knee knocks against something solid. They've

reached the platform at last. Gingerly, she climbs up, not at all easy if you can't see what you're mounting and can't even see your own arms and hands and legs. Helping Pax is no less of a challenge, but then both of them are up, and there is a dim light straight ahead. Dayna takes a tentative step forwards and her stretched-out fingertips brush at glass.

'We're here,' she gasps to Pax, eager and breathless and scared. There are blurry shadows inside the cube. One of them comes closer, raps on the glass, moves to her right, his left, raps again. Dayna follows, pulling Pax with her. A door out of nowhere is opened a crack, and a hand grabs Dayna's and tugs her, as she tugs Pax, into the cube and sight and air. The moment they're inside, someone else slams the door shut quick, and they're safe, or as safe as anyone can be in this situation.

Dayna looks at Jason, who grins at her, his skin paler in the cube's fluorescent lights.

'I only just got here myself,' he says. 'Bloody difficult, moving in the mist, isn't it? I'm glad you changed your mind anyway, it'd probably be too risky waiting for each other in the open with all of them loose ...'

Behind him is Evie, who only gives Dayna a quick, uncertain smile before turning again to stare out through the glass walls into the pink mist enveloping them from all sides. Behind him is the Eggman, hunched in a far corner with his head between his knees. Jean is propping the metal chair back against the door. And when she's finished, she pulls Dayna into a tight hug.

'You crazy, crazy girl,' she whispers. She hugs Pax too, who squirms and laughs and coughs.

Dayna has torn off her mask and is coughing too, the clean air stinging her throat.

Someone says her name, and Dayna turns – and freezes. Because that someone is Mother.

Mother is standing in another corner, separate from the Eggman, separate from Jason and Jean and Evie. Her hair has come loose from her bun as if she ran – and ran fast – to be where she is. Just held her breath and ran.

She says: 'I'm so glad you're all right.'

She says: 'How could you do this? You've jeopardised the entire project. The entire future! How could you be so stupid?'

And Dayna says nothing.

But Pax does: 'You lied to us! You said that you'd let Evie and Jean go, and you never! Day didn't believe it, but I did. I'm not ever gonna trust you again, not ever ever ever.'

Mother shakes her head, gives Pax a sad, wise smile. 'I explained before, Pax. Sometimes you have to do the hard thing to do the right thing. We have to plan ahead; years, decades, not just days—' She locks eyes with Dayna. 'You may have saved your friends for today, but ultimately, you've doomed all of us, them included.'

(She's right.)

(She's wrong.)

(She's both.)

'Or you could have done,' finishes Mother. 'It's not over yet.'

'Oh, yes. It's over. For us, anyway,' says Jean, her voice cool and dismissive, her hand suddenly on Dayna's shoulder, an anchor point.

And Dayna finds her voice again: 'We're leaving.'

She turns to Jason, hand outstretched. He understands, fishes into his pocket and hands her the FFP2 masks. Dayna passes on one to Jean, then starts knotting the elastic band of another so that it will fit Evie's smaller head. She will take no chances, even though Evie is immune. The spare masks they came in with are just enough to go around.

'The little girl doesn't want to go with you,' says Mother. 'She wants to stay here and help us save the world. Isn't that right, Evie?'

Evie turns from the glass, her eyes flicking from Mother to the Eggman. To Jason, to Jean, to Dayna, to Jason again. She shakes her head. 'No, I don't like it here, and you hurt Dayna and you almost hurt Jean and I don't want to stay here any more.'

'Not even to save all the world?' coaxes Mother. 'Because that's what you can help us do.'

Jean snorts. 'Listen to yourself,' she says to Mother. 'Save the world? Have you ever looked out of the bloody windows in the last decade? The world is *thriving*. The only endangered species is us. Which, well, let's face it, is nature justifiably getting her own back.'

Mother stares at Jean. 'Are you saying you don't consider humans worth saving?'

'I'm saying everyone left now has found a way to adapt to this new state of normal, or they wouldn't be left in the first place. I'm saying it's not the world you're trying to save any more, but *your* world. Which puts your ethics here into perspective, doesn't it?'

Mother opens her mouth, but Dayna says: 'Stop. We can't convince you, and you can't convince us, so just stop.'

(Although Jean *has* convinced someone else. Dayna feels better now, clearer in her mind and in what she is doing. And by the looks on the other kids' faces, it's not just her.)

'Let's go already,' urges Pax. 'I don't want to stay here with her. What're we waiting for?'

'Not for me,' says Evie, jumping forwards. 'I'm going too!'

'Here.' Dayna gives her the newly adjusted mask.

'I don't need that. I'm—'

'Yeah, I know. Stop bragging about it, will you? Do it anyway.'

'But *why*?'

'You're not taking her,' says Mother.

Everyone ignores her. Even the Eggman, who looks at Jason and speaks for the first time: 'If you go off again, I won't come running after you like last time.'

'Good,' says Jason shortly.

'You'll be on your own, and if they do bring you back here, you'll be just another patient. I won't help you. You won't be my son any more.'

'No one's gonna bring me back here,' says Jason. 'And I won't be on my own.'

'YOU'RE NOT TAKING HER!'

Mother is standing in front of the door, and she's holding a small metal knife in her right hand, its blade tiny but the sharpest Dayna has ever seen.

'You won't hurt me,' says Dayna, although suddenly she isn't at all certain. There's a crazed glint in Mother's eye, which is fixed on Evie and Evie alone.

'I will if I have to,' says Mother. 'Because it's the right thing to do. You can leave if you must. Not even I could save you from the others after what you just pulled off. But she stays. We need her. There's a very good chance she has the cure in her. Talk about ethics all you like, about how you don't mind living in this hell. You wouldn't say no if I offered you a fully working vaccine right now, would you? No one in their right mind would.'

Dayna chews her lower lip, sizing up the situation. She

doesn't know how quick Mother can be with this blade, but she's outnumbered by a long shot. The Eggman, still crouched in his corner, seems to have no thought of assisting her.

'OK,' she finally says. 'Here's what we do. Jason, you come at her from the left, Jean from the right, me from—'

'Oh, for God's sake.'

Jean pushes Dayna aside and makes a break for Mother, completely ignoring everything Dayna has just said. Mother takes a hasty step back and slashes her knife left to right, and Jean's hands come up to meet it. A moment where anything could happen, where both women struggle and strain and push – hand around wrist, hand around knife – then the blade is rammed into Jean's leg. Her right leg, beneath the knee, because that's where she's guided it to. Evie squeals and the Eggman winces and Dayna meets Jason's eye, and then Pax's. Mother lets go of a triumphant cry. But that is before she sees Jean's smile. And before she tries to pull out the knife and discovers it won't budge.

'Meet Mr Smith,' whispers Jean, and punches her right in the face. Mother is knocked to the ground with a whimper that makes Dayna's stomach tighten. But apart from a rapidly swelling left cheek, she seems fine, if dazed.

Jean is trying to get the knife out of her prosthetic leg herself now, and not getting any further than Mother did.

'Someone give me a hand with the scalpel?' she appeals to the room at large. 'My palms are too sweaty.'

Jason helps her out and manages to wrench the knife free. 'Nice move,' he comments. He makes to pocket it, but Jean holds out her hand.

'Can I see?' asks Pax, intrigued. 'What did you call it? Scull-pel?'

'Let's go,' says Jean. '*Now.*'

'Right,' says Jason. 'What's our formation, Sarge?'

'Our what?' asks Dayna, momentarily distracted from Mother.

'Who goes first, who last? You know. Don't tell me you haven't got a system this time.'

Of course she has.

Masks on, even Evie, they leave the relative safety of the cube. They leave behind them the Eggman and Mother, who seems to have had all the fight knocked out of her by one woman and her prosthetic leg. She watches them as, one by one, they slip out of the door, taking care to close it right after them so that only the bare minimum of mist has a chance to pass through. Jean leaves first. Next Pax, without so much as a glance in Mother's direction. Next Evie.

Dayna hasn't taken her eyes off Mother, which is hard because Mother is crying silently. Whether over the loss of the immune girl or of her own children, Dayna can't tell and would rather not know in any case.

Jason follows Evie, leaving Dayna alone with the two doctors. She hesitates, then says: 'I don't have any spare masks and I probably wouldn't trust you with one if I did. But you'll be OK if you stay here. Someone will come get you at some point. You're the leader, aren't you?'

Mother wipes her eyes and shrugs. 'I wasn't at first. I am now.'

Dayna nods. 'Like me.'

'Dayna …' whispers Mother. Dayna waits, but nothing else comes. Maybe Mother herself doesn't know what she wants to say to her daughter. So Dayna swallows, and says it for her.

'Goodbye.'

And then she leaves.

(Mother, whose favourite colour is blue. Who was named after the night sky, after a woman whose lock of hair turned into the stars. Mother, whose smiling, beloved photograph is in the picture archive even now, waiting for them. Mother, who wants so badly to be a hero.)

53

Hand in hand and with Dayna in the lead, the five of them walk through the mist. Finding her way out of the auditorium is easier than going in. Dayna has a good memory, and now has a fair idea of the distance and layout of the place. Once they enter the hall, things change, become louder and more scary. They can hear trapped people coughing and trying (and failing) to scramble away while they gradually lose more and more control over their limbs. And there are more purposeful movements too, of people running. Some of the Hummingbird soldiers must have grabbed their masks by this time and are wading back into the mist to — what? Rescue the stragglers? Lock up the infected before the craze takes over? Find them? Find Evie?

All these things, surely, but which has the highest priority?

Whenever the sounds of these marching thumping footsteps come too close for comfort, Dayna squeezes Jason's hand, who passes the message on to Evie, who passes it on to Pax, who passes it on to Jean. It takes around one second, then all of them will freeze in place, as silent as the moon, and wait until the danger has passed them by. The only real weapons they have are Mother's scalpel in Jean's free hand, and a thin lock-pick hook in Dayna's. Two chances, but not very big ones.

They don't need those chances, though. No one sees them. No one hears them. Dayna keeps her troop close to the side, the wall to their right, and out of the way. If everything had gone according to plan, they would have just left by the main doors. But nothing has gone according to plan, and if anyone is waiting for them, this will be where. So they walk on in this stop-and-go fashion (and now Dayna is following Jason's whispered instructions and turns) until they reach a corner, double back, feeling more intently, find a door.

'This is it,' says Jason, his voice muffled by the mask.

Dayna tries the handle. Locked, of course. Her eyes are stinging again, her head throbbing. FFP2 masks are all very well, but prolonged exposure to the mist is bad because they can't keep everything out.

'It'll take too long to pick it,' says Dayna. 'We'll have to find another way out.'

For an answer, Jason's hand lets go of hers (and it's like being untethered, suddenly all alone in a cloud of toxic mist), and then comes back with an array of small metal objects, warm from Jason's pocket. A key ring with three four five keys attached to it.

'Took this from my father before you came,' whispers Jason's voice. 'Most of these lab doors open to the same key; they couldn't have things too complicated. Try them.'

Dayna does, one by one, feeling for the slit with one finger and nudging the keys blindly into it. Of course none of the keys fit until she tries the last one.

They enter this room the same way they exited the cube, slipping through the door like eels. This time Dayna is first, and she watches as, one at a time, the others join her, dishevelled and slightly red-eyed, but otherwise all right.

'Let's never do that again,' says Pax in between another fit of coughing (not infected coughing, just a-tickle-in-your-throat coughing).

'Ooh, look!' exclaims Evie, who out of all of them is completely unaffected, of course. 'Look!'

She's pointing towards the far end of the room, where there are cages beside and stacked on top of each other, just like in the Hummingbird lorry all that time ago, only many, many more. In these cages, Dayna sees glimpses of all sorts of animals, mostly smaller mammals like cats and ferrets and foxes and rats, but larger ones too. The largest is a doe, trembling at the very back of her cage.

'Yeah, this is where they keep all the animal test subjects,' says Jason, who is rubbing his eyes. 'I figured no one was gonna run in here because if something goes wrong you don't want to be anywhere near infected animals.'

(Yes, some of the animals are hissing and spitting and banging their weight against the mesh bars.)

'Good thinking,' says Dayna. But she locks the door again, just to be safe. Then she strides to the window and scans the outside. The world seems not to have realised what is happening in here. The rain is still falling and there isn't a trace of pink mist in the air. It seems like none of the hummingpeople have been careless enough to leave any outside doors open. Yet. But even if they did, the heavy moisture in the air would prevent the spores from spreading very far. Dayna isn't sure if this is lucky or unlucky, but it's what they have to work with.

She opens the window and a rush of sharp and fresh and safe air hits her full in the face. She closes her eyes and breathes in deeply. Immediately, the throbbing in her head calms itself.

She turns to the others and says: 'All right, listen. Me and Jean have picked out the escape route. Which way are we facing now, Jason? North?'

Jason shakes his head. 'South.'

Dayna looks at Jean, who nods. 'OK, then we know which way to go. If we go now, the hummingpeople might not be outside yet. They will be as soon as they stop panicking and start looking for us properly. But at the moment it's chaos. And they probably think Evie's still in the auditorium, and it's Evie they care about.'

'You don't have to explain every little detail,' says Pax. 'Let's just go, please?'

Dayna ignores him and takes them through all the important steps: where they're heading – the Wood Green tube station – and by which route and where they meet if they should get separated.

'So, we'll do the same thing we did in Clapham?' asks Jason. 'Take the underground way?'

'It worked then, didn't it?' Dayna shrugs. 'Spy flies can't find us there. We just have to make it that far.'

'OK, OK, whatever you say, can we GO now?' urges Pax.

'Yes,' says Dayna.

'No!' cries Evie. 'We have to free the animals first!'

Evie is adamant and deaf to all reasoning that they have no time to spare. When Jason tries to pick her up and take her towards the open window, she SCREAMS, and is quickly dropped again.

'Shit,' he says, then he takes the keys, which Dayna has left in the door lock, and hurries to the cages.

'What're you doing?' demands Dayna. 'We don't have time!'

'You have a better idea?' asks Jason. 'We don't have time

to argue with Evie either. There's about ten animals here that don't have the craze. Give me five seconds for each.'

Pax screws up his face in an effort of mental arithmetic, then says: 'That's almost a whole minute!'

The first animals are already scurrying over the floor towards the open window. Jean hurries towards Jason, hissing, 'Wait! Wait! I want to make sure they're not infected.'

Pax turns to Dayna. 'Evie's so spoilt. And we keep on doing what she wants.'

'I know. But now's not a good time to teach her. We'll do that after we get out. Come on, let's go.'

So Dayna and Pax are the first to lower themselves out of the window, amidst a weasel, a cat and two frantic rats, and land on the squelchy ground. Luckily, the rainstorm masks any sounds Evie's freed animals make as they dart in all directions and out of sight. It doesn't take too long before Jason lowers Evie down – Pax ostentatiously lets her drop into the mud without trying to catch her. Dayna shoots him a dirty look as Evie starts to whimper on the brink of howling.

'Quiet,' she whispers, helping the little girl back to her feet. 'You'll put us all in danger.'

And, amazingly, Evie wipes her eyes and nods.

Jason jumps down next, and then Jean, who almost loses her balance after hitting the ground, but this time Pax is willing to help. She's unsteady because she's holding something in both her hands. Dayna squints at it through the heavy rain. A puppy, black as soot, stares back.

'Look at her,' smiles Jean proudly.

'You can't—'

'I can, at the moment anyway. She doesn't seem to mind. I think she likes me.'

'I want a doggie too,' demands Evie. 'I'm the one who said to free them!'

'You're so annoying,' says Pax, shoving her.

'No, you are!'

'Everyone, shut *up*,' hisses Dayna. 'If they find us, they'll kill us. OK?'

That shuts them up, all right.

'Good. Everyone put your masks into your pockets so they won't get soaked through. Jason, hang on to Evie. Jean, give the dog to Pax because you and me are the only ones with weapons. We ought to go first. Pax, let go of the dog as soon as there's a problem. We sprint to the trees, and then we walk on in a straight line. We'll have cover for about ten minutes before it's houses and streets again. OK? OK. Let's go.'

The last Dayna sees of the Station is the shadow of a doe leaping out of the window they left open, and skittering off into the woods and rain. Then she pushes through some shrubs, and when she turns again there are only leaves.

54

They move quickly without actually running, weaving their way through the dripping undergrowth as silently as they can. At first, Dayna can't hear anything over the heavy rainfall and the rustle of thickets and leaves caused by their progress. But then her ears pick out individual sounds further away; a *creak* here, a *snap* there ... And once she's homed in on them, they become much easier to make out. She says nothing at first, hoping she's mistaken. But the sounds continue, and continue to come in their direction.

'We're being followed,' she finally mutters, just loud enough for the others to hear. Of all of them, only Jason and Evie are surprised.

Evie whimpers and Jason asks: 'What? You sure?'

'Shhh. Yes.'

'Not too many, right?' says Pax. 'They'd be louder if it's a lot.'

'Only one, I think,' says Jean, nodding. Dayna hopes she's right. She herself can't tell. She's never been stalked by men before and all she knows is that whoever they are, they're human, not animal.

'What, you all knew this already?' demands Jason. 'Thanks for sharing with the rest of us.'

'I thought it was obvious there was something,' says Pax.

'I wanted to be sure it was following us,' says Dayna.

'I was waiting for Dayna to tell us what to do,' says Jean with a breathless laugh.

Dayna finds herself smiling in spite of everything. 'Yeah, I know what to do. It's kind of obvious, though.'

'Run?' asks Jean.

Dayna nods. 'We get to the road, and then we sprint for all we're worth. If we can only get to the town bit without being seen, they'll never guess where we went. Jean, can you run?'

'Of course,' she says, although her limp has become worse and worse in the short time they've been here. 'Don't look at me like that. I can if I have to, and I'll have to.'

'OK,' mutters Dayna, still not quite convinced. 'And Jason, can you carry Evie piggyback?'

'I can run too,' says Evie at once.

'Your legs are too short, you won't keep up with us. Can you, Jason?'

'*Yes*, what do you think?' Jason sounds almost as indignant as Evie.

All this time, Dayna has been leading them in the direction the main road should be, but there's one more obstacle they have to pass. She forgot all about the Hummingbirds' barricade, or maybe she's just been hoping it doesn't go all the way around. But here it is, the rusty metal panels snaking through the trees, forming a wall almost twice as high as Jason. They come to a halt in front of it. And the person creeping behind them in the distance keeps on moving …

Dayna pushes at one of the joints, and maybe they've been welded together, or the panel is just too heavy, but she can't budge them an inch.

'Not a problem,' says Jason. He cups his hands together

and turns his palms upwards to form a bridge. 'You first, Sarge. It'll be a bit of a drop on the other side, and you can help the others.'

Dayna hesitates. 'What about you? How will you get over?'

'Take a running start. I've got long legs. Now come on, even I can hear this guy now.'

Dayna steps on to his cupped hands, and from then over the panel easily, landing on the ground with a thump that rattles her kneecaps. Through the trees on this side, she can see a paved road. Almost there … Next comes Pax, who jumps right into her, knocking them both into the damp ground.

'What'd you do that for?'

'Sor-ree. I thought you were gonna catch me.'

She does catch Evie when it's her turn. And the terrified black puppy, when Jean lowers it down from the other side as far as she can and then lets go. Jean herself manages to stay upright when she lands, although it's clear that her leg is hurting something fierce.

'Get on my shoulders, Dayna,' she says through gritted teeth. 'You can help Jason over from this side.'

Jason has to try four times, but he finally manages to grasp her hand and pull himself up and over. Dayna is just about to follow him down when something on the other side catches her eye. Human, not animal. Human, with dark hair plastered to his scalp in the rain, a gas mask over his face. Its goggles lit up in an eerie green light. An insect man. A soldier. Sir.

'He's here!' shouts Dayna as she jumps down to the others. There's no point in being quiet now. He's seen her. 'Everybody, RUN!'

★

They run. Tearing through the last of the undergrowth. Down the battered road slicing through the wilderness. Towards the brick houses in the distance. Dayna is fastest, which means she keeps having to glance back to make sure they're all there. Pax puffing just behind her. Then Jason with Evie bobbing on his back, arms around his neck. Then, way, way behind, Jean, her limp a hobble now, further back every time Dayna looks. The puppy is in her arms again.

'Jean!' shouts Dayna over her shoulder. 'Let go of the dog!'

Jean won't at first, but when she falls back further still, and further and further, she gives up and lowers the puppy gently to the ground.

'Don't stop, keep running!' shouts Dayna. She can't see anyone behind Jean, and maybe the barricade gave him as much trouble as it gave them. And maybe it's just too difficult to see far in all this rain. And maybe he's right behind that curve there, just out of sight ...

'Day! Come on!' screams Pax's voice, from somewhere ahead, and she realises that she's been stationary for at least ten seconds. Jean is limping up to her, breathing heavily, the puppy dog trotting by her feet (one human, one artificial).

'I said she liked me,' pants Jean. Then: 'What are you doing? Get moving, don't wait for me.'

'You're too slow,' says Dayna. 'Lean on my shoulder.'

'No. Go *on*, what are you playing at?'

'Come on, he'll get you!'

'And he'll get both of us if I slow you down too. I can take care of myself. Just GO.'

The exact same thing Father told her beside the Hummingbird lorry, the same thing in different words, and Dayna believed him because she always believed him. Not again. She couldn't save Father. She couldn't save Mother. But she is not going to abandon Jean. She takes Jean's arm and puts it around her shoulder, then pulls her forward.

'Dayna, for God's sake, this isn't getting us anywhere—'

'I'll help too,' says Pax, suddenly in their midst. Just like Jason and Evie.

'Come off it, shrimp,' says Jason. 'Jean, put your other arm around my shoulder, then me and Sarge've got most of your weight.'

'You've got Evie—'

'No, he doesn't!' Evie wriggles down from Jason's back. 'I can walk. I can RUN. Faster than any of you!'

And to prove this, she darts off, thankfully in the right direction.

'Pax—' begins Dayna.

'Yeah, yeah. I know. Why do I always get lumbered with her?' But he runs off after her obediently.

'Come on, Jean, you're only wasting time arguing,' Jason tells her. 'Let's move before the little kids beat us to it.'

It's amazing how much difference another person makes. Jean feels not heavy at all, and they can even jog along at a fairly decent pace, the puppy lolloping just ahead of them. Dayna glances back, sees no one, turns to face forward again. There are houses behind the trees now. Pax and Evie, holding hands (and Dayna can imagine how much both of them resent this) are halfway up a small slope when Jean calls out to them: 'No, come back!'

But she's so out of breath, only Dayna and Jason can hear her, so Dayna repeats her words at a bellow. The kids turn and trot back, weaving in and out of dead cars.

'In here,' gasps Jean, nodding to a bunch of creepers. 'Push through,' she tells them, when they look at her dubiously.

Pax does so first, and vanishes into the green with a surprised laugh, dragging Evie after him.

'You can let go of me now,' Jean tells the other two. 'Too narrow. Jason, can you take the dog?'

Dayna pushes through the leaves next and comes out on a little overgrown path between a railing and a wall. You have to move through the ivy like through spiderwebs, but the leaves offer little resistance, and flex and bend to accommodate her. A secret doorway of green.

Now Jason is pushing through with the puppy. Now Jean is. Still panting heavily, she reaches out and prods and nudges the leaves and vines back over the opening. You can still see the indentation their bodies made, but only if you know what you are looking for.

'Come on,' hisses Pax, who is furthest down the narrow alley with Evie by his side.

But instead of coming on, Jean slides down the wall into a sitting position. She shakes her head. 'I can't,' she gasps. 'You go. I'll catch up.'

'No, you won't,' says Dayna impatiently.

She tries to pull Jean up by her arm, but Jason says, 'SHHH!'

Everyone falls still at once, Dayna's hand freezing on Jean's arm. Jean presses her own hands to her mouth to muffle her panting. On the other side of their ivy door, someone – Sir – is jogging down the street in the tireless lope of a soldier. The black puppy emits the tiniest of whines.

He'll have a gun with him. He won't take any chances. He'll take Evie. He'll shoot all the rest of them. *Bang bang bang*. William taught them that a revolver can hold six bullets, a semi-automatic handgun up to seventeen rounds. He'll only need four. *BANG*.

I had a chance of stopping this, all of this, thinks Dayna. If

I had just triggered the Echidna without giving warning ...
But she knows she couldn't have done that, no matter how much she hates them.

She closes her eyes.

And Sir passes by their hiding place without slowing down and moves onwards, the way Pax and Evie almost went, and his footsteps are swallowed up in the rain.

Everyone seems to breathe out at the same time.

'Oh man,' says Pax shakily.

'Jean did magic,' says Evie.

'How'd you know this opening would be here?' asks Jason.

And Jean smiles and scoops up the puppy and nestles her face into its damp black fur. 'I used to live here,' she says. 'I took this path almost every day. To commute to the city.'

The path leads on to a small bridge over train tracks and a station house that looks like a sleep-enchanted cottage from a fairy story, and then to the street on the other side. Like magic, Evie is right.

'We should have lost him now,' says Jean as she and Jason emerge last. 'No need to run.'

'Just be as quick and quiet as we can,' says Dayna, taking up her position on Jean's right and motioning for Jason to imitate her. Jean accepts their help without complaint.

It takes another ten minutes, but nothing bad crosses their path. Dayna sighs in relief when she sees the circular building of the Wood Green tube station. She ducks from under Jean and runs to the entrance, where they left the bag of supplies only yesterday. It's a canvas bag, and inside is an electric torch and all the weapons they could scavenge at such short notice: two children's wooden swords, a wrench and a hammer.

55

Almost done now. Almost over.

The tunnel is just as black and dank-smelling as the one in South London, and has just as many rats creeping in the shadows. It's a risk, being down here, but it's far riskier to stay up top where all the Hummingbirds and their spy flies will soon be searching, or are searching already.

The Hummingbirds won't find them here, in the darkness, in the shadows, underground.

They're heading northwards, where two stations on, the archive is waiting for them with its new motorised engine. To take them right away. Where to, neither Dayna nor Jean has discussed because neither, not truly, believed that they would ever get this far.

To Oxford, perhaps. Or further still. Scotland. There are many sights in Scotland that will enrich the archive. There may be other things as well. Almost certainly. Bad and good and in between …

There's no need to run any more, but it looks like Mr Smith has given all he's willing to give today, and Jean still has her arm around Jason's shoulders as she matches her limp to his step. Her spare hand is holding the wrench. His, the wooden sword. Pax has snagged the other sword, as Dayna knew he would. Every now and then he swishes it from left to right, or from right to left, making small squeaks of protest rise up from the dark. The pup, whom Jean has dubbed Dog III, pads beside him warily, fur bristled and back arched. Evie is the torchbearer and takes this very seriously; keeps the beam steady, on the tracks before them. Dayna's long shadow walks ahead, with herself a close second. The hammer's weight in her hand is heavy and reassuring.

They walk in silence, and she knows it's not because they have nothing to say, but because they have too much. And because they are bone tired.

If this was a story, thinks Dayna, then we'd be its heroes. The word sends a shiver down her spine. Are they like the other heroes of Now? Did they just make things worse?

By taking the immune girl away from the Hummingbirds.

Or the other way around. And worse perhaps: By letting the Hummingbirds live and carry on.

No vaccine, or hope for vaccine, in the near future.

No peace from the Hummingbirds.

Still, Dayna can't see how she could have acted any other way than she did. And why should one person believe they can save the world anyway? Not Liam, and not Mother, and not Dayna either.

They reach Bounds Green station without incident and go further still. Dayna smiles when their tunnel burrows out of the ground near Arnos Grove. This is where the archive is waiting for them. And something else besides. She has just time enough to register what it is before it's upon her: another crazed rat, just like the one that began all of this. That rat bit, and so does this one. It tears at Dayna's trousers, and tears through right to the flesh of her ankles. In her shock, the hammer comes down hard on the gravel beside it, missing it by inches, and when has this ever happened before? But what does it matter? Once is enough. And she thinks: Father didn't miss, and still he died.

The pup is yapping and Evie is shrieking and Jason swings his wooden child's sword with such force that all there is, is white-hot blinding pain. But where is the rat? To her left now, dazed but still savage and squeaking, still trained on her. And here it comes again, and – *THWAK* – this time Pax gets it – and now it's by Jean, who brings down the wrench in one smooth movement, like she knew this is exactly where it would end, its skull crushed, its limbs twitching twitching and then still.

'No,' she says sternly, as Dog III begins sniffing at its carcass.

'Day! Day, did it get you?' asks Pax, rushing to where she's sprawled on the tracks. Dayna can't answer because she doesn't know. Her whole lower leg is throbbing and painful. And that might be from an infected bite. And it might be from Jason's whack.

'Sarge?'

'I don't know.' Her teeth are chattering. Frantically, her fingers pat the skin around the torn trouser leg.

'Here, let me look,' says Jean. 'Evie, give me the torch.'

They all crowd around her. Dayna's skin is red, and there are scratch marks criss-crossing up and down. But no blood or openings. It didn't break through.

'You're all right,' breathes Jean. 'Oh, thank God.' And Pax emits a high, wobbly laugh. And Evie asks: 'Is it over? Have we won?' And Jason punches Dayna in the shoulder and says: 'Don't scare us like that!'

And on the cold, wet, muddy ground, Dayna closes her eyes, and smiles, and savours the feeling – (I'm alive. The others are here. The Station is behind. The archive and new stories are ahead) – of Now.

Acknowledgements

I lived around the corner from Marine Court for a couple of years as a kid and always loved the building, which is why I decided to set a portion of the book there. Once I had Marine Court, I naturally needed an equally impressive setting for the big finale – this turned out to be Alexandra Palace. It was my dad's suggestion when I asked him for location ideas (he used to live in London), so thanks, Dad! I can't imagine the Station being anywhere else now. Thanks also to Bella Milton, Jane Bruce and Chris Milton for their help with Marine Court, and to Momo LG Kolwe for answering my Alexandra Palace questions – but any mistakes in the depiction of either building are mine and mine alone. I repurposed both locations for their new inhabitants; I had Marine Court's ballroom restored, bricked off many of Alexandra Palace's entry points, changed rooms, and added solar panels, soundproof glass walls and observation cubes. So, I took liberties, but never lost sight of the magnificent buildings themselves. It was great to have my characters walk and creep and run through them.

As a first-time author, it seems amazing to me how many people are involved in the publication of one novel.

I'm beyond grateful to my agent, Oli Munson, who believed in this story (and in me) from the beginning, and found a perfect publisher for it in a very short space of time. Also, to his then-assistant at A. M. Heath, Harmony Leung, who started all this by reading my submitted manuscript and getting it to Oli in the first place.

A huge thanks to my wonderful editors at Bloomsbury YA, Alex Antscherl and Cathy Liney, for their enthusiasm, insight and great ideas, and for always staying true to what I had in mind. I loved working with them!

The whole team at Bloomsbury YA are fantastic, and I really appreciate all their hard work and dedication – special mention here to Jessica Bellman, Jess White, Sarah Taylor-Fergusson, Tim Hardy, Isabelle Tucker, Laura Bird, Grace Barnes and Nicholas Church. Thanks also to Sophie Kamlish for her valuable feedback on Jean and Mr Smith. Simón Prades illustrated the beautiful cover which I absolutely love, and somehow managed to bring the Echidna fungus on to paper just how I had envisioned it.

I want to thank my friends and family for all their support, and also just for being so happy and excited about this publication. Some I do need to mention by name: Anne Rabbitt, for helping and encouraging me so much when I first began to write just after leaving school. My first readers – Leonie Griepentrog (who has read every story I have ever written), Lea Lubs and Emily Marx, for cheering Dayna on before anyone else had heard of her. Or almost anyone, because my very first readers were my parents, Tony and Andrea Reason; I'm so lucky to have them and know that they always have my back. And, finally, my brother Benni, who inspired so much of Pax (although I suspect Jason would have been his favourite). Benni never got to read this story, but without him, it wouldn't be how it is now.

LOOK OUT FOR THE THRILLING SEQUEL

COMING SOON

About the Author

Miranda Reason grew up in an Anglo-German household, spending part of her childhood living in Hastings on the coast of Southern England and part in a small village in Bavaria. Alongside writing and reading, Miranda is passionate about films and film history. She works as a film restorer of classic German movies. Although now living in Germany, she still prefers English for writing and storytelling, thanks to all the classic and contemporary English children's books her dad read to her as a child. *Day of Now* is her debut novel.